Netta Muskett was born in Sevenoaks,]
Kent College, Folkstone. She had a varie
first teaching mathematics before working ᵤₛ ₐ secretary to the then
owner of the 'News of the World', as well as serving as a volunteer
during both world wars – firstly driving an ambulance and then
teaching handicrafts in British and American hospitals.

It is, however, for the exciting and imaginative nature of her writing
that she is most remembered. She wrote of the times she experienced,
along with the changing attitudes towards sex, women and romance,
and sold millions of copies worldwide. Her last novel 'Cloudbreak'
was first published posthumously after her death in 1963.

Many of her works were regarded by some librarians at the time of
publication as risqué, but nonetheless proved to be hugely popular
with the public, especially followers of the romance genre.

Netta co-founded the Romantic Novelists' Association and served
as Vice-President. The 'Netta Muskett' award, now renamed the
'RNA New Writers Scheme', was created in her honour to recognise
outstanding new writers.

AFTER RAIN	A MIRROR FOR DREAMS
ALLEY CAT	MISADVENTURE
BLUE HAZE	NO MAY IN OCTOBER
BROCADE	NO YESTERDAYS
CANDLE IN THE SUN	NOR ANY DAWN
CAST THE SPEAR	OPEN WINDOW
THE CLENCY TRADITION	THE OTHER WOMAN
CLOUDBREAK	PAINTED HEAVEN
CROWN OF WILLOW	THE PATCHWORK QUILT
THE CROWN OF WILLOW	PHILIPPA
A DAUGHTER FOR JULIA	QUIET ISLAND
THE DURRANTS	RED DUST
THE FETTERED PAST	THE ROCK PINE
FIRE OF SPRING	SAFARI FOR SEVEN
FLAME OF THE FOREST	SAFE HARBOUR
THE FLICKERING LAMP	SCARLET HEELS
FLOWERS FROM THE ROCK	SHADOW MARKET
FROM THIS DAY FORWARD	SHALLOW CUP
GILDED HOOP	SILVER GILT
GIVE BACK YESTERDAY	TAMARISK
GOLDEN HARVEST	THIRD TITLE UNKNOWN
THE HIGH FENCE	THIS LOVELY THING
HOUSE OF MANY WINDOWS	THROUGH MANY WATERS
HOUSE OF STRAW	TIME FOR PLAY
JADE SPIDER	TODAY IS OURS
JENNIFER	THE TOUCHSTONE
LIGHT FROM ONE STAR	THE WEIR HOUSE
LIVING WITH ADAM	THE WHITE DOVE
THE LONG ROAD	WIDE AND DARK
LOVE AND DEBORAH	WINGS IN THE DUST
LOVE IN AMBER	WINTER'S DAY
MIDDLE MIST	THE WIRE BLIND

WINTER'S DAY

Netta Muskett

HOUSE OF
STRATUS

This edition published in 2014 by House of Stratus, an imprint of
Stratus Books Ltd, Lisandra House, Fore St., Looe,
Cornwall, PL13 1AD, UK.

www.houseofstratus.com

Typeset by House of Stratus.

A catalogue record for this book is available from the British Library and the Library of Congress.

ISBN 07551 4333 7
EAN 978 07551 4333 7

Chapter One

Jennifer sang as she put up the last of her curtains.

There was nothing very much to sing about. Outside a dank and dirty day was coming to a close, and in the atmosphere drifted perceptibly, endlessly, the tiny specks of grime which would soon make the starched white Nottingham lace black again. Inside was the cheerfulness which a born home-maker like Jennifer could produce almost anywhere, and here her indomitable spirit and tireless hands and her imagination had made it out of the poorest material: out of cheap, shoddy furniture, rag rugs on the scrubbed floor, a table laid with a coarse cloth, and with chipped oddments of china and worn cutlery.

Only the fire was lavish, for coal is the only thing easily come by in a mining village, and it had to do everything for which electricity, gas, or oil is used elsewhere. It made endless work and kept the house insufferably hot all the summer and smoky all the winter, but it never occurred to anyone to complain. That was life as Werford understood it.

And Jennifer sang as the birds sang, because it was her nature, and this her native place, the home in which she had lived all the twenty years of her life. She sang as the birds sang – pure, sweet notes welling up untrained, notes of happiness, of contentment with the mere gift of life.

The door opened and a head appeared.

'Can I come in, Jen?'

'Sure. Wait till I move the steps. I've just done. Look nice, don't they?' descending the step-ladder gingerly and surveying her handiwork with pride.

'What's the use? They'll be dirty again tomorrow,' said her friend gloomily.

Jennifer laughed.

'What's the use of eating? You'll be hungry again tomorrow,' she said, picking up one of the dirty curtains and beginning to fold it neatly before she put it into the wash-basket to wait till Monday.

A stranger might have been disappointed after hearing the song to see the singer, though once people came to know Jennifer, they never even realised that she had no claim to beauty, that she was too tall and gaunt, that her mouth was too wide, her dark eyes too deeply set, her strong, wiry hair of the sort that refuses to set in snug waves.

To those who knew her she was just Jennifer, old for her twenty years because for so long she had had to mother her menfolk, old with the premature age which comes to these women whose men go to the pits every day and do not always return. She was Jennifer, their friend and confidante, a safe receptacle for their tales of joy and sorrow, old enough to understand, young enough to be having a love affair of her own. She was Jennifer, who could soothe the most fractious baby, who could bind up wounds or kiss the place to make it well – Jennifer who could sing like an angel and yet who could keep a straight bat on the village green and had been known to knock a four three times running off Danny Corker's googlies.

She turned a cheerful face now to her friend.

'What's wrong, Lottie?'

Lottie Marsh sat down on one of the hard wooden chairs. She was only a few years older than Jennifer, but her face was lined and thin. She had a young family to rear, and it was a marvel sometimes that the mothers contrived to live at all. Very few miners were on full time work for more than a few weeks of the year, and even such work as they had was continually interrupted by the heartbreaking strikes which, it seemed, brought them nothing but added difficulties and poverty, though they embarked on them time after time in the same pathetic hope of making themselves heard by their indifferent countrymen.

'Some of them have gone to Lighton, Jen,' she said heavily.

Jennifer frowned.

'What do you mean?' she asked.

'That sound again. Mrs. Batty says she heard it herself this morning and Len says the men have heard it underground for more'n a week.'

Jennifer's eyes grew stormy. They all lived in the shadow of tragedy, though as a rule they managed to make themselves proof against it by the simple expedient of not thinking about it. They could not have lived otherwise. But they were not really proof against that shadow, and lately there had been such persistent rumours that the Lighton pits were not safe that the women had taken to watching their men go down the street and going indoors reluctantly when at last they were out of sight.

'What's Beaton doing about it?' asked Jennifer.

Lottie snorted.

'Beaton? Do you think he cares? His only thought is to get his tonnage and collect the cash. What are a few men's lives to him and the owners? Plenty more where they come from!'

They were silent for a few moments, each living in the griefs of the past. Lottie's father and brother had lost their lives in the same disaster which, four years previously, had taken Jennifer's two older brothers and cost her, eventually, her mother's life as well. Mrs. Jenks had waited through a night of sleet and snow, with hundreds of silent, despairing women, and when they had brought up the body of her second son to lay beside that of her first-born, she had dropped senseless in the blood-stained snow which had mocked with its white mantle the grime and dirt at the pithead.

She had lived for two incredible years after that, her mind alert but her body as helpless as a baby's, and Jennifer had taken on the almost superhuman task of being nurse, mother, housekeeper, and of keeping up what attendances she could at the continuation school in Belsdale to which she had won a scholarship and which Mrs. Jenks had insisted she should attend.

Her father, and young Joe still at school, had shared with her the task of waiting on the helpless woman they adored, but the bulk of the work and all the responsibility fell on Jennifer's young shoulders, so that it was no small wonder if, at twenty, she were old beyond her years.

They were glad when the suffering woman died, though even now they turned their eyes away from the old couch in the corner on which none of them could ever bear to sit.

Now, staring at her from Lottie's frightened face, the spectre walked again. There had been no serious accident since, nothing beyond the constant 'small' casualties, a life here, a limb there, a man half crushed to death but still able to go on living a helpless existence, or smitten with a painful and disfiguring disease but getting no compensation because the doctors could not, or dare not, place the responsibility where it belonged – on the men for whose enrichment he had played with death and disease and lost. These trifles were not even 'news'. Not even in the silly season of the newspapers would such items have been considered worth reporting. What's a miner, anyway? Those fellows were always complaining, always making trouble, striking for more money or something. Shoot the lot!

For five years there had been no disaster which the country at large considered worth the name. Owners had grown more complacent than ever. They drew their profits, but of course one could hardly expect them to *visit* the filthy places. That was the job of their managers and paid assistants – Beaton's job at Lighton, for instance.

Lighton belonged to Sir Jervis Patney – Lighton amongst other collieries. They seldom saw him, though he had an estate ten miles away, at Belsdale. A convenient hill hid from him and his guests most of the colliery workings, and a belt of forest trees completed the screen. In spite of that, Lady Patney felt it was not reasonable that she should be asked to breathe into her aristocratic lungs air which might be polluted by a breeze which blew across Lighton before it reached Belsdale, so the Manor House was seldom occupied. Sometimes an excursion from Werford, the village for Lighton Pits, was organised to Belsdale, by charabanc and, if suitable representations were made in good time, parties were even permitted within the grounds of Manor House – provided always, of course, that neither Sir Jervis nor his lady was in residence. The miners and their womenfolk understood that, of course. Sir Jervis and his lady could not be expected to undergo the shock of looking out of a window or walking across a lawn and seeing anything like a miner or his inconsiderable female belongings breathing the same air.

But there were occasions when the sacred grass might be trodden by the feet of the proletariat, when the trees and the flowers which the mind of God had conceived for the delight of Sir Jervis and his lady and their chosen friends might be viewed by eyes suitably grateful for the change from coal and the bowels of the earth. So nice for the miners, poor things, to see the grounds, and the house (the outside, of course) so different from the wretched hovels where they lived! It must be such a pleasure for them – not, of course, that they *understand*. Poor dears, they *prefer* to live their way, you know.

Just in the same way, people drawing their incomes from the slums of our great cities are so sure that, My dear! These people *like* living in slums. Why, if you gave them anything else, they'd make slums of them within a year, and as for bath-rooms – my dear, they'd keep their coals in them!

'The rich man in his castle,
The poor man at his gate,
God made them high or lowly,
And ordered their estate,'

sang the village children on Sundays, and Lady Patney, at least, believed it. If the miners and their wives did not believe it, well, that was their fault for not going to church and being shown the truth about God, wasn't it?

So Lottie said, in answer to Jennifer's demand: 'What is a miner more or less? Plenty more where they came from.'

Jennifer's face softened a little and she laid a hand on the older girl's shoulder, a large, strong, work-hardened hand that had never had time to be beautiful.

'Don't, Lottie. Don't let's get bitter. It's so damned easy, I know.'

'You haven't got children to think about, Jen. If—if anything happens to Len, what are we all going to do?'

'Don't meet trouble half way, dear. This may be nothing at Lighton. There are people who are always ready to make trouble by spreading rumours – making a band out of a tin whistle!'

But her own heart was heavy with fear. Down in Lighton were her father and her brother, and Bob – Bob Haling, who had lately begun to mean so much to Jennifer.

'I've a mind to go to Lighton myself,' said Lottie. 'I can't just sit and—wait.'

The door was open and two women hurrying by paused to look in.

'They say there's been a fall at Lighton, Jennifer,' said one, and the other pulled at her to hurry, her face red with crying.

Jennifer went to the door.

'Does anyone actually know, Mrs. Moss?' she asked anxiously.

'Well, everybody says so,' and they hurried on. It was two miles to the pit and already the clattering of wooden clogs on the flinty road was growing into a definite sound, fraught with meaning for anyone who has once heard it. The women were going to the pithead!

Lottie jumped to her feet and drew her shawl about her shoulders.

'I'm going, Jen. I can't stand it any longer.'

'What about the children, Lottie?'

'They're asleep, and I've left a note for Polly in case she wakes and finds me gone. She'll look after Jackie and Prue.'

Jennifer nodded. Polly was eight, quite old enough and able to look after the younger ones in a land where childhood never lasted long.

'All right. I'll come with you,' and she took a coat from the peg, twisted a scarlet handkerchief over her head, and went out with Lottie after a last glance at the huge fire and the two big kettles which stood on the hobs in readiness for the men's baths when they came home.

When they came home! Jennifer's mind repeated the words, and then thrust them from her. They would come home. It was all rumour, lies, stupid, wicked lies of that man Mallinger and his crowd. Mallinger whom her father said was a paid agitator and whose job it was to keep the miners in a state of ferment and unrest, though no one seemed able to decide who paid the alleged money to him. Some spoke of the communists, talking a lot of nonsense about Russia.

Some suggested that it was to the owners' advantage to keep the men always discontented, to encourage the frequent strikes which in the end petered out, leaving the men and their trade unions more impoverished and doing the owners no harm because they seldom wanted or needed to keep the men working full time, and even a small strike sent up the price of coal and increased the demand.

Jennifer had wondered quite a lot about Mallinger. Bob Haling had been seen in his company several times lately, and Bob's usually mild speech had been coloured afterwards by strange words and violent expressions of opinion.

'I expect it's only that Mallinger,' she said, as she and Lottie hurried along, her thick shoes soundless beside the clacking of Lottie's clogs.

Mrs. Jenks had never worn clogs nor let the children wear them. She had been considered to be 'a cut above' most of the other miners' wives, though she had never given herself airs nor set up a different standard of living for her family. The children had gone to the village school like the rest of them, but somehow she had managed either to bequeath to them or implant in them a certain delicacy of speech and manner which even now set Jennifer a little apart in the eyes of a good many.

'Even Mallinger can't make noises come out of the earth,' said Lottie with a little shiver, quickening her steps as one or two women caught up with them and joined them, all talking at once, all afraid to say the things that lay closest to their thoughts.

Jennifer strode along, her gallant head held high, her eyes looking straight ahead save when she paused for a moment to wait for Lottie's shorter legs to catch up with her and to smile encouragement at the little, panting figure.

Lottie was going to have a fourth baby. Of course she ought never to have had even three. District visitors, self-appointed, came in their cars to tell her so, though they looked shocked and went away quickly when Lottie asked them point-blank how she could prevent it. Jennifer knew that her heart was heavier with the thought of an extra mouth to feed than ever her body would be heavy with the unwanted scrap of humanity which would be born to love but to nothing else that was beautiful.

As they came in sight of the pithead, with its gaunt structures stretching up above it, the giant cranes, the elevated railway with its belt of trolleys, it was evident to all of them that something more than rumour had brought them there. The women had not been allowed to go near the shaft, but stood in a silent ring some hundred yards away, patient as yet, their fears under the control taught by a lifetime of waiting for just such an hour. The trolleys were at rest for the moment, and near the shaft was a group of men, overseers and foremen, and one or two well-dressed, prosperous-looking men who had probably come out of the cars which stood in the open space behind them.

Jennifer and Lottie joined the ring of women and listened to the disjointed jumble of words to which most of them seemed anxious to contribute something, no matter how unlikely.

'There's been an explosion down Number Three—gas, they say— no, water coming through. The pumps can't carry it—my boy's down in Number Six, been down there since the first shift—O God! Have mercy! Don't take him! Spare him to me, God—you've got so many more men without taking my one!'

This last from an elderly woman who stood near Jennifer, apart from the rest, her eyes closed, the tears raining down her sweet, lined face, rugged with grief and work and privation. Coal had taken from her whatever the Great War had left to her, and it was for her grandson she prayed, the only living thing she had left to her of the sons she had reared.

Jennifer laid an arm about the bowed shoulders.

'That's right, Mrs. Evans. Pray to God,' she whispered fiercely. 'Up there, where there are stars, there must be a God, else who made the stars? Pray to God for all of us.'

Her voice broke a little on the words, and the old woman opened her eyes and saw who it was.

'Ee, Jennifer, it's you. Are your men down? It's you should pray to the Lord. You're young and strong. I'm thinking my time's over, anyway, and it's not much good I am now to anyone.'

Jennifer stood with her arm about the old woman's shoulders whilst Lottie pushed her way amongst the crowd, which was gradually growing restless, and here and there a high note of hysteria broke upon the low murmur of voices.

Suddenly a man detached himself from the little knot near the cages, and Jennifer recognised him for Bob Haling. He stood over six feet, was broad in proportion, and his magnificent physique marked him amongst the men who, as a race, were small built and whose manner of wresting a livelihood from the earth itself did not incline them to develop size and weight.

She moved forward with that long, swinging gait of hers, and he saw her coming and turned aside to meet her and draw her away from listening ears into the shadow of some trucks.

'What's wrong, Bob?' she asked.

He put an arm about her and held her strongly, aware of her gallant courage, of the strength on which a man might rely in time of need. Here was no puling girl, but his mate, born and bred of this strenuous, unyielding, cruel life of the coal-fields.

'Plenty, they're afraid, Jen,' he said quietly.

'What is it?'

'Number Three's had a fall between that and the new cutting they made in Four last week. That's what they think, anyway. They're waiting for the engineer to come up again. He's been taking soundings. They've got extra pumps working on Four and when they've done what they can with them, we're going to try to get through.'

'We? You mean—you're going down, Bob?'

Her own men were down in Three.

'I must, dear. They called for volunteers, and of course everybody spoke. They're a fine lot. Beaton picked out the first eight, and of course I was the first to be chosen. I know more than anyone how Three and Four lie.'

Weak suddenly and momentarily, Jennifer clung to him and laid her cheek against his shoulder. She did not argue or implore. It never occurred to her to do so. Of course he would go. That was just simple duty.

'How long before you go down, Bob?'

'Any minute now. They're testing the gas masks. I came to look for you. I knew you'd be here. Jennifer—darling.'

He was not a man of words. She knew it and would not have had him different by a hair's breadth.

'I know, Bob.'

They stood there for a few moments in silence. Then she spoke again.

'What are their chances?' she asked him steadily.

'Fairly good if we can make it quickly. We're going to try to tunnel through to them. We daren't blast because of other falls. It's too thin there.'

She did not comment on that. She knew what it meant. The same old story – a few extra tons or a few more lives, one or the other, but not both. Her father had said they were taking a risk, that Beaton had known it was a risk, that the engineers had warned him.

The men near the shaft began to split up and to move towards the waiting women with the guarded information which had been agreed upon.

'First volunteers ready,' said a voice.

Bob held Jennifer for a moment that was both agony and rapture.

'If I don't—see you again, Jen,' he whispered hoarsely.

She set her firm young mouth on his to silence the words she could not bear to hear spoken aloud. They had not kissed before.

'You'd better go now, Bob,' she said, and she tore herself from his hold and slipped back amongst the women whose tears would no longer be denied.

Gradually they pressed forward, a dense, surging mass, quiet, orderly, making no panic or scene, just waiting – waiting, hoping, some of them praying in whispers, clinging together or, like Jennifer, standing in silence and alone.

She saw a small, black-clad figure threading its way amongst the groups of women, a little, elderly man whose wisps of white hair were blown about his almost bald head by the chilly evening wind, whose mouth was as tender as a woman's and whose blue eyes were as innocent and trustful as a child's.

'Father Flint,' they called him, though he made no pretensions to representing any particular creed or order or religion, and he ministered to the needs of their bodies just as freely as he ministered to their souls. He had come amongst them as a young man, with a little money and a lot of hope. He had less of either now, but he counted himself as blessed beyond the bounds of ambition by the riches of their love for him and his for them.

He had built a little church when he first came to Werford, but scarcely anybody came to it for the purpose for which it was built. It served as a dispensary and casualty station for the sick, a free hostel for the homeless, reading-room, writing-room, unofficial club. A dart-board hung under an illuminated script of the Ten Commandments, and the rush seats had long been arranged round the room so that the young people could dance where Father Flint had once dreamed of a congregation.

Orthodox church and chapel were horrified for a long time, but Father Flint never came into his 'club' without seeing the face of Christ, and never left it without leaving behind him the memory of the Man he called Master.

He saw Jennifer and came towards her. She went to meet him, towering above him so that she had to bend to him.

'You ought to have brought a hat, Father,' she said. 'The wind's cold.'

'And the thatch growing thin,' he said, his china-blue eyes wearing a special smile for Jennifer. 'I didn't stay. If it hadn't been for Mrs. Brett, I should have had even less on for I was just going to bed. I hadn't much sleep last night,' he added apologetically.

'I know. You stopped with that poor Lucy Jones, didn't you?'

'Ah, poor girl, poor child. The world's a hard place for lonely women, Jennifer,' he said, shaking his head.

Poor, frail Lucy, who had come home to die in her fine clothes and her furs, and who, but for little Father Flint, would have died in the street or in the poor-house instead of in the arms of her mother.

'Women are fools,' said Jennifer.

He smiled.

'So are most men, my dear,' he said. 'I always feel so helpless when I come face to face with the real things of life—and with death.'

Her mouth quivered and she clenched her hands.

11

'With things like—this, Father,' she said in a low voice, and her eyes travelled to the skeleton arms above the shaft.

'Your father and brother are down there?' he asked.

'Yes. Bob's gone down too. He volunteered, of course,' she said steadily.

'I wish there were something one could do,' he said sadly. 'Words—words. What is that to offer at a time like this? And platitudes about God's will. I don't believe it is God's will that His people should suffer. He fought suffering and want with every means in His power, and I don't believe He ever intended that we should accept suffering as by His desire.'

They stood together for a few moments in silence, though all about them the murmurs of the crowd were growing louder, more broken, and hysterical. Women sobbed and did not try to hide their tears. Here and there were angry voices raised in condemnation of their leaders, of the owners who not only permitted these accidents to happen but even sometimes made profits out of them through clever insurance.

The temper of the waiting crowd was growing angry. Fear and suspense found an outlet in words which had little or no meaning, which were just an effort at finding relief, no matter how absurd and unjust the allegations they made.

Father Flint looked anxious and suddenly was inspired.

'Sing to them, Jennifer. They are keyed up, overwrought. It needs so little to lead them. They are like children. They are frightened.'

Jennifer did not hesitate. Simple of heart and of manner, she lifted her head and her voice rang clear and beautiful above the murmuring of the crowd, above the anger and the tears, above the bitterness and the heart-ache, above the hope that was so surely turning to despair as no sound or sign came from the pithead.

'Oh! for the wings of a dove!
Far away, far away would I fly.
In the wilderness build me a nest
And remain there for ever at rest.
In the wilderness build me a nest.'

Gradually the murmuring ceased, the other voices were still, and only Jennifer's remained, soaring above them as if the very music itself were wings to bear their hearts to heaven.

Many of the women dropped on their knees, their eyes closed, or wide open to the starry vault above them. Little Father Flint stood with his lips moving soundlessly, and they knew that he prayed for them and took comfort to themselves because he did so.

Unnoticed, a huge grey Rolls had drawn up on the outskirts of the crowd, and from it had stepped one of its occupants, leaving the other there, lying back on the cushions and indolently watching the scene which meant very little to him, a southerner, paying a short visit to Sir Jervis Patney at the Manor House.

Slowly he became conscious of the sound of Jennifer's voice and he sat forward and stared into the gathering darkness. He could not see the singer, but he recognised the quality of the voice, its volume and sweetness, the purity of tone. He knew it was quite untrained. Its values were uncertain, it was not always absolutely true, and the enunciation of the words set his teeth on edge.

But it was a voice! By heaven, it was a voice!

He leaned out and spoke to the chauffeur, who stood like an automaton by the side of the car waiting for Sir Jervis to return.

'Who is it singing, Blunt? Do you know?'

'I'm afraid I don't know nobody 'ereabouts, sir,' said that worthy stiffly.

'Could you go and find out, do you think?'

The man hesitated. Sir Jervis was a stickler for perfection of service.

'I'll take full responsibility if Sir Jervis comes back before you do,' said Rothe, and the man did as he was asked.

'A young woman by the name of Jenks, sir,' he said when he came back. 'Jennifer Jenks is the name. She's waiting for 'er father and 'er brother as is darn the mine.'

Rothe made a moue of distaste. Jennifer Jenks and the voice of an angel! What a misnomer!

There was a cry, and the crowd surged forward, the song ceasing abruptly as Jennifer herself was swung forward with the rest.

'They're coming up!' was the cry, and it took all the strength of the men at the top of the shaft to keep the women back so that the cage could discharge its load.

But no men from Number Three were amongst them, and only six of the eight who had gone down. Jennifer could see that Bob was not amongst them, and she put a hand to her throat, which had suddenly gone dry and hard.

'What is it? What's happened?' everybody was asking.

Nothing had happened. They could not get through and the gas down in Number Four was so deadly that six of the rescue party had had to be hauled up.

Bob was all right then. Bob was still working, still hoping that her father and Joe would be brought back to the surface from the pit of death.

Another six went down, and first-aid was administered by the ambulance men to those who had come up. As soon as they could speak, they told a story which struck death into the hearts of the women who listened and understood. It seemed certain that behind the fall of earth and coal, where sixty-four men were entombed and trapped, were poisonous gases from which nothing could hope to come back alive.

'It'll take us all night to get through to them unless we can blast,' said one.

'Gregory himself's been down and says it would be certain death to blast,' gasped another, who still fought for the air his lungs could not draw in.

'The stuff that's coming through is worse than anything any of us have ever tasted before,' said a third.

And these were all seasoned men, experienced men, men who would not easily be scared or give up hope.

Jennifer prayed as she listened. Prayer came naturally to her mind. She came of a race which is essentially religious, easily excited to emotional fervour, and though she was too sane and well-balanced to reach either the heights or the depths so easily attained by her fellow-countrymen and women, there was in her the same deep-rooted desire for expression of emotion which is the basis of all religious beliefs.

She tried not to think of her own two down there: of the grave, kindly, generous-hearted father; of Joe just on the threshold of life, sixteen only last week, gay, happy, laughing, full of plans for the future, plans in which she was a lady in a silk dress with a maid to do the work, a dog at her heels, a cat by the fireside, and a parrot in a cage.

How they had all laughed and teased her, telling her she would be an old maid when all the time there had been that lovely, secret knowledge that Bob Haling loved her and she him.

Oh Dad – Joe – Bob! She choked down the thoughts of them and remembered other men who were down there, remembered one by one nearly all of the sixty-four men and boys and of the weeping women whose hope was by now as faint as hers. Husbands there were whose wives would be left destitute, to survive for a while on charity whilst people remembered, and then to live God alone knew how. There would be so many worse off than she, Jennifer, who would have only herself to provide for, and soon Bob would do even that for her.

She went back to the other women, and through the dreary hours of the night they waited, shivering beneath their shawls, their clothes never at any time adequate protection against the winter and hopelessly inadequate for this night of drifting rain and eddying wind.

The cars had gone, the grey Rolls amongst them. Sir Jervis had felt that nothing more could be done than was already being done. It was too late for him to do anything, in any case. He had had his chance when first he had been told that the Lighton was not capable of the output he demanded of it. He had been brief and to the point about that.

'That's the quantity I was told the mine would yield and that's the quantity it's got to be made to yield,' he had said. 'You're not denying that the coal is there?'

Oh no, they were not denying that, but they began to go into figures, to use words that meant nothing to him. Why should he be expected to know what these things were? He paid other people to understand all about coal. He could not be expected to do anything but draw the profits from it.

So by the night of the Lighton disaster, he had had most of the required output. It was a nuisance, of course, that this affair should have happened whilst there was still coal in the pit, but possibly later on it could be reopened. In the meantime he might as well go back to Belsdale. Beaton would ring him up there if there were any further developments.

Beaton was a decent man at heart, though as the mouthpiece and paid servant of Sir Jervis he was hated and distrusted by the men. The scenes at the pit-head this night sickened and appalled him. It was his first experience of an actual disaster, and he blamed himself out of all proportion for the part he himself had played in it. He had known that the workings should have been abandoned at least three days earlier, but he had preferred to keep his job rather than say so more definitely than he had.

Someone else would have taken the job over, of course, with the same tragic result, but at least his own conscience would have been clear.

Sir Jervis had looked round nervously when he was preparing to go. He liked neither the weeping women nor the scowling men who pressed a thought too closely to the barricade which had been hastily thrown together to keep the crowd back.

Beaton caught the look and his lip curled.

'No, there's nothing you can do here, Sir Jervis,' he said in answer to a question which he felt was merely rhetorical. 'The people might get nasty if you did.'

'I really don't see why. After all, I didn't make the coal fall. They can't hold me responsible for an Act of God.'

'I don't suppose they'll be looking at it in that light if their men don't come up,' said Beaton grimly.

There was a low sound like the incoming wave of an angry sea. It died away again, but Sir Jervis did not wait to be sure of that. He reached the grey Rolls, got in beside his friend Rothe with unseemly lack of dignity, and did not draw a comfortable breath until the great iron gates of the Manor House had clanged to behind the car.

'My sheylde is mine honour' was the motto emblazoned beneath the lion and the leopard which did valiant battle over the gates.

The Patneys liked their family crest. They had spelled shield with a 'y'; they felt it looked much more dignified and blue-blooded than the normal way. In any case, it did not in the least look as if it had only recently been added to the lion and the leopard. It fitted in so *well* on that sort of screen thing, my dear! It was Jervis's idea. Excellent, don't you agree?

And back at the pithead the women still waited, silent again, hopeless, dreary, infinitely desolate. Dawn came with that ghostly whispering of the world which is the first stirring of a new day, and the cranks of the cages turned again and brought up for the last time the ghastly-looking, staggering figures of the rescue party.

It had been decided that nothing more could be done, that no living thing could still be entombed in Number Three, that further attempts at reaching the bodies of the men would only add to the toll of the victims, for poisonous fumes were pouring into the channel which had been made from Number Four, and during the night dozens of the volunteers had been brought to the surface only just in time to save their lives.

And at the last minute came that extra catastrophe which it seemed the devil himself must have devised for tortured women and half-dead men.

Half way up, one of the chains which held the cage broke, and the platform with its human cargo went hurtling to the bottom of the pit again, flinging the men like so many lifeless sacks against the floor and iron-barred walls.

A shriek went up and instantly fresh rescue work was begun. They knew what must be done, and almost before the news of the disaster had reached the outer fringe of the crowd the unconscious men were already being hauled up in the second cage and the ambulances which had waited all night were rushed to the top of the shaft.

Jennifer, white-faced, watched them carry the broken form of Bob Haling past her on a stretcher.

'Is he—dead?' she asked, her voice sounding queer and cracked.

'No, only stunned, Jenny. May be a bone or two broken, but it takes more than that to kill young Bob,' said one of the stretcher-bearers, and she dropped back amongst the crowd again.

She had lost sight of Lottie, but now she found her again, a pathetic figure with her face buried in her shawl, her shapeless body rocking backwards and forwards in the helplessness of her grief.

Jennifer took her home, made her go to bed in the big old four-poster which her father and Joe had shared and would never need again, brought her hot drinks, covered her shaking form with extra blankets and rugs, sat down beside her at last and let her own head droop against the pillow, longing for the tears which would not come.

Lottie looked out of red, heavy-lidded eyes.

'The children, Jen,' she said.

'They're all right. Father Flint's staying with them till your mother can get here,' said Jennifer.

'Oh, Jen—Jen! I'll never see him again!'

'Don't, dear—don't,' said Jennifer, and she stroked the aching brow with her tender, strong fingers until at last Lottie dropped to sleep and she could be still and alone.

She sat there staring into the new day, and now there was no song in her heart.

Chapter Two

The grey Rolls drew up before Jennifer's house – the house which was still called hers, at least, though she would not be able to go on paying the rent if she did not earn a living, and how was she to do that in Werford? At the best of times they seemed to live by taking in one another's washing at Werford, and at a time like this no one knew how they lived or were going to live.

The Lighton pits were definitely closed and Beaton had told them that Sir Jervis did not propose to open them again. A requiem service had been held at the pithead for the sixty-four men by whose tomb they stood, and that was all. Just another tragedy to add to the story of the coal-fields, a story for the papers, a subject for people to write about, to collect money for, a mild sensation with that piquant touch of horror which is so intriguing to the minds of the safe and comfortable sections of the community. Just that – and then on with the dance! On with the next horror, and for this, forgetfulness.

Sixty-four miners! My dear, how perfectly *ghastly*! Have you seen that new film at the Empire? My dear, too devastatingly male!

But for Werford there would be no forgetfulness on this side of the grave. Women took up their lives again, broken, crushed, hopeless, despairing. Children laughed and played, babies were born, old people died. Life was the same and yet eternally different.

Jennifer looked out of her open doorway to see the grey Rolls pull up. She recognised it. It had been pointed out to her on the night of the disaster. Her lip curled and her eyes narrowed a little. What did Sir Jervis Patney want of her? Was he going to offer her sympathy, charity? How dare he come even to her door?

But it was not the dapper little figure of Sir Jervis. It was an older man, a man in the fifties, grey-haired, erect, alert, a little pompous perhaps but with a face that would have inspired confidence had its owner not stepped out of Sir Jervis's Rolls.

Julian Rothe smiled at her and walked straight into the living-room, aware of storm in the air but not a whit dismayed by it, 'Miss Jennifer Jenks, I believe?' he asked pleasantly.

Jennifer inclined her head, but made no other answer.

Rothe disguised marvellously his disappointment at this close view of the singer. She had been pointed out to him at the requiem service, and he had realised that she was no beauty, but there had been an air of strength and vigour about her which had distinguished her from the bowed and weeping women about her. Seen at close quarters and alone, however, she certainly had little claim to distinction.

'I am Julian Rothe,' he said, and was amused rather than piqued to see that the name conveyed nothing to her.

'You wanted to see me about something?' she asked, and the clear tones of her speaking voice gave him the pleasure he had not been able to find in her appearance.

'Yes. I heard you sing the other night at the pithead. Forgive me if I am clumsy, if I have—intruded on your grief too soon, but I am obliged to go back to London in a day or two and I wanted very much to see you before doing so.'

Still she said nothing. He thought he had never seen anyone with such a capacity for stillness, and yet there had been storm in her eyes. This was no cold, lifeless clod.

'I am interested in you, Miss Jenks. I see my name means nothing to you, but I am what they so gracefully call nowadays an impresario – a teacher of singing, a discoverer and launcher of opera singers, variety stars, and a lot of other often useless and unnecessary people. You would be neither of those. Do you, I wonder, realise how great a gift you have?'

'My voice, do you mean? I have always been able to sing,' said Jennifer without enthusiasm.

'You have had no training?'

'No. I have always been too hard at work to bother with things like that,' she said indifferently.

'I have to believe you, of course, but it seems incredible that you shouldn't know, that no one has ever told you.'

'Told me what?' asked Jennifer.

'That you have untold wealth in your throat. You live amongst coal-mines and in your own self is a gold-mine. What are you going to do about it? I know—forgive me again—that you are singularly bereft by this terrible disaster—'

'Don't trouble to say things like that, not to me,' said Jennifer brusquely, all the lovely softness of her tones gone. 'I know just what you and your kind think of us sort of people – those poor, wretched miners, who are always squabbling and striking. I know just how much of a disaster it is to you and your friends when we women lose all we've got in the world. Oh, go away, please! We don't want you here, any of you.'

What she said did not matter to him in the least. He rejoiced in her voice, in the verification of his impression that there was fire as well as ice. He loved the ups and downs, the major chords, the soft minor cadences dying away into silence.

'Tell me what you're going to do, how you're going to live?' he said.

She stared at him, finding it hard to realise that what she had said had made absolutely no impression on him.

'What business is it of yours?' she demanded curtly.

'Probably none at all, though I'm trying to make it my business,' he said with a smile, aware by now that his famous charm of manner was entirely lost upon this strange, gaunt girl with the exquisite voice for which apparently she cared nothing at all. 'I came to see you today with a quite definite proposition to offer.'

She waited with that same stillness and patience she had shown at first.

'I want to train your voice, to teach you how to use it,' he went on, a little nonplussed by her stoical calm.

'Why?' she asked.

'Well—er—why, to make a great artiste of you, a great singer, an opera star—concert singer—you could be anything you wished—

almost,' adding the last word as he remembered her gaunt frame, her lack of beauty, and hoped she would not desire to become a star of musical comedy.

'You mean go away from here?' she asked.

'But of course. You could hardly study in a place like this. And I have to be in London for my other pupils, my work. You would start in London, but before you were ready you would have to spend time in Berlin, in Vienna, in Paris, Rome—everywhere. A great artiste must be cosmopolitan.'

'I don't know what that word means,' said Jennifer gravely. 'I understood all the rest, though, but I don't want to, thank you.'

He stared at her. He had felt self-righteous, coming with gifts in his hands to turn the pauper girl into the princess – but she spurned them!

'Do I understand that you don't *want* to have your voice trained? Why, there's a fortune in it, girl!' with a little spurt of impatience. 'Don't you understand? I can make you famous, one of the greatest singers in the world. With your voice and my skill and knowledge, you can have the world at your feet.'

She stood looking down at him, for he was several inches shorter than she, and he had the unpleasant and ridiculous feeling that she looked down on him metaphorically as well as physically.

'And what are you going to get out of it?' she asked calmly.

He flushed. Heaven, what a girl! What an impossible, ungracious creature!

'Money, obviously,' he said curtly. 'One doesn't do things for any other reason in business, and this is a business proposition. I should assume full responsibility towards you, provide you with everything necessary to you for an agreed time, which I estimate roughly would be about three years. During that time you would learn to the best of your ability everything I asked of you, not only how to sing but also how to comport yourself, to speak other languages. Then, when you were launched on your career, you would be bound to me for another stated period, during which I should recompense myself for what I had spent on you, taking a reasonable profit, and then you would be free, famous, wealthy. How old are you?'

'Twenty,' said Jennifer.

'A glorious age, though I could wish I had had you two years earlier. One can do much between eighteen and twenty.'

'Taking things for granted, aren't you?' asked Jennifer. 'You haven't got me yet, you know.'

'What do you mean by that?'

'That I'm not going to do it. I am glad you've put it all so plainly because I see that all you're after is money for yourself, so I need not feel badly about turning it down, as I should have done if you'd offered all that in friendship. Not that you would have done that, of course!' with a curling lip.

He could have kicked himself for having been so clumsy, but he had naturally assumed that a girl of the people, a mere miner's daughter, would jump at the chance of selling herself in so high a market. After all, these people can't have the sensibilities of the well-to-do, can they? How could he have dreamed that she would respond more readily to an offer of friendship rather than to one of money?

'I don't think you can understand, Jennifer. Do you mind if I call you that?'

She neither consented nor demurred, but just stood waiting.

'You don't understand. You will be wasted here. What will you do for a living even? I know something of your unfortunate circumstances—'

She cut him short with a gesture that had grandeur in it, a gesture which he could appreciate.

'I don't want to discuss that with you or anyone,' she said.

Lottie popped her head in at the open door at that moment and would have withdrawn it again. Jennifer knew quite well that her curiosity regarding the visitor who had come in Sir Jervis's car had overcome her.

'Come in, Lottie,' she called. 'This gentleman is Mr.—Mr. Julian Rothe,' picking up the card which he had laid on the table near her and reading the name with a little difficulty. 'What do you think he wants? To take me to London with him and turn me into a famous singer?'

Her voice was derisive, and Lottie's eyes darted from one to the other of them in uncertainty.

23

Rothe turned to her.

'I am trying to persuade Miss Jenks that she has a great future before her if she will let me take her in hand and train her,' he said.

'You think her voice good?' asked Lottie shyly.

'Definitely. Raw and untrained, of course, but definitely good.'

'We all think it's lovely,' said Lottie. 'Oh, Jen, are you going to do it?'

'No,' said Jennifer, closing her lips with a little snap.

After a moment's hesitation, Lottie threw the weight of her influence on Rothe's side. In vain they argued and explained. Jennifer just said 'No' in that firm tone, and at last he could do nothing but go away as he had come, disappointed and angry.

'If you change your mind, you have my address on that card,' he said shortly. 'I warn you, though, that in six months' time *I* might have changed *my* mind. It's no use starting too late, and you've lost two valuable years already,' and he bowed ironically in his anger to the two girls and walked out to the waiting car.

Jennifer stood quite still. It had all happened so quickly, much too quickly for a mind which had not been trained in the necessity for quick decisions and which was still numbed by the bitterness of her loss and her anxiety for Bob, who lay in his hospital bed at Belsdale, torn with pain, struggling not to let Jennifer know his actual condition.

His legs had been crushed by the force of the cage's fall, and though the doctors were doing everything in their power for him, it was very doubtful whether they would save the limbs. They had tried to hide the gravity of the position from him, but he knew too much to be deceived, and his magnificent strength had been his enemy, for he had retained consciousness when most men would have been granted merciful oblivion.

Lottie had been to see her brother and to her he had told the truth.

'I'm done for, Lottie,' he said quietly. 'I don't suppose I'm going to die. They're kinder to the beasts than to us. They'd shoot a horse or a dog, but we have to go on living, if you can call it life to be dragged about in a chair or roll about on two stumps.'

She had broken down and sobbed at his bedside.

'Don't say it, Bob. It can't be true!'

'They won't admit it, but I know. I'm no fool. They've left the thinking part of me alive, worse luck. Lottie, Jennifer mustn't know, not yet. She's got all she can stand up to at the moment. You see—I can't ever marry her, Lottie, and I've got to work out how to make her understand it and give me up without knowing the truth. She'd make me marry her if she knew, wouldn't she? She's like that. She'd ruin her whole life to stick by a helpless clod.'

Lottie nodded, broken-hearted. There seemed no ray of light for any of them just then. A huge fund had been started all over the country for the relief of the women and children of that tragic sixty-four, and she supposed, in an apathetic way, that they would all live somehow. The position of the miners was such that, by long usage, their womenfolk had come to accept the idea of living from hand to mouth, never knowing where the next day's food would come from, but blindly accepting it when and where they could get it. When their men were working full time, every spare penny had to go to repaying the money borrowed, the goods allowed on credit during periods of enforced half-time or of one of the tragic, hopeless strikes which in the end accomplished nothing. When they were on half-time, or not working at all for any reason, the men could borrow, so when they were on full-time they were little better off because of the mountain of debt that had accumulated and which, for the most part, they strove honestly to repay.

So to Lottie this tragedy that hung over Jennifer and Bob was only another thing to be accepted, to be lived through.

'I know, Bob. Yes, Jennifer's like that. She'd marry you somehow, whatever you said or did, if she knew you were a cripple.'

He winced and turned his head away so that she should not see the look in his eyes. A cripple – he! So proud of his strength, so jealous of it, making himself hard and firm by exercise, living the decent sort of life, with no excesses, which kept him fit. He had been so proud to be able to offer Jennifer, whom they all loved, something worth while.

And now? There would be some beggarly compensation given him, he supposed. Compensation! What in this world could ever compensate him for the loss of his limbs, of the very power to walk?

And it would even be a grudging gift then. He knew so well what happened. It would be pointed out to him that he had not received his injuries whilst actually in performance of his duties. He had not been told to go down the pit to try to rescue his comrades. He had offered to go, *wanted* to go, not in the way of paid duty, but for personal reasons. Of course, had he been *told* to go, it would have been a different matter – oh yes, he knew! He had heard it all before, seen the miserable subterfuges whereby compensation had been refused, or reduced to a pitiable minimum on some technical excuse which just provided a loophole for the people who would have had to pay.

'You won't tell her, Lottie?' he had said, and she had promised and gone away, blind with weeping.

And now had come this offer which would have provided a way out for Jennifer, for poor, broken Bob – and she had refused it!

After Rothe had gone, Lottie renewed her persuasions.

'You ought to accept, Jen. It's your right. Think what it would mean to you. What are you going to do down here? There's no work for anyone. You'd have to go away anyhow, take a job in one of the big towns as a servant. Jen, why won't you?'

'Bob needs me,' said Jennifer simply, and would add nothing to that.

Where she gave, she gave royally. Where she loved, she loved with no mean withholding. She and Bob belonged to each other. Where he was, there she remained. Where he went, there she went too. She made no heroics of it. That was just as she saw things. It just did not occur to her to try to see them differently.

'Bob needs me,' she said, and that was all there was to it.

But Lottie had gone a little further down the dark road of life than had Jennifer. She knew what it was to despair, not for herself but for her man and her children; knew the agony of a mother who cannot give her children enough food, of the right sort of food, to make them strong and well. She knew what it was to watch them grow thin and pale, develop all sorts of weakening diseases, knowing all the time that if she could give them just food, the simple right of everything living, they would be well again – food, not just margarine and bread, the cheapest of meat once a week, an egg between four as a treat, skim milk or cheap powder mixed with water for her babies when her own under-nourished body could no longer give them their birthright.

Oh yes, Lottie knew. And Jennifer could not know. Her father and brother had been luckier than most, for they had been on work which kept them at full pay when others had been 'stood off' for a time or forced to work only three days a week, with pay in proportion. The Jenks's had never been badly pressed, and there were no young children to keep when Jennifer had taken over her mother's job.

But if she married poor Bob, she would descend to the very depths. There might be children. She did not know the extent of Bob's injuries, but Jennifer would ardently desire children. She had mothered everybody else's for years and she could administer nauseous medicine, cleanse and bandage wounds, perform minor operations in the way of removing splinters, lancing boils, applying poultices, where often the mothers had to admit defeat. She loved everything small and helpless, agonised over wrongs she could not put right. What a hell, then, would her life be if she married Bob Haling, having to work for him as well as herself, seeing his physical and mental torture, bear his children and suffer for them and with them, or deny herself forever the joy for which she seemed to Lottie to be made.

Oh, she must take this man's offer, she must! She could come back and marry Bob later, if she still wanted to, if she had by then not gone too far from them, and a lump came into Lottie's throat as she thought of that. They would lose Jennifer anyway!

So, when all else had failed, Lottie went back to the hospital to Bob, filled with the courage that was utterly selfless, and for a long time they talked. She told him everything about Rothe's offer, about Jennifer's proud refusal of it.

'She won't go because of you, Bob,' she ended brokenly. 'Oh, you poor dear, it's too much to ask of you! Too cruel!'

His eyes stared into space, seeing far beyond the white hospital wall, seeing life stretch endlessly ahead – life as a cripple, life without his glorious Jennifer. Sternly he made his mind turn away from that picture and to see Jennifer's future, clearly, with cruel truth.

When he spoke, his voice was flat and his face grey with pain.

'I understand, Lottie. Thank you—my dear,' he said. 'I think I'd like you to go now. Will you ask—Jennifer—not to come Wednesday? Just that. Don't say I'm worse or anything. Just not to come. Perhaps on Sunday she'll come.'

And on Sunday she found him sitting up for the first time and had no means of knowing that he had dragged himself to that position as soon as the nurse had thankfully withdrawn and left the ward to the visitors. Sweating with pain, almost fainting before he had accomplished it, he had at last achieved it, his neighbour in the next bed able to reach over and make a support with his pillows for his back.

'Oh, Bob, you're sitting up! That's grand,' said Jennifer happily, but the next moment the smile faded and gave place to a puzzled, hurt look from which Bob averted his eyes.

'Oh, I could have sat up before if I'd wanted to, but it's fine being made a fuss of by the pretty nurses and making yourself out to be an invalid,' he said brusquely. 'Matter of fact, I'm glad you came today, Jen. I wanted to see you.'

'Then why did you send a message for me not to come Wednesday?' she asked him, and he knew she had been hurt.

'Oh, I had other people to see, a man who was coming specially to see me,' he said indifferently.

'Oh. I see,' said Jennifer slowly, the hurt look deepening into a sort of lost bewilderment. 'What man, dear?'

'Oh, a man who comes here visiting. Matter of fact—I'm not coming back to the pits, Jen.'

'Bob! Your injury's worse than you told me!' she cried at once.

'No. How you jump at things. I'm all right, I tell you. The doctor says I shall probably be about again in a week or two. It's not that. I've decided not to go back to the pits, though. For one thing they'll never open Lighton again, or so Beaton says, so there won't be much work for anybody this winter. For another, I'm sick of Werford, sick of the whole business, never want to see a coal face again. I'm thinking of going out to Canada. That's what I wanted to see that man about. He arranges it sometimes, and he thinks he could get me out there. I dare say Clowes will manage to get me enough compensation money to pay my fare, and there'll be nothing to keep me here if I don't work in the pits again.'

It was the longest speech of his life, and he had made it without once looking at Jennifer. He had known, however, just how she would be looking hurt, puzzled, with eyes wide and incredulous, with her mouth, that tender mouth, trembling a little until at last she would bring pride to her rescue and sit quite still, with nothing at all in her face that anyone might read.

She did not speak for so long that at last he had to turn and look at her. She was staring straight ahead of her, and, just as he had known, there was no expression on her face at all. It was just wooden, blank.

Her tone was the same when she spoke.

'I see, Bob,' she said. 'Are you going soon?'

That was all. No passionate outcry, no protest, nothing. Just, 'I see, Bob. Are you going soon?'

He choked back his own passion of grief.

'As soon as Clowes can arrange the compensation and I can get out of here. The doctors talk of my being able to leave next week.'

It was true – but he was not to be discharged as cured, as he tried to imply. He was to be moved to the City Hospital as soon as they thought he could stand the twenty-mile ambulance journey. With the equipment and the vast resources of the great hospital, they hoped to be able to do something more for him than could be undertaken in the little Belsdale institution.

Her eyes came slowly to meet his, to hold them for a moment's exquisite, blinding pain, and then to look away again.

'That will be—fine for you,' she said slowly, her lovely voice all strangled and harsh.

She longed to be able to break down this dreadful, unexpected thing which had risen between them, but she could not. There seemed nothing to do, nothing to say. 'What is it, my love, my dear? Where have all the lovely things of life gone? Why do you look at me as if you had never loved me? Speak to me as if I were a stranger?'

Those were the things her heart said, but her lips spoke no word of that. She would have done exactly what he was doing, had circumstances been reversed, but how was she to know what he was doing? It just did not occur to her. She was a humble person. She did not find it incredible that she should not have been able to keep his love. The incredible thing was that she had ever had it, even for so short a time.

So all she said was 'That will be fine for you,' and presently she rose to go, though still ten minutes of the visiting hour remained.

He made one last effort.

'Jen—you—what will you do?' he asked her desperately.

'Oh—I don't know. I haven't thought about it. Things have all been so—uncertain. I think I'll go now, Bob, if you don't mind. Goodbye. Good luck. God bless you, my dear,' and she was gone, leaving behind her such intolerable pain of body and mind that for hours he was dazed and dumb and broken.

And Jennifer went back to her cottage and put in order what was left of her life, saying no word to anyone, not even to Lottie.

There was not very much to do. The rent was paid up to the end of the week and she had already told the landlord that she would not be able to remain there. The furniture was of little value and she gave it away, keeping for herself only such little intimate belongings as she could not bear to part with or destroy – an old carved pipe of her father's, a fretwork photograph-frame which Joe had made for her birthday and which held a snapshot of the four of them before her mother had died. There were one or two books, too, that her father had bought for her – Shakespeare's plays, *David Copperfield*, Stevenson's *Virginibus Puerisque*, and a volume of Rupert Brooke's poems which she loved without understanding them very well.

She opened it, looking for something she remembered, something she had been able to understand without knowing that some day it would find an echo in her own heart.

The way of love was thus.
He was born one winter morn
With hands delicious,
And it was well with us.

Love came our quiet way,
Lit pride in us and died in us,
All in a winter's day
There is no more to say.

That appealed to her quiet spirit. For her 'there was no more to say'.

She had a little money from her father's insurance club, enough to get her to London, to this place where Julian Rothe would help her to forget.

At the last she told Lottie.

'Bob has decided to go away from Werford, go away from England altogether and start afresh in Canada. There's nothing for him here,' she said. 'So I am going to London, to this man Rothe, to be turned into a great singer.'

Her voice told Lottie none of the things she wanted to know, asked for neither sympathy nor pity, just stated facts as if they were no more to her than last week's washing.

'I shall miss you, Jen,' she said in a small, tearful voice.

Jennifer held her in her arms in a rare moment of emotion and in her eyes lay a world of pain.

'I shall come back, Lottie. I shan't be able to stay away. My body will be there, but my heart will be here for ever.'

'You'll forget us, Jen, when you're a great lady, a famous singer,' said Lottie sadly.

Jennifer shook her head.

'I don't think I'm the kind to forget very easily,' she said slowly.

Chapter Three

Jennifer settled herself grimly in the corner of an empty third-class compartment.

She had refused to let anyone come to see her off. No one had even seen her leave Werford. She had just walked out of her house, leaving Lottie to dispose of the last oddments of furniture and hand the key to the agent, as they had arranged.

Her friends would have been amazed had they seen her, for she was in a print working dress, a shawl and wooden clogs, and in her hand she clutched an ancient rush basket secured with a strap. Jennifer had never looked like that before, and she had so arrayed herself in a spirit of defiance, as a gesture to show Julian Rothe just what he had undertaken. She could not have explained to herself why she did it, but it gave her a queer feeling of courage when she most needed it.

She was going to this man Rothe with the gloves off.

It was a long and weary journey, for the train was a slow one and people got in and out at the various stations, glancing curiously at Jennifer in her shawl and clogs, though she gave them nothing but a detached, indifferent glance in return.

Several times she looked at Rothe's card, memorising the address and having not the faintest idea where Highgate was, save that it was 'London', and when she got out of the train at the huge terminus she looked round her with her first real fear.

It was early morning, not quite six o'clock, and there are few more desolate spots on earth than a London station at six o'clock on a winter morning. Not many people had arrived by her train, and those who did went at once about their business, leaving her standing forlornly on the platform, tired and hungry.

A porter came up to her.

'Want 'ny help, miss?' he asked her with gruff kindness, and she produced Rothe's bit of pasteboard.

' 'Ighgate? That's quite a decent way from 'ere. Won't be no trams runnin' from 'ere for a bit,' he said. 'Julian Rothe. That's the man as puts on the shows, isn't it?'

'I don't know,' said Jennifer. 'Where shall I have to wait for the trams?'

'Well, you can wait in the station. You can get a cup o' corfee over there. Buffy's not open yet, but you can see where them men are. You go in there.'

Jennifer took her place gravely with the line of men waiting at a stall for coffee in thick cups, and they eyed her curiously but with the rough kindliness that is in most men who work hard for a living. She told them, in answer to their questions, that she wanted to get to Highgate, and they exchanged glances, nudging and whispering together, and then the spokesman of the party moved next to her.

'Say, miss, we got to go right up near this place o' yours. We got a lorry artside. If yer don't mind it being a bit rough-like, it'd take you nearer than the tram and it won't cost you nothink. We're movin' orf right away.'

Jennifer, warmed by the coffee and the men's rough kindness, accepted gladly and climbed into the lorry, consenting cheerfully to being covered up with sacks 'till we get clear o' the cops a bit'. The unconventional mode of travelling was nothing to her, country-bred as she was, and when presently the men began to sing as they jolted along, she joined in with them vigorously, to their delight.

They set her down at the bottom of the road which they told her would take her to Rothe's house, and she parted with them regretfully, feeling lost again as she stood on the path and watched the lorry vanish in the cold morning mist.

It was barely daybreak, and she had to peer at the names of the houses as she went, growing more frightened as she realised how far apart the gates were and what enormous houses must lie behind them.

She found the one she wanted at last. 'Pesante' was its curious name, and only when she began to understand both musical terms and the slightly mordant wit of Julian Rothe did she appreciate his choice of a name for the huge, gloomy-looking place which for some reason or other he had chosen to inhabit.

She walked slowly between two ilex hedges which depressed her still more, coming out on the semi-circular stretch of gravel which lay in front of the house with its enormous double doors defaced with hideous brass knockers which a blue-faced maid was vainly trying to polish in the foggy atmosphere.

She stopped to stare unbelievingly when she heard Jennifer's clogs on the gravel, and Jennifer herself flushed very pink. She had long repented the foolish trick she had played on herself by coming to Rothe's house dressed like that, but there was nothing for it now to go through with it.

'I want Mr. Julian Rothe,' she said in a clear tone to the astonished girl.

Florrie burst into a spasm of laughter and fled into the house, leaving the door with its half polished brass hanging open. Jennifer walked in, put down her preposterous double basket, and sat on one of the carved hall chairs, looking round her and beginning to feel as absurd as she felt she looked.

The hall was as big as most of the entire houses she had known, and on its dark, gleaming floor lay rugs of beautiful soft colours. From the centre ran up, in two wide, curving branches, a magnificent staircase with another landing above, semi-circular, with deep windows to the floor and heavy curtains drawn back from them. On either side opened a wide corridor, and from where she sat she could see closed doors at intervals.

From the lower hall were other doors, massive, carved affairs designed in the spacious days when the harbouring of dust and dirt was either of no consequence, or could be removed by the host of servants which such decorations made necessary. Jennifer, who had always done her own work, shuddered at the thought of keeping a place like this clean. Why, a woman would never be done with her work!

The maid who had been cleaning the brass returned.

'Why, she's come inside—the cheek of it!' said the girl, and the pompous-looking man who had returned with her came to stare at Jennifer. She thought his outfit peculiar. A man who wore half dress clothes and half baize apron and red woollen cardigan at seven o'clock in the morning had surely no call to stare so hard at what *she* wore, and she gave him back look for look.

'My good girl, you can't come in 'ere,' he said with dignity.

'I've come to see Mr. Julian Rothe, by appointment,' said Jennifer composedly, sitting firm.

'By appointment? At seven in the morning? Ho no, miss. Not Mr. Rothe. That won't do. You'll 'ave to think out another one, *h'if* you please.'

'I have come over two hundred miles to see Mr. Rothe, because he asked me to, and I'm not going until I have seen him,' said Jennifer. 'If he is not up, I will wait here until he is.'

Simmons scratched his head, realised thereby that he had not yet brushed his hair, and decided to waste no more time on such nonsense as this.

'Well, Mr. Rothe is not up, and won't be for another hour or more, and you can't sit 'ere for an hour. You better come back.'

'I haven't anywhere to go. I have been travelling all night. I am tired and hungry and I have no intention of going out of this house until I have seen Mr. Rothe,' said Jennifer with spirit.

Simmons and Florrie exchanged glances, not knowing what to do with this extraordinary visitor. The butler had a wholesome respect for his employer, and he could see nothing but trouble resulting from having allowed this young person to remain for an indefinite period in the hall.

'Well, if that's 'ow you feel about it, miss, all I can say is I shall 'ave to call the police and 'ave you removed,' and with that he walked majestically towards the still open front door.

Jennifer had made up her mind what to do in any such emergency, and she did it now. Rising to her feet and moving so as to be immediately between the two wings of the staircase, with the domed vault of the roof high above her, she lifted her head and began to sing.

'Oh! for the wings, for the wings of a dove,'

she sang, her voice high and clear, soaring up into the roof, reaching Rothe as she had hoped and believed it would, coming to him out of his dreams and seeming a part of them translated into actual, living sounds.

For a few moments he lay there, whilst downstairs the servants stood stupefied, and Jennifer sang on, knowing that if he heard her, he would associate that song with her. Then suddenly he sprang out of bed, pulled on a dressing-gown, thrust his feet into slippers and came out to stand in the arc of the landing above her, looking down at her.

For a moment he stood there, bewildered at her appearance, at her bare head with the shawl thrown back from it, the print dress, the wooden clogs. Then he was down the stairs in a bound, taking her hands in his, smiling at her, crying to her: 'Jennifer! Jennifer, my dear—oh, my dear!'

Simmons melted away to return in the twinkling of an eye minus apron and cardigan, plus coat and the ministrations of a hair-brush, and he shooed Florrie off to her brass-cleaning and stood waiting for orders with breathless interest.

Jennifer had stopped singing, but he made her go on, stood listening, frowning now and then, smiling for a brief second, and nodding his head. She'd do! She *was* all he had dreamed her to be. The capacity was there, the volume, the depth, the clarity. God! What could he not do with a voice like that?

'When did you come?' he asked her. 'How? Where did you sleep? Have you had breakfast?'

The questions were fired at her. She could scarcely believe he was the quiet, composed, businesslike man who had stood in her little room and offered her a bargain.

'I have travelled in the train all night and I came here on a lorry,' she told him gravely.

He stared at her and then laughed.

'On a lorry? Why? Were there no taxis?'

'I haven't the money for taxis,' said Jennifer. 'The men offered to bring me here, so I came with them. They were very kind.'

'I'm sure they were,' he said.

'I sang with them coming along. It was fun. We laughed quite a lot,' she said in her serious way.

'Jennifer, you're going to be the toast of the town,' he said.

She shook her head.

'I'm afraid you may be disappointed in me, Mr. Rothe,' she said.

'I don't think so. But what about breakfast? Did you say you had had some?'

'No, I haven't.'

'Come along then. Simmons, breakfast for two, and tell cook a good one, please. Come along, Jennifer. It looks as if I'm going to call you that, doesn't it? Jennifer Jenks—that won't do at all, you know.'

She was letting him lead her up the stairs, his hand beneath her arm. It seemed strange to her and not quite right that he should be so familiar, but she did not like to draw her arm away.

'Why won't it do?' she asked.

'My dear, no prima donna was ever called Jenks. No prima donna ever could be called Jenks and still be a prima donna. We must find you another name.'

'Yes, Mr. Rothe,' said Jennifer. Everything was upside down and she was so completely lost that what did it matter if she lost her name as well?

The way she spoke his name gave him an idea. He noticed for the first time that there was a trace of accent in her speech. That must be eradicated, of course, and her terrible figure must somehow be given grace, her complexion improved – but for the most part he must leave her as she was.

On second thoughts, he rather liked the way she said Rothe.

'Rothe,' he said aloud. 'I wonder? Why not? Jennifer Rothe. That would be amusing and intriguing. Jennifer Rothe. How would that appeal to you, my child?'

'You mean—pretend that my name is that? Jennifer Rothe?' she asked.

'Yes. Yes. We'll do that. It will give the gossips food for thought. My pupil I shall call you, but they will be torn between wife, daughter, and mistress.'

He chuckled, and Jennifer thought him a little mad, not quite catching his meaning.

He opened a door for her and ushered her in, but she drew back instantly, her face flaming, for they were in his bedroom.

'I—I can't come in here,' she said.

'Nonsense! Why not? Everybody does. I don't get up as a rule till eleven or so, and anyone who wants to see me comes and has breakfast with me. Sit down and don't be stupid. That's the one thing I can't stand – stupidity.'

Jennifer simply turned and walked out of the room and down the stairs again, meeting Simmons, who was carrying a folded table.

Rothe hesitated, frowned, and then, with a chuckle, followed her.

'Put breakfast in the morning-room, Simmons,' he said. 'This way, Jennifer,' and he ushered her with an ironical smile into a small room where a bright fire burned and two large cats were asleep on the rug.

'Meet Gog and Magog,' he said, introducing her gravely to the furry aristocrats.

Jennifer acknowledged the introductions, stroked the great heads, one grey, one jet black, and was somewhat at a loss until Simmons brought in the breakfast and drew up a chair for her.

'I trust you will pardon my *déshabille*, Miss Rothe,' said Julian airily.

Jennifer looked across at him sedately, and then laughed. It changed her completely, that laugh, and the sound itself was a beautiful one, as a singer's laugh should be, but as, alas! it not always is.

'You think me very ignorant and stupid, don't you?' she asked.

That laugh of hers had worked wonders for him, and he smiled across at her as he helped her to bacon and eggs in such quantity as she had never seen on one plate before in her frugal life.

'I think you're quite likely to make a howling success of life, my dear,' he said, with a wry smile at his own choice of words.

The sound of voices outside sent Jennifer into the depths of shyness again, and she was scarlet and tongue-tied when at length the door opened and three people came in, two girls and a pretty young man.

They greeted Rothe with amused laughter.

'Entertaining royalty, darling Julian?' asked the young man. 'Or couldn't you sleep?'

Rothe introduced them.

'This, my dear Jennifer, is Godfrey Mere, usually referred to as Merely God, and as completely vacuous as he looks. God, *where* did you get that atrocious tie? Would you mind putting a table-napkin over it if you must remain in this room? And this is Jane Bettle and the other one, the small one with too much rouge on her lips, is May Chance. And this, though none of you is worth an introduction to her, is Miss Jennifer Rothe, who is to be the world's greatest contralto.'

They all stared at her with speculative interest and Jennifer wished she could sink through the floor. For one thing, she had never heard anyone who could be so rude to guests as Rothe had been, and for another she felt that they regarded her, quite rightly, as an oddity.

As a matter of fact, they were all impressed by Rothe's words, for he was not given to superlatives and they knew that this queer-looking girl must be quite out of the ordinary to have been deemed worthy of such a prophecy.

May Chance broke in shrilly.

'Heavens! What a rage she's going to be! What a rave! Those clothes—and clogs, my own! They are clogs, aren't they, Miss Rothe? Er—Miss *Rothe*, did you say, Julian?'

'I did,' said Julian grimly, offering no other explanation.

Godfrey sniggered.

'But, Julian, how priceless! Do we tell the world, or what?'

It was obvious that Jennifer did not understand the imputation, so Rothe merely smiled.

'Whatever you like,' he said. 'And now would you go, all of you?'

But the two girls pulled up chairs and sat down at the table.

'Not me,' said Jane Bettle, a marvellous and incredible blonde. 'I've been dancing all night with God, and if that isn't enough to wear a poor girl out, I'd like to know what is. We've come to breakfast. I couldn't find anything in that ghastly hole of God's.'

She threw off her coat and revealed herself in a very low-cut evening frock which made Jennifer stare.

'Can't you even feed your women, God?' asked Rothe, ringing for more coffee and pushing the electric breakfast warmer nearer to his self-invited guests.

'My dear, he can't do a thing but dance with us!' said Jane. 'Or *can* you, my precious lamb?'

'I'd often wondered myself,' said Julian. 'More kidneys, Simmons, please. Jennifer, my dear, nothing else? Come along then. These people will sit here and make it do for lunch. We'll leave them to it. I hope you people will go before it actually is lunch-time as I am expecting guests, and I'd hate my friends to meet anything like your tie, God, or your lips, May, or your morals, my sweet Jane.'

Jennifer followed him, wide-eyed, but he offered no explanation of the amazing scene and his rudeness, and she saw as she left the room that none of the three of them thought of resenting it, but fell to on the breakfast with relish.

But in the wide and lovely room to which Rothe took her he seemed to change and become another man. He went first to the telephone, dialled a number, and then waited.

'You, Claire? Would you honour me by lunching with me? ... Yes, here, if you will ... Half past one? ... Till then, my dear.'

That was all, but Jennifer was bewildered. It was difficult to believe that that invitation had been issued by the same man as the one who had been so insufferably rude to his other guests, and Rothe, catching the look in her eyes, smiled and took her hand.

'You are going to meet one of the most charming women in England, my dear Jennifer,' was all he said. 'You will then see how very unimportant the *canaille* in the other room are. Have you any other dress than that?'

She felt utterly humiliated. She had thought to shame this grand London man in his fine house, to show him how little she cared for all the things he thought would dazzle her. Instead she had shamed herself. He was treating her with honour and she had thought to offer him dishonour.

She shook her head.

'No. I—I came just like this, with nothing else,' she said in a low voice.

Rothe smiled. He understood her far better than she thought he did. Indeed, she was a simple soul, direct and without artifice.

'That is of no consequence to me, nor will it be to my friend, Mrs. Ferring. I am afraid you will, for your own sake, however, have to conform to custom. You will be happier being unremarkable until your voice makes you the most remarkable woman of my particular circle. Now I expect there is a room ready for you, and I am sure you must be very tired and glad of a rest. Suppose you go and lie down until lunch-time?'

She was only too glad to get away from the curious, slightly quizzical smile he gave her. He was sizing up her possibilities, wishing he dare let her continue in her print dress and her clogs. But she would be unhappy. She was not the type to carry off anything like that.

In the room to which the round-eyed Florrie led her, Jennifer stood quite still and looked round with eyes a little blurred.

She had been so deeply hurt by Bob that she had thought to put on a mantle of hardness and defiance which should carry her through the rest of life. She had vowed that nothing should ever touch her again, nothing be allowed to reach the inner place where she herself dwelt. And here, in the house she had thought she would hate, she was already finding kindness against which the mantle of defiance would not be proof.

She took off the horrible clogs which were all she had for footwear and stole softly about the room. Rothe had shown his understanding of her in having this room prepared for her rather than one of the usual guest-rooms. It was a small, corner room with deep windows set in an angle and looking out over a garden which she imagined would be a paradise in summer. It was a virginal little room, bare and white, with a narrow bed and furniture of some plain wood built into the walls. There was a strip of carpet on the polished floor, a wicker chair with cushions to match the chintz curtains, and nothing else at all.

Its exquisite cleanliness did something to the soul of Jennifer.

It made her feel humble and grateful, but it did more than that. It began to heal the gaping wound with which she had fled from Werford, to show her that such healing was possible.

It gave her a strange feeling of peace. Rothe had known how great was her need of just that. He had not studied men and women in vain, and he had known at once that this bare, white little room was what she must have.

She opened a window and drew deep breaths of the dank, earthy air filled with the smell of wet leaves. Something elemental in her loved that smell and she steeped her senses in it. Already she had the unexpected knowledge that she was going to be happy here.

She had not thought she could sleep, but peace wrapped her round in that small, white room, and she woke with a start to find the maid standing beside her with a can of hot water, with brushes and a comb.

'Sorry to wake you, miss, but the master says would you please ring when you're ready and I'll show you the way,' said the girl, with respectful curiosity in voice and look.

Shame came again to Jennifer. How could she have done so hateful a thing as to come to Mr. Rothe's house looking like that? She would have been glad to have even the maid's outfit at that moment.

'I wonder if you could lend me some shoes?' she asked nervously. 'I—I haven't any.'

She was too proud to make an excuse. She let the girl think she habitually wore the wooden clogs, which actually made her ankles ache with the effort of keeping them on.

Florrie, who was small, looked doubtfully at Jennifer's large, if shapely, feet.

'I don't know as mine would go on you, miss, but I could go and try the others downstairs for you.'

'Please don't bother,' said Jennifer hastily, picturing at once the result of such a quest amongst the servants, of whom she had caught glimpses whilst she had been downstairs.

Florrie went away, and Jennifer made herself at least as neat as she could, though nothing could disguise the poverty of the faded print or those dreadful clogs in which, presently, she clattered down the stairs in Florrie's company.

But when she had been for a few moments in the room where Rothe and his guest awaited her, she forgot everything save the woman whom he had said was 'one of the most charming in England'.

Claire Ferring had been lovely at all ages, but now, at forty, she was entering on what was probably the most attractive period of her life, for to it she brought the added charm of experience, of maturity, of conscious appreciation of her own possibilities. Of medium height, with that lovely combination of golden bronze hair and brown eyes which is so rare, her delicate colouring enhanced by art most skilfully employed, she was a joy to society photographers and to paragraphists who so often have to prostitute their adjectives.

And she had more than just physical beauty. She had the innate good breeding which may make an ugly woman beautiful and with which she soon had Jennifer at her ease, making her forget the print dress and the clogs save when she caught sight of them or had to move.

'My dear, Julian has been telling me about your wonderful voice and what he hopes to do for you,' she said as they waited for lunch to be announced. 'May I be allowed to say that you are both fortunate to have found each other? And to hope that we are going to be friends?'

'I hope Mr. Rothe will not be disappointed in me,' said Jennifer shyly. 'He is taking such a risk.'

Mrs. Ferring laughed and glanced at Julian.

'Mr. Rothe never takes a risk,' she said, and Jennifer was aware of some undercurrent in their laughter, aware of the perfect understanding between these two who were soon discussing her and making for her plans which gave her a dizzy feeling. Was all this to be done to her, Jennifer Jenks?

Presently they let her slip from their talk, and she sat and listened to these two cultured, well-bred people talking of things she only vaguely understood. She was to listen to them many times, and to learn much that helped to make up the new Jennifer. She saw Julian Rothe as he really was and as she came to know him, kindly though always a little cynical, disillusioned about most things in life and yet keeping somewhere, unpolluted, the spring of the waters of hope without which life is a desert. She was to know him bitter, angry, incredibly rude, but to Claire Ferring he was always as he was now, charming, witty, beautifully mannered with the ways of a passing generation.

Once they touched on something which Jennifer could not fathom, sensing the deeps without actually being aware of them.

They had been talking lightly of Claire's husband, evidently a man of some importance, and then they seemed to pause as if by mutual consent and to wait for something.

'And the boy, Claire?' he asked.

'Well, as ever, thank heaven. He is in Switzerland just now, at Wengen for the winter sports. He tells me he can manage skis already, and of course he has always been able to skate—or I believe he has. I can't remember when he couldn't. He sent me some snaps,' and she found them in her bag and passed them to him, and some to Jennifer with a smile and an explanation.

'Derek, my large son.'

'He is like you,' said Jennifer, but though the boy's short, wide face and his eyes and his smile were like Mrs. Ferring's, there was some other likeness that eluded her.

Rothe changed the subject abruptly.

'Will you take Jennifer in hand, Claire? Get her the right sort of clothes and so on?'

'And the right sort of friends?' asked Claire with a smile.

'No. Give her all sorts and let her pick,' he said, and, after the guest had gone, he enlarged on that.

'You can learn something from everyone you meet,' he said. 'That's what I want you to do. Take that appalling trio who came this morning. You can learn from all of them. From Jane Bettle you can learn how never to behave and from May Chance, Mischance, how never to look.'

Jennifer smiled her slow, grave smile, never quite sure how to take him.

'And the young man?'

'From Merely God you can learn the sort of young man to avoid. He is the epitome of all the worst in man. I'd rather hobnob with a wife-beater or a murderer personally.'

'And yet they come here to see you?' frowned Jennifer.

'Because they can get a cheap meal when they're hungry,' said Rothe.

'Hungry?' asked Jennifer, startled. 'You don't really mean that?'

'Oh yes. They are the Bright Young Things clinging on to the edge of Mayfair, living on twopence a year and on their friends and God knows how else.'

'Why don't they work, if they haven't any money to live on?' asked Jennifer.

He laughed.

'My dear, that's the only thing they won't do for money,' he said.

'But their clothes!' said Jennifer, remembering the fur coat Jane had worn and the lovely frock that had partially concealed May's meagre flesh.

'They either owe for them indefinitely, or wheedle them out of their dressmakers or tailors by introducing new clients to them, clients who *will* pay. They'll make quite a nice bit out of you, you know.'

'Out of me?' asked Jennifer, shocked.

'Or me. We're going to a party on Monday night, you and I, and you'll probably meet them there—almost certainly, I should say, because I dropped a hint to Mischance that you would be going. Before the evening's out, I'm willing to bet you'll be committed to going to at least two dressmakers' establishments and one tailor's for clothes.'

'But—I haven't money to buy the sort of clothes they wear,' said Jennifer in her direct fashion. 'I have only just begun to realise, Mr. Rothe, that—that I shall be living on your charity until I can begin to earn by singing.'

'That's the last thing for you to worry about, Jennifer. You can take it from me that Julian Rothe never lost on any of his deals. You'll earn me enough money for you to draw on with reasonable lavishness, and Mischance and company will be quite well aware of that and will be most assiduous in their attentions.'

Jennifer was red and uncomfortable. She felt that it was dreadful to talk in that way of people who came to his house as friends and ate at his table. But it was also dreadful to think of them living on others in that way.

'I shall keep away from them,' she said.

'Don't do that, my dear. Let the poor things live!' laughed Rothe. 'Why bear them any ill-will? I don't.'

She frowned.

'I think it is all very difficult to understand,' she said. 'I can't really believe that they are poor, as you say. They—they looked so rich and prosperous. I know what poor people look like. I've lived amongst them. I suppose to people like you I've been poor myself.'

'There are none so poor as the poor of Mayfair, as you'll soon learn. I don't suppose any of those three who came here this morning to breakfast gets a square meal except when they receive the invitations to lunch or dinner for which they have to angle so cleverly. I've never been to visit any of them, but I'm willing to wager that none of them has more than one shoddy little back room for which they pay the whole of their slender income so that they can have a good address. Mayfair, my dear! When they came here this morning, they were really hungry, *really* hungry, and couldn't hold out without a meal any longer, possibly hadn't managed to get a lunch invitation, and dinner might be uncertain. So they came here, quite prepared to accept my rudeness and knowing that I see through them and despise them, but deciding that it was worth it. They probably got Simmons to pay their taxi, which, of course, will be duly charged up to me.'

'I think it's terrible,' said Jennifer.

He laughed.

'Oh, I don't grudge it to them. It's my form of charity. And now, my dear, you'd better come and have your first lesson, after which I expect there will be clothes and things ready for you to try on and choose from. Mrs. Ferring is going to take you shopping tomorrow, but she says she would send you things to go on with.'

'Will Mrs. Ferring be there on Monday?' asked Jennifer shrinkingly. His smile was enigmatical.

'No. Mrs. Ferring does not go to that sort of place nor meet people like the Mischance,' he said. 'Later I am hoping she will take you up and then you will meet the right sort of people, but just at first I am going to take you to places like Lady Horrit's. It will amuse me—and you, I hope. Now come and let me hear what you can do. I'm horribly afraid you're going to disappoint my memory of your voice. What are we going to do with you then?'

Chapter Four

Jennifer was tired, frightened, and confused when she and Rothe entered the crowded room where Lady Horrit was receiving such of her guests as paid her the compliment of speaking to her.

All day Rothe had worked the girl mercilessly, sparing her nothing, giving her little praise or encouragement, and she had grown more and more despondent. Her voice responded uncertainly to the demands made on it by exercises which were monotonously uninteresting. She had sung as the birds sing, joyously, naturally, letting her voice go where and how it would. Now Rothe was limiting it, forcing it to do things which seemed unnatural.

'Good God, girl!' he raved, leaving the piano and walking up and down the long, bare music-room, his spluttering little figure duplicated time after time by the long mirrors which formed almost the only furnishing apart from the grand piano in the middle. 'Let your voice go! Up! Up! And *can't* you sing in tune? Can't you feel that you're not? Keep on that note—now—hold it! Up, up!' And he ran to her, caught her hands and dragged them above her head, his smaller figure on tiptoe, his head strained upwards absurdly.

Jennifer, roused to a sort of frenzy by him, did wildly as he bade her, and when he barked at her 'Enough! Enough!' was the more bewildered by his going down on his knees before her and kissing her hands whilst the tears ran down his face.

'Divine! Divine! Oh, my beautiful, I could worship that note of yours!'

Then, before she had recovered from her amazed discomfort, he was at the piano again, drumming out a fresh exercise, reviling her rendering of it, singing it with her and then spinning round on the stool to rest his elbows on his knees, bury his head in his hands and tell her he was ready to weep at her imbecility.

Jennifer, stolid, bewildered, unhappy, stumbled through as best she could, but in the end she burst into tears and rushed from him, finding her own room the refuge from storm which it was destined so many times to be.

Flinging herself on the bed, she finished her tears and then lay and looked at life and wondered what it was going to be. Could she endure this strange, wild, inconsistent man who both terrified and inspired her? Was it going to be worth it? She saw herself as she had done so many times lately, ever since Rothe had come to see her in her cottage as a great singer, with the world at her feet, but, more than all, with money at her command, not for herself, but for the people she had left behind, her friends who suffered so deeply, and whose voice, it seemed, would never be heard, had grown weak with the years of despair.

Yes, it was going to be worth it, and when presently a maid came to the door and brought two or three large cardboard boxes, she was ready to rise to her feet and try again.

The contents of the boxes brought her mingled consternation and excitement. Claire Ferring had tried to hit the happy medium between her own sense of what was suitable and fitting for Jennifer and Rothe's command that the girl was to be made to look striking.

'She'll hate to be paraded and shown off, Julian,' Claire had said.

'Her loves and hates don't count—yet,' he told her. 'She's got to be someone at the very outset, and she's not good-looking enough to be left to make her own impression. I'd like you to dress her in red velvet—or gold lamé—or emerald.'

She laughed.

'Savage! I'll do nothing of the sort, Julian. If you insist on her looking like something out of a circus, you'll have to go to someone else. I won't have anything to do with it, or with her.'

'Or me?'

'That follows. I know quite well that you and this girl are going to be inseparables from now on. Is she so wonderful, Julian?'

'To no one else would I say this, Claire, but my soul is on its knees to her. Her voice is the sort that's born only once in a century.'

'You're going to let me hear her?'

'Not even you yet. She's not going to sing anything at all except exercises for at least a year. After that, we'll see. And you'll dress her, Claire?'

'Not in red and gold, my dear.'

He shrugged his shoulders.

'All right. Have it your own way. Only she's to make a stir, mind.'

So the frock that Claire had chosen for her was of velvet, deep rose and cunningly contrived so that it would help to conceal the unlovely angles and general gawkiness of the girl's figure. The few measurements which they had taken had served for sufficient guide for a gown for a not too important occasion, and when Jennifer, wide-eyed and conscious of how much the gown revealed, at length summoned up courage to go downstairs Rothe nodded his approval.

'Claire is clever,' he said. 'You look charming, my dear. Do you feel it?'

Jennifer swallowed hard. She had to readjust herself quickly to his reversion to the man she had known first and forget that emotional, terrifying figure he had presented to her in the music-room.

'I feel naked,' she told him briefly, and he laughed.

'You'll be far more covered than most people you meet tonight. We shall have to get someone to groom you and exercise you, show you how to do your hair, how to walk and so on. We must do something about your figure too—take you in here and fill you out here,' prodding her unconcernedly.

'Not mistaking me for a horse, are you?' asked Jennifer unexpectedly, and he laughed and slipped a hand under her elbow to take her out to the waiting car.

'I'm frightened,' she said to him on the way.

'Pooh! What for? What of? That crowd of nitwits?'

'It's all very well for you, Mr. Rothe, but I've never been to anything like this before, never worn an evening dress before, and I shan't know what to do or say. I wish you hadn't brought me!'

'Just be yourself, my dear, and if you feel you can't find anything to say, say nothing. That'll impress them. In no time you'll find yourself the fashion, and they'll think you're silent because you're too clever for them.'

Jennifer did not answer for a moment. Then: 'Why are you so bitter about everybody, Mr. Rothe?' she burst out suddenly.

He paused a moment before he replied. Then he spoke in a quite different tone.

'I suppose because I am a spoilt child, Jennifer. I've had so much. I still have so much. But because I can't get the one unattainable thing, everything else turns to dust and ashes in my mouth. Don't be like that, my dear. Keep something that you have that is very precious, irreplaceable – your sweetness.'

She was touched, drawn towards this strange, difficult man with the haunted eyes, the bitter mouth, and caustic tongue.

What was this thing that was unattainable? She wondered whether she would ever know him well enough to ask him, or if he would ever think her worth being given such a confidence unasked.

'Mr. Rothe—' she said impulsively.

She saw that the mood had passed.

'One favour I'm going to beg of you, Jennifer,' he said.

'Of me?'

'That you won't call me that. I prefer to be Julian to you.'

'But—of course,' she said in confusion, and was careful for a long time after that not to speak his name to him at all.

And then they stopped at the house with the strip of carpet across the pavement and the red awning and the little crowd of the curious and the envious on either side. Rothe handed her out and she paused a moment to look at the people who watched her.

'Coo, that one ain't much to look at, for all 'er pink velvet,' said one voice quite distinctly.

Jennifer looked in the direction of the voice and laughed at the girl who had spoken.

'You're right. I'm not,' she said. 'I've seen my face a lot oftener than you have.'

The crowd laughed and liked her. Julian hesitated between a frown and a smile and finally propelled her forward with an expression that was neither.

'Lady Horrit's guests don't talk to the proletariat, my dear,' he said.

'Well, a week ago I'd have been amongst the starers myself—and enjoying it a lot more,' retorted Jennifer.

He chuckled.

'We're going to get on fine, Jennifer Rothe,' he told her. 'Don't shake hands with the first gentleman we meet, the one at the top of the steps. That's Lady Horrit's butler. The little man with the walrus moustache apologising for his existence a step or two further on is Lady Horrit's husband. You can greet him if you like, but as he's the host, it's unnecessary and unusual to acknowledge his existence.'

But Jennifer noticed that, for all his words, Rothe spoke with punctilious courtesy to the little man and presented him to Jennifer.

'Sir John Horrit, my dear – my ward, Miss Jennifer Rothe, Sir John.'

Sir John seemed overwhelmed with surprise and gratitude for the introduction. His wife's guests did not, as a rule, think it worth while to notice him.

'How shall I find you again?' asked Jennifer in trepidation as a musical-comedy maid offered to conduct her to the cloakroom.

'I'll come back here for you and then we'll go and find Lady Horrit—not that we could possibly miss her. I might almost have said: "I'll meet you at Lady Horrit, south side." '

The rest of the evening passed in a maze of bewilderment and unhappiness for Jennifer.

She was passed from one to another, names flung at her, odd things said to her, things to which she could find no reply. She stood looking and feeling an outsider, aware of Rothe's amused, sardonic smile, furious with him and with herself, longing to rush away out of the place, back to her own sort of people, back to poverty that was at least open and honest, to simplicity and kindness and the things she understood.

Her only bearable moment was when Jane Bettle, finding her alone for a moment and beyond the watchful eye of Rothe, bore down on her and asked her to come and sing for them.

'Not to all this crowd, Miss Rothe, but just to a few of us in here—look, it's empty and we'll shut the door. Do you play for yourself?'

'No, I can't,' said Jennifer uncomfortably.

'I'll find someone,' said Jane.

'There's Snooty over there. Ask him,' said a languid and exquisite young man in a dark wine-coloured evening suit.

'Snooty' appeared to be willing, though supercilious.

'What do you know?' he drawled to Jennifer when they had reached the little room off the main reception-room and the half-dozen or so of them had grouped themselves round the piano in sprawling attitudes.

'Oh—just simple songs like—oh—"Rose in the Bud". Do you know that?' asked Jennifer innocently.

They exchanged glances and she flushed unhappily, but Snooty, with a grin, began to improvise an elaborate accompaniment to the old song, making her the more confused.

Realising it, he dropped into simpler phrasing and she began to sing, feeling strange and uncomfortable at first but gradually regaining confidence as she sang.

Snooty ceased to elaborate the accompaniment, keeping it soft and very simple, giving her voice every chance, and the little group about her ceased to grin and giggle, but remained quite still to listen to her. Pure and sweet, the lovely voice of Jennifer reached something in them which they had not known they possessed, something left untouched by all the jazz, the blues, the hot rhythm they loved.

Suddenly the door was flung open, the heavy curtain thrust aside, and Rothe stood there, his face white with anger, his eyes blazing.

He strode towards the piano, his eyes fixed on Jennifer, and Snooty stopped playing and the song trailed off into silence.

'How dare you sing? What possessed you? Are you stark, staring mad, or am I?' he flung at her, and she stared at him in amazement.

'Does it matter?' she asked. 'I didn't know.'

'Matter? Of course it does. You'd better come home,' and he grasped her wrist.

The wine-coloured exquisite laughed indolently.

'If you're afraid of the big, bad wolf, Miss Rothe, we'll come with you,' he drawled. 'I rather think he's going to beat you.'

Jennifer's face flamed and she shook Rothe's hand from her wrist.

'You don't have to drag me out,' she said sharply, and when the others laughed, she wanted to die.

Somehow she got her cloak, found Rothe waiting for her white and silent, was helped into the car, was being borne swiftly away through the quiet streets.

He did not speak. Her mind was in a turmoil. She had been so angry with him for his treatment of her, for speaking to her like that in front of others – and suddenly, when one of them had laughed, she had been on his side, against them, against herself.

When they were back in his house, he held open the door of the morning-room for her and she went in. It was the small and pleasant room which she found he used a great deal when he was not entertaining. A cheerful log fire burned in the grate and on a little table were sandwiches and a silver thermos jug of coffee.

She bent automatically to hold out her hands to the warmth of the fire, and he took her cloak from her shoulders and laid it over a chair.

'Coffee, Jennifer?' he asked.

She turned swiftly.

'Oh, I'm sorry. It was hateful,' she said. 'I didn't understand, I still don't—only—I hated it when they laughed.'

He poured out coffee for her and brought it to her, standing looking down at her with that inscrutable expression of his.

'Some of us are fools all the time, but all of us are fools some of the time,' he said. 'I think it was the thought of your prostituting your voice for those apologies for human beings that made me so angry—but I should have been angry anyhow. "Rose in the Bud"! *Rose in the Bud*, indeed,' and the contempt in his tone would have withered a rose garden. 'See here, Jennifer Rothe. Your voice belongs to me. Do you understand that? It's mine, and I won't have it spoiled, wasted, squandered by all and sundry. You will sing how I want, when I want, and where I want—and none of those things belong to "Rose in the Bud", to a lot of half-wits in Lady Horrit's back drawing-room. Understand?'

'But I have always sung at parties when people asked me,' said Jennifer simply. 'I was just being polite.'

'Polite fiddlesticks! You don't have to be polite any more than I do. You're going to be Someone, with a capital "S", and ordinary standards of convention won't affect you. You're going to be extraordinary, not just ordinary. Understand?'

Jennifer made a gesture of helpless bewilderment.

'No, I don't, and I don't like the idea. I want to be polite to people. I like it. Why do you tell me Mrs. Ferring is such a charming woman if you don't like politeness? She's polite.'

'I know. But people like Mrs. Ferring don't have to push and work to get anywhere. They're there from the start. You aren't. You've got to arrive. And you've got something to sell. Don't forget that.'

'You couldn't want me to be like Mrs. Ferring, then?' demanded Jennifer.

He hesitated and then smiled at her, took her empty cup and set it down.

'You couldn't be,' he said succinctly, and Jennifer felt she was left in the air.

If Rothe demanded rudeness of her, he certainly set her an example. She was alternately attracted to him and repelled by him, hating him and yet knowing that she would follow him and go wherever he sent her. She was a little bit frightened at the thought that inevitably she would also become just what he wanted her to become. What sort of woman was he going to make of her? A being to be admired possibly, but also to be hated.

She shivered as she laid aside the velvet gown and arrayed herself in the blue silk pyjamas which Claire Ferring had bought for her and which felt uncomfortable and strange.

How far already she seemed to have gone from the Jennifer of Werford, house-mother to her two men, philosopher and comforter, friend of Lottie – lover of Bob.

Lover of Bob.

That gave her uncomfortable pause. The thought of him had of necessity been crushed down in her mind by all these new experiences, and Rothe worked her so hard that at night she was too tired to lie awake with her memories. Life held too many possibilities now to spend her days in useless regrets, but it was something of a shock to her to realise how little she had actually been grieving for Bob.

He had held an unique place in her life for as long as she could remember. They had always been friends, and friendship had ripened into love so imperceptibly that she did not know when the actual thought of marriage had been born.

His secession from that loyalty of theirs had been a tremendous shock to her and she had left him in a daze of grief which should have turned to a sword-thrust when she wakened. And instead of that, the wound was healing with no agonising pain.

She scorned herself for a light, fickle woman, marvelled at the ease with which she had accepted their separation, and fell asleep with not even a dream to disturb her peace.

Chapter Five

If at first Jennifer had thought to exchange a hard life for an easy one, she was quickly undeceived.

Rothe was a hard taskmaster and she was completely under his dominion, living every minute of her life according to rule, eating, working, resting, going to bed, getting up, walking, driving in his car, strictly by schedule. Her days were almost unvaried, save that her work, apart from actual singing and piano lessons, altered a little with the days of the week, Italian alternating with French and elocution with what Rothe called, with his sardonic grin, parlour tricks. These consisted in instruction in the ways of the polite society, and the instruction was given by a little shrivelled-up spinster, the Hon. Amelia Birke, whose indubitably blue blood was her sole asset and who spent a weary life trading her name for dinners and week-ends to keep her body alive and for clothes wherewith to cover it. Rothe maintained that neither was necessary, for her life could be of no value even to herself, and why trouble to cover a body which could be of no interest to anybody else?

Jennifer was gentle with the odd little woman and learnt from her something of the habits and manners of a bygone generation, thinking them slightly stupid but adopting them out of deference both to Rothe, whom they amused, and to little Miss Birke, who had to justify the money she was paid to turn the miner's daughter into the semblance of a fine lady.

The girl's natural modesty and innate consideration for the feelings of others made her an apt pupil for the standard of manners which Miss Birke desired for her, and Rothe, amused though he was, had to admit that the slightly out-of-date courtesies which she acquired suited her and gave her added charm.

'No one else behaves like that nowadays, of course,' he would tell her. 'You will have noticed that, no doubt. But the modern style of rudeness and boorishness does not suit you and that is one reason why I put you in the hands of a decayed gentlewoman rather than in those of decadent Bright Young Things.'

But the lessons in deportment were the lightest of her duties. The heaviest were the singing lessons, the endless exercises, the breathing, the unlearning, it seemed, of everything she had ever done and the formation of a new habit in exchange. Rothe spared her nothing, gave her grudging praise and abundant blame, seemed never satisfied, reduced her often to a frenzy of tears which he would watch sardonically, would time by the second hand of his gold repeater, and then insist mercilessly on her starting again even though sobs choked her voice and blurred her utterance of the 'mee mee mee's' and 'mai mai mai's' to be repeated endlessly.

Rarely, very rarely, he let her sing something more tuneful than those exercises, but it was always something of his choosing, an aria, a scrap from an opera, nothing easy or what Jennifer would, a short time before, have called 'pretty'. She longed to be allowed to sing some of the old songs again, and yet she knew that they would bring to the surface that almost unbearable longing for the old life, the loved friends whom she felt could never have their substitutes in the people she met in this strange, new, artificial existence she led.

Yet as the weeks went by and turned imperceptibly into months, she had to admit that Rothe knew his business. Not only was her voice gaining in quality, her breathing easier, her powers of phrasing infinitely improved, but her whole physical and mental being showed signs of the work that was being put into them. Her hours of physical culture, Swedish drill, exercises of all sorts, the massage which at first she had hated but gradually began to enjoy, the visits to hairdresser, manicurist, chiropodist, dressmaker, and milliner – everything added its quota towards making the best of her, and Rothe watched the process with cynical amusement.

'You've got to be something more than a voice, my dear,' he had told her when she demurred about the multiplicity of his arrangements for her. 'You've got to have a personality, without which nobody in the world can succeed at anything. Mere beauty of feature, figure, or voice may give anybody a start, but it's only personality which will get them anywhere, and that's what all these things are developing.'

And through it all, Claire Ferring was her guide and commentator, encouraging her, smoothing the way for her, arranging certain small functions, dinners, cocktail parties, informal gatherings of all sorts to which only specially selected guests were invited with the idea of accustoming the girl gradually to the kind of life Rothe desired that in the end she should lead.

Privately she thought he was taking the wrong line, and told him so.

'Aren't you digging up a wild flower and expecting it to become a hothouse plant, Julian? Do you think she will ever settle down with us and make our sort of life her own? Wouldn't you have been better advised just to train her voice and let it go at that?'

'No. It amuses me, for one thing, and God knows there isn't much amusement to be got out of life at fifty-two. It satisfies something in me to deck up a miner's daughter, give her all the airs and graces to which she was not born, and make the people of our world accept her and fawn on her. If I let her keep the ways and customs and manners of her class they would just admire her voice but treat her as a curiosity, just a singer.'

'Might one be permitted to suggest,' said Claire, 'that the ways and manners and customs of Jennifer's class are in many ways infinitely more desirable and pleasing than those of our own young people? She neither smokes nor drinks nor wears men's clothes. I have never heard her swear, her mind is as virgin as her body, and she possesses the amazingly out-of-date quality of reverence.'

Rothe smiled at her.

She lay stretched on a couch in front of a roaring fire in her own sitting-room, a room of soft greys and blues, a room of infinite peace and quiet where only the chosen few of her friends ever penetrated. Outside roared the February blast which had laid her low with the chill from which she was recovering, having nursed herself for a couple of days at the urgent behest of her husband.

It was bitter-sweet to Rothe to be there with her in the intimacy of that room, to see her a little pale and fragile and inviting the small services which he was so seldom permitted to perform for her: flowers, a cushion for her head, an extra cover for her feet, a screen to be moved, another log to be thrown on the fire. He tore his heart by the pretence that he belonged there, that this lovely, desirable woman whom he had loved for so many hopeless years lay there in his own home – his and hers.

'Most of those qualities are yours, Claire,' he said.

'Are they? I smoke, I drink within reason. I don't wear men's clothes because I know they wouldn't suit me, and I don't swear because it doesn't attract me. I lost the virginity of both my mind and my body years ago, and—do I reverence anything? If I do, I wouldn't dare admit it to anyone!'

'I wonder if I am unconsciously modelling Jennifer on you?' reflected Rothe. 'Perhaps I am. I'm toying with God's job—trying to create someone. In reality, of course, I'm only taking the prepared material and twisting it into another shape. You think I've chosen the wrong shape? That in trying to achieve perfection by modelling her on you, I'm trying to make a silk purse out of a sow's ear?'

She smiled and laid her hand for a moment on his arm, the merest touch for a fragment of a second.

'You make me feel very humble, Julian,' she said softly. 'As for the silk purse—I rather think it's silk you're working on, not a sow's ear. Jennifer is fine quality. Perhaps I have realised that you are trying to make her like me, and that is why I feel you may be—belittling her, robbing the silk of some of its fineness.'

He lifted her hand and laid it against his lips.

'I always liked my own opinions better than anyone else's,' he said. 'Claire, it's February.'

'I know. You aren't the only one counting the months, my dear.'

'You won't let anything get in the way?'

'Not if I can help it. You know that, Julian.'

'Yes. Only every year it seems a miracle that it should ever come to pass, and one has lived too long to believe overmuch in miracles. There are so many things which might keep you here. Looking at May from February, everything seems impossible.'

'It seems like that to me. I am trying to keep it all clear ahead, though. Nearly every night I'm fitting in something or someone, and you wouldn't credit the work Miss Spears and I put in dovetailing them all so as to leave me free in May. This year there's the possibility of a general election, of course, but I don't think Guy will want any entertaining done as early as that. He knows that I claim May for my own and he has never attempted to intrude on it.'

There was the faintest note of bitterness in her voice, and he rose and paced the room restlessly.

'Oh, my dear, I hate all this mockery—'

'Please, Julian.'

He broke off and came to sit beside her again.

'Forgive me, Claire. I always get so restless and anxious between January and May, and the years are going, and—'

She broke in on his words again, gently.

'Don't you think it's exactly the same for me, Julian?'

'I both like to hear that and hate it, my dear.'

'You'll have to go now if I'm going to be at all presentable this evening. You're bringing Jennifer to dinner?'

'If you'll have her.'

'Of course. I'm enlarging her circle a bit. She'll have to meet strangers now. Derek's coming. It's his half-term. I've asked Brenner Mayne to come too. He knows the Patneys and will help me to mix the ingredients a bit. Thank heaven you know them too. I simply can't get on with them, and I know I've got to because of Guy.'

'You know Jennifer comes from that part of the country, don't you? That her people were killed in that disaster in the mine that Patney owns?' asked Rothe.

'I know. You must use your own judgment about bringing her, though I don't see that it need make any difference. To them she'll just be Miss Rothe, and she can't know them socially. She probably doesn't even know he had any connection with it.'

Certainly Jennifer had never spoken of Sir Jervis nor revealed to Rothe any of the bitter hatred that seethed in her mind for him, and Claire had no idea of the feelings that surged through her when, later that day, she made 'Miss Rothe' known to the mine-owner and his beautifully gowned and jewelled lady.

Derek took it off a little, annexing the girl and taking her to the other end of the room to meet his model and hero, Brenner Mayne, the rising young barrister for whom was predicted a great future.

Jennifer saw him, at first glance, as a tall, spare man in his forties, though she discovered later that he was still in the early thirties. His fine, unremarkable hair was receding from his broad forehead unkindly, but in his case it served to make the more noticeable his keen, grey eyes deep set beneath heavy brows, and the fine, strong lines of his lean face.

He was taller than Jennifer, for which she experienced a second's relief, for most of the men she met were, at the utmost, only on a level with her. The grooming she had had, the exercises, and Miss Amelia Birke's lessons in deportment, had succeeded in making her carry and hold herself so as to disguise a little her unusual height, but the fact remained that she was half a head taller than most men, and it gave her a painful feeling of mental inferiority to balance the superior physical height.

He smiled and something happened to Jennifer. It was as if somewhere in the room a lamp had been lit – or as if the curtains had been drawn back and, instead of a February night, it was noon-day in June.

'I've wanted to meet you,' he said. 'Mrs. Ferring and Derek are Philistines, I tell them. They have a box at the opera and fill it almost nightly with people who go there to see and be seen. Even Claire is usually there for political reasons, and when they're good enough to give me a seat I edge my way into the corner where I am least likely to be disturbed. I have been promised the box to myself when you first sing "Delilah". Are you going to?'

There was nothing artificial or gushing about it. It was simple sincerity, and Jennifer answered likewise.

'It may be a very long time and you may be disappointed,' she said. 'I am very raw yet—and if you could hear Mr. Rothe and see his face when I'm having a lesson, you'd come to the same conclusion as I have done, that I shall never sing anything more important than "Mee, Mai, and Moo"!'

He shook his head.

'No. I've known Julian Rothe too long. He never makes a mistake about a voice. When you do sing "Delilah" I shall make you recall this conversation. How, I wonder? The banal thing will be to say it with flowers, but you won't be able to pick mine out from all the rest.'

'Send her a lock of your hair, Brenner. That'll be a fitting tribute after she's shorn Samson,' grinned Derek.

'If I'm to do that, you'll have to be very quick getting into opera, Miss Rothe,' laughed Mayne with a regretful hand passed over his head. 'I'll send you—a camellia,' catching sight of a vase filled with them. 'Actually I never like to see them in a vase like that. They ought to be growing, or given just singly for a beautiful woman to wear.'

'I've never seen them growing,' said Jennifer, who, until that moment, could not have told even what a camellia was like. Camellias don't grow round coal-mines, nor do they grace the tables of the miners' cottages.

'Some day, before you are too great a prima donna to have become blasé about everything,' said Mayne with a smile, 'you'll see them growing in Italy. You want to travel?'

Derek drifted away and left them alone, and she was grateful to him for the way in which he made it easy for her to talk, and when they went in to dinner she was pleased to find him her neighbour.

Opposite her flashed the diamonds of Lady Patney, who revealed her plebeian origin in their number and size, though time and zeal and money had overlaid her essential vulgarity with a veneer of good manners. At the end of the table, on his hostess's right hand, sat pompous little Sir Jervis, and Jennifer was both fascinated and repelled by the skilful way in which Claire dealt with this important, undesired guest. From the other end of the table, Guy Ferring showed his approval by an occasional glance at his beautiful and witty wife and by keeping entertained such of their guests as might have detracted from the impression she sought to make on Patney.

Before the end of the meal the conversation turned inevitably on political issues, in spite of Claire's clever avoidance of too controversial subjects, and the smug voice of Sir Jervis rose a little at the bait which a renowned newspaper man dangled before him with the mention of coal.

'Coal? My dear Pronter, that is, if I may put it that way, a warm subject, very warm,' said the little man, and those near him gave a polite ripple of unamused laughter at his joke. 'Heaven knows where we're all going to end with these beggars always shrieking out for more money and less work. Where should any of us be if that were our cry? Where should I be, I wonder, if I didn't work my five days a week and rest content with what I earned in them? I tell you, these miners are a positive menace to the community.'

'What would you do with them, Sir Jervis, if you were a dictator?' asked Pronter.

'Put them under martial law, make them servants of the State like the army and navy and treat 'em as deserters if they behaved as these beggars do.'

Jennifer leaned forward, and Mayne spoke in his measured, easy tones, contrasting so vividly with the little man's heated speech.

'But, Sir Jervis, to do that you'd have to make the coal all State-owned, you know,' he said. 'Our army and navy, by repute at least, protect the community as a whole, not personal and private possessions.'

Sir Jervis spluttered and Claire flung at Brenner a warning glance which he answered by his whimsical, one-sided smile, whilst Guy Ferring cut in suavely: 'If we didn't know you so well, Mayne, we might take your communistic utterances seriously. When Mr. Mayne is a judge, Sir Jervis, he will no doubt delight his courts with a wit which must be a great relief to the Bar—if, of course, it is in keeping with the nature of the case. I must admit, however, that there are times when levity on the part of justice jars a little. After all, when a man—'

But Sir Jervis was not to be cajoled off his hobby-horse, and when he had politely heard his host to the end of a discourse calculated to turn the tide of the conversation, he acknowledged it briefly and returned to his own subject.

'You can't satisfy these fellows, you know. After all, they are free to choose their own work just as much as anyone else, and they are paid as good a wage as the industry can afford, a perfectly reasonable wage in my opinion—'

Jennifer's voice broke in, startling them all. She was leaning forward, a bright spot of colour in each cheek, her dark eyes glowing angrily, everything about her instinct with life and vigour. She seemed to those who knew her a creature transformed, a Galatea come to life.

'Thirty-one and sixpence a week, Sir Jervis Patney? Is that a reasonable wage in your opinion? Reasonable for what? For keeping a wife and family on, paying rent for one of your cottages, buying food and clothes and warmth, paying doctors' bills? Not comforts and pleasures, holidays, amusements, toys—those don't come their way at all. Reasonable pay for the sort of work they do? For lying on their backs deep down below the ground picking away at the coal, never seeing the sun except at earliest sunrise or at sunset, and then only in the middle of the summer, working in foul air, in horrible attitudes so that their limbs get cramped and their bones grow out of shape in time, in constant danger of death from the fall of a prop, from an engineer's mistake, from gas and flooding—thirty-one and six a week! A reasonable wage, is it? How far would it go with you—any of you?' her eyes sweeping a glance from one end of the table to the other, including all the startled, uncomfortable guests and their unfortunate hosts. 'How much of this meal could be bought for thirty-one and sixpence? I don't know the cost of food like this, or wine, or flowers. They don't have these things where I come from, but I don't suppose you could get more than one of those bottles of champagne out of a miner's whole weekly wage, earned by the sweat of his brow, by living in hourly danger of his life, with the knowledge that at the end of his life, or when he isn't able to work in the pits any longer because he's old before his time or injured or diseased, there's nothing in front of him but starvation or public charity.'

Her voice, that lovely, throbbing, deep-noted voice of hers, paused quiveringly, and Sir Jervis attempted to bluster in reply, aware that the tide of sympathy was with this impertinent girl rather than with himself.

'Nonsense, my dear young lady, nonsense! I am afraid you are not aware of the true facts, but have been reading some trashy newspaper paid to keep up a public agitation. The wage you quote is the very lowest, if it really is a correct figure at all—'

'It is the wage paid to many thousands of miners, Sir Jervis, as you ought to know,' cut in Jennifer.

'As for being left to starve if they meet with an accident, you are ridiculously misinformed, which shows what damage ignorant people can do, if you will pardon my saying so. I can give you an example of the sort of thing that gives rise to such statements. In one of my own pits there was a regrettable disaster some few months ago—very regrettable and sad, of course, but absolutely unavoidable. A young man was injured during the attempt to rescue some poor fellows entombed in the mine. Something happened to one of the cages. Those are the lifts they use for getting down to the coal face. He has a permanently injured leg and will have a slight limp for the rest of his life. I went to see him in the hospital the other day and offered him a—er—a sum of money as compensation for his injury, but be flung my offer back at me, positively flung it back with rudeness and not a word of thanks, and I found out afterwards, through my agent, that this fellow is receiving an allowance from some society or other to be a public agitator when he gets out of the hospital. You see the situation? He will go limping about amongst the men, saying he has to live on charity and always stirring up trouble and keeping the miners in a ferment of dissatisfaction.'

'That's not true!' blazed Jennifer.

Sir Jervis, knowing that his last speech had begun to turn the tide in his favour, flung her a look which he tried to make bland.

'My dear young lady, may one be permitted to ask what you know about coal-mines to set your opinion against mine—one who actually owns them?'

'I have lived all my life in the coal-fields,' said Jennifer, her voice breaking and her face working in emotion which she could no longer control. 'I am a miner's daughter. My mother died a lingering death, broken in body and mind after my two eldest brothers were killed in a pit explosion, and my father and my only remaining brother are lying dead at this moment in that pit you spoke of just now, the pit that had to be sealed up with sixty-four bodies in it—the Pit of Death, they called it in the newspapers whilst they remembered it and people here doled out their charity to us who were left … Oh—I must go,' and she rose from her chair precipitately and rushed from the room, the tears pouring down her cheeks, her hands stretched out blindly towards the door which a scandalised servant held open for her.

Claire rose from her seat as if to follow the girl, but Mayne forestalled her.

'I'll go, Claire,' he said. 'You stay and pour oil on the troubled waters,' and a little sigh of relief went up from the discomfited guests at the ordinary, cheerful tones of his voice.

Jennifer had not known where to go. She stood uncertainly in the hall, looking like a hunted animal, and she gave a little gasp as she felt Mayne's hand at her elbow and heard his reassuring voice.

'Better come in here,' he said, and took her to Claire's own sitting room, switched on the light, poked the fire logs into a brighter glow and busied himself at a cocktail cabinet to give her time to recover.

'Get this inside you,' he told her, bringing her a glass, and she gulped it down, the fiery liquid burning her throat and making her tear-wet eyes smart.

'I'm—sorry,' she said shakily.

He took the glass from her and set it down.

'You've properly put the cat amongst the pigeons,' he said with a smile.

'It was—unforgivable. Mrs. Ferring will never forgive me. I went mad,' she said. 'You don't know how awful it was to sit there and hear him—and know—'

Her voice began to break again, and he pushed her gently into a chair, tucked a cushion behind her head and a footstool under her feet, talking to her the while in his nice, comforting voice.

'I should just sit quietly for a moment and get over it, and then if you still want to get it off your chest, we'll talk it out, and—I'm terribly afraid that the only thing for you to do in the end will be to forget it.'

He was standing by the fire looking down at her with his kind eyes, lined at the corners from innumerable smiles. Her tired, bewildered spirit seemed to stretch out towards the kindness he offered like cold hands to a fire.

'I can't ever forget it,' she said in a low voice. 'It's born in me, part of me. I live here, am learning to speak and behave the way they do here, to dress like them and look like them, but in my heart I am still what I was before. I can't forget.'

'But is there any alternative?' he asked her gently. 'Is there anything we can do, either of us, for the miners?'

'Yes. There's something I can do, anyway. They need money, not just to exist on but to fight for better conditions. Their funds have been dipped into so often that there is so little left. These constant, futile little strikes help the owners because it keeps the Federation poor. Some people even say that the owners make the strikes themselves for their own purpose, I don't know whether to believe that or not, but the miners desperately need money, and that's how I am going to help them some day. That's the only reason why I stay here, live this life that without my work would be so empty, pretend to be contented, to like these people.'

It never even occurred to her that Mayne was one of 'these people'. That bond of sympathy between them, without cause or intent or explanation, made her think of him as being with her rather than with them. Mayne noticed it without comment. She attracted and interested him. As one of the most eligible of bachelors, he had been much sought after and flattered for years, paired off with one girl after another, had his name coupled many a time by a hopeful mother to her daughter's. But he had never had a serious affair in his life. Deep within him there dwelt his ideal woman whom unconsciously he compared with every woman he came to know at all intimately, finding that living woman wanting inevitably and knowing that it would always be so, that no man ever yet found his ideal because no woman is perfect.

Oddly enough, there was no thought of his ideal in his budding interest in Jennifer. She was of no type, no known variety of woman. Her gravity, her serenity, the discovery of the fire that raged beneath it, set her apart from all other women he had known or his mind had conceived.

'You want to give your life for your friends?' he asked her.

'That sounds—what word do I want? Pretentious?'

'I didn't mean it to sound like that. I think you've got a fine ideal and I honour it because—well, ideals seem to have got a bit mislaid for most of us. They so seldom stand the wear and tear and the friction of everyday life.'

'I hope mine will,' said Jennifer wistfully. 'Sometimes I think I shall never be able to sing at all, and it makes me go cold when I know that Julian thinks so too. I daren't think of the possibility of—failure.'

'What if you want to marry?'

She shook her head, and there came rushing back to her a memory that in that moment of frenzied escape had slipped her mind.

'Mr. Mayne?'

He heard the new note in her voice, a startled, questioning note.

'Yes?'

'Did you hear something Sir Jervis said? About a man who had been injured doing rescue work? Was still in hospital and would be a cripple for always?'

'Yes, he said something like that,' agreed Mayne.

'Mr. Mayne, would you do something for me? Something I can't possibly do now? Would you go to Sir Jervis and find out who the man was that was injured like that, his name? It's—it's most desperately important.'

He realised that it was.

'Of course I will. You think he would know the name?'

'Oh, perhaps not,' she said bitterly. 'Miners don't exist as people to Sir Jervis Patney. Still, as he went to see him, it's just possible, don't you think? Could you try for me, anyway?'

'At once. You'll stop here?'

'Yes. I—oh, however shall I face Mrs. Ferring?' she said in panic at being left alone with that possibility.

'I shouldn't worry. Claire's the most understanding person I know. I think you'll find she'll be ready to forget it even sooner than you are.'

'But I spoilt her party.'

'Don't you believe it! Except for the fact that Ferring wants to keep on Patney's soft side for some dirty political game they're all playing, Claire will be glad that you provided her guests with such a thrill in place of the polite inanities that one expects at a dinner-table. Anyway, I'll see you through it. You wait here till I've tapped Sir Jervis.'

Jennifer was a prey to a turmoil of unhappy thoughts during the minutes of his absence. In spite of what he had said, she felt that her outburst had been unforgivable to Claire Ferring and she was frightened of Rothe's reaction to it. What should she do if he cast her off now, half trained, deeply in his debt, and with no possible means of repaying him? Crowding in on that thought came the consideration of what she would feel and do if, as seemed certain, that injured man proved to be Bob.

She closed her eyes on the thought that agonised her sensitive mind – Bob a cripple; Bob who had been so strong and so proud in his strength; Bob who always won the best of the prizes at the miners' annual sports, which were organised by Beaton, the prizes being provided by Sir Jervis and occasionally presented condescendingly by her ladyship. The mile running race, the weight-lifting, the javelin-throwing – Bob had always won them hands down. His magnificent form had always been at the crucial point of the tug-o'-war solid as a rock. He had done feats of lifting and endurance in the pits which had become traditional, and if he had done them a little vaingloriously and unnecessarily nobody wanted to cavil at it, for his workmates were almost as proud of his strength as he was himself, and all the girls admired him and envied Jennifer.

And he was a cripple, would never walk again without a limp, never run or climb or throw. At the sports he would be amongst the onlookers, skulking in the background, impotently enraged.

The tears pricked her eyes and made her throat ache at the pictures in her mind. She knew him so well, knew that he could never accept such a destiny with resignation. He was not of the type to endure with courage such a fate. He would grow bitter, resentful, hurting himself and everyone with whom he came into contact.

And she had deserted him. She, who loved him, had not been able to see through that pitiful pretence, that sorry tale which now she marvelled she had believed so easily. And Lottie had been in this. Lottie had known, had connived at it, had helped him destroy the only thing that life had left him – the love of his girl.

She was on her feet when Mayne came back, pacing the little room restlessly, and she turned to him at once with her quick demand.

'Did he know?'

'Yes. Haling was the name, Robert Haling. My dear, what is it?' he added in distress, for she had dropped into a chair and hidden her face in her hands with a little moan.

'Oh, Bob—Bob—my poor dear,' he heard her whisper, and again, 'Oh, my dear, my dear!'

Presently she told him, sitting there in her chair with her hands loosely clasped in her lap, her eyes dull with misery, her voice a mere whisper of sound. She made him go through with her the agony of that night, the pictures which her crude, stark words painted for him following one another in swift, terrible succession through his mind. He felt something of the horror of these entombed men, of the women waiting above in the darkness, of the men going down in their vain, heroic efforts, of the crashing cage, of the slow dragging of the injured man through the underground tunnels until they could get him into another cage, of the rush in the ambulance, and then of that last scene where he had made his great sacrifice and Jennifer, in her hurt ignorance, had accepted it.

'I've got to go back. I've got to see him. I can't let him go on like that,' she whispered.

The dull misery in her eyes hurt him.

'Is that going to be wise or right, for either of you, my dear?' asked Mayne gently, seeing this girl, with all the promise that lay in her future, giving it all up to marry and slave for a crippled man who might not go on being a hero just because that one great moment had been possible.

Jennifer let her eyes waken to life for an instant.

'Wise? Right? Why, of course. There can't be any question about it,' she said.

'Look at it from his point of view, as I, being a man, find it easier to do. He's brought himself to the point of being able to make a supreme sacrifice. Realising what life would be to you with him crippled, he did the decent thing, the thing which proved him a man, and gave you up. Are you going to fling his heroism back at him and make all that agony he must have endured count for nothing? Is he going to be glad, do you think, if you go back to him and make it count for nothing?'

'It won't make any difference what you say, Mr. Mayne. I'm going back to him,' she said steadily.

'What to do? Give up everything here, your work, your future?'

He did not know why he was pleading with her, why there was born in him this passion to prevent her from making such a mess of her life. He only knew that it was vital to him.

Her face contracted in a flash of pain, but her voice was as steady as ever.

'I don't know. That's not a thing which I can decide now. All I know is that I must go; must see Bob. What happens after that—well, must just happen,' she said.

They were silent for a moment, Jennifer trying to sort her twisted, painful thoughts, Mayne standing looking down at her and wondering why it should matter to him whether she went or stayed.

He broke the silence abruptly.

'Do you love this man?' he asked.

Her face flushed. The question had in some strange fashion flung a cloak around them, shutting them within its folds as if for an instant they two were close and the world shut out. She shook the enveloping folds from her mind and answered him as directly as he had asked.

'Yes. I was engaged to marry him,' she said. 'We have been sweethearts for years. We have always been going to be married, since we were children.'

Why should something make his mind lighter, make him feel less resentful at her going? There was no answer to that question and he put it aside, merely accepting the fact that these things were. They were 'sweethearts', tender, old-fashioned word – they had always been going to be married. This man, Bob Haling, had been the lover of Jennifer, the child, had gradually become, through the years, the lover of Jennifer, the girl – but of Jennifer, the miner's daughter. What of this new Jennifer which he sensed had been created by Rothe and, in lesser measure, by Claire Ferring?

He bent to take her hands and draw her to her feet, his eyes smiling and kind.

'Well, if you have definitely made up your mind, for good or bad, shall we go to find Claire, to make our peace with her? And Rothe, who will want a good many explanations? What are you going to say to him, by the way? Do you think he will let you go?'

'He can't keep me,' said Jennifer simply, and he loved the pride of her, the courage, the simplicity.

'Let's go, then,' he said, and they went together.

Chapter Six

Jennifer was in the train again, in a first-class carriage this time, with dark blue coat, fur-collared, and smart little hat in place of the print dress and the shawl she had worn on her last journey, and with thin silk stockings and narrow grey suede shoes instead of wooden clogs.

In her pride she would have preferred to go as she had come, but Rothe had been kind to her, unexpectedly understanding, and she could not hurt him as that would have done. She could change into a third-class carriage before she reached Belsdale, and none of them would actually appreciate the value of the simple clothes she wore.

Rothe had put on the seat beside her a stack of magazines and a box of chocolates, the latter with a three-cornered smile.

'That shows how complete is my surrender of you,' he said, for chocolates had been taboo for her as he believed they spoilt not only the figure and the complexion but also the voice.

'I can't bear to go,' she said unexpectedly, tears at the back of her eyes.

At this final moment she realised how much he had grown into her life, or perhaps it was that her life had been grafted on to his. In so short a time had her familiar background become dimmed, so that she could almost think this background which Rothe represented had become the familiar one.

Claire Ferring had sent her a note, graceful and gracious, showing her understanding and not even speaking of forgiveness but more than hinting that she expected them to meet again, that this was only an interlude and not the final break which Jennifer had decided it must be.

And now Rothe waited by the carriage, immaculate as ever, his trim figure upright, his grey head bare, his eyes unusually kind, his voice offering neither word nor tone of reproach or of disappointment. He was a wise man, and Jennifer was too simple of heart to realise his wisdom. She only knew that his generosity and kindness were almost unbearable.

'I can't bear to go,' she said, and surprised herself.

'I'm not sending you away, my dear,' he said.

'I know. I wish you wouldn't be so—so nice about it, though,' and she managed an uncertain smile.

'What would you prefer? Wrath and recriminations? That I should drag you back by the hair of your head and keep you under lock and key and say "Sing, damn you, sing!"?'

She laughed a little at that.

'There are moments when I could almost wish that,' she said.

At the first shock of discovery, there had seemed nothing for her to do but go. She had recognised no alternative, had sought none. But now, after the first hectic excitement, she was beginning to feel afraid, to wish she had not rushed at it like this, had at least waited to write to Lottie or to Bob and to get an answer. Suppose Bob really didn't want her, was sorry she had come and could not let her see it? What if it were all a mistake, the story Sir Jervis had told, this mad rush of hers? What then?

She laid a hand on the one which Rothe had placed on the carriage door.

'Julian—'

She stopped after that quick, whispered word and he looked at her with his head a little on one side in whimsical inquiry.

'Jennifer?'

'Julian, I—am I being an idiot in going away like this?' she asked him, her words coming in a rush, her voice quivering.

'My dear, that's a question no one but yourself can answer. That's why I haven't ventured to advise you from the very first, either to encourage you or to deter you. Only—there's one thing I've meant all along to say to you, and to say at this very moment, with the train just about to start. This isn't irrevocable, Jennifer. If you do find that you've been an idiot, that you've made a mistake, that things aren't quite what you think they're going to be—well, I'm still here, still ready to carry out the contract—still waiting for my prima donna.'

His look and tone, no less than his words, affected her deeply and, lacking the power for adequate reply, she bent her head and laid her lips on his hand.

A moment later the train was gone and she saw him for an instant through a mist of tears and then no more.

By the time she reached Belsdale she was calm again and able to look forward more cheerfully with every glimpse of things familiar, things dear to her because they had been linked with so much of her life. Even the tall chimneys, the gaunt frames of giant cranes, the huddle of nondescript buildings marking a pithead, added to her rising spirits, and by the time the slow local train puffed into Werford she was able to meet Lottie with a smile and a hug in which there were no reserves.

'Jen, it's fine to see you again, and you're looking great—and grand! Oh, Jen, ever since I had your wire I've been dreading seeing you in case you were different,' said Lottie.

Jennifer was shocked beyond belief at Lottie's looks, for she had more than the natural fragility consequent on her recent confinement. She looked thin and haggard, and almost transparent, as if a breath of wind could have blown her away.

'I'm just the same, Lottie—oh, my dear, it's good to see you, to be at Werford again ... Hullo, Bill, how's life? That you, Mrs. Rickets? I thought it was, but I couldn't believe that was Effie. Hasn't she grown?'

'Any luggage, Jennifer?' asked Job, the solitary porter-cum-stationmaster-cum-clerk, and she wheeled round in warm greeting to the wizened little old man who had wheeled her and her brothers about on the station trolley many a time.

'Oh, hullo, Job! Hullo! It's like coming back to life after a bad dream to see you all again. How's Mrs. Denny?'

'Not so bad considerin'. She don't get over Jim in a hurry, though. Them things come hard on us old 'uns, you know, Jen.'

They had lost their only son in the recent pit tragedy, and Jennifer's face grew pitiful.

'I know, Job. They come hard to us young ones, too,' she said in a low voice.

'Yes, Jen, I allow they do. Well, we're glad to see you back. Will you be stopping now?'

'I expect so, Job. I've decided that my place is here, after all.'

'That's good hearing. We've missed you sore. Will there be a trunk or anything?'

'No, only this case. They'll send on the rest of my things if I want them.'

'Right. Young George Rickets'll carry that up for you presently. Where'll you be staying?'

'At my place,' said Lottie. 'So long, Job. See you later,' and the two went out of the little station together and began to walk up the hill towards the two rows of cottages and the huddle of small shops which constituted the village.

'Can you really make room, Lottie?' asked Jennifer doubtfully, for she had decided to get a room at the Rose and Crown, rather than strain still further the resources of her friend.

''Course I can. What do you take me for? Unless you've come back too fine for a shakedown in Polly's room if Jackie and Prue come in with me.'

'Of course I haven't, Lottie. It hurts me when you say things like that. Don't I belong here the same as you do? Isn't this my home? Aren't you my friend?' asked Jennifer with a fierceness which made Lottie realise how strongly she was feeling.

'Sorry, Jen. You know I didn't mean anything. Only—we're wondering what's brought you back like this, all of a sudden, you going off with such fine hopes and all.'

'What do you mean by "we", Lottie?' Jennifer asked more quietly.

'Oh—oh … well—everybody, you know,' said Lottie confused.

'Do you mean Bob?'

Lottie looked at her quickly, saw that she knew, and nodded.

'How did you know?' she asked.

'Never mind. I'll tell you another time. Lottie, I've got to know the truth now. No more lies. How is he? Is he home yet? Is he—can he—walk?'

'He's still in the hospital,' said Lottie soberly. 'He'll be coming out tomorrow or the next day. They're going to let me know. Was that what brought you back, Jen?'

'Partly that, though I didn't know whether he had come out or not. Is he lame, Lottie?'

'Yes.'

Jennifer drew a deep, gasping breath. Until her friend had spoken that uncompromising monysyllable, she knew now she had been hoping against hope. Now she could hope no more. The thing was true.

'Poor Bob,' she said simply, but Lottie knew every tone of her voice, every fleeting expression of her sensitive, mobile face.

'Oh, Jen, why did you come?' she asked. 'Why didn't you stay away? He'd have got over it and so would you. You were getting over it already, weren't you? Your letters sounded happier, more settled—and then your wire came and now you ... Oh, Jen, why did you do it?'

'I had to, Lottie. Do you think I could possibly stay away when I knew the truth? Oh, I know why you did it, you and Bob, but don't you see that I can't accept it? He needs me now more than ever he did, and my place is with him, sharing whatever there is to share, helping him as he would have helped me if things had been the other way round. What sort of girl do you take me for, Lottie?'

'Oh, Jen, I take you for a fool—and someone very splendid,' said Lottie, her voice shaking, her hand catching at her friend's as they turned the corner into the village street.

Everybody stopped to speak to Jennifer, coming out of their houses or their shops, or crossing the street to have a word with her. She wondered how she could ever have thought it foolish to come back, ever imagined that her background had shifted, that Rothe and Claire and their friends could blot out this simple, unquestioning, sincere friendship of her own people, friendship that had stood the test of time, that knew her for what she had been and was and loved her for that rather than in expectation of the future.

She greeted them all with loving words and a misty smile and came at last to Lottie's cottage, never quite as neat and well-cared-for as Jennifer's had been; but, then, Lottie had four little ones to look after and she had had only her two men.

The children eyed her shyly in her London clothes, but a moment later they were swarming about her, clinging to her with grubby, sticky fingers, pulling off her hat and burying their noses in her fur collar with surprised delight at its warmth and softness.

And then Jennifer became aware of Bob.

He was sitting by the fire and making no attempt to come to her, and in the first moment the dimness of the crowded little room had been enough to hide him from her, though Lottie had seen him instantly and put a hand to her mouth to catch back the instinctive cry of surprise at his unexpected presence.

Slowly Jennifer put the children down, and Lottie in the background hustled them away and closed the door, and they were alone.

She went to him with hands outstretched, and as he rose with difficulty, gripping the arms of the wooden chair, her eyes and her lovely voice grew soft with pity.

'Bob—my dear!'

He managed to stand upright, but he was a wreck of his former self, gaunt and thin, his skin wrinkled where the firm young flesh had shrunk beneath it, and on the table, eloquent messenger, lay a thick, rubber-shod stick.

'This is a bit of a surprise, Jennifer,' he said slowly.

'To both of us, Bob. Lottie said you weren't expected till tomorrow or Friday,' she said, feeling unaccountably awkward, as if they were strangers meeting for the first time and shut into this tiny, cluttered room to make conversation.

He shot her a suspicious glance.

'Lottie said? Did she get you here then?' he demanded brusquely.

'No. She knew nothing about it until the wire I sent her just before I started from London. She's as surprised as you. Aren't you glad to see me, Bob? You aren't—looking as if you are.'

He steeled himself against the appeal in her voice, against the new charm which these clothes gave her, and the unfamiliar way of doing her hair, and a certain new quality about her to which he could not give a name. Claire would have called it poise, but the people who lived in Werford knew nothing about poise.

'Did you expect me to be?' he asked her slowly. 'Haven't we— finished with things, got the other side of them? What's the use of seeing each other again, raking up things best forgotten?'

She came to him and laid her hand on his arm and looked into his face, seeing with infinite compassion the new lines there, lines of pain and misery and bitterness and despair – lines which took away his youth and gave him something hard and repellent in its place.

'I want to rake them up, Bob. That's what I've come back for. I know what you did, you see, you and Lottie. I was so simple and easy to deceive. I believed you about going to Canada and starting a new life with new friends and forgetting the old. I never realised the truth, but now that I know, and know why you did it, you won't be able to send me away again so easily. I've come to stay, Bob—to stay with you.'

For an instant there was a hunted look in his eyes and his face worked unhappily. Then he put on the mask again and she saw that she had lost him once more.

'That's rubbish. You can't stay here,' he said harshly. 'There's no place for you in Werford. How're you going to live, for one thing? They're all taking in one another's washing now, and God knows what any of them will do when there are not even rags to wash. You'd better go back again and stay there.'

Her heart ached for him, for the dumb misery and despair and loneliness that had robbed him of his youth.

'No, my dear. My place is here and these are my friends. You can't send me away. I've come back to stay.'

'What for?' he asked roughly.

'Because—I love you, Bob, and I believe that you still love me, and even if you don't need me, I need you. I've no one else, no one in the world. I thought my heart would break when you sent me away, let me believe you were tired of me. Now that I know it wasn't true, that it was because you loved me you sent me away—I've come back to be happy again. Bob, you do still care, don't you?'

But he stood staring straight in front of him and her pride would let her go no further.

'Care? What right have I to talk about caring for anyone?' he asked bitterly. 'The best advice I can give you is to go back where you came from, as I've said before, and stay there,' and he picked up his stick and lurched painfully from the room.

Agonised for him, Jennifer stood and watched him go out and down the street, slowly dragging one leg as he went, lifting himself step by step with an obvious effort, pausing every few yards to rest – Bob, whose step she had known from a thousand others, his swinging, easy, confident stride.

She turned away blindly and sat by the fire, the slow tears coming painfully from eyes which had learned not to shed them. Then, hearing Lottie, and feeling that at this moment she could not face that good friend's lamentations, she snatched up her hat and went out of the house, taking the other direction from that down which Bob trod his difficult way and never pausing until she came to a small, white stone house with a crazy, much repaired shed of corrugated iron beside it – Father Flint's 'church', with its door hanging crazily off its hinges, a door which would not even shut, let alone lock.

'What should God's house want with a lock and key?' he had said many years ago when someone had suggested that he ought to lock it at night. 'Who or what would He ever want to keep out? "Him that cometh to me, I will in no wise cast out", was what the Lord Himself said,' and when they hinted that it would tempt burglars, the old man had laughed.

'What is there to steal? Nothing I could not replace with a little time and patience myself, and if there is something there that someone badly wants enough to steal it, why, he must want it badly enough to provide his own justification.'

So the door had never had a lock and key, and now it hung by one hinge until Father Flint had time to climb up on top of the steps to repair it, or until someone else did the little job for him.

'Bob would have done it,' thought Jennifer with a lump in her throat as she went past the building and up the path, brave with its borders of stunted, grimy little shoots which Father Flint fondly hoped would soon be showing spring flowers.

He gardened as he did everything else, never defeated, always hopeful, looking forward to the next season if this one had proved fruitless and never looking back, seeing the flowers bloom where no one else saw anything but arid ground. And it seemed to Jennifer that the flowers did bloom for him better than for other people, that he left everything he touched a little brighter, a little happier, a little more fruitful than he had found it.

She knocked now at his door and went in. His house was no more barred and bolted than his church, and for the same reasons.

She found him in his little workshed at the back of the house, bent over a bench with a tiny, frightened kitten in hands that were as gentle as the voice with which he soothed it as he attended to it.

'Sit down a moment, will you?' he said, hearing a visitor but not leaving his work to turn round. 'This poor little thing has run a nasty jagged splinter into its pad and I've managed to get it out, but if I don't dress the wound it'll turn septic – another case of casting out one devil and leaving the place open for seven worse than the one. There, I think that'll do, my scrap. Now a drop of milk for a stirrup cup and then you can go ... Oh, Jennifer! You!—' turning round to reach the saucer of milk which he had placed in readiness for his patient.

She came to him with that smile which even the surliest of people usually found for Father Flint, and Jennifer was by no means that.

'I came on the London train, Father,' she said. 'I needn't ask you how you are. You're a miracle. Aren't you ever tired or sick?'

'Oh, now and then, now and then,' he said. 'I really haven't time for such luxuries, though. I always think half the doctors would be out of work if all other people were in work—and hard work at that. Well, my dear child, it does my heart good to see you. Come into the house and have a cup of tea with me whilst you tell me all about it,' and he thrust a hand through her arm and took her back into the living-room which was bare of everything save actual necessities. The only exception was one really good, comfortable chair which someone had given him a year or two previously for his own use, though he was very seldom in it, for almost the only occasions on which he sat down other than for meals were times when he had a visitor, whom he insisted should occupy the chair of state.

Jennifer, protesting in vain, occupied it now whilst Father Flint busied himself with a kettle and a gas-ring and cut bread-and-butter and apologised for the absence of jam or cake as if he usually had it, though she knew he never did.

'Mrs. Kimble resting as usual?' asked Jennifer with a smile.

Mrs. Kimble was his daily housekeeper whose only absolutely regular day for attending the White Cottage was Saturday, for on that day Father Flint paid her her wages.

He smiled like a boy caught at the jam cupboard.

'Well, she isn't getting any younger, you know, and it's a climb for her up here twice a day, so I told her I'd manage,' he said apologetically. 'And now, my dear, pour the tea, will you? It makes me feel quite a swell to sit at the table and have so grand a lady opposite me drinking tea with me—or ought we to be having cocktails at this time of the day?'

She laughed and poured the tea from the old brown teapot into two odd cups and looked across at the old man affectionately.

'I'd rather have tea from this old pot than the most marvellous cocktail ever invented,' she said. 'Oh, I'm glad—glad—to be home again!'

'Well, let's gossip, shall we? I haven't had a really good gossip since you went away, and I do hope no one's got ahead of me in detailing the village scandals yet,' said Father Flint, drinking his tea and seeing to it that she took her bread-and-butter from the proper side of the plate. One side held bread with butter, the other, nearest to him, bread with margarine on it. He did not know that Jennifer, aware of that old trick of his, had slyly turned the plate round when he was not looking so that he got the buttered pieces. He cared so little what he ate that he remained unconscious of the exchange, and Jennifer felt he needed butter much more than she did.

In spite of having congratulated him on his looks, she thought he had grown thinner, that his cheek-bones were more prominent than she remembered them to be, and that his clothes were beginning to hang loosely on him. She knew that he half starved himself so that he need not turn away the hungry from his door, and some of the people who came to him to be fed were, in fact, better nourished than he was. She must look after him again as she had often done in the past, making him big pots of soup and seeing to it that Mrs. Kimble put in an appearance at least once every day.

Oh yes, there was need of her here, she thought with a deep feeling of peace.

They talked of village matters, Father Flint telling her little happenings with a turn of humour which was never malicious and which he knew she always enjoyed. Where in London Jennifer had been tongue-tied and won a reputation for dullness and lack of humour, here in this bleak little cottage, drinking weak tea and eating bread and margarine in the company of one shabby old man, she was both bright and entertaining and showed herself to possess a fund of quiet humour. She was always at her best with Father Flint. The same could be said of most people who knew him. He had a knack of bringing the best out of people by the simple method of always believing the best of them, and no one liked to let him down or disappoint him.

After tea they sat over the fire, a good, hot fire because coal was cheaper than gas for lighting the room, and Jennifer told him quite simply the story of her break with Bob and her return to him.

'You've seen him, Father? Talked to him?' she asked.

'Yes. I've been to the hospital most weeks since he has been there. I think he liked me to go, but—he takes it hardly, Jennifer.'

'Yes. He's so changed. He's so hard and bitter and—old, somehow. He's made my heart ache.'

'And mine. What are we going to do for him, Jennifer? He's so fine actually. All this bitterness and anger are only on the surface. At the core he's the same as ever.'

She opened her heart to him as she could never have done to anyone else, knowing that he would understand, would see things not from a worldly point of view but as she wanted to see them.

'I want to marry him, Father. That's what I came back for. I tried to make him understand, told him I cared still, but he made it so hard for me, and I know that everybody will be against me, even Lottie. You think I'm right, don't you?'

'I always hesitate to advise anyone on a matter like this, my dear, but to you I can say what I might not dare to say to anyone else – do what your heart dictates. Is this actually what it dictates, Jennifer? You are not acting from pity or a sense of duty?'

'No. I want to marry Bob. I love him. I could never care for any other man.'

Yet why, as she spoke, should the memory of another man flash across her mind, a tall, thin man with a smile that warmed her, with kind eyes set amidst a network of wrinkles which smiles had etched there? Perhaps it was because Father Flint had such eyes, though his were blue and those other eyes had been grey.

'You are of the faithful kind, Jennifer,' said the old man. 'If you feel like that about Bob, I think you are right to marry him. I think it is the only way to save him from himself, to dig him out of this slough of bitterness and despair in which he is sunk. Through you he will realise that life still holds something for him, and between you I am sure you will make good. There is always the practical consideration, of course. What are you going to live on? There isn't much chance of a job for him here, and I understand he has turned down a clerical job Sir Jervis Patney offered him in Belsdale.'

'He offered him charity and Bob refused it,' said Jennifer proudly. 'I've thought a lot about the practical side of it and I've got a scheme, if Bob will agree. Mr. Rothe—you remember he is the man who is teaching me to sing? I think he could be persuaded to go on with my lessons. He practically said so when he saw me off today, and I think he knew I was coming back here to marry Bob. He is keeping me, of course, lending me money for my present needs, the idea being that when I come out as a singer I shall earn enough to pay it back. I don't see that it need make any difference my being married to Bob. He will

85

come back to London with me and we can live very simply and quietly, and then when I have finished my lessons and Mr. Rothe lets me begin to earn, I can pay him back the money he has lent to Bob and me.'

'Do you think Bob would agree to that?' asked Father Flint doubtfully. 'I don't. No decent man would let his wife work for him and keep him, and Bob is terribly proud.'

'I know,' said Jennifer quickly. 'I've gone a little further with my thoughts, though. Whilst I am finishing my training with Mr. Rothe, Bob could be learning a trade. Mr. Rothe would lend him the money, I feel sure, and that, too, we could repay in time so that we could both be independent. There are lots of skilled trades which Bob could learn even if he is—even if he cannot walk very well. Father, he'll get better than that, won't he? Walk better in time?' she asked urgently, the question forcing itself in front of the other issues and showing him how deeply it was on her mind.

He reassured her.

'Oh yes, my dear. You need have no fear of that. You know they thought at first he would lose his leg, but a surgeon they had down from London managed to save it and they told me at the hospital that in time, probably six months or so, he would be able to walk with only a slight limp and would not even need a stick.'

'Thank God for that,' said Jennifer earnestly. 'Oh, to see him limping along like that, so slowly, so painfully—it was terrible.'

'You needn't dwell on that, nor need he. Look, Jennifer, shall I see him for you? Talk to him? Show him that it's going to mean happiness to you to marry him? It is, isn't it, my dear? I must be sure of that.'

'Oh yes, Father,' she said in her sincere way. 'It is the one thing I want in the world.'

And on that note they parted, the old man promising that he would, if possible, see Bob that evening.

Jennifer went slowly back to Lottie, half afraid that Bob would be there and relieved to be told that he was staying in his old lodgings at the other end of the village.

For three days they neither saw him nor heard anything of him, but on the Sunday evening, as Jennifer sat alone over the fire mounting guard over the sleeping children so that Lottie could go to church, the door opened quietly and Bob came in.

Jennifer waited for him to come to her, and after a moment of agonised uncertainty, he stumbled across the room and came close to her and laid his head against her shoulder without a word.

With the mother-note in her voice, she whispered to him: 'Oh, my darling, rest there a moment. Don't let's talk. Just rest.'

And presently he spoke, his voice muffled and uncertain.

'I've wanted to come, Jen, but I couldn't. I daren't. I haven't any right now, but I can't stay away from you any longer. Oh, Jen, I love you so—I love you so. I've wanted you so terribly.'

And she held him against her as if she mothered a tired, penitent child, soothing him with words of sweet foolishness and with no least idea that it was as a mother rather than a lover that she comforted him. This was the love she had always known, the safe, gentle, peaceful love which had satisfied her childhood and her girlhood and to which, as yet, her womanhood had nothing to say.

They spoke of marriage, Jennifer the pleader, Bob the reluctant.

'I thought at first that nothing could make me marry you, Jen, once I knew about my leg. When you came back and we spoke to each other, I still felt nothing could make me. Then Father Flint came to see me, and we talked and argued for hours, and he told me that I was making one of my legs out to be the only important part of me, body or soul, and letting it be more important than you and your happiness. It sounded queer, putting it that way, but I suppose that is really what I have been doing. Jen—'

'Yes, dear.'

'Jen, is it true what he said? That I am spoiling your chance of happiness by refusing to let you marry me?'

'Quite true, dear,' she said, for so it seemed to her in her pity and her passionate desire to heal his bruised and embittered spirit.

'He said you proposed to go on with your lessons in town and that I should live on you, Jen,' went on Bob, sitting down painfully in the chair and stretching out his injured leg to get it into the most comfortable position. 'You know I wouldn't do that, anyway.'

Eagerly she told him of the rest of her scheme for getting him trained in some skilled craft, mentioning two or three trades which had occurred to her, but he shook his head doggedly.

'No, dear. I'm not going to live on you or let that fellow Rothe keep either of us. If you want to sing, sing to the people here, sing in our home, sing because you're happy and want to, not because people have paid money to hear you. I've got a plan, Jen. I can get work, here in Werford. I've been offered it already. In fact, I—well, I've said I'll take it.'

'What sort of work, Bob?' she asked a little sharply, for there had been something in his tone she had not liked, something furtive and utterly at variance with his nature as she had known it.

He hesitated.

'Well—it's rather a confidential sort of job, working for the Federation in a way,' he said at last.

'You mean you're to be paid by the Federation? A sort of official?' pursued Jennifer.

'The money won't come out of the Federation funds. There are one or two people who are putting up the money, rich people, you understand, who couldn't afford to have their names mixed up in anything but who are privately in sympathy with us—'

'Bob, you're not going to work with Mallinger, are you?' cut in Jennifer quickly.

'No, of course not. What made you ask that?' came the reply, but she was not satisfied.

'Won't you be able to tell me, at least, Bob? You know I'm safe.'

'Perhaps I shall be able to later. I'll find out and let you know. It'll be a decent job, Jennifer. Three quid a week and the Union dues paid for me.'

'Three pounds a week? Bob!'

It seemed a colossal sum to Jennifer Jenks, though to Jennifer Rothe, a week ago, it would have seemed barely adequate. One changed one's standards so quickly when one became a part of the Werford community, and to most of the women there three pounds a week would seem a fortune.

'So you see, Jen, there won't be any need for you to go back to London to this man Rothe and learn to be a singer. I'll be able to take care of you, if you can put up with a cripple for a husband. You won't have to work for a living.'

It never occurred to him that he was asking her to sacrifice anything in giving up her career. He had never thought of it as other than a means of livelihood, the best she could find when her two breadwinners were taken from her and he no longer available. His only reluctance towards this marriage was on the score of his lameness, and Father Flint had managed to beat down much of his resistance where that was concerned, pointing out to him that Jennifer would find comfort in the knowledge that he could never work down the pits, and that she was not of the type to think more of a man because he could win races and dance.

It had not been so difficult, in the end, to persuade him to change his determination not to marry her. His own heart was her advocate. He loved her so desperately, wanted her so much, had hungered and thirsted for her during the months of their separation, that it was almost impossible for him to go on denying himself when both Jennifer and Father Flint urged him to do what he longed to do.

And so Jennifer wrote to Rothe that evening, wrote painfully and at length, telling him many things that she had no idea she was saying, making him both smile and rage when he read it.

I feel terribly conscious of the burden of my debt to you, dear Julian, she had written, *after she had told him that she and Bob were to be married almost at once. I would never have let you do so much for me if I had had any idea that I should let you down like that and never be able to repay it. I know it will only make you smile when I say this, but I am still going to say it — that I shall remember you always with gratitude and in my prayers and I think that some day you will find your reward. I don't speak of a reward for the money you've wasted on me, but for your kindness to me, your patience, and your consideration.*

She added in a postscript: Will you please tell Mr. Mayne?

Rothe answered her briefly and characteristically, not bemoaning her decision but accepting it without criticism. He expressed the conventional wishes for her happiness, and then he added something which she felt he had not intended to write when he began the letter but which touched her deeply.

For all my polite and discreet sentiments, my dear, don't forget that the cage is still open if ever the nightingale wants to return and perch there a little while – or remain there for always.

He enclosed a cheque for fifty pounds which Jennifer dare not show Bob, but which Father Flint advised her to put safely away in the savings bank 'in case'.

And on her wedding morning the postman brought her a little square wooden box marked: 'Fragile. Urgent. For immediate delivery.' The handwriting was strange, but when she looked inside she had no need to search for the card which she eventually found and which said, *'May all your dreams come true'*, for lying in their bed of damp cotton-wool were half a dozen camellias, pink and white and red against the glossy leaves.

Bob watched her take them from their wrappings and expressed his surprise.

'What a funny thing to send anyone, specially a bride. Do they take it for a funeral?' But Jennifer only smiled and went to put the fragile blooms in water.

Her eyes were very tender and the faintest possible sigh escaped her. She had given up other things beside her career for Bob. She had given up dear friends who so soon would be but a dim memory to her.

She touched the waxen petals of the camellias with gentle fingers.

Chapter Seven

Jennifer pushed open the door of Father Flint's 'church'. It still hung crazily from one hinge, for he had never found that spare half-hour and nobody else had troubled.

Anyone who pushed open that door expecting to find a church would have had a shock, for anything less like the orthodox 'house of God' could not be imagined, though anyone not hidebound by creeds might well have pictured the Carpenter of Nazareth meeting His friends there.

At the far end, men were playing darts and chalking up the score on a board hung below the Ten Commandments; two of the older men were hunched seriously over a chessboard at the foot of the pulpit steps, and in the middle of the room a space had been cleared and some youths were playing ping-pong on a home-made table-top supported by two pews.

In a corner, half a dozen women sat in a circle 'ragging', that is knotting small strips of rag into a large piece of sacking. By making rugs in this way, each a communal labour, the work was done quickly and easily and the women enjoyed the gossip and laughter which inevitably accompanied a ragging party. They took it in turns to become possessors of the finished rugs, and, if the sacking were not too large, a rug could be finished in a day. The woman who was eventually to own it provided cheap refreshments, usually tea, with bread and margarine, or oven-cake, which was a large, flat cake made chiefly of flour and water and eaten hot from the oven.

The children played about in any available space, chidden shrilly now and then by the mothers, or by the darts or ping-pong players when they got in their way, though for the most part they were left to do what they liked and no one seemed even to notice the noise.

It was November, a bad month for the poor, a month when winter seems to stretch endlessly ahead and mothers' eyes grow anxious and their hearts fail at the sound of the first cough, at the first shiver and the drawing about the thin little bodies of the inadequate clothes. In the mining districts there was usually the alleviation of more regular work because of the added demand for coal, but the output of the Belsdale Collieries was chiefly steam coal, and year by year the demand for that grew less as the ships burned oil in increasing quantities.

The men were busy with strike talk again. The women were weary of such talk, hated the very sound of the word on the lips of their men, and yet when the time came they would bear their terrible share in the struggle with courage and in the knowledge that they had reached the lowest limits in which life could be maintained.

The first fogs of the year were finding the under-nourished bodies ill prepared to meet them, and ordinary colds developed with tragic speed into bronchitis, influenza, pneumonia, and a hundred kindred ills. Men and women were crippled with rheumatism and children were rickety from want of proper food. Skim milk and the cheapest margarine provide no fortification against an English winter, and children died whilst in Whitehall they argued as to the least sum which might be spent in order barely to maintain life. Pompous members of Parliament caused to be drawn up for them schedules showing the number of vitamins and calories contained in certain of the cheapest forms of food, proving by figures on paper that a woman could feed her husband and children on less than a generous State was already allowing them, totally ignoring the fact that, in order to carry out the demands of the schedules, she would have to be not only a skilled mathematician but would also have to do her day's shopping in fifteen or twenty different parts of England to buy at the prices quoted. After arriving at the satisfactory conclusion that no one in this land of ours is being starved, the pompous members would be driven home in their cars to a five-course dinner whose vitamins and calories would have kept a whole family fed and warmed for a week.

Jennifer felt herself to be amongst the more fortunate, because, out of Bob's wage and what she herself was able to earn, she had only two people to feed, warm and clothe. That did not prevent her from looking at other people's children and knowing that her own heart and arms were empty. She had given up nursing and playing with the babies of her friends, but they did not know why she had given it up. They said Jennifer was 'stuck-up' since her marriage.

She looked into the 'church' on that afternoon without much hope of finding Father Flint there. All day and most of the night he might be met trotting about from place to place, a basket over his arm, a smile on his saint's face which was persistently cheerful in spite of his torn and bleeding heart. He was an irresistible beggar, and the basket usually contained food, tinned soups, sometimes butter and eggs and cod-liver oil, whilst over his arms hung miscellaneous parcels of clothing, blankets, toys for sick and fretful children, or for the infinitely more pathetic ones who never complained but just lay in unchildlike patience which had ceased to try to understand why these things should be.

But Father Flint left more behind him than the food, the blankets, or the toys. He left new hope, cheer, the memory of a smile and a heartening word, the feeling that someone cared, and few could hear his brisk step coming their way without a lifting of the head and heart and a brightening of the eyes.

The 'raggers' paused in their work to look at Jennifer as she stood in the doorway.

Marriage had already set its seal on her, for these had been difficult months, months in which hope fought a losing battle with despair, when the solid ground seemed to have shifted beneath her feet leaving her no place in which she felt she could stand with safety.

The women were curious about her, for her marriage had been a matter for wonder and speculation in the village, and there had been very few who thought it had any chance of success, especially after Jennifer's stay in London in the fine house of which Lottie Marsh had boasted.

But Jennifer, with an open ear for all the confidences which were still poured into it, had a still tongue for her own affairs, and beyond the knowledge that their little cottage was spick and span with its new furniture, and that Bob Haling limped off every morning to catch the 7.50 to Belsdale and limped back again from the 6.40 every evening, no one knew anything about the Halings.

They eyed her slim, upright figure with interest, obviously speculating how much longer it would be before she showed signs of the family which they regarded as inevitable. Jennifer felt and recognised their curiosity, resenting it and yet realising that there was kindliness behind it.

Contrary to their expectations, her form grew thinner rather than bulky with fertility, but though she was losing weight, she kept herself fit with a queer inward pride, religiously performing the exercises on which Rothe had insisted in spite of her husband's jeering comments. She never retaliated when he made fun of her for doing her 'physical jerks', as he termed them. Her tender heart saw more deeply than the surface, and she knew that beneath the scoffing was an aching sense of his own incapacity. She spared him all the humiliation she could, thinking out little services which she could ask him to perform, knowing them to be within his power, but often the look with which he rewarded her cheerful request told her that he knew and bitterly resented the motive which had prompted it.

She had very little to do when she was not occupied with the needlework which she did for a shop in Belsdale, and she was employing her spare time in painting and papering the cottage which had been let to them cheaply because of its bad state of repair. She invented excuses, however, for abandoning her work when Bob was in the house, knowing how embittering it was for him to be able to do so little to help, for it seemed even the simplest job in house-decorating necessitated climbing a ladder or a pair of steps.

But Jennifer kept resolutely cheerful for his sake, making light of his crippled state so that he should not guess what anguish it was for her to see his superb strength reduced to the helplessness of a cripple, and his pride of manhood exchanged for querulous complainings and bitterness. He could not accept his lot, could not make the best of it, and by that very fact increased a thousandfold the difficulties which Jennifer had to face.

Her one consolation was that she was able to practise, for Bob had bought her, out of the remains of his 'compensation' money, an ancient, wheezy piano.

'That'll keep you from missing your fine toy in London, lovey,' Bob had told her, and she had hugged him and held him very closely because of the childlike happiness he had found in giving the piano to her. It never occurred to him that she might miss anything else, and he was content in the belief that now that she had a piano of her own and could play and sing when she liked, she could have no possible hankering after her life with Rothe.

And Jennifer let him think so, deeply compassionate as she was for him and desiring above everything that she might give him happiness.

But in her heart she knew that she dare not think of any other kind of existence, must not let herself think of it. It was not the soft luxury she craved, for she was of hard stuff and the ease of Rothe's house had never affected her very greatly and she never missed the luxurious chairs and couches, the rich food and the wines. She had enjoyed all these very sparingly, and actually felt more fit on the simple, wholesome food she prepared for herself and Bob over her kitchen fire.

What she would miss, if she allowed herself to do so, was the talk on many things of which Werford had never heard, not the gossip and the scandals, the 'darlings!' and the superlatives which constituted the conversation of such as Jane Bettle and the Mischance, but the talk of Claire Ferring, of Rothe, of their intimates, men and women of letters and culture and of diverse interests, men and women with knowledge and the intelligence to apply it. Jennifer had been learning something of the world of art, had been to exhibitions with Claire and discovered undreamed of beauty in line and colour and thought. She had gone to old churches, to the museums so that she might be able to talk with understanding of a variety of matters, and though Rothe had sent her to these, always with a knowledgable companion, with the idea of giving her topics for conversation and an ability to hold her own amongst cultured people, Jennifer had found there something satisfying to the quiet needs of her mind, had found wonder and enchantment. Derek had suggested books to her, and she had begun to read voraciously once she got over her first surprise and difficulty with a new style and phrasing. Claire gave her a library subscription and a list of modern novels, and Derek went with her to choose books of non-fiction, showing an unusually wide knowledge of a range of subjects and inviting the girl's comments, which were fresh and unspoiled by having been instructed previously as to what she ought to think about these books.

Rothe had formed a habit of talking to her when they lunched or dined alone, taking her in imagination to many countries of the earth, for he had travelled extensively and found places where the ordinary tourist never penetrates, seeing nature in the raw. She had come to look for and enjoy these talks, his pungent commentary on life and his apt descriptions and flair for unusual adjectives a delight to her opening mind.

These were the things she missed without admitting it even to herself.

Bob was a devoted husband, proud of her and delighted with the open admiration and envy of less fortunate men, but she had come to look for other things with which to satisfy her mind. She felt as if, after galloping ahead in boundless space, she had come suddenly up against a brick wall at which her mind beat unavailingly.

Debarred from any other interest in sport save the watching of a match or the filling in of football coupons, Bob Haling was utterly bereft of an interest in life, for sport had been his god ever since he had won the hundred yards handicap in Standard Two. Occasionally something would escape him which showed Jennifer that he still took some sort of interest in the miners' difficulties and problems, but at such times she noticed that he would cut himself off short, with a glance at her which held something furtive, something which made her feel vaguely uncomfortable because she could not understand it. She could see no reason why he should not take an interest in his former comrades, and yet he was adroit in avoiding any discussion of their problems which she tried to introduce as a relief from his one topic of conversation, which was his own physical condition.

He seemed never to tire of discussing his symptoms, of comparing yesterday's pains with today's and today's with last week's. He described in detail sleepless nights which she knew existed entirely in his imagination, for he slept soundly in the bed beside her whilst she lay awake, planning, thinking, scheming for a future which was so shadowy and unreal.

Now, with a new trouble on her mind, she turned where she knew she would find courage and fresh hope.

'Where's Father Flint?' she asked one of the ping-pong players who came near her to retrieve a ball.

'Just gone, Jennifer. He was going to call at the Fosters'. Their Jackie's bad.'

'Oh, poor Mrs. Foster! I'll walk down there,' she said, and was glad of the excuse to occupy her mind with the troubles of others.

She met Father Flint coming slowly from the cottage whose drawn blinds told her a pitiful tale. The old man's eyes were dim and Jennifer thought how old and frail he looked without his smile.

She slid a hand beneath his elbow and insisted on taking from him his empty basket.

'Is little Jackie dead?' she asked.

'Half an hour ago. I'll go back later, but just now they're best left alone. I said what I could, but what is there anyone can say, Jennifer?' he asked heavily.

The distress and want were taking toll of him as no mere wants of his own could have done, and everybody's trouble was a personal one to him.

'Why should such things be?' asked Jennifer fiercely. 'Isn't there enough for everybody in the world? God made the earth fruitful for the people He created to fill it, for all of us, not just for the few who have managed to get hold of more gold than the rest of us! A mineral of the earth, and because of it they keep all the food that grows above it!'

The old man sighed and wiped his eyes.

'Ah, my dear, if only all the women of the world thought like you! I think sometimes of something Ruskin wrote about women. "Oh you queens, you queens, among the hills and happy greenwood of this land of yours, shall the foxes have holes and the birds of the air have nest; and in your cities shall the stones cry out against you that they are the only pillows where the Son of Man can lay His head?" The women of this land could do so much—so much—and yet how lethargic they are! How wrapped up in their narrow little lives! How atrophied are their brains and their hearts!' He broke off with a little whimsical smile of apology and opened his gate for her, for they had reached the White Cottage. 'Forgive an old man, my dear. That isn't what you came for, is it? To listen to my diatribes, which are by no means directed at you, bless you. Are you coming in, Jennifer?'

'May I, for a little while?'

'No one in this world is more welcome. Come in, child, and we'll put the kettle on.'

She gave him the smile few could deny him as she went into the house with him.

'After you're dead, Father Flint, I can imagine the job they'll give you. They'll put you at the gate of heaven with Peter, and as the people come in, you'll say to each of them: "Come in, brother—come in, sister. I've just put the kettle on." '

He chuckled.

'Well, I can think of worse jobs. It wouldn't suit me at all to have to sit on a golden throne with a harp. I can't sing "God Save the King" in tune, and I'd be much handier with a kettle than a harp, as the Good Lord Himself will know without my having to apply for a change of job.'

He busied himself with the tea-things, Jennifer helping him, and after a while he looked at her with kindly inquiry.

'Well, my Jennifer?'

She swallowed a lump in her throat.

'We're in a new sort of trouble, Father. Bob's lost his job,' she said with a quiver in her voice. 'Did you know what the job was?'

'Not definitely,' said the old man with caution.

'He was working with Mallinger,' she said scornfully. 'A paid agitator, a parasite living out of our own people's troubles and privations. Oh, he hasn't admitted it, any more than Mallinger will admit the source of his money, though no one ever sees him working, and he has always money to jingle in his pockets or spend at the "Rose and Crown". But, whatever he's doing, Bob's been working for him, taking his money for helping him with his dirty work, and now I suppose Mallinger's boss has cut him down, so Bob has lost his job—and I'm glad he has,' she added defiantly.

'I was afraid of something like that, Jennifer. I didn't think it fair or right to tell you, but I used to see Mallinger at the hospital, and I suspected that he was after Bob.'

'Bob's always hidden it from me, given me to understand that he was working for the Federation, though I could never understand why it should be such secret and private work. Well, anyway, it's finished now and I'll see that he doesn't get it back.' 'What will you do now?' asked Father Flint anxiously, setting the two cups on the table and opening the bottle of milk.

'That's what I want to talk to you about. I don't see how he is ever going to get a job in Werford, and Belsdale seems as bad. He isn't trained for anything but cutting coal, which is out of the question, and his leg closes heaps of jobs to him, driving a lorry, doing decorating, building, almost everything, and he'd never make anything of an office job, even if he could get one. Father, he'll have to have training for something, and I think the only plan is my original one.'

'You mean for you both to live in London whilst you go on with your singing?'

'Yes.'

'What does Bob say?'

'He won't hear of it, won't even talk about it, goes off into heroics about supporting his own wife and never living on a woman and so on, but what's the *use*? We took each other for better, for worse, for richer, for poorer, in sickness and in health—oh, Father, I meant it, every word, and I believe Bob did. He'd carry it out if I were sick or incapable, so why won't he let me carry it out for him? Oh, Father, will you see him, talk to him, make him realise that it's the only way for us?'

'I'll try, my dear, though you know I hate coming between husband and wife in anything vital. You think you would be able quite soon to earn and repay Mr. Rothe, Jennifer?'

'I think so. I should work very hard, and I have tried to keep up my exercises and to look after my throat—just in case I wanted to sing again. Of course I've lost a year, but if I worked hard, I think I could almost make it up.'

'There's another eventuality, my dear, which you've got to consider. You're no longer a single woman, you know. What if there are babies?'

All the expression went out of Jennifer's face, leaving it a mask.

'There won't be babies, Father,' she said steadily.

He looked shocked.

'No babies? Not for *you*, Jennifer?' for ever since she had been old enough to be trusted to hold a baby in her arms she had mothered the Werford babies, nursed them and played with them, comforted and spoiled and loved them. He had so often pictured her with a baby of her own, with half a dozen children playing about her whilst she rocked the latest and littlest in her arms and her beautiful voice sang a lullaby to it.

No babies for Jennifer! He had often deplored the glut of babies to worn-out mothers who could not even nourish those they had already, but Jennifer was different. Jennifer had the sense to look after herself, to apply to herself the principles of family limitation which he himself dare not advocate or preach. Jennifer's babies would be intentional babies, wanted, provided for before birth, cared for with wisdom and prudence.

She was still looking straight before her with that expressionless face.

'Not for Bob, Father,' she said, but for all her self-control there was a little quiver in her voice, and, the next moment, she had broken down and laid her head against his shoulder with a broken sound that went to his heart.

'My dear—my dear,' he said gently, stroking her dark hair.

'He didn't know. Neither of us dreamed of it. The doctors must have known and they ought to have told him. He—he was as blessedly innocent as I was, perhaps more so. Father, have you ever been married?'

'Yes, my dear, a long time ago, so long that it seems like someone else's memory rather than my own,' he said, and his faded blue eyes looked out above her head, looking back down the years to the dead yesterdays which were now but frail, sweet shadows to him.

'What happened, Father? Did she die?' asked Jennifer, who had never associated Father Flint with a wife.

He shook his head.

'No. She ran—away and left me,' he said. 'Oh, I wasn't always so tolerant or so well able to understand, my dear. I was young and hot-blooded and hot-headed. She was so gay, so young, and I was a dull dog, always either in my books or shouting at street corners in an attempt to reform the world. I was going to do great things, marvellous things, for the world—and I couldn't even make one girl happy. My poor, laughing, weeping little Dimity.'

'And you never saw her again?' asked Jennifer, aware of the deeps that lay beneath his quiet words and in his gentle blue eyes.

'Yes. She wrote to me that she was happy, but I knew what she really wrote for and, when she wrote again, I went to her. She was dying quite alone. I had divorced her as she had begged me to do, but the man had never married her and she was dying of two things, and the one that the doctors never diagnosed was a broken heart.'

'Poor little Dimity,' said Jennifer softly. Poor Dimity who had thrown away the substance for the shadow, who had thought that another man could be a fitting exchange for Father Flint! 'What did you do, Father?'

He smiled. It was a very tender, sweet smile.

'We were married again an hour before she died,' he said simply. 'It was a poor little room, but we could not move her, so I brought flowers, and a gay cover for the bed and something she had always wanted. They were rare things then. A gramophone. I think we called them phonographs then. They played cylinders instead of the discs we have now, and I bought her a song she used to sing to me, an old and foolish song we had loved. I would have prayed with her, but—well—I somehow think God understood why I let her listen to that old song instead. I don't think He would hold it up against me. She was smiling when she died—little Dimity.'

He had forgotten that she had been nearly forty when she died, that her bright hair had grown thin and dull, that her mouth was sagging from grief and bitterness, that her eyes had seen dreadful sights and her lips spoken of unpleasant things. To him she had been just that – little Dimity.

He roused himself with a smile and a word of apology.

'My dear, I forget myself. I am becoming a doddering old man. Do you know that when I have another birthday I shall be——'

Jennifer put a hand over his lips.

'No. Don't say it. You'll always be as young as your heart, my dear,' she said. 'Anyway, I shall have to be going. You'll speak to Bob? Try to persuade him?'

'I will, child. Keep up your courage and remember what I've said so often to so many people – "I have had many troubles in my life, most of which never happened." Good-bye, my dear. God bless you and show you the way.'

She walked back with lightened heart. Not that she really thought Father Flint or anybody else could do anything with Bob once his mind was made up, but the talk they had had strengthened her belief in herself.

She had never told anyone else about the babies. It was a thing too deep for discussion, even with Lottie, who was somehow managing to scratch along with a little work and a little charity and a lot of courage. Since Jennifer and Bob had known for certain that he ought never to have married, she had not seen so much of Lottie. The sight of the children, especially of the baby (who was named Jennifer and was altogether adorable, as if she knew that she had come at a time when there was little sunshine otherwise for her mother), was too much for her when she knew Bob could never give her a child.

The knowledge now made a deep cleft of bitterness in her relations with her husband. She herself, made of finer clay, could have stood the test and come through the fire, but Bob had gone all to pieces, saying despairingly that he had spoiled her life and ruined any chance of their continued happiness.

That was what lay at the roots of his objection to her scheme in going to London. He felt that here he stood a faint chance of justifying himself in some small measure by providing for her, whereas in London he would be nothing but a parasite on her. He did not believe in that job for which she hoped so cheerfully. If he could not get a living in his own place, how could he hope to get one in a great city, amongst strangers?

He was sitting hunched over the fire when she returned, bringing with her the sharp tang of the outside world.

'I've seen Arthur Spence,' she said with determined brightness. 'What do you think he's going to do?'

'God knows,' said Bob listlessly.

'Marry Miss Little!' she laughed. 'Can't you just imagine how *thrilled* she is? He wasn't going to give her an engagement ring because she had told him it wasn't necessary at her age, not as if she were a young girl, but I've egged him on and I left him going into Gutterly's to buy one. She was only trying to save him expense, poor little soul, and he has no idea what self-denial that was. She'll just love to sparkle it at the chapel social.'

'Well, he's lucky,' said Bob.

She managed to laugh.

'That's a nice thing to say to your wife, Bob Haling!'

'I didn't mean that, Jen. You know I don't envy any man in the world his girl or his wife. I meant—he's got a job and two legs to go to it on, and—how old is Miss Little?'

She knew what he meant and dropped down on her knees at his side and pulled an arm about her.

'Darling, why let yourself dwell on what can't be helped? It isn't going to spoil everything for us for always. We've got each other. We're happy together—'

'Are you, Jennifer? Are you happy? Truly?' he demanded, searching her face with his eyes, seeking the very inmost soul of her.

She kept her steady eyes on his and would not belittle that moment by lying to him.

'Not perhaps as happy as we thought to be, Bob, but happy in a different way, an older and wiser way, happy because already we have shared sorrows and known suffering and come through with our love still undimmed.'

His arm gathered her closely and held her.

'Oh, Jen, I'm such a rotten sort of husband for you, and because I can never forget that, I get even worse and more beastly to you. Jen—'

'Yes, dear?' gently, as he paused, and she saw, looking up at him, that his face was torn and ridged with suffering, that his eyes were haunted and tragic.

'Jen, do you realise that—that you can get free from me?' he said at last desperately.

'Get free? But why, Bob?' she asked, startled.

'It's part of the law. I've been to see a man in Belsdale, a solicitor, and he says that—that our marriage can be annulled, that means wiped out, not counted as a marriage at all. You'd be free, Jen, not Mrs. Haling any longer, but Jennifer Jenks again.'

She put her arms about him.

'Oh, my poor darling, is that what you've been doing? Is that what you think of me? As if I should do such a thing, or even want to! I'm Mrs. Robert Haling for keeps. Jennifer Jenks is dead and gone and I don't want her back ever. Kiss me, Bob. Tell me you don't want her back either.'

They clung together, afraid, tormented, hiding from each other in the secret places they could not share, and presently she rose to get the supper, talking of village gossip, of Lottie's new job at the vicarage, and how long it was likely to last, of anything and everything that was not of themselves.

Father Flint was as good as his word, seeking out Bob the next day and trying to put Jennifer's proposition before him in a different light, but nothing he could say would ever shift the younger man's determination not to leave Werford.

'Up there I'd be lost, just a poor thing living on Jennifer, known to her friends as Jennifer Haling's husband. Up here people remember me as I was, are decent to me because they know it's no fault of mine that I'm a hanger on, as it looks likely I'll be. There's another thing, too. There's a chance I shall get my job back later if I stay here.'

Father Flint saw the wisdom in his attitude, though he repeated again the need for Jennifer to earn, or at least to get herself into a position to earn, so that, if need arose, she would not be left stranded.

For an hour or more they argued, made plans and discarded them, but in the end the old man went away defeated, and yet with the feeling in his heart that right had triumphed.

Jennifer looked at her husband when he returned from the club, as Father Flint's church was usually called, to the satisfaction of the vicar, who dispensed Christianity from his pulpit twice on Sundays and from his arm-chair in his comfortable vicarage for the rest of the week. It was unthinkable that God's house should be used as a place of rest and recreation rather than as a place where people sat, stiff-backed and uncomfortable, to hear the Rev. Charles Auber explain to them their duties of resignation and patience. How could the Lord be expected to enter a place where they played darts and where other carpenters played and did odd jobs of work? The Church had long outgrown the simple Nazarene.

So Father Flint's 'church' was called the club, and Father Flint himself was glad. He much preferred the society of the Carpenter of Nazareth to the Lord whom the Rev. Charles Auber patronised.

Bob's face was expressionless, and Jennifer, after that quick glance, returned to the preparation of the supper.

Presently he spoke. 'I suppose you put Father Flint up to talking to me, didn't you?' he asked.

'Yes,' said Jennifer without hesitation. 'He is wiser than I am and I thought he could help me in showing you that what I suggest is the only way out.'

'Well, I'm not taking it, Jen, and that's that,' said Bob.

She was silent for a little while, stirring the cheese over the fire for the welsh rarebit which was a favourite of his.

'Haven't you got anything to say about that?' he asked her.

'What is there to say that I haven't already said, Bob?'

'Nothing, I suppose.' Then, after a pause, 'Jen?'

'Yes?'

'Are you mad with me about this?'

'No, not particularly. In a way I admire you for it, but I think you're trying to do something too difficult for us. What are we going to live on if you don't get a job? I've got the rent money for this week and there's three pounds fifteen in the jar. There's four shillings a week to find for the extra furniture we got when we did the middle room and two and sixpence for the wireless instalments, and after this week there'll be the rent, sixteen shillings, and two shillings for the gas. We shall want more coal too—'

He spent on her last words the frenzy to which her calm reckoning of liabilities roused him.

'Yes. Other men can go and get what they want from the tip, enough to bank the fires, anyway. I've got to buy every bit of stuff we burn. That's one of the pleasures I got down Patney's blasted mine, amongst others! Pay, pay, pay all along the line. To those that hath shall be given—you bet it will, but not for always. The time will come when we shall pay them back for every life lost, for every woman widowed and every child orphaned, for every disease and every accident—'

'Bob, why go over all that again? What's the use? It doesn't get us anywhere. If this new measure goes through Parliament—'

'Yes, *if* it goes through, but the whole thing's only eye-wash for the next election. They'll probably put one small unimportant point in the bill through and throw out the rest, postpone the discussion of wages and hours and unemployment, and then they'll go to the country and say: "Look what we've done for the miners! We're your friends, we are. You vote for us and we'll see that everybody has a nice cushy job at five quid a week and pensions at fifty. Jolly fine fellows we are! You vote for us and see", and so the fools all over the country will vote for 'em and they *will* see. Not half they won't!'

Jennifer dished up the rarebit and drew her chair up to the table.

'Well, sit down and have your supper now,' she said. 'I dare say you're right. You know more about these things than I do,' for Jennifer was a wise wife, and if she did not know much about men in general, she knew quite a lot about Bob. Welsh rarebit would go a lot further to pacifying him than any discussion of politics.

After supper, they sat together to talk things over, Jennifer realising that she must either accept Bob's decision and remain with him here, or fly directly in his face by leaving him and going to London alone. She had written to Rothe and had his reply in her pocket. The knowledge that though he was still ready to have her now, time was slipping away and would soon make him reluctant to train her, gave her food for bitter thoughts. She would not think them, however. She was Bob's wife, and she had been brought up in the belief that marriage was binding and that the wife must say, with Ruth, 'Whither thou goest I will go. Thy people shall be my people and thy God my God.'

Jennifer did not know who was her husband's God. In these days he followed strange ones whose faces were not like that of the benign, merciful, uncomplicated God of their childhood. His 'people' were few, Lottie in Werford and a few obscure cousins.

But whither he went, she would go.

Under her counsels and encouragement as they talked, Bob grew more hopeful.

'People know me here and I've met a good many men in Belsdale who might give me a job. I'll go in and look them up tomorrow,' he said.

'Bob, will you promise me something? That you won't take up with Mallinger again?'

He flushed and avoided her eyes.

'He's a decent chap, Jen. I can't see what you've got against him,' he said.

'He makes things worse for our men, Bob, and you know it in your heart. They suffer terrible injustice and wrongs which I believe all the really decent-minded people in the country would try to put right if it were put to them fair and square. Don't you see, though, that they only get people's backs up by being always on the grouse, always looking for something fresh to make trouble about? If they would only leave it to the Federation and let them do what they can gradually, tackling the biggest things first, I believe, in the end, the miners would have justice and reasonable conditions. It's all these little, secret agitators like Mallinger who give the miners a bad name in the country.'

'What has the Federation ever done? They go up by and large to the Government with a big stick and a lot of wind, and some big nob says "Boo!" to them and they turn round and run back. It's only because they know they've got to face people like Mallinger that they ever stay and do something.'

Jennifer sighed.

She was not as well up in local affairs as she had once been, for whereas her father and brother had been reasonable, temperate men who could see things from both sides and would discuss them freely with her, Bob had always been secretive and she had little knowledge of current events as regards the men in the pits. She knew, however, that Mallinger and his crowd were extremists, and that Bob really did not go below the surface in these subjects. Primarily a physical animal, his physical incapacity had not turned him into a thinker, and his mind was all for action, fighting, winning by force just as he had always been wont to settle any argument with his fists, quickly.

'Well, anyway, even if you don't agree with me, do this for me, Bob—for love,' she begged him with her lovely smile.

'All right. If you make such a point of it,' he said grudgingly. 'It seems a mug's idea to me, though, because Mallinger's the man most likely to give me a job.'

She did not stress the point, having won it, and they made a list of the likely people. Hesitatingly she suggested Sir Jervis Patney, but Bob flamed again.

'That swine? Not so likely! I wouldn't take a penny piece from him or anyone like him. I'd rather starve than eat his bread,' and Jennifer ran her pencil through the name, reflecting that he might have to do just that, for Sir Jervis owned so much of Belsdale, the shops, the factories, the various business concerns, that if he cared to be vindictive towards Bob few people would give him a job.

He folded the paper at length and tucked it into his pocket.

'Well, that's all for tonight. I'm tired. Come on, mate. What about a spot of shut-eye?'

Chapter Eight

The bank manager bowed Jennifer out with the same courtesy he would have accorded to a duchess or a depositor.

'I'm sorry, Mrs. Haling,' he repeated regretfully, and she managed to smile before she turned away to wait for her bus.

It was November again. The streets were covered with a film of greasy mud and a fine, cold drizzle made everyone hurry shiveringly under cover.

Jennifer scarcely noticed that it was raining. Mere weather could not be as bleak and hopeless as her thoughts.

Two women got into the Werford bus with her, but she did not even notice them, taking a seat near the door and looking out with a fixed, expressionless intentness.

'See who's by the door?' whispered one of the women to the other. 'Jennifer Haling. Looks bad, don't she?'

'My old man was sayin' only the other day as he didn't know what she and Bob was living on.'

'She's been doin' bits o' work for a dressmaker in Sun Street. *That* don't keep 'em, though. My Alfie's young lady used to work there and she says the pay won't keep one alive, let alone two, and a hearty eater like Bob Haling too.'

'Well, I'm downright sorry for Jennifer. She should 'a' stopped in London and done her singing, and Bob Haling isn't the man I thought he was to fetch her back and marry her.'

Jennifer caught a few words, and her lips set more tightly. She was proud. She hated their pity. She had come back to Bob, married him with colours flying, had such fine ideas about what she was going to do – and here she was, down to her last half-crown, with her work dwindling into a mere five shillingsworth a week, and not a hope of getting more. And women like Ellen Mark, with her husband on the lowest grade of pit work, had the right to pity her.

Bob was sitting hunched over the fire when she got home. That was his usual attitude now and the sight of it roused her to sudden, unreasonable anger.

'Can't you do something?' she asked sharply without greeting. 'Couldn't you at least have got coal in before dark?' and she seized the hod to go outside and fill it.

'There isn't any more coal,' he said sulkily.

The year of idleness had made deeper marks on Bob than the year of hard work had done on Jennifer. She was thin, worn, and aged by it, but he was soured and embittered, his heavy shoulders were hunched and his muscles slack by sitting about, and whilst there was still courage in Jennifer's eyes, his own were mere dull pools of misery.

'No more at all?' she asked incredulously. 'What about the lot Bill Sterling was going to bring down from the tip?'

'Well, he didn't, that's all,' growled Bob, not moving from his chair.

'Why not?'

'Oh lord, you going to start nagging again? Well, if you must know, because I didn't go up to the tip and shovel it, and now are you satisfied?'

She picked up from the table the parcel of work which she had brought from the shop with her, a small enough parcel of the cheap sort of frocks which brought in almost nothing for the neat, conscientious work she put into them. Her body was sick with tiredness and want of proper food and her mind was sick with the thoughts which filled it.

'Satisfied? Yes, I *am* satisfied, Bob Haling, that if anybody brought you a job of work to your door, you'd be too darn lazy to bend down and pick it up. You sit here, day after day, and don't even *pretend* to go after a job now whilst I work and slave for the two of us, and you can't even rouse yourself to go and shovel the coal that's to keep the fire going for you to sit over.'

'Well, perhaps if I were a whole man, perhaps if I had two legs same as you have, I might go and get work too. I tell you it's killing work for me to use the shovels. It's agony every time I bend,' said Bob sulkily.

'It didn't seem much agony that I could see when you were playing bowls all the summer,' snapped Jennifer.

He turned round to face her at last, and the sight of his utter wretchedness sent her tumbling to her knees beside him, her parcels dropping on the floor, her arms going about him.

'Oh, my dear, my dear, is that what we've come to? You and I? Forgive me, Bob. I'm so miserable and worried and I simply took it out of you because—well, you were the only person here.'

He put his arms about her and rested his head on hers.

'It isn't me to forgive you anything, Jen,' he said humbly, and that note in his voice hurt her terribly. Bob, who had been so gay and proud, to have that humility! 'I know I ought to have gone to the tip. It does hurt, but not as much as all that. It was just that—well, that I seem to have grown to this chair, and nothing seems worth while any more. It isn't that I don't mind you working for me and never bringing in a penny myself. It's because—well, I reckon it's because I do mind so much that it's taken the guts out of me and left me just what I am, worse than a bit of furniture, because that doesn't cost anything to keep and you could always make a bit by selling it. I'm no use to you alive at all, and if I do myself in, you've got to bury me. I wish to God I had been down in the pit with the others that day.'

She comforted him in her arms, her voice holding its deep and lovely notes of pity, mother-love for this man who had to be both husband and child to her and yet who could be neither. In moments like this the strange bond between them held them closely, though neither of them could have given a name to that bond. For Jennifer it was a deep, abiding tenderness and pity, for Bob it was all the frustrated, unsatisfied, insatiable longing of his broken manhood. He did not want children. He wanted only Jennifer, and with every hopeless day he saw her drifting a little further from him for all his longing for her.

'Don't talk of things like that, Bob,' she was saying. 'You're my man, my own, and brighter days will come. It's always darkest before dawn, but the dawn always comes at last.'

'Darkest? I reckon it's about its darkest now, so it should be near dawn, though I don't see any signs of it,' said Bob bitterly.

It was that bitter despair which she could not lighten. It was sapping away his manhood, making him an impossible man to live with, morose, soured, never smiling, saying little, and that little only self-pity and vituperation of society in general.

How could she tell him at this moment the things that had to be told? Last week she had drawn the sole remaining pound from the bank where she had placed the fifty pounds of Rothe's wedding gift on which they had been existing for a year, eking it out by Jennifer's sewing. She had never dared to tell Bob of that gift in the first place, and once they started to live on it, the telling became impossible, for he nourished in his heart an unreasoning anger against the man who might have made Jennifer's life one of luxury instead of the grinding poverty to which he himself had reduced her.

And now Scrimshaw's, in Sun Street, had told her regretfully that this parcel of work would probably be the last for some time. It had been dwindling for weeks, and she had lived in fear of this, and, now that it had come, it found her still without plans for their future.

She left Bob at last to mix the flour and cheese which, with a tin of skimmed milk, was to make up their supper. She knew that this dish, once a prime favourite with him, had become nauseating by the frequency with which she served it, but it was cheap and nourishing and had the advantage, to Jennifer, of not being repulsive in the raw. She had come down a long time ago to the shelf under the counters of the various shops, shelves where the oddments and throw-outs, the scraps and the not quite fresh pieces were thrown so that the poorest buyers could have them cheaply. She would always remember the time when she had come down to that sort of buying, for she had had a proud way with her in the shops, had always marketed with skill and discretion and suspicion, able to pay the prices asked and therefore to demand what she considered her money's worth. Shop-keepers had welcomed her with a smile and bowed her out. Now she skulked in, asking for cheaper things, for smaller pieces, for the leavings of such buyers as she had been previously, and there were no smiles for her, only half-pitying, half-contemptuous looks.

Only a woman can appreciate what that meant to Jennifer, and how reluctantly she went to the shops, how hot and humiliated she felt every time she came out.

And very soon now she would not be able to pay even for things off the counter shelves. She would have to ask for credit in the knowledge that it would probably be refused, for whereas the miners' wives had a reasonable hope that their men would ultimately be earning again, Bob Haling had nothing to mortgage and everyone in the community knew it. In a place like Werford, everybody's business was common property.

Bob did not complain about the supper when Jennifer served the flat cheese cakes, but he picked at them with no relish and she was ashamed of herself for feeling glad that he had left enough on his plate for her dinner the next day. He would probably be going into Belsdale in his vain search for work, though very soon now he would not be able to afford the bus fare even once a week, and he could not walk it as other men could and did.

'You'll have to go and see if they'll give you the dole again, Bob,' she said, putting as brave a face on it as she could. 'Scrimshaw's can't give me any more work.'

He scowled, jabbing at the cloth with the point of his knife, cutting holes which Jennifer would have to mend, but she felt too intensely for him to say anything about it. All she did was to clear the table and move the cloth as quickly as possible.

She knew how hateful it would be for him to go and plead for that thing which was so unjustly called 'the dole' and which had come to be regarded as charity. Rich people insured everything they had of value, their houses, their furniture, their cars, their furs and jewels, even their holidays, and when they collected the insurance for the loss of these things no one thought of calling such payments 'doles' or regarded them as charity. Yet when the poor, who had nothing of value save their earning powers, insured such powers just as the rich insured their possessions, payments under their policies of insurance were contemptuously termed 'the dole'.

'They wouldn't give it me, Jen,' said Bob at last. 'That money I got for compensation wiped it out, it seems.'

'Well, why not at least try them again, Bob?' she had to insist, hating the necessity and knowing that she was asking him to give up even the last little rag of pride to which he had clung.

'What's the use?'

'But, Bob, what am I going to do? We've got to get money from somewhere. The shops won't give us credit, and even if they do, they've got to be paid sometime or other.'

'Oh, let me alone, can't you? I'll get work if you only give me a chance,' he told her roughly.

She went on with her work silently. They both knew that his long, enforced idleness had sapped his energies to such an extent that he no longer really desired to get work, would probably not be able to hold down a job if he were given one. He, who had been so proud of his strength, so scornful of the men he had termed 'pub-crawlers', was a pub-crawler himself, idling away the heavy-footed hours somehow, anyhow, until the public-houses opened again and then hanging about at the door of the 'Rose and Crown' until he could find one of his former pals still good-natured enough to ask him to come in and 'have one'. He seldom was so fortunate as to find enough of such friends to get really the worse for drink, but Jennifer saw with a sick helplessness that the constant 'tippling' in small quantities was sapping away such manhood as his other failures had left to him. His eyes and his brain were dulled by it, his manners had become an increasing trial to her, and his slovenly personal habits were making it repulsive to her to share the narrow limits of their little cottage with him. She was by nature fastidious, and the months she had spent in the house of Julian Rothe had given her an appreciation of dainty habits which she fought hard to retain in the midst of all this poverty and the squalor into which they could so easily have plunged.

After a while he rose and went out, muttering some excuse, but she had no need to glance at the clock to see what time it was. She knew.

She had desperate thoughts of appealing to Rothe for help to tide them over until she could get some sort of work again, but she felt she had treated him too shabbily already. Not only had he gone to considerable expense whilst she had been with him, but there had been his fifty pounds on which they had been living, and she had not even answered his last letter in which he had again hinted that he would be glad to have her back. She had not found it possible to answer it. Everything within her longed to do what he asked, to throw off this burden which had become well-nigh intolerable. When he had first put his proposal to her, she had been able to refuse it without difficulty because she had had no idea what it had meant, and there had been Bob, loving and loved, to pull her the other way. Now she knew the peace, the security, the beautiful orderliness that might be hers again, and the only thing to hold her back was cold, unlovely duty – Bob whom she no longer loved, who surely could no longer love her.

There remained only stark charity for them, the Public Assistance Committee whose very name was hated and feared by the people for whose help it had been instituted. It should have been charity in its loveliest guise, the help given to those who had fallen by the wayside by those who were more fortunate. It should have represented the ideal of Christian teaching – universal brotherhood. It was none of these things. It was operated for the most part by men and women whose zeal was to work for 'good causes', for 'charity', rather than for love and brotherhood's sake.

Jennifer had seen the methods of these people and knew why they were so hated, with a bitter, deadly hatred which made death by starvation preferable. They poked and pried into the pitiful secrets people had striven to hide from others, stripped them bare before neighbours to whom they had showed so gallant a front. The few shillings scraped together from their meagre earnings to save them in their old age from the dreaded 'poor-house', a piece of furniture for which they had screwed and saved for years – piano, perhaps, or gramophone or wireless set – all these things were taken from them before help was otherwise doled out to them, the pieces of furniture dragged out of the house, loaded on a truck for all to see, trundled off to some second-hand shop not so far off but they could sneak along some dark evening and see them displayed for twice or thrice as much as the few shillings for which they had had to part with them.

After that, when there was nothing left but the barest necessities of living, money would be trickled out to them in a thin, grudging stream. Often they had to line up even for that, for all to see their shame, and how carefully it had to be spent, how poor and cheap must every article be, lest the eagle eyes of the 'Committee' catch sight of something which they might conceivably have done without, and the meagre sum be cut down even further.

Oh, Jennifer had seen it! She knew what heart-aches there were behind the receipt of such assistance, what shame and fear and bitterness and humiliation. There is no pride like the pride of the poor, for it is all they have. Better, she felt, to let them die rather than keep them grudgingly alive to go on suffering. It was the refinement of torture from which the old Inquisition could have learned.

Yet eventually Bob had to go to them, and Jennifer watched him go and knew that nothing else in her life would give her just that intensity of pity again. She had held him closely for a moment.

'Oh, my darling, I'd give the world for you not to have to go,' she whispered brokenly.

He had stood there without response. Then he had kissed her roughly and broken away from her and she had understood and let him go.

He came back with a jaunty air of defiance which did not deceive her. She had managed to get two days' housework that week, and she had recklessly spent half a crown of her five shillings on dinner for them both, a hot, savoury stew which would feed them for several days with care and plenty of water.

She had made him eat it before he talked, but after the meal the thing had to be discussed.

'I'd rather have gone to the poorhouse,' he told her. 'At least when you get in there they close the doors on you and nobody sees you again.'

'What did they say, dear?' she asked him pitifully.

'Nothing much. Said they'd see. That means some nosy parker of a woman'll come round here and want to poke into every nook and corner. I'd better not be here or I'll throw her out.'

The woman who came was a plump, comfortable little person in a fur coat and a car, the wife of a prosperous tradesman in Belsdale who thought that by doing social work for the poor she would ally herself with social play amongst the rich. She was a vulgar, kindly enough little woman, but puffed up with importance and a sense of well-doing.

Jennifer received her with the quiet, dignified manners which little Miss Amelia Birke had taught her and which had so easily become a part of her own personality. Unfortunately they had the effect at once of making Mrs. Townsend feel an inferiority complex, and her plump bosom expanded like a pouter pigeon's in resentment.

'I've come from the P.A.C. to ask you a few questions and have a look round, Mrs. Haling,' she said importantly.

'I think my husband answered every possible question and we have nothing whatever to conceal, no money put by or any means at all,' said Jennifer with proud humility.

'I'll take a look round, though,' said Mrs. Townsend, and pushed past Jennifer and proceeded to do so. 'A piano! Good gracious, what extravagance! Why, do you know that *I* haven't a piano in my own home?'

She forebore to say that, since no one ever used it and it had become damp-infected and tuneless, she had, with the grand gesture, presented it to her son's wife as a wedding present and decided not to have another.

'My husband gave it to me when we were first married,' said Jennifer with a lump in her throat, remembering the pride and joy with which that not too reliable gift had been made.

'What's it worth? Can you play it?'

'A little. I was having lessons at one time,' said Jennifer.

'Oh, were you? It would have been wiser, wouldn't it, if you had put the money by so that you had something to use now? Music lessons are all very well for people who can afford them, but of course people in your position should realise that the first consideration is food and rent.'

'The lessons were before I was married,' said Jennifer, with cold eyes and a heart in which burnt fierce, scorching anger.

'Oh. Well, you seem to have made a very foolish marriage, if I may say so,' began the woman, leaving the piano to examine the cheap little ornaments on the mantelpiece, wedding presents most of them and of little value save to the donors and the recipients, to whom they stood for friendship, affection, and the knowledge that each meant personal sacrifice and self denial. How many wedding presents mean that? Jennifer hated the supercilious look with which Mrs. Townsend regarded them.

'You mayn't say so,' she said. 'That's my own business.'

The visitor was unperturbed. She had the skin of a rhinoceros, an almost necessary equipment for her job. She was used to what she called rudeness from these people, and could not see the pride, the shame, the bitter crushing in the dust, from which the pitiful attempt at holding their own came. They had no defence save the useless words which such as Mrs. Townsend called 'rudeness', nothing else wherewith to hide their tortured spirits.

'Well, Mrs. Haling, I'm afraid it's got to be ours as well now. Any other luxuries in your house beside the piano?'

Jennifer swallowed.

'Nothing. You can go and look,' she said.

The furniture that had been in the second bedroom and in the little parlour had gone back a few weeks before as they had not been able to keep up the instalments on them, and they were so much in arrears that the amount they had already paid was overset by the amount owing, so the furniture dealer had merely taken the things away and closed the account. The neighbours had seen the van taking them away. That had been horrible for Jennifer as she knew that Bob had let it be believed that he had paid for everything they had had when they married, though the neighbours had thought them extravagant to furnish all their four rooms. Now they knew that it had been only prideful boasting and that they, like most other couples, had begun their married life on credit, that insidious parasite on modern homes.

Mrs. Townsend opened the parlour door and sniffed, went upstairs and had a good look round the room which Jennifer shared with Bob, that room which would always have tender memories for them, the room which had known their love and their grief, their happiness and their bitter sorrow. It was sacred to them, and Mrs. Townsend was poking about in it, fingering the quality of the eiderdown which

Claire Ferring had sent them, its delicate satin shrouded for protection in cheap sateen.

Jennifer offered no comment or explanation but stood in proud, tortured silence as the visitor opened cupboards and drawers, satisfying an innate curiosity over other people's affairs by grossly exceeding her duty, though the people who suffered from it had no means of knowing that, accepting it as part of their martyrdom and necessary humiliation.

They returned to the living-room at last, and Mrs. Townsend made notes in a little book, sucking the pencil as if she were licking her lips over her job.

'Well, I think we can allow you something,' she said. 'You'll have to sell that piano, though. I'll make inquiries in Belsdale and see if I can get a firm to take it off you, though of course second-hand pianos don't fetch much nowadays. People like you buy such luxuries at half a crown down and half a crown a week and then can't go on paying for them, so that there are hundreds of second-hand things on the market. Well, I'll be getting along. I've got a lot of people to see and it's beginning to rain again. Terrible weather, isn't it?' becoming affable as she drew on her expensive gloves and fastened her fur coat.

'I shouldn't think that matters with a car and a chauffeur,' said Jennifer stonily.

Mrs. Townsend gave a smug little laugh.

'Well, of course, it is nice, isn't it? I must come and take your husband for a drive one day. That would be nice for him, wouldn't it?'

Jennifer knew so exactly what Bob would look and say were such an invitation issued.

'Thank you,' she said steadily. 'I don't think he would really enjoy it. You see, we don't live your sort of life, Mrs. Townsend, and the contrast would be a little difficult.'

'Yes, I suppose it would. Well, well, it takes all sorts to make up a world, doesn't it? And what a good thing it is that some of us who have plenty think of you poor people who haven't, isn't it?'

Jennifer's gorge rose. Through the open door she saw the car, the uniformed chauffeur standing to attention outside it with a fur rug over his arm and a wooden expression on his face, the perfect automaton. Between her and the street stood plump Mrs. Townsend, a silk dress beneath her fur coat, an expensive hat on her carefully waved hair, shoes on her feet whose cost would have kept Bob and her for a week.

'If some had less, there would be more for the rest of us,' said Jennifer sharply. 'It is just because the few are so greedy that the many haven't even enough to eat, and whilst rich people live in luxury and idleness, there will be poor living in want.'

Mrs. Townsend coloured uncomfortably and edged nearer the door. She had neither the knowledge nor the intelligence to discuss economics with these people who had a disconcerting habit of revealing that they often had both.

'Well, there will always be the rich and the poor,' she said. 'It says in the Bible "the poor we have always with us".'

'Yes,' said Jennifer crisply. 'It also says "Sell all that thou hast and give to the poor", and if that were carried out by these people who call themselves followers of the Man who said that there wouldn't any longer be any poor.'

'I don't like talking about things like that, Mrs. Haling,' said Mrs. Townsend with excessive dignity, aware that the eyes and ears of her chauffeur were open for her reply. 'I think such discussions are better left for the people who understand them, the Church. Good afternoon. I will see that your case has full consideration and you will be hearing from us,' and she went to her waiting car quickly so that this annoying and stuck-up young woman should have no further opportunity of routing her.

Quoting scripture to her indeed! That was the worst of educating that class of person. It only made them think themselves as good as other people.

It took a fortnight for the wheels of the Public Assistance Committee to grind out help for the Halings, and during that time Jennifer had run into debt. There was no money for the rent and the tradesmen had to be asked to give her credit, which they did with a reluctance that humiliated her.

When help was given, so little was granted that after the rent was paid, only the cheapest of food could be bought, in small quantities insufficient for Bob's bulky frame, for he had always eaten heartily and Jennifer was glad enough to let him have her share of the bread of charity, which tasted bitter in her mouth. The piano had not been sold. Jennifer had, on Father Flint's advice, pleaded that she might later on be able to give music lessons if she retained it, so it still stood in its corner of the living-room, though Jennifer had no heart in these days to play or sing.

A fortnight before Christmas Father Flint managed to find a job for Bob. It was a poor enough one and it was possible that it would be only temporary, though the firm who offered him work hoped to be able to make it a permanent one. He could sit at the machine in such a position as not to affect his crippled leg.

There were several drawbacks to it, of course, and here Father Flint showed that his kindly mind was also a shrewd and wise one. The factory was in Belsdale, and the wages would neither allow Bob to travel to and from Werford every day, nor enable him to keep a wife.

Bob realised that and was for refusing the offer, but Jennifer pointed out to him, doubtfully, that if he did so, he would be disqualified from further assistance.

'But what will you do, Jen?' he asked wretchedly.

He could not fail to see how their troubles were telling on her. She looked thin and faded and her shoulders stooped a little. Her eyes seemed to have receded into her head and the shadows beneath them accentuated the prominent cheekbones. She had never been physically beautiful, but now she looked old and unattractive from anxiety, from the reactions to Bob's uncertain temper and from actual want of food, for he ate most of the food she could buy out of the Committee's allowance, carelessly ignorant that he did so.

Jennifer had worked out the answer to that question as to what she would do, but still she hesitated to put it into speech.

'Where will you go, Jen?' he repeated. 'We've fought the Committee about giving up this house and moving into two rooms, but I can't possibly pay the rent if I take this job, and rooms in Belsdale are so dear unless we go into the sort of place you'd hate.'

She faced him bravely.

'Bob, I want to go to London,' she said.

He coloured and there was a defeated look in his eyes which hurt her, which she had known would be there but which she could not avoid.

'You mean—back to Rothe?' he asked dully.

'Yes. Oh, my dear, can't you see it's the only way? We can't go on like this, and if we had to give up our home, what would happen to us? It's the one thing to which we've clung, the only thing we've got left out of all we started with or almost the only thing. We've lost hope and comfort and—almost our love, Bob. They say money doesn't make happiness, and I know it's true, but it's just as true that the terrible want of it makes unhappiness. It wears away everything that's fine and decent in people unless they're saints, like Father Flint.'

He sat moodily before the fire, seeing no way out – but, after all this time, to accept defeat.

'It's a long time,' he said at last. 'He may not want you now.'

'Who? Mr. Rothe? I think he will,' said Jennifer.

He glanced at her quickly.

'How do you know? Have you been writing to him?' he asked suspiciously.

'Well, we've not kept up a correspondence, but he wrote to me some weeks ago,' she said.

'You didn't tell me,' said Bob moodily.

'No. I thought it might upset you so I just tore the letter up and tried to forget it.'

'Tried to? But you didn't, did you?'

She laughed a little at that.

'Bob, are you *jealous* of him?' she asked.

'Why shouldn't I be? He's got everything I haven't, and he can give you everything I can't,' he growled.

She touched his hair with light fingers.

'My dear, he's about fifty-four and I'm still only twenty-two, though sometimes I feel a hundred and two, and I know I look it now,' she said with the faintest touch of regret in her voice.

He caught her fingers and held them against his cheek.

'I've made an awful mess of things for you, Jen,' he said humbly, 'I was going to do such wonders for you once, wasn't I? Nothing was to be too good for you, and now I can't even give you a home and enough food to eat. I'm a failure all round.'

She put her other arm about him and held his head against her side, the mother-look in her eyes deepening, her face softening.

'No one is a failure who has done his best,' she said. 'Life has beaten us down for the moment, dear, but we shall come up again and look back on all this as a bad dream. Let's just make up our minds to this and get it over, and in the spring it may all be different.'

'But you won't come back to me in the spring, even if it is,' said Bob with conviction. 'How can you? If you go to Rothe this time, he'll make you stick it, and you won't be trained in a few months, especially after all you'll have lost by stopping with me.'

'I know. I shall have to stick it out this time. But I can look for a job for you, and maybe in a few months, even less, you'd be able to come up and we can live together and I can go to my lessons every day. I'm sure it will be that way, Bob. Mr. Rothe knows a lot of people and there is his friend, Mrs. Ferring, Guy Ferring's wife, you know, who's sure to be able to do something.'

'Rich people,' commented Bob bitterly.

'Well, of course they're rich. If they weren't, Mr. Rothe wouldn't be able to do this for me, would he? And naturally his friends are rich people just as ours are poor ones.'

'You call this Mrs. Ferring his friend. It sounds queer to me, a man having for his friend somebody else's wife.'

It flashed across Jennifer's mind that it had seemed queer to her once, but that time seemed now a million years ago. It had become so customary to her to couple Rothe and Claire Ferring in her thoughts that she realised, with a shock, how often they had been there during the time of her separation from them, nearly two years now. Was it odd? Well, perhaps it was, and yet life as they lived it permitted so many things which life at Werford could not possibly contain. How could she explain that to Bob, however?

'Well—she's very popular, you see. She has to know everybody and go everywhere, being the wife of Guy Ferring,' she said.

'Is he going to be Prime Minister?' asked Bob.

He was trying to place Jennifer amongst these people, but he found it impossible. She belonged here, to Werford and to him, and yet already these other people, these cursed rich people, were drawing her to them.

'I don't think so. You see, he is the heir to Lord Bordray, and if he succeeds to the title he would have to resign from the House of Commons because he'd have a seat in the Lords,' said Jennifer.

Bob sneered,

'You seem to know a lot about them,' he said. 'The titles roll off your tongue.'

She laughed, irritated a little by his lack of perception.

'Oh, my dear, I've lived amongst them long enough to have got used to it,' she said.

He rose heavily, brushing aside roughly the hand which had been lying on his shoulder. He wished he could be gracious in his defeat, but he could not. He dreaded her going, had no doubt at all but that he was going to lose her, no hope that she would ever return to him as she was now. These rich people would take her. She would belong to them and not to him. They would make her successful, rich, and he would be still what he was, a failure earning, at most, a pittance which would not even let him buy her food and a roof.

Jennifer stood watching him as he lurched across the room, took his coat and cap and went heavily out.

Her heart ached for him, but not even she could guess the bitterness of the cup which she had held to his lips for so long and which at last he had had to drink.

Chapter Nine

Rothe sat at the piano picking out slow, soft notes with one finger, a habit of his when deeply buried in thought.

Jennifer could scarcely control herself. She had been back in London for two days, but this was the first time Rothe had let her sing, insisting on her having massage, gargling with some special preparation, exercising and sleeping, anything and everything except sing. He had been afraid. So much might have happened to her voice, must have happened to it.

And actually nothing had happened to it.

Sitting there picking out the meaningless notes, he realised that and was astonished and bewildered. Her voice was dulled from lack of proper exercise, but otherwise it was just the same clear, effortless, completely unemotional organ, beautiful but to Rothe's mind, colourless. It was like a machine which a little attention and use would make perfect mechanically, to be switched on and off without effort or variation.

'Oh, do say something,' said Jennifer quiveringly, unable to bear the silence any longer.

He spun round to look at her. Except that she was thinner, that her hair lacked care and lustre, she too was unchanged by marriage.

How? Why?

'What do you want me to say, Jennifer?'

'The truth. I can bear it. I've faced it ever since it was first decided that I should come back to you. Whatever it is, I want to know. Is my voice still any good?'

'It is just the same,' said Rothe, and she gave an audible sigh of relief. 'I wish you hadn't looked quite so unctuously pleased about it,' he added with a twisted smile. 'I didn't want it to be the same.'

She stared at him.

'Why not? I thought you—didn't you want it like that? Why did you bring me here in the first place if you wanted my voice to be different?'

'I wonder if you'll understand? You ought to. You were a young single girl before, untouched, inexperienced. You lacked that vital something which every artist must have, no matter what his art. Well, you still lack it. I thought you'd come back to me experienced—how shall I put it without offence? Sophisticated, emotional. Why haven't you? This man you've married, do you care for him?'

She flushed. Bob seemed so far away, just as, whilst she was with him, Rothe had seemed far away. Shadow had become substance and substance shadow. She felt ashamed by the knowledge and was quick in her own defence and in Bob's.

'Of course I do. He's all I have to live for. He's my life,' she said, her head high, her eyes defying him.

'Then how is it, I wonder, that you've come back to me with your clear boy's voice again, still so terribly young?'

He sighed and turned back to the piano, and Jennifer could find no answer. How could she tell him, this cynical, worldly man to whom nothing seemed sacred, the real truth of her marriage with Bob? That it was no marriage at all, but only a union of – what? Hearts? He would laugh at that. Lives, certainly, and she felt instinctively that he would not scruple to tear them apart were he ever to know the truth.

'Do you mean I—shall never be able to sing as you hoped, Julian?' she asked presently, keeping her voice low and steady.

'I wonder? I think you will. You'll have to suffer before you do and then you'll be a great artist, Jennifer. If you don't—well, you'll always have a nice voice to sing to the old ladies in the almshouses with.'

The little sound she made was between laughter and a sob.

'Do you think I haven't suffered?' she asked him. 'Do you think I've enjoyed life, eking out an existence by making cheap dresses at starvation pay, living on charity sparingly doled out to us, having horrible women poking about my home and tearing open every poor little secret, watching my husband change before my eyes, knowing he was losing everything that had made him the man I had fallen in love with and yet not able to do a thing for him? To have no future? No hope? You think I haven't suffered?'

She was transformed by her impassioned speech. Her eyes glowed and something flamed within her. There was strength, vigour, emotion, where before there had been too placid acceptance.

Rothe caught her hands, his face alight and eager.

'Hold it! Hold it!' he cried, and let her go and spun round to the piano again. 'Now sing!' and he dashed into the opening notes of Ruth's impassioned plea – 'Entreat me not to leave thee!'

Jennifer obeyed him, but after a few bars, he broke off and sat helplessly before the piano whilst her voice drifted into silence. The passion had left her voice directly she began to sing. It was quite impersonal again, unemotional, meaningless.

'Suffered?' he asked scornfully. 'No. You've suffered nothing. With your body, yes, but not with your mind. You haven't been tortured, wrung with pain, torn to pieces with unendurable agony. You've suffered nothing.'

She stood there and heard him, knowing in her inmost heart that it was true. Until that moment she had believed that she had indeed suffered, but what he said was true. Nothing had done those things to her, and yet something within her told her that some day she would suffer as Rothe, in his merciless ambition, had hoped she was suffering.

'Better go and get some fresh air,' he told her curtly, and she was too well used to him and his ways to resent them.

'Julian, you—you'll go on with my training?' she had to ask him desperately.

'Oh yes. I've said so, haven't I? I don't break my word,' and Rothe turned his back on her.

She went slowly to her room, no longer the little conventional place she had had before, but a large room on the first floor, a room with everything striking a note of modernity, very simple, even crude to eyes which had grown unaccustomed to anything later than Edwardian style. Limed oak and chromium plate had not reached Werford, and she felt strange and at sea amongst the expensive simplicity of her setting.

What should she do? She must find diversion somehow. She dare not sit and let herself think about what Rothe had said, about the future that lay before her and Bob if actually she never did become a singer.

She decided to go to see Claire Ferring. It would give her something to do, even if she found her not at home. Something she could not explain urged her to take up the threads again, not to let any of them slip, to identify herself once more with this life which already she was beginning to find amazingly familiar. She paused to let her thoughts go to Bob, working away in bitterness and despair, and for a moment she hated the luxury of her surroundings, the clothes she wore, the money which Rothe had insisted on her taking.

'Mind, it's for you, Jennifer, not for this husband of yours. You understand? You must go about, do what other people do, dress well, know everything that is to be known.'

She had nodded, though it had hurt her mind to think of Bob. She knew she must do these things, and that even if she sent money to her husband he would indignantly return it, knowing that it was Rothe's. She must wait until she was earning something herself, and even then she knew it would be gall for him to accept it.

She shook from her mind the thought of things she could *not* remedy, and got ready to go to Mrs. Ferring's. She had spent part of her two days shopping for necessities, and though she had had to order most of the things which she knew would be necessary, she had managed to get a dress and a coat of soft grey, with a big collar of grey fox and hat and shoes to match. She looked rather as she liked to look than as Rothe and Claire Ferring had decided she would have to look. She felt neat but undistinguished, and the fact that she should never have worn grey had not deterred her from buying this one outfit which expressed her own personality rather than that which she was required to develop as a prima donna in embryo.

She took a taxi, feeling guilty at the satisfaction she had in travelling luxuriously again, and she had not yet got over the comfort of seeing money in her purse, silver and nice new notes, and not having to count the balance every time she spent anything.

The Ferrings' staid butler welcomed her with a discreet smile of recognition which warmed her, and she stayed a moment to speak to him. Claire had very early taught her that it is far from derogatory to repay one's servants with kindness and courtesy, and Jennifer compared that attitude with the one which she knew people like Mrs. Townsend took towards their overworked little generals.

'Madam is out at present, Miss Rothe, but we are expecting her back at any moment. Will you wait?'

'Thank you, Gage, I'd like to,' said Jennifer.

It felt strange to be called Miss Rothe again. It gave her a feeling of guilt which was exaggerated by the knowledge that she liked it. Rothe had made it a condition of her return that, except for the favoured few who knew it already, no one was to know of her marriage.

'It's always a doubtful experiment for a great artist to marry, but for a singer to start on her career with a husband already in the background would be a calamity. Keep your professional name, my dear,' and Jennifer had no option but to agree. She took off her wedding ring and put it safely away, and after the first little shock of seeing her finger bare, she knew it gave her a feeling of lightness and freedom, though she did not put it to herself in those terms.

Now, as Jennifer Rothe, she was picking up another thread, the thread of silver which led her to Claire Ferring's scintillating charm.

Gage showed her into Claire's own private room, and as she entered it someone rose from a chair and came through the dusk of the winter afternoon to greet her.

He held her hand, and she knew in that instant that he held so much more than her hand that she dare not keep the knowledge in her mind. She scattered it with words strung on a golden thread of laughter.

'Mr. Mayne! I had no idea you were here—or am I flattering myself when I take it for granted you even remember who I am?'

But she knew. She knew by the eager warmth of his hand, by the light that leapt into his grey eyes, by that spark that leapt between them at sight of each other.

And Brenner Mayne knew that the image of this girl had been engraved on his memory, had been eating its way into that inner, secret place where no woman's image had ever been for even a day, an hour. It was a thing without reason, without cause, without even sense, without desire or wisdom.

'Of course I remember. The girl who defied all things holy and told the great Sir Jervis where to get off!' he laughed. 'I didn't even know you were coming back. Are you back, by the way?'

She laughed. How easy it had suddenly become to laugh!

'Yes, I'm back,' but the very word caught her up in the memory of all that had to be remembered, and her face grew grave again.

His eyes searched her remembered features, saw that her eyes were deep and shadowed, that she had grown thin, had a transparent look which caught at his heart. What had they been doing to her whilst she had been away from him?

But convention must be served and no hint of what he felt must reach her.

'How is everything with you? I wasn't really surprised to hear of your marriage.'

'Weren't you?'

'No. I thought somehow that was what you would have to do.'

She opened eyes that were a little startled at his choice of words.

'Have to do?' she repeated. 'But—no one forced me to do it.'

'Only your implacable conscience.'

She was silent at that, unable to find an answer. She ought to have defended herself, to have protested her love for Bob, to have refused the imputation that she had married him from a sense of duty. Instead she said: 'Thank you for the camellias.'

'I wondered if you would understand. I thought then that I should never have a chance of sending them to you on the stage. You remember that you were to sing Delilah?'

'Yes. Perhaps I shall, even now, though Julian thinks—well, I don't know quite what he thinks about me.'

'When will you sing to me?'

'I don't know. I'm not allowed to sing yet, though I should like to sing to you,' she said with great simplicity.

That was one of the things that charmed him so much. In a world that was over-elaborate, full of artifice and scheming, she was like a clear light, and the essential simplicity of his own nature responded gratefully to that of hers.

'Will you, some time? Not at Rothe's, though. Somewhere else. We shall find a place.'

He thought he did not want to be with her in Rothe's house with its continuous stream of professional people, openly professional like the actors and concert artists whom Rothe invited and secretly professional like Jane Bettle and Godfrey Mere and their kind. She did not belong there any more than she really belonged in the elaborate simplicity of the Ferrings' big London house.

Claire came in as he thought that, and her beauty smote Jennifer anew. She had seen nothing like her since she had gone away to Werford. Claire sparkled like a jewel and yet there clung about her a subtle perfume that was not just of one sense but of all of them.

She held out her hands to them.

'Oh, my dears, it's heaven to come in from the freezing outside to find you both here! Jennifer, how are you? You've grown thin, Julian tells me, and he says your eyes are too big. Brenner, ring for Luigia, will you? I simply can't go upstairs.'

She took off her exquisite fur coat as she talked and threw it over a chair, pulled off her hat and ran her fingers over the sleek hair with a gesture which would have ruined any ordinary hairdressing but which made her deep, natural waves set more closely.

'Oh, thank God for a fire! Or should I say, thank the miners, Jennifer?' with a little mischievous smile that showed the girl she remembered.

'I've always been so—mortified in my thoughts, Mrs. Ferring,' she said, embarrassed by memory.

Claire laughed and held out her well-kept hands to the fire, and the jewels on them sparkled and shone.

'Why? It caused quite a sensation, and as there wasn't an election after all, I was sincerely glad to have witnessed so complete a rout of one of my natural enemies. Let's talk of something else—of you, my dear, and of this husband of yours who, I understand, is to be a dark secret. How is he?'

'He will never be very well, I am afraid,' said Jennifer, and knew that she did not want to talk about Bob, not here in Claire Ferring's beautiful house – not here with Brenner Mayne listening.

'I'm sorry, Jennifer. It's his injury? Julian told me.'

'Yes. That—and of course the trouble about getting work,' said Jennifer.

She was thankful that she had not told Julian of her own personal struggle, of the hours of sewing, of the pittance she had received in exchange for her health and her strained eyes and her tired brain. Those things, at least, should remain locked away from these people, who would not have been able to understand why she did it, with Rothe ready to have her back.

Luigia, Claire's Italian maid, entered the room and began to gather up her mistress's belongings.

'We've got Miss Rothe back, Luigia,' said Mrs. Ferring to her, and the girl acknowledged Jennifer's smile with her expressive dark eyes.

'That is nice,' she said in her pretty English. 'You sing soon, signorina, yes?'

'I hope so, Luigia, but I'm feeling very rusty and out of practice, and my throat feels tight,' said Jennifer.

Claire laughed.

'It's this terrible weather, Jennifer, with which I know Luigia will agree, won't you? She spends ten months of the year longing for the other two, which I spend as a rule in her beloved Italy.'

The maid smiled again and withdrew. Footmen came in with the tea and Jennifer felt herself to be lapped again in the luxury which was so easy to decry when one was in Werford, so delightful to accept when one was in houses like this, with the logs blazing in the hearth and the soft glow of the concealed lighting giving everything a delicate brilliance.

'You're going again this year, Claire?' asked Mayne, and she nodded, and Jennifer had a strange fancy that there was something defiant in the glance which she gave him. Why should there be?

'I'm desperately trying to,' said Claire. 'With a general election always looming ahead, I never know whether I dare plan anything, though.'

'You'll love Italy, Miss Rothe,' said Mayne calmly.

Jennifer stared at him.

'Why do you say that to me?' she asked. 'I haven't any expectation of going there.'

Claire flung that odd challenge at him again, but it was to Jennifer she spoke, her voice cool and smooth.

'I expect Julian will come to stay for a little time whilst I am in my villa on Lake Como,' she said. 'I have asked him if he will bring you with him, if you would like that.'

Jennifer's eyes lit up, then the light was dimmed again.

'I should love it,' she said. Then, 'You don't have to invite me just because of Julian, you know. I can stay in his house and practise whilst he is away.'

Claire laughed and touched her hand in a fleeting caress.

'No, my dear. I'm not asking you just because of Julian and your work but because I want you. It's my annual holiday when I go to Menaggio, and I never invite people there because of any sort of duty or obligation. Only my friends come to me there, and we are all at peace because we like one another and we never talk politics.'

Jennifer's face softened again. How good they were to her, how kind and gracious, without hint of condescension or patronage. She remembered the way Bob spoke of people like this, hating them with a bitter hatred which she would unhesitatingly have shared had she not known them herself.

Yet they were wealthy, living in every luxury on money which, according to Bob and his friends, could only have been made by dishonesty, by 'grinding the faces of the poor'. Certainly Claire never ground a face of the poor in her life – nor did Brenner Mayne, with his quick smile, his kind eyes, his gentleness which was never unmanliness, but which was the supreme gentleness of the strong who know and respect their strength.

For a little while they talked. Then someone rang up and Claire had to excuse herself and go.

'Forgive me. The wife of a cabinet minister leads a dog's life in these days. My dears, do what you like, won't you? Stay or go, but forgive me for having no choice.'

'What shall we do?' asked Mayne when she had gone, and Jennifer's heart leapt because he so naturally included her in his immediate doings.

'Anything you like,' she said.

Again he knew that delight in her simplicity and met it as simply.

'Shall we walk, then? The park's like a fairyland and the trees like a Christmas card.'

She rose and he helped her with her coat, which in the intimacy of Claire's room she had taken off, and they went out together into the frosty air, her eyes bright and her cheeks tingling and new life flowing through her being with every step she took.

She had done little walking lately. She had had no time, for one thing, whilst she had been working for Scrimshaw's, and when she and Bob went out it was always with a definite object and by the shortest route because of his lameness. It was an exercise she loved, and, even though it was getting dark and was very cold, she felt a wild exhilaration.

Mayne could not see her, but he could hear it in her voice, that unfailing telltale.

'All right?' he asked her. 'Liking it?'

It was an unnecessary question, but he wanted to hear the thrill with which he knew she would answer it.

'Loving it,' she said. 'Rather guilty though.'

'Why?'

'Because—I can't help thinking of my own people, my friends at home. The cold isn't any pleasure to them. It is a bitter enemy, filling them with all sorts of misery and fear. You see, they haven't warm enough clothes, or big enough fires, or enough food to eat, the children especially. It makes me ashamed to be enjoying it.'

He liked her frankness, her complete lack of pretence.

'Why shouldn't you enjoy the good gifts of nature because they are not enjoyed by everyone? It doesn't make it any better for your friends. The wrong is not in your enjoying them but in their being prevented from enjoying them,' he said.

She gave him a bright and eager look.

'Oh, you feel that too? You know how topsy-turvy is everything in the world? How wrong it is that the things that were created for all of us to enjoy should have been taken by the few so that they could withhold it from the rest of us?'

His last thought had been to become involved in any such weighty discussion with her, but they found themselves talking long and earnestly, and when at last he took her in a taxi to Highgate and left her outside Rothe's house he realised that they had not talked personally at all and yet he had come to a much greater personal knowledge of her than if they had.

He would not come in, though she gave him a somewhat uncertain invitation to do so.

'I've got a lot of work to do,' he said. 'I'm working on a case, and when I come up against a problem such as the one I'm dealing with I like to cut it right out of my mind for hours at a stretch and then come back to it and attack it with vigour, preferably when everybody else has gone to bed and the world's not quite as feverish as it has been during the day.'

'I've loved discussing things with you,' said Jennifer wistfully.

'And I've loved it too. When do we continue it? Tomorrow? In the morning? Do you ride?'

She laughed and shook her head.

'I scarcely know one end of a horse from the other,' she said. 'I'd rather be on my feet.'

'Shall we walk, then? Will you ring me up, or may I ring you?'

She sketched out for him her probable programme for the next day now that her lessons were starting again, and there seemed no time left.

'I'll call you just the same,' he said, 'Early? Ten o'clock?'

'That's late for me,' she said with a smile. 'I get up soon after six.'

'All right. I'll ring you at half past six,' he said laughingly, and the next morning he was as good as his word, though a surprised housemaid was cleaning round her feet and listening to every word.

They could not meet for a few days, but when they did, almost by chance, they knew so much more about each other for the days between. They met with a smile, holding each other's eyes and looking away again, with the smile still lingering.

It was at a dinner reception, and they were going on to the theatre afterwards, but Mayne could not go because of pressure of work, and they had only a few moments together. Afterwards it seemed to Jennifer that they had been together all the evening, for she could not remember what she did during the rest of the time.

'No time for walking yet?' he asked her.

'Only when you're too busy,' she told him regretfully.

'Never mind. The time will come. I'm not always as busy as now. I shall see you, anyway, before the end of the year. We're going to meet at Claire Ferring's.'

'Are we? Will you be there?'

'Yes, and you will, she tells me. We can dance together,' and in his voice was a satisfaction that thrilled her.

'I don't dance awfully well,' she said.

'You will, with me. It's because most men are shorter than you and it gives you an unfair advantage. You look down on them all the time,' he laughed.

'I can't look down on you,' said Jennifer in her slow and lovely voice.

'I don't want you to—ever,' he said, and then someone came to separate them, to hustle Jennifer off, wrapped in furs, to Rothe's car, leaving Mayne standing to watch her go, to smile at her and have her secret smile in return.

Rothe watched her curiously, speculatively. She was attracted to Mayne. So much was clear. And he to her? Rumour had connected his name with many, but without any foundation, nor had he been caught up in any of the toils. What if he fell at last for this girl of the people, with her uncertain future, with her divine voice, with her crippled husband in the background? He did not concern himself so much with Brenner Mayne. He was quite able to manage his own life and to extricate himself from anything without help.

But what of Jennifer?

He knew so well what she lacked, what her life needed to make her voice the perfect instrument rather than the perfect machine. This Bob, what sort of man was he that Jennifer should have retained her ice-cold innocence through two years of marriage? Had he made his first mistake over a voice? Had he staked so much only to lose it? Was she going to let him down after all?

Or – was this the solution?

He watched her covertly during the journey home, but she was serene and calm and cool.

Chapter Ten

'Happy new year, Jennifer!'

'Happy new year, Brenner.'

Her tongue had tripped a little at his name, but she had managed it, and their hands clung, and their eyes, as the last note boomed forth from the wireless that had given them the farewell and hail of Big Ben.

They were both absorbed immediately afterwards by others, by greetings boisterous, gay, hilarious, as glasses were raised and toasts drunk and kisses exchanged and laughter.

Soon he found her again. She was standing a little apart, strange to his eyes, and so nearly beautiful in the low gown of oyster-coloured velvet in which at first she had felt overdressed, too elaborate.

'You're lovely tonight,' Brenner told her, and though she laughed and shook her head, she was glad that he had said so.

'I could never be that,' she said, her voice not quite steady, her eyes like stars.

'I shall remind you of that when the press are burbling about you, printing all manner of photos of you, describing what you wear and what you eat, how you look on every possible and impossible occasion. Have you had any supper?'

'No. I waited,' she said.

His eyes gleamed.

'For me, Jennifer?'

'I hoped you would want to,' she said simply.

He found a reasonably quiet corner of the supper room and foraged for food for her, for champagne in its pail of ice, for sandwiches and all sorts of queer, delicious food.

She disliked caviare intensely, and was glad that he agreed with her.

'They say it is an acquired taste,' he told her, 'though it passes my comprehension why anyone should want to acquire a taste for anything so expensive and only to be acquired after much diligent and nauseating practice. Have some of these queer little black things. I don't know what they're called, but Claire always provides them for the initiates.'

They talked gaily as they ate, Jennifer at her ease with him, he with a feeling that he had come home after many wanderings. She satisfied so much of his need, not only the need he had known and recognised, but undreamed of, secret needs which, without her, he might never have known himself to possess.

After supper they danced. He had come very late and there had been no time before midnight, but now he took her to the dance floor with a little sigh of contentment.

Jennifer had danced assiduously in preparation for this moment, taking extra lessons and working hard with them, so that now she was reasonably proficient – not that she even thought of her feet or where they went after the first minute or two in his arms.

She was both thrilled and frightened by the feelings she had, and now and then her eyes would find his fixed on them with a questioning, half startled look that found an echo in her heart, so that she looked away and was afraid to look again – and yet did look again.

Rothe, dancing with Claire, smiled at them enigmatically as they passed and stooped to say something to his partner, something which made her pause to cast a questioning, reflective look on the tall, beautifully matched pair who were so absorbed in each other.

'I don't want to dance any more,' said Jennifer breathlessly.

'Tired?'

'No.'

How could she tell him the truth? That she could bear no longer the exquisite delight of his nearness, of his arm about her, of that feeling that, out of all the world, she belonged to him for just this hour?

'Jennifer.'

'Yes?'

Sweet to hear him speak her name like that.

'You promised me that you would sing to me. Did you mean it?'

'I always mean what I promise,' she said gravely.

'Then—now?' he asked.

'Here?' with startled eyes on the crowded room filled with lovely women, with laughter and jewels, with faces that looked as though hearts never broke.

'No. At my house. Will you? It isn't far and there are people to play propriety and I'll bring you back again, or take you home.'

She hesitated. What would Rothe think if she broke her tacit bond to him not to sing without his permission? Or would this not come within the bond at all?

'There'll be no one else there?' she asked.

He misinterpreted her words and was disappointed in her. She should know him better.

'I've told you, the servants,' he said. 'Can't you trust me?'

'Oh, not that,' she told him swiftly with rising colour, and she explained. 'I don't think he could count just singing to you though, could he?'

'You get your coat and meet me in the hall. I'll tell him,' he said and threaded his way, when she had left him, to where Rothe stood, alone for a few minutes.

'I'm taking Jennifer home with me for an hour,' said Mayne without preamble. 'I want to hear her sing and she says she has promised you that she won't do so without permission from you. You don't mind?'

Julian looked at the younger man with an inscrutable smile. Was his Galatea to come to life then, after all?

All that Mayne saw was the courtesy of a man who was Claire's guest as Rothe inclined his head.

'Not in your case, no,' he said. 'What will you do with her? Bring her back here or take her to Highgate? I may be very late.'

'Take her to Highgate probably. I won't keep her long.'

'All right. She oughtn't to be out too long in the night air, or up at all at this hour. I'll make her adieux to Claire.'

And a few minutes later they were in his car, Mayne at the wheel, Jennifer tucked into a fur rug beside him, the moonlight making the frost a fairyland about them.

'Where do you live?' she asked him.

'In one of London's forgotten streets,' he said. 'A little street behind Clement's Inn where there are still some old houses which have escaped the ruthless maw of the flat-builder, though I have had notice that it is on the destruction list. I shall be sorry. It isn't very light or very convenient, and the servants say it is impossible to make it look as if they had spent hours cleaning and polishing its crannies, but I've grown fond of it in ten years there. This is the street,' turning into a narrow gap that led off from the wide, busy thoroughfare. 'And this is the house. Will you mind if I run her into the garage? It is so cold that she may be a bit of a bother to start up unless I protect her from this icy wind.'

It was sweet and a little frightening, this sudden intimacy, this feeling of being separated from their kind, and when he had stopped the car in a dark, narrow slipway between two houses, roofed over and provided with ends, she turned wide, startled eyes on him.

'What's the matter? Afraid of me?' asked Mayne with a tightening of his throat.

She looked so young, so entirely at his mercy. Impossible to think of her as a wife of two years' standing!

'No, not afraid. Just—that it is queer to be shut up in this little space with you.'

'Yes. Nice though.'

She did not answer that, but climbed carefully out of the car and let him take her into the house through an old oak door, heavy and black, which opened on a small square hall, oak-panelled and dim, with soft Persian rugs on the shining floor and electric light in an ancient lantern swinging above their heads.

A baize door at one side opened and an elderly woman came to them, stiff and starched and rustling in black silk.

'Oh, Mrs. Dodds, have you been sitting up for me? I didn't mean you to do that, but I appreciate it.

'This is my housekeeper, Jennifer. Miss Rothe will not be here long, Mrs. Dodds. She is going to sing for me for a little while. Take a good look at her for the day will come when all the world will want to do the same but will have to pay heavily for the privilege.'

The old woman gave her a funny little curtsey and a respectful smile.

'Will you want anything, sir?' she asked.

'Port, perhaps, and biscuits. Nothing else?' with an inquiring glance at Jennifer, who stood fascinated by the quiet, dim old house. They might be miles from anywhere, and yet she knew they were in the heart of London.

'Oh no, thank you,' she said.

'Come in here,' and he took her into a low-ceiled, dim room, a room which smelt of books and leather and pipe-smoke, a man's room, comfortable, as simple as Mayne's tastes could make it yet lacking nothing necessary.

He took her coat and laid it across a chair, poked up the fire and put another lump of coal on it, turned off one of the lights and switched on another over the baby grand which occupied a place of honour.

'What will you sing?' he asked her.

'I don't know a lot of things,' she told him. 'Julian keeps me to arias and scraps of opera and recitatives and Gregorian chants.'

He laughed.

'None of those tonight, then. Sing what you yourself like to sing, Jennifer. Here is a stack of music of all sorts. Let's go through them.'

They pulled from the pile songs that she knew, a curious medley which delighted him, for it showed so many facets of her nature. Some of the songs she chose were frankly sentimental ballads which Rothe would have thrown aside as 'tosh'; others bordered on the classical and yet had a tunefulness which appealed to her.

'I'm not really musically educated at all, you know,' she admitted ruefully. 'Julian is doing his best, but I still like songs with tunes in them.'

'So do I,' he agreed heartily. 'Come along. Let's start with this,' and he showed by the way he tackled the opening chords that he was no mean musician himself.

Jennifer's voice trembled a little at first. She felt selfconscious and nervous. But soon the nervousness went and she was at her ease, singing song after song to him with sweetness, with pathos, gently and unemotionally, her voice rising to power and volume now and then but leaving him with just the feeling that enraged Rothe and made him feel helpless.

'She's still asleep,' thought Mayne. 'How marvellous and incomprehensible. I wonder why?' but his manhood rejoiced to know her still untouched, even though his reason told him that it could not, must not, be any concern of his.

'Your voice is very lovely, Jennifer,' he told her.

'Julian is disappointed in it, but neither he nor I can alter it,' she said with a little frown and a sigh.

He looked up from his seat at the piano. She stood framed by the circle from the one lamp, and he thought how splendid was the picture she made in her oyster velvet with the dim old room behind her and her dark head against the light.

'I think time and—life will do that,' he said very gently, almost regretfully. 'Would you like to rest? Then I must take you back. Rothe made me swear I'd not let you be late.'

She sat in the chair he drew near the fire for her, aware of his thought for her comfort, of the extra cushion at her back and the stool for her feet. She had never been so cherished before. It was both beautiful and hurtful.

He went back to the piano and played to her softly, and presently he sang to her, his voice not strong, but mellow and tuneful in the dim quietude of this old, forgotten house. The slow, difficult, unaccustomed tears forced themselves between her closed lashes for no reason at all as he finished the song.

'I did but see her passing by,
And yet I'll love her till I die.'

Why should that make her stupidly weak and want to cry? She swallowed hard and blinked the tears away before he could see them, glad of the shadows in which she sat, but when she spoke to him, he heard the tears in her voice and wondered, and remembered them long after she had gone, after she had herself forgotten them.

Why should Jennifer cry because he had sung that song to her?

And why had he sung just that particular song to Bob Haling's wife?

He took her back in his car to Highgate and they were very quiet on the journey.

'Warm enough, Jennifer?'

'Yes. This rug's lovely.'

'Happy?'

'Yes.'

'Hadn't you better come in?' she asked him when he drew up at the door. 'Julian's back.'

He did so reluctantly. This thing between them was like a windflower, fragile, easily crushed and withered by the touch of rough fingers. He dare not give it a name himself nor could he bear that anyone else, Rothe least of all, should give it one.

Rothe glanced at them with a gleam of amusement in his unhumorous eyes. A tubby little man was with him.

'That you, Jennifer, my dear? Come in, Mayne, and have a drink.'

'Thanks. I don't think I will. The roads are bad and I've got to drive back and the faintest smell of one's breath is enough for the police nowadays—D and D if your car goes into a lamp-post off a skid.'

He was talking for the sake of talking.

'There speaks the prudence of the law,' said Rothe. 'Jennifer, you've heard of Pelledew, the baritone. My ward and pupil, Miss Jennifer Rothe. You know Pelledew, Mayne, don't you?' The little man squeezed Jennifer's hand and smiled at both of them.

'I'm afraid I shall never be given the honour of singing with you, Miss Rothe,' he said ruefully from his lower eminence.

'I'm afraid my height is going to be one drawback Mr. Rothe can't hope to deal with,' said Jennifer. 'Thank you, Julian, I will,' as he offered her a drink.

'Ah, but you'll make a glorious Brünhilde,' sighed Pelledew, rolling his eyes.

'When we've filled her out a bit,' said Rothe. 'She's not exactly on the lines of the heroic Norsewoman yet, is she?' Mayne found himself resenting unreasonably the proprietorial look Rothe cast on the girl and wisely took his departure after remaining with them only a few minutes.

Rothe went to the door with him.

'Did she sing to you?' he said.

'Of course. That's what she came with me for as you won't let her sing where there's a crowd,' said Mayne coldly.

'And at your house I take it there wasn't a crowd?' asked Rothe blandly.

He had the satisfaction of seeing the younger man look irritated.

'Naturally not,' he said shortly, and without another word turned to go.

Rothe went slowly back into the room, a faint smile playing about his lips and behind his eyes. So Mayne had resented that vague suggestion, and there was only one reason why he should. Jennifer rose to say good night.

'Will you forgive me if I go up? Mr. Rothe makes me keep such early hours, Mr. Pelledew, that I am like a child after a party when I do have a late night.'

'What's tired you so much tonight?' asked Rothe. 'Singing to Brenner Mayne?'

She flushed and he saw the little pulse in her throat beating. 'No, not that,' she said. 'Mrs. Ferring's party was very gay and I suppose I'm not used to London life yet. Good night,' and she went quietly away.

After his guest had gone, Rothe sat over his night-cap by the embers of the fire. Jennifer's slight flush had not escaped him any more than had the brightness in her eyes when she had come in with Mayne, the look of aliveness which she had not worn before.

The next day he went to see Claire Ferring. It was not an unusual procedure with him, but she had not expected him so soon after an all-night party.

'I'm feeling a wreck, Julian, and don't really want you to see me,' she said when he came in. 'Say your little piece and go, there's a sweet.'

But he was so long coming to the point that she really began to think he had come, as he had said, on a casual impulse. Just as he was preparing to go, however, he spoke of the Italian holiday. 'Will you do something I'd like, Claire?'

'My dear, of course.'

'Then will you invite Brenner Mayne whilst we are there?' His voice was completely unemotional and cool and he was lighting a cigarette, his whole attitude one of complete unconcern, but Claire's eyes narrowed a little.

'Why?' she asked.

'I'd like it. After all, we don't want to have Jennifer with us all the time, do we?'

'Derek will be there.'

'A boy of eighteen might have been sufficient company for her two years ago, but do you think he will appeal to Jennifer as a companion for a married woman?' asked Rothe placidly.

'Julian, what exactly are you up to?' demanded Claire.

His air of innocence was too real to be true.

'Up to, my dear? In what respect?'

'That might do for some people, but not for me. I know you too well, my lamb. What are you trying to do to Jennifer and Brenner?'

He met her eyes steadily and at last he smiled, shrugged his shoulders, and looked away.

'You know as well as I do what's wrong with her voice,' he said. 'I watched Mayne carefully last night and I rather think he can put it right.'

'Julian, you're a devil.'

'Not at all, my dear. On the contrary, I'm playing the little blind god's game for him. Did you know that she went with Mayne to his house last night when they left here?'

She stared at him.

'Julian! I don't believe it!' she cried.

'"Grandmother, what big eyes you've got" – and what a nasty mind! She went there to sing to him because I won't let her sing in public. That's all.'

She gave a little laugh of relief.

'You're an idiot, Julian. You gave me a fright.'

'But, my dear, why? Isn't it natural? They're both unusual people, and isn't that what he, at least, has been looking for for so long?'

'Don't forget she's married, Julian.'

'Poof! How much will that matter when she falls in love, do you imagine?'

Her eyes flamed suddenly.

'Julian, you're horrible. Do you realise that you're deliberately trying to wreck the lives of at least three people?'

'Aren't you getting the wrong angle on this? Isn't it going to complete their lives rather? Can they ever be complete without emotional experience?' argued Rothe.

'Why should you suppose that Jennifer hasn't had it? She must have been in love with this man she married, or why did she go back for the purpose of marrying him?'

'I notice that even in your defence of her, you put it in the past tense—that she *was* in love with the man, suggesting that she is no longer. It is my conviction that she never was in love with him, that she has never been stirred to any emotion other than pity, sympathy, resentment against social conditions, and the strong faithfulness which is the essence of her character. I am just as much convinced that she is ripe for the completion of her emotional life and that, no matter what anyone does or omits to do, she is going to find it.'

'With another man than her husband.'

'My dear, be reasonable. If the man were going to fulfil her destiny for her, don't you think he'd have done it already, with two years to do it in, and not sent her back to us with that look of a strayed and inquiring angel in her eyes and nothing whatsoever in her voice?'

'I still think you're playing with fires which may become— catastrophic for them all,' said Claire gravely.

Rothe suddenly tossed aside his air of being outside all this, of being an impersonal onlooker. There was fire in his voice and in his eyes, passion in his words.

'Catastrophe? What can be a greater catastrophe in this life for man or woman than to be denied the greatest experience, the most primitive experience, destined for all living things, common to all, desired by all? Would you have been without it, Claire, in spite of the cost? Have you ever, at any time, counted the cost, and found it too great? Have you?'

She sat looking into the fire, her face the battlefield for conflicting emotions. He could not see her eyes, but his ears, attuned to every least shade of tone, heard all he needed in her soft, low voice.

'No. I've never found it too great,' she said. 'I've had something else to put in the balance though, Julian.'

'Derek?'

'Yes.'

'That need not be denied to Jennifer.'

'To love a man like Brenner Mayne and bear a child to this man she married?' asked Claire, and she lifted her eyes at last and looked deeply into his. He saw in them the pain that never died, the longing, the sorrow, the deep regret, which underlay all her brilliance, of which no one in the world knew save two men – the man she had married, and Julian Rothe.

He took her hands and carried them to his lips.

'Forgive me, my dear,' he said, and his voice shook. He could not bear to look on the naked soul of this woman he loved, and she knew why he asked her forgiveness in that moment of memory.

'There is never anything to forgive between you and me, my dear—my dearest,' she said, and for a long time they were silent.

He spoke at last,

'About Mayne, Claire?'

'"Vaulting ambition that o'erleaps itself",' she quoted sadly.

'What sort of life do you think lies before her if she doesn't make a success?' he demanded impatiently. 'She'll have to go back to Haling, to that wretched life about which she says nothing but which left its marks on her for all the world to see. If she hadn't been so foolish as to marry him, she would probably have married someone here, Mayne possibly, and turned into a nice, comfortable, capable housewife and forgotten in time that she might have been a great singer. What can she do, married to Haling, if she fails? And you know as well as I do that she has no earthly hope of becoming a great singer until she has developed every part of herself, gained her own experience of life, known every emotion. With that, she can get anywhere, be anything, and she can choose her own form of happiness, either with Haling or with any other man or with no man at all. She'll be free and prosperous instead of turning into a weary, embittered drudge for a man who doesn't know the worth of her.'

Claire knew the truth of what he said and yet, completely ignorant of Haling as she was, she could offer no argument or defence.

'All right,' she said at last. 'If he'll come, I'll have him there, though I shall always look on it as a diabolical scheme and shall hate to see either of them suffer.'

'He'll come all right,' said Rothe with satisfaction. 'I don't think I'll tell Jennifer he's expected, though.'

'There's time enough for almost anything to happen,' said Claire. 'I've known four days to change the universe, and they'll have four months. You understand that I can't have any scandal there, Julian?'

He laughed and prepared to go.

'Can't you trust me yet, my dear?' he asked.

When he had gone, she sighed over her reflections. Julian was so masterful. He treated the world as if it belonged to him, as if the people on it were pawns to be moved at his will, to be made or destroyed as he thought fit. Even she moved at his will. Otherwise how had she come to give her promise about inviting Brenner Mayne to Italy so that he and Jennifer might know the heady seduction of the lotus life they led there by the shores of Como for those blessed, wonderful weeks?

The door opened and Guy Ferring came in.

He was a man in his fifties, tall and spare, with a keen, clever face and an uncompromising mouth, a man to rule other men but with no dominion over the hearts of women.

'Was that Rothe?' he asked.

'Yes.'

She waited for what was to follow the pause.

'I should like you to go down to Challissey this week-end,' he said.

Challissey was the seat of the Bordrays where one day, in all human probability, she would reign. At present it was occupied by the childless widower, Lord Bordray, a surly, morose, lonely old man who neither gave nor won friendship for anything living save perhaps a dog or a cat, and whose death was impatiently awaited by Ferring and would be regretted by none.

Claire loved Challissey but she hated Bordray, and she lifted her eyes to meet those of her husband levelly and with understanding. She was being asked to pay the price for that visit of Rothe's, and he knew she would pay for it without question just as she had paid for eighteen years and would go on paying it to the end.

'Very well, Guy. Will there be a party?'

'No. Just you and I and the boy.'

Claire rebelled a little at that. It would be Derek's last week-end before he went back to school, and she knew that he wanted to spend it in town in a last celebration.

'Why need Derek go, Guy? He will be going back to school in the week following,' she ventured, daring for her son what she would not have ventured for herself.

'Because I choose that he should go. He has not suggested going down during the holidays, and as the place will some day be his, it is only right and fitting that he should show some interest in it and pay respect to the head of the house. Tell him, please.'

'Guy, you're hard, aren't you?' she asked him with a rare note of bitterness in her voice.

He stood looking down at her, his eyes like steel, his mouth set in a firm line, his whole expression one of unyielding determination. At such time Claire saw his uncle in him and shuddered for an old age at Challissey.

'Why shouldn't I be hard?' he asked coldly. 'We made a bargain. We are both prepared to keep it. That is all. You'll tell Derek?'

'Oh yes,' she said with a little helpless gesture, and he turned away and a moment later she heard him giving some order on a different matter, completely unmoved and unaffected by the little scene.

'Thank God my Derek will never be like that!' she cried in her mind fiercely. 'Thank God! Thank God!'

Chapter Eleven

'I can't bear not to earn,' repeated Jennifer.

Rothe put a hand on her shoulder and smiled at a face which was not as placid as usual. He liked these little storms. They augured well for the eventual transformation of his Galatea into flesh and blood.

'You'll earn far more if you can make yourself be patient for another year, my dear,' he said.

'A year! Julian, not a year?' she asked dismayed.

'I put it at that, but of course everything depends on you. You're doing well, much better than when you were here before, and I'm pleased with you. It is amazing how the time goes, though. In May we shall be going to Italy, first to Mrs. Ferring's villa for a holiday. We cannot go to Milan until September, so I propose in the meantime to go to Germany, to Berlin, Strasburg, perhaps on to Vienna before we go further south, though of course Vienna does not offer the attractions and advantages it did formerly. Milan and Rome in September, probably on into October and November. If we come back here by Christmastime, we could then think of your first concert, which must be carefully planned and arranged so that the right people will be in London.'

Jennifer had heard little of the arrangements. She had caught at the central idea, that it would be a year before she began to earn, a year – and Lottie's letter crushed in her hand and burning into her heart.

Things are bad here, Jen [Lottie had written]. I think they get worse every day and you can't expect the men to stand it for ever. All this talk in parliament and nothing ever done, and Sir Jervis riding about Belsdale in his car and saying the men are well off and got nothing to grumble at and his wife in a fur coat and us in thin coats three years' old and bitter weather too. They keep talking about striking and that's how it will have to be though Father Flint is always talking against it and begging the men not to and men like Mallinger always about making the others desperate. Bob's still friends with him and it won't do him any good though I don't see him much now he's in Belsdale in rooms. Have you got anything you can send me for some of the kids, Jen? Mrs. Riggs three have got bronkitus and you know she lost her Archie with newmonia this time last year and the doctor keeps on about all sorts of stuff they ought to have and how can she get it with Rigg on short time for weeks and weeks? They want blankets too and there's lots more like them. Lucy Potter is having her third next week and she'll have to go into the infirmary and nobody to do a turn for the other two except I go in and I can't afford to buy things for them though they want things badly. So if you could send me a pound or two, Jen, if you can spare it, and Bob wants things. His coat is shabby and I can see he isn't wearing his overcoat and I think he sold it when you were so pressed before you went away and I don't think he's getting enough food.

There was more of it, local gossip and talk, for Lottie was a ready writer if her spelling and construction were not always up to standard, and she knew that Jennifer would be interested.

Jennifer had thought furiously and wretchedly, and as an outcome had gone to Rothe to beg him to let her take engagements, little private ones at dinners and receptions which she thought she would be able to get. She felt desperately the need to earn, to get money to send to Lottie, not only for the cases she had quoted but for the hundreds of others who were in need. She knew what it was like to be terribly poor, to have hanging over one's head the fear of the landlord, of the grocer and the baker and the milkman – fear day and night, indoors and out, at every street corner and at every door – stark, crushing fear.

And Rothe had flatly refused.

'You're going to undo everything we've done,' he said, 'There's nothing in being just a singer, a third-rate concert artist, which is all you could ever be if you had already cheapened yourself as you suggest. Why do you think I've cherished and guarded you, dressed you and chosen your friends and timed your programme to such a nicety if all I wanted of you was that you should sing to fat men after their gross dinners, or warble on the wireless at five guineas a time to make an accompaniment to people's conversations or to drown the noise of their soup?'

She had pleaded and argued and all but wept, but he was adamant.

'If you must have money for your friends, I'll give it to you,' he said, but she refused.

'That's not the point. Don't you see? Can't you understand? They're my people, my friends. I want to work for them, not just to sponge on people like you for charity. That's one reason why I came back to you, not to make money for myself so much as to be able to do something for them.'

'Well, don't let's argue the point any more. You can have the money within reason, but you may not sing a note anywhere, to anyone, without my permission and in my presence, and that's final. Now it's time for your Italian lesson, isn't it? I saw Signor Alberti go by the window just now. How is it going? Remember that a good knowledge of Italian and a good pronunciation of the vowel sounds is absolutely essential for you.'

But it did not end there for Jennifer. She was determined that she would earn money somehow, and as she had no assets except her voice, it was with her voice she must earn.

The idea came to her one evening, a few days later, when she was going with Mayne and his married sister, Mira Dennis, to the theatre.

She was not seeing much of Brenner, accepting without question his lightly apologetic explanation of important cases on hand, but it seemed that wherever she went she heard his name. He was making it a household one through his masterly handling of cases which, in the ordinary way, would have been given to an older man. He seemed to make up in quickness of wit and alertness of brain what he missed in experience, and he was chosen as junior by famous counsel who could have named almost any of the younger barristers.

This visit to the theatre was a pleasant surprise. Mrs. Dennis had rung her up during the afternoon.

'I've had a box absolutely flung at me for the thriller at the Vanity tonight,' she said. 'Do come, Miss Rothe. I'll dig up two men and make it a foursome,' but when the Dennis's car had driven up to the door for Jennifer, as arranged, she found Mayne seated in it with a gay, apologetic Mira opposite him.

'This is positively all I could get in the way of men,' she said. 'That's one of the disasters that follow marriage, Miss Rothe. You have to go to the theatre with your brother if your husband's too busy. Will you make do with him?'

In the dimness of the car, Jennifer and Mayne's eyes met, clung and parted again. Supremely well they could 'make do', though neither knew the truth about the other's feeling.

And just as they reached the theatre, Jennifer's idea came to her.

A woman stood at the edge of the pavement singing. Her face was haggard and unlovely, but her voice must once have been a thing of beauty, for even now it was full and sweet, though the fog was choking her throat and making it rasp now and again.

Mayne helped the two women from the car and then turned to the street singer and, with a gesture of exquisite courtesy, put some money into her hand, raising his hat to her and smiling.

'Brenner, was that ten shillings you gave her?' asked Mira suspiciously. She was a few years his junior and a privileged person.

'It was. It was—a thanksgiving,' he said quietly, and though he spoke to his sister, it was Jennifer at whom he looked and Jennifer who, with a little thrill of wonder, understood. He was glad to be with her – perhaps almost as glad as she to be with him!

She thought about that woman quite a lot. Whilst they had waited for Mayne to get from the box office the ticket which was waiting for them, she had seen quite a number of people stop to give the woman money, not perhaps as magnificently as Mayne had done, but in shillings and half-crowns for the most part, and it only needed eight half-crowns to make up a pound, she reflected – and how very far anyone like Lottie, like poor Mrs. Rigg, could make a pound go!

A few nights later she crept out cautiously with a bundle under her arm, her evening frock exchanged for a quiet day dress. She knew exactly what she was going to do, and she did it without hurry or confusion. She let herself out of the french window from the morning-room, walked noiselessly over the wet grass to a little side gate, and from the street outside took a bus towards the West End, getting off when within easy walking distance of the theatres. In the shadow of an archway, she took off her beret and pushed it into her pocket and arrayed herself in a long cloak of grey velvet which reached to the ground, and tied over her eyes a mask of the same material. She had bought the things that afternoon at a theatrical costumier's, and a careful inspection of herself had satisfied her that she was quite unrecognisable.

Slipping through side streets, with more luck than skill she came out into Shaftesbury Avenue and her heart gave a great leap and she felt horribly sick as she met the lights and the crowds and the curious eyes of passers-by. Then two urchins began to jeer at her and make impish remarks which brought answering smiles from the onlookers, and Jennifer realised that her whole scheme would be frustrated from the start unless she acted quickly.

Walking slowly along the kerb, she began to sing, her head flung high, her glorious voice clear and pure and honey-sweet in the garish lighting and the crowds jostling one another along the wet streets.

She chose old songs, sentimental ballads, and sang them with a simplicity that touched many hearts. She carried a little bag which she had made herself, and soon the coins began to drop into it, silver and coppers, and presently there was the crisp rustle of a note and an elderly man, in evening dress and opera hat, touched her hand as he tucked the folded paper through the open mouth of the bag.

'Where do you come from, beautiful?' he asked her thickly, and Jennifer drew back, snatched the note from the bag and pushed it into his hand again.

'I don't want it,' she said, but he laughed, hesitated and then put the note back into his pocket.

She regretted her action at once. Nothing could happen to her in the crowded street. She was safe from discovery and yet she had been fool enough to refuse ten shillings, she thought scornfully. Well, she would not refuse again, but true to life, no other came her way, though a good many invitations and inquiries did.

She knew where Rothe had gone for the evening and kept an eye on the time so that she should get back before he was likely to return and would be able to let herself in with her latchkey. After he came in at night, he fastened the door.

It was all ridiculously easy, and her only regret was that she had not stayed an hour longer, for she had been home much more than an hour when she heard Rothe. Her first act had been to count her money, and she was delighted to find that she had collected nearly two pounds as a result of her first adventure.

Night after night, whenever her engagements and Rothe's, and the weather, permitted, she slipped out with her grey cloak and mask under her arm, and very soon people began to look for the 'Singing Lady', as one of the papers called her in a little paragraph which she was frightened to find one morning. She exercised even greater care in her comings and goings, took great pains to find out where Rothe would be and avoided a large circle around that particular spot.

She concentrated on the theatres and the places where they had supper and a cabaret show in the very late hours. For one thing she did not interfere with the regular entertainers of the queues by doing that, for she was ever on the side of the poor and needy; for another, she could leave home later and run less risk of her absence being discovered. Also, she found people generous at that hour and did not scruple to exploit the open-handedness of the men who had done themselves very well during the evening. To Jennifer they were fair game, for she felt she was taking from those who had money to burn so that she might give to those to whom it was precious beyond words.

And then Brenner Mayne found her out.

More than one of the London newspapers had now commented on the mystery of the Singing Lady, doubling both her takings and her need for caution, and she had to exercise great skill to avoid being 'drawn' by enterprising reporters who dogged her footsteps and had more than once tried to track her down to Highgate. There was always the possibility of trouble with the police as well, for though they were friendly to her and one was nearly always about and ready to protect her, she knew that she was walking on the very thin ice of the law.

On the night that Brenner discovered her, she was almost ready to go home. She was tired and it had started to rain and she dare not risk a cold, but just as she decided to go a gay, laughing party came out of a popular club and stood talking on the pavement whilst taxis were found for them. Little groups of people like this were usually fruitful for her, and she moved a few yards nearer to them and began to sing.

'Oh listen! The Singing Lady! I've never heard her before. Do stop a minute,' cried one of the girls, and they crowded about her, their chatter and laughter dying as the pure, clear voice thrilled them with its almost unearthly sweetness.

And gradually, by that unerring sixth sense which is given to most of us at some period of our lives, a gift of God and the devil both, Jennifer became aware of Brenner.

He stood close to her. She could have touched him by lifting her hand. He stood quite still, and when the song was over and they were raining their gifts on her, trying to make her speak because the papers said she never uttered a word except in her songs, he did not move.

'Come on, Mayne,' said one of the men. 'We can drop you.'

'Thanks, I'll walk a bit,' he said. 'Will you take Maisie home? Good night, everybody. Good night—'

'Good night—and to you, Singing Lady!' cried one of them, and a chorus of good wishes to her followed.

She stood quite still on the pavement, smiling a little and inclining her head in acknowledgement, a strange, mysterious figure in her grey cloak and mask. If only he would go! Even when the taxis had driven off, leaving the place quiet and dim, something kept her rooted here and she knew that Brenner had not moved.

He came nearer to her.

'Jennifer,' he said quietly, and she gave a revealing start, half turned to face him, and then turned back again and drew her cloak about her ready to flee.

He laid a hand on her arm, gently, possessively, and she knew that he would not be deceived.

'Please let me go,' she said in a very low, shaky voice, and at that moment one of her policemen friends strolled up, cleared his throat to speak and then recognised Mayne and visibly felt at a loss what to do.

Jennifer spoke to him quickly.

'It's all right,' she said nervously. 'This gentleman is—a friend of mine,' and the man went reluctantly away.

The Singing Lady had become a figure of romance even to London's stalwart police.

'Can't we slip away, Jennifer? So that I can talk to you?' urged Mayne in a low voice. 'I won't give you away. You know that.'

She looked round anxiously. A little way away there was one of the furtive little passages which lead off most of the big London streets, and she slipped within its shadow, pulled off the cloak and mask, rolled them into a small bundle and brought her old beret out of her pocket.

He had waited for her without moving a step, and she appreciated his act. If she meant to remain with him, she should find him there, but if she did not, he had given her an opportunity for escape.

He threw her a glance that was both question and smile and hailed a passing taxi, told the man to drive towards Highgate and got in beside her.

'Well, young lady?' he asked her.

'How did you know?'

'Have you forgotten an evening when you sang to me?'

'Was that—enough to recognise me?' she asked him with a catch in her voice.

It was so unbelievably dear to be here in this dark little space with him, with a secret shared, with she knew not what to come. For the first time she realised how dear it was, and would not herself realise anything else.

'I think I should know your voice amongst the celestial angels—or at the Cup Final at Wembley!' said Mayne, his voice between love and laughter. 'Oh, Jennifer, you mad child, what is it all about? I never dreamed for one wild moment that you were the Singing Lady, but I knew instantly, before I even saw you, and I don't know now how I contained myself whilst you sang and that crowd jostled you and gave you money. Jennifer, tell me the story.'

Quite simply and honestly, she told him, made him see with her eyes something of the poverty and want, of the unhappiness which a little money could relieve, of the vast distress which only violent upheaval of the whole scheme of things could touch.

'You're almost a revolutionary, Jennifer,' he said.

'So would you be, Brenner, if I could take you there, not as a visitor, to poke and pry and say "poor things" and go back to your comfortable living, but to live there as I did, to know what it is to want for almost everything that people like you consider a necessity, not to know whether you will be able to pay the rent next week, to go round and round your rooms to see if anything—*anything*—is likely to find a buyer so that you won't be without food when your last shilling has gone, to walk when your feet are swollen and blistered, to sew when your fingers are numb with cold so that you don't even feel the needle if it pricks you—oh, you'd understand then!'

He loved her eager passion, her ardent defence of her own people, still her own people though she lived in the luxury of Rothe's house, in ease and plenty. He worshipped her for her loyalty, for the absolute simplicity of heart which kept her loyal.

'I want to understand, Jennifer. I want to understand every thing about you, all you care for, all you know and feel and want, your ideals—everything,' he said.

His voice shook, and they sat together for a little while without speaking, aware of this thing that was happening to them, afraid of it, yet unable to check its approach or to move an inch out of its way. This thing that was to happen to them must come. It was destiny, and they were quivering and expectant at its approach.

'I won't take you right to the house,' he said as they came near the road in which Rothe lived. 'You can get in all right?'

She nodded.

'I do, every night almost. I'd like to get out and walk now,' and they held hands for a moment, looked into each other's eyes, and then she was gone.

He had made no attempt to dissuade her from her self-appointed task, but several nights she became aware of him near her, watching her, protecting her silently, and giving her courage and a glow of happiness. Afterwards they went in a taxi towards Highgate, and though she felt that she was jeopardising her secret and making it possible for people to trace her, the wonder and delight of it was worth the risk. Her greatest fear was lest Rothe should discover what she was doing and cast her loose from him because of her broken contract, but she was earning so much money to send secretly to Lottie that she could not bear the thought of being forced to discontinue it.

She tried to salve her conscience about Brenner by sending money to Bob, by writing him long letters which remorse made more affectionate than she knew and which served to create in Bob an increasing frenzy of resentment against his own impotence to provide for her, to be able to demand her return, to do anything but accept from her.

Lottie says you aren't wearing your overcoat, dear [she wrote once]. I am sending you some money and please do get yourself a new one, a warm one, won't you? I know how you're looking at this very moment. Your jaws come out like a prize-fighter's and your lips have gone thin and there are blue devils in your eyes, but, darling, try to look at it as I want you to. I'm earning the money, really and truly. I'm not sending you a halfpenny from Mr. Rothe. I've managed to get some little jobs, privately of course, so as not to interfere with the splash I am supposed to be going to make next year. Next year! What a long time it sounds, doesn't it? I shall of course see you long before then, but it would interrupt so much of my work to come now, and I am going to stay with Mrs. Ferring in Italy in May because of my Italian. Isn't it funny to think of me speaking Italian? I can, just a little. It will make you laugh when you hear me. Oh, darling, I do hope you're getting on all right and not missing me too much. Be sure to wrap your throat up well in this weather, won't you? I am learning to be ever so fussy about things like that and you'll call me an old hen with feathered legs, like Mrs. Batter. Do you remember?

She was thankful when the spring came with a rush, bringing new hope, relieving some of the want in the land, setting Jennifer free to some extent from the necessity for sending money to Lottie, who wrote gratefully that the worst seemed to be over for the moment.

Of course most of the men are still on short time, and everybody is disappointed because the increase was refused. It looked as if it would go through and then when your friend Guy Ferring spoke against it in parliament, they all seemed to turn against the miners again and here we are worse than we were before. I saw Bob the other day. He looked a lot better and has got his new coat, a brown one. He says the men are sure to come out before another winter and all us women dred that but know its the only way to get the country to remember them. It's all right not to send any more money, Jen, if your going away. Fancy going to Italy. I wish I was you. But perhaps I dont after all. Send some postcards when you are there and dont forget us and go off with some Italiano hokey pokey and go to live in a palace.
Your loving friend,
Lottie.

They were to go to Italy early in May. Mrs. Ferring was doing a last round of her husband's constituency, paying a final visit to Challissey, performing every duty she could think of so that she might be free for the one holiday of the year which she reckoned as a holiday, the magic weeks when she was free from duty, from the round of entertaining and being entertained, from the intrigue and the matching of wits, from her husband's constant demands on her. He never went to the Italian villa. Tacitly it was agreed between them that the weeks of her holiday there were to be free ones on which he intruded neither his presence nor the duties which, as the wife of a cabinet minister, fell on her.

Ferring himself seemed never to need or want a holiday, and his friends wondered what he would do when, at no distant date, he should succeed to the earldom of his uncle and give up practical politics. He was a hard man, but he was as straight and honest as he was allowed to be. He had no shares in armament firms, no financial interest in war, and took a feudal attitude towards the working classes, who constantly irked him by their increasing objection to being so looked upon. He was an honest man according to his lights, but a short-sighted one; he would have been a great man had he lived five centuries sooner.

To their intimates, it was a somewhat curious *ménage à trois*, each of them so individual, the boy Derek a link between parents who were studiously polite to each other. Claire loved her son devotedly but seldom cared to show it; Ferring was scrupulous about his upbringing, choosing his school, his curriculum, his friends in so far as he could, with the undeviating aim of making him his ideal of what a future peer of the realm should be; Derek steered an easy course between the two, loving his mother without approving of her and approving of Ferring without loving him.

They never quarrelled. They were all too well bred for that, and self-control was their creed. Yet no one could ever be in the presence of all three of them without feeling that there lay all the ingredients of a bomb which might go off at any moment and yet which one knew instinctively would never go off.

Derek was to be in Italy with Claire for a time and was to spend the rest of the summer at Challissey, going up to Cambridge in September.

'How will you endure Bordray for three months?' Claire asked him with interested amusement on the last week-end they spent together before she left England.

Derek smiled and helped her with the tea things. He had his mother's charming manners.

'But, darling, I like him,' he said. 'He's so honest and so utterly natural. If he feels like a beast, he acts like one—and why not? We've most of us gone so far from nature that none of us any longer knows what the rest of us really feel.'

'That was very complicated, my dear, but from it I gather that you would like us all to gnash our teeth on occasion, go berserk and generally behave like the wild animals we all feel at times.'

Derek looked at her critically, cool, self-possessed, exquisite as always.

'I wonder what one would find in you, Claire, if that could happen?' asked her son.

She laughed.

'You'd be surprised,' she said. 'However, if you have to go to Challissey for the summer, it's a mercy you like it. What do you do there all the time, alone with Bordray?'

'Oh—fish, shoot, hunt, anything that's in season. Mostly we tramp about. There's always heaps to be done now that he doesn't have a steward for the estate.'

'Just meanness?' asked Claire, drinking her tea.

'No, it isn't meanness,' said Derek with warmth. 'I think he's quite right. It's his own job, so long as he is able to do it. I respect him for it, and he gets a knowledge of the tenantry and conditions first-hand, as a landowner should do.'

'Darling, you're positively feudal,' said Claire with amusement. 'Bordray always was more pleased with you than with anyone I have ever seen with him. How very fortunate that, in all human probability, you will eventually succeed him!'

The boy flushed. He often suspected an undercurrent of laughter in his mother's speeches, and in such discussions as these she seemed alien to him and to Ferring and to all the heritage of thoughts and manners and customs which they felt were their own.

'Yes, it is fortunate,' he said shortly, showing a most unusual touch of temper. 'Fortunate that I am much more my father's son than yours, I think.'

She raised delicately protesting eyebrows.

'Darling,' she murmured in a voice to match.

'Sorry, Mother. That was unpardonable,' said Derek stiffly.

'No, my dear. The truth often is unpardonable, but not in this case.'

When he had gone from the room on an obvious excuse, she turned to Rothe, who had been a silent, interested spectator.

'Amusing,' was her light comment, but there was a faint shadow in her eyes.

'You thought so?' asked Rothe.

She looked at him defensively.

'Didn't you? Isn't it amusing?'

'I suppose it is,' he said thoughtfully. 'Derek—Ferring—Bordray—Challissey—yes, I suppose it is.'

She left her chair suddenly and came to him, knelt at his side and rested her cheek for a rare moment of self-revelation against his shoulder.

'Let's be amused at it, Julian, and glad and happy about it. Isn't it marvellously right? Isn't everything for the best?'

Her voice was low and full and amazingly sweet.

His hand touched her hair for a second.

'Almost everything, my dear,' he said.

They were silent for a while. Then she rose to her feet and smiled down at him. It was a smile of hope and courage, those unquenchable lamps within her.

'I shall be in the sunshine in three days' time,' she said. 'Think of that!' for April in England was going out in rain and dull skies and shivery wind. 'With the sunshine and with you, my dear. Julian, are we wise, or fools, to do this year after year?'

'Fools because we have to do it year after year, Claire,' he said with passion.

'Ah Love! could thou and I with Fate conspire
To grasp this sorry Scheme of Things entire,
Would not we shatter it to bits – and then
Re-mould it nearer to the Heart's Desire!'

quoted Claire softly. 'Don't spoil anything with regrets, my dear. If we haven't learned by now to live for the moment, to take what we have and not grasp after what we can never have, we are no wiser than we were twenty years ago.'

'When I am with you, I am no wiser,' said Rothe unsteadily.

'Then I must be wise enough for two,' said Claire. 'If I'm to be that, you'd better go now and leave me to my packing and my last minute duties. We shall be together so soon now.'

'Au revoir, my dearest dear.'

'Bless you, Julian.'

Chapter Twelve

In the middle of May, Jennifer and Rothe went to Como.

She had never enjoyed anything quite so much in her life as she did that journey, once she had managed to shake from her mind the oppression of Bob's angrily resentful letter, his threats to her and her own feeling of guilt in going, in spite of Rothe's reasonable arguments.

She liked the crossing of the Channel, for she stood it well in spite of some pitching and tossing, and she was enthralled by the scene when they reached Boulogne, the blue-bloused porters clambering on the boat with their unceasing chant of *'Porteur, porteur,'* their businesslike briskness, the way in which they dealt without waste of words with inexperienced, nervous passengers who hesitated to allow their luggage to vanish from before their eyes in exchange for a metal disc or a scrap of cardboard.

She had her first lesson in travelling *en prince*, for Rothe engaged one of the porters exclusively, offering him fluently in his own language sufficient payment to compensate him for having no other passenger's luggage, and with swiftness and ease the two of them passed through the customs in the man's wake and were transferred to their first-class compartment in the train for Bale, whilst others were still struggling with opened cases and argumentative porters.

Rothe had engaged a sleeper for her, and she was surprised to find that she slept for hours, somewhat disconcerted by waking in the early morning to find a uniformed attendant unconcernedly busy in the compartment and arranging her breakfast-tray for her.

'Of course, I shouldn't have undressed had I realised what was going to happen,' she told Rothe afterwards.

He laughed.

'Jennifer, you're really priceless. How do you manage to remain a prude amongst us all?' he asked. 'Come over this side to get your first glimpse of the snow peaks. God, how I envy you! You've got the first experience of everything worth while in life still in front of you!'

Both of them seemed to have forgotten that she was married, that she had presumably had her first taste of much of life's experience. To her no less than to him, life seemed to be opening before her. She stood tiptoe, expectant, her face touched with the wonder and glory of things to come, viewing life much as she stood to view, awed, marvelling, with caught breath and no words, the grandeur of the eternal snows with the glory of the morning still upon them, and below them the rich green of the valleys and the rush and flung spray of the mountain torrents.

Jennifer's eyes filled with tears.

'It's—almost too much to bear,' she told him shakily, and he watched her curiously, exultantly. Here was no ice maiden but a living, pulsing woman with the fires in her heart waiting to be kindled.

They lunched on the train as it rushed through the lovely valleys of Switzerland, and Jennifer could scarcely eat or drink because of the steeping of her soul in unimaginable beauty.

'I didn't know anything in the world could be like this,' she told him, in breathless wonder. 'I wish we were going to stop here amongst the mountains.'

'Some day we will. You'll love Italy, though,' and he told her enough about Claire's villa, perched beside the lake, to reconcile her to the gradual changing of the scenery to gentler, more gracious valleys and mountains, though still in the distance they followed the snow peaks.

They had to spend a couple of hours in Lugano, and again Jennifer revealed herself as Rothe had not dared to hope she was. She found the streets of shops, the conventional public gardens, the white promenade along the edge of the lake, praiseworthy but uninteresting. Apart from the scenery round and above the town, which remained unchangingly lovely, she found nothing to inspire admiration save the huge fountain with its many gushing waters and its high-flung spray, iridescent in the sunshine.

'You're missing your cue, Jennifer,' he told her laughingly. 'Lugano is one of the show places for the tourist. They come hundreds of miles to spend ten days in it. What's the matter with it?'

'Oh—nothing's the matter. It's all very fine and splendid, of course, and everything shines and is very clean, but—that's what I really love,' lifting her eyes to the ridge of the mountains standing in their invulnerable might, unchangeable, silent, far above the petty frets and struggles of mankind.

'You're going to be a primitive, after all,' said Rothe, with satisfaction.

She turned her clear eyes on him, not understanding but glad if for once she came up to his desires.

The unhurried little steamer took them aboard and she was blissfully content to sit in the bow and watch the panorama of Italy unfold before her enchanted eyes, no longer resentful of man for adding to nature his fussy, ephemeral handiwork because even the houses had caught the magic of the lakes and the mountains, and lay dreaming in the sunshine, poised above the still water, hung with roses and wistaria which drooped over the pink and white walls and made the balconies places of fragrance and shadow.

Casually she was aware of officialdom on board, of the exchange from the polite, smiling Swiss to the remote Italian Government servants in their feathered hats, who seemed so suspicious of the foreigners who sought the hospitality of their country.

'I don't think they want to let us in,' remarked Jennifer when, after keeping their passports for an unconscionable time, they stamped and returned them with reluctance.

'Oh, they're the officials whose business it is to look important and maintain their fellows in salutary awe of them. You'll find the Italian people delightful. They are simple folk whose lives have not been complicated by too much knowledge. They don't belong to themselves and apparently don't want to. Their bodies are owned by Mussolini and their souls by the priests, and therefore they need take no responsibility for anything. The real trouble will begin here when

Mussolini falls out with Rome, if he lives long enough to do so. When the people have to choose between the owner of their bodies and the arbiter of their souls, they won't know what to do, and that's when Italy's likely to blow up. Anyway, it won't be during our holiday, so take that anxious look off your face and look at the little place in the corner. That's Porlezza, where we are going to get off and take the little railway for the last stage of the journey. You've stood it well.'

'I've loved it,' she said, and there was a touch of wistfulness in her voice.

'Yes?' he said.

'Nothing—only—I was thinking of my husband,' she said, and the inhuman devil that dwelt in Rothe at times chuckled to hear her tone and see the shadow in her eyes.

'Not out here, my dear. Husbands belong to England,' and she had a guilty feeling that Bob seemed even more unreal and incredible here than he had done in London.

At Porlezza they found the dirty, noisy little train awaiting them and belching out fire and smoke whilst Rothe claimed their registered luggage and conformed with the customs requirements, and at last they were chugging along the narrow track that wound along the hillside, clinging to it precariously, now high enough to see the waters of several lakes set like jewels amongst the mountains, now dropping down in the narrow valleys with their vineyards and pasturage and grazing cattle, their little bubbling streams fed by miniature waterfalls, which peeped in and out of the rugged mountain sides, losing themselves amongst the rocks and finding themselves again in laughing spray a hundred feet below.

They saw Como itself at last, suspended above it for a moment of unforgettable beauty. Like a sapphire set in a ring of emeralds, Italy's loveliest lake offered them the same unchanging beauty of which the ancient poets had sung, of which Virgil and the Plinys had written, which will still hold its deathless loveliness when we, too, shall be dust.

Jennifer's eyes were wet and even Rothe, hardened traveller and cynic, found no words with which to smirch that moment.

In a little while the lake was hidden again as the train took another of the bends which have made the Italian engineers world-famous. She turned misty eyes to him and her hands went out to him impulsively.

'Thank you for—that,' she said shakily. 'I shall never forget it. I shall never see anything so lovely again. It's—on my memory for ever.'

As they descended gradually, they passed through the tiny villages, scarcely even that, with their colour-washed cottages, the gardens and the little vineyards cultivated so assiduously by the industrious people who loved every inch of their country's soil as they loved and tended the many children of their body.

Jennifer thought of the thousands of acres of uncultivated land in her own country, where even a slight rise in the ground was enough excuse for the owner to abandon it to the grass and the scrub as not fit for cultivation. Here the peasants made the steep hillside yield its fertile crops of vine and maize and corn in their orderly rows, buttressing with stone walls, tier after tier, and making nothing of the toilsome climb up the rough paths which were serpentine because the hill was too steep for straight tracks.

At last they were dropping down towards the level of the water, and there was Claire in white frock and wide-brimmed hat, and Derek beside her with open-necked shirt and shorts showing his sunburnt skin, and behind them an ancient horse-drawn *carrozza* in which the driver slept peacefully and the old horse dozed between the shafts.

'Julian!' cried Claire, a younger, happier, strangely more beautiful Claire.

'My dear,' said Julian, and they stood clasping hands and looking at each other for so long that Derek, with a laugh, protested.

'Claire, my sweet, there *are* other people present,' he said, and she turned to greet Jennifer, to make her feel delightfully welcome.

'Derek, see to the luggage, and Julian, go and wake Benedetto up, will you? Come and get the first glimpse of the villa from here, Jennifer, before we go down. I always think it is such a welcoming sight. Look—the pink one at the edge of the water, with the wooden balcony and the two little towers on top. Can you see?'

Jennifer drew a deep breath.

'How—lovely,' she said softly, and Claire laughed a little low laugh of satisfaction and led her back to where Julian was completing the task of getting the smiling Benedetto back on the box whilst Derek and a porter loaded the luggage on to a truck.

'Everybody is smiling,' observed Jennifer, catching a glimpse of the white teeth of the brown-faced porter.

'Everybody's happy in Menaggio,' said Claire. 'I don't know if it's the air, or the scenery, or the sunshine, or just—Italy. I think a long-dead and obscure ancestor of mine must have been Italian and bequeathed to me a love of his country, for I always feel my very best and happiest and most beautiful in this lovely land.'

And, indeed, they all seemed different here, thought Jennifer, as they rumbled along behind the leisurely old horse, through Menaggio's narrow, cobbled streets, which were just waking after the mid-day siesta, and along by the water's edge to wards the pink Villa Felicita, so aptly named.

Smiling maids came out and the brother of Benedetto, Alfredo. Amidst chattering and laughter, the visitors and their luggage were brought into the dim, cool hall of the villa and made to feel that all life had been standing still waiting for this supreme hour of their coming.

Jennifer was taken to a wide and lovely room whose windows opened on to the balcony overhanging the lake. The walls were blue-washed and on them hung pictures of saints and of bovine madonnas and impossible babies. The furniture was of unstained, polished pine, and on the pinewood floor was a strip of gaily coloured matting.

Her Italian was, she found, good enough to ask for a bath, for the times of meals, and she discovered why her phrase books had taught her how to ask which was the electric light switch and which the bell, for they were both alike.

Maria, who was to attend to her, gave her information with smiling delight, and Jennifer went on to the balcony and looked out over the jewelled lake, sapphire water, emerald hills sloping down to its edge, and above them, against the sky, the eternal snows.

Her soul, starved of beauty through the childhood and girlhood so near the coal-fields, drank it in and felt a little dizzy from too much delight. It did something to her. She could scarcely bear it. She put her hand to her throat and felt the wild throbbing there which was like a bird struggling for release. She understood why Italy was the land of song, of romance and music. Surely, surely here she could sing as she longed to do, feel at last that the barrier which she had striven to break was gone. She had not needed the look in Rothe's eyes, the tone of his voice, the gesture of shrugged shoulders, to tell her that always there was something lacking, something which she did not know where to search for or to find.

Julian had said it was love that she needed.

Had she not known it? Hadn't she given and received in full measure from Bob?

For some reason she shivered suddenly and went back into her room, glad that the sound of the dressing-gong promised her other companionship than her own thoughts and that strange, intangible fear that had come to her.

They were very gay at dinner, Claire unbelievably lovely in some soft, misty blue which seemed the very spirit of Como, that indescribably delicate haze which invests everything with a bloom of enchantment which is the love and despair of the artist. It seemed so to invest Claire, to hide her enchanting spirit and yet to reveal it. Her eyes were veiled by it, her subtle and delicate wit, every movement and expression, coloured by it.

They sat by the long windows which were open to the flagged terrace overhung by the balcony, and a faint sweet wind made the stars of the jessamine tremble, and waft their fragrance into the room. The deft, dark-haired maids waited on them with smiles which brought the last touch of perfection to the unfamiliar Italian food with its little dishes of rice, of spaghetti, of the inevitable cheese.

Rothe seemed to Jennifer to be transformed into another man. His appalling rudeness, the bitter flavour of his speech, the apt, cruel aphorisms for which he was famous, had no place now in his words or looks. He was as simple as Jennifer herself, smiling at other people's little foolish jokes, adding to them bits which were pungent without being cruel, and so often his words hung in the air whilst he and Claire exchanged long, secret looks from which Jennifer found herself turning her eyes instinctively.

They had their coffee outside on the terrace, Giulio himself coming from his kitchen to serve them, a round, fat, little Giulio freshly arrayed in spotless white coat and apron, and high cook's hat.

'The signora is content?' he asked, with his wide smile touched with such an anxiety as might be caused by the balancing of the fate of nations.

'Supremely content, Giulio. You have excelled even yourself,' said Claire, and she raised her hand, broke off a spray of jessamine and gave it to him.

The balance of the nations was safe. Giulio bowed to the ground, came up smiling, lifted the jessamine spray above his head to contemplate it with rapture, laid it softly to his lips with eyes closed in ecstasy, and then pinned it to his breast with a pin miraculously produced from the lapel of his coat.

'Signora—signorina—signore ...' and he bowed himself out without the need for mere, inadequate words.

Claire laughed softly, affectionately, when he had gone.

'Dear Giulio! I love my Italian servants. One has a feeling for them which is quite impossible for English servants. Can you imagine Mrs. Purvis, my cook, coming to ask me after a dinner whether I were content? And can you see her face if I were to present her with a carnation from the decorations? That's where the people of the south score so much over us cold northerners. We are so afraid to be natural, so afraid to show our feelings, so afraid to deviate by one hair's breadth from the standard laid down for us by generations of people exactly like us. Here they are natural, free, individual. At home one scarcely knows, even after a fortnight's visit, the difference between the servants of the house. Here no one could possibly mistake Giulio and Benedetto, or Maria and Caterina and Elena.'

'You'll have to pension off old Benedetto, Claire,' said Derek from the depths of his chair.

He had definitely refused to change into conventional dinner clothes, though for this first night Rothe had done so. He wore a white-silk sports shirt, open at the throat, and white flannel trousers, with Italian sandals on his sockless feet.

'Why?' asked Claire.

'He does nothing but sleep, and why should you pay good money for people to sleep?'

Derek was a business-like young man, brisk and energetic, with little use for the idlers or the people who did nothing with their lives. He was a constant source of amusement to his mother, who complained because she had so little time to idle.

'But think what a glorious life I am able to give to just one human being, my sweet,' said Claire. 'It makes me feel god-like—or even more than a god, for they decree, according to the socialists, that to live man must work. What is it they say? He who will not work shall not eat.'

'You're encouraging a human being to waste his life,' argued Derek.

'My darling, can any life be wasted which is spent in the heavenly contemplation of this lake?' said Claire drowsily. 'Besides, Benedetto has worked hard all his life.'

'That's impossible, seeing that he has been working for you for twenty years at least,' retorted Derek.

'That's cruel and unnecessary,' said Claire, with a smile. 'Here in Italy I like to believe that the years drop from me and that the only person who could have worked for me for twenty years is my nurse. Go away, Derek. Go and walk off some of your beastly energy; climb mountains, swim across the lake, walk to the Villa d'Esta and see if Lotta is still there.'

He rose from his chair, flung a cushion at her and held out his hand to Jennifer.

'Come and rhapsodise over Como with me and leave our elders to their mutual admiration society, Jennifer,' he said. 'You don't mind my calling you Jennifer?'

'I like it better,' said Jennifer gravely, as she walked beside him out of the little garden and on to the white, dusty road behind it.

'Your name isn't really Rothe, is it?'

'No. It's Jenks, but Julian says no prima donna was ever called Jenks, so I have to let people call me Rothe.'

'Julian's a queer bird,' said Derek reflectively. 'He's such a stickler for doing the right thing in some ways, but in others he's so darned free. Coming out here to Como, for instance.'

'Does he often come?' asked Jennifer, as he broke off.

'Yes. Every year almost. Claire goes on strike about this time, tells Dad she can't stick London any longer, and bolts off here, and Julian generally bolts too.'

'It seems odd to hear you call your mother Claire. You don't call your father by his Christian name.'

'No. Dad's different. I'm terribly fond of Claire, of course. We've always been pals. But Dad's so fine, you know.'

'Is he?' asked Jennifer, vaguely but politely. She had been frightened and almost repelled by Guy Ferring, finding it very difficult to associate the cold-eyed, grave-voiced, unsmiling man with either Claire or Derek.

'Yes. You only meet him at Claire's parties and he hates things like that. He doesn't like women at all.'

'He must have liked one of them once, to marry your mother,' said Jennifer.

'I don't think so. He had to marry somebody. He's the heir to Lord Bordray, you know, and if he hadn't produced a son the title would die out. Claire thinks it's all tosh and wouldn't care a bit if titles all died out, but Dad's feudal. That's why he had Claire and Claire had me. Bit idiotic to have stopped at me, of course, because I might rub out and then they'd be in the soup, but that isn't my affair. Of course, I hope I don't rub out. I'm—oh, well, I suppose I'm a bit feudal myself.'

'You want to be a lord, you mean?' asked Jennifer, in her grave way.

'Well, I do, rather. Claire and Julian laugh at me, but I think I'm really more Dad's son than hers, though she always adopts the attitude that I belong to her and her alone, and that Dad's only incidental.'

'You're still at school, aren't you?' she asked suddenly.

He coloured and glanced at her quickly, suspecting that she was laughing at him, but she was quite serious and without *arrière-pensée*.

'I'm going up to Cambridge in September. I'm going to read for the Bar eventually. It's Claire's idea, though personally I think it's a bit waffey, and I'm never likely to want to practise. Still, I think everybody ought to have a living, a trade or a profession. Of course, when I'm Lord Bordray I shall have enough to do looking after my estates and my tenants and all that. I shall want to be a pukka landowner, and do the job well, so as to justify my ownership ...'

'Could anything ever do that?' put in Jennifer unexpectedly.

Derek stared at her.

'What do you mean by that?'

'Well, do you think anyone has any right to own things they haven't worked for?' she asked.

'Of course they have. Isn't that the very foundation of—of civilisation?' asked Derek, dumbfounded.

She had seemed so simple and meek and he had been enjoying himself, airing his pet themes to anyone so uninformed as he had supposed her to be.

'It is, but it shouldn't be,' said Jennifer firmly. 'Why should you, just because this man Lord Bordray happens to be a relation of your father's by no choice of yours, decide that you own hundreds of acres of land and buildings, industries, mines, and goodness knows what? Why should you rake in thousands of pounds from the sweat of other men's bodies, live on oysters and champagne which they've earned whilst they have only enough left for bread and margarine, keep your half dozen houses empty most of the year whilst they live in a couple of rooms and let the other two to pay the rent? Why do you go to Eton and Cambridge, holidays in Switzerland and Italy and Madeira, whilst the children of the men who earn the money for you go barefoot, hungry, and get half a day on a crowded beach once a year if their fathers have been allowed to work hard enough and long enough hours for you?'

She stopped, breathless, as amazed at herself as he was.

'Good lord,' he said at last. 'What are you? Communist? Bolshevik? Or what?'

'I'm sorry. I got a bit lost. You see, I don't belong to your sort of life. Your people aren't my sort of people, and I shall never belong with you. I see everything from the point of view of the poor, and you see it from that of the rich. It—well, it made my blood boil suddenly to hear you talking about being a lord, a good *owner.* Where we come from, we hate the owners like poison, and we should be glad to see every one of them wiped out.'

Derek managed to laugh a little at that. He could not believe that she was really serious. Of course, he had heard people talk like that. He had helped at the last general election, and the other side, fighting with the result a foregone conclusion, had said things like that – not that anyone took any notice of them, of course. There must be owners and workers, or where would you all be? The money must be in the hands of the people who knew how to spend it. Why, what would all these poor people do if they *had* money? Just spend it in ridiculous things, buying cars for themselves, fur coats for their wives, sending their children to expensive schools, where they would get quite wrong ideas. They wouldn't have the sense to save it, invest it in foreign securities or in the safe British concerns like armament factories, battleship-building and fighting planes. They'd simply squander it.

'I know you don't mean quite all you say,' he said. 'You wouldn't really like to see people like—well, like Claire and Julian wiped out? They're what you'd call the owning classes, I suppose?'

'Julian works,' said Jennifer shortly.

'And Claire?'

She frowned. That was the worst of it. She got so quickly out of her depth.

'I don't think I mean women quite as much as men,' she said. 'I suppose in her way your mother does work. There will always have to be politicians, and she must have great influence amongst the people she entertains for your father, and she is—good and kind and helpful.'

He laughed again.

'You're a fraud, Jennifer. You're just like the rest of us. You like to see people like Claire decorative and beautiful, and yet how could she be if she were poor and had to work, as you suggest? And take yourself, by the way. Aren't you living like the rest of us, and enjoying luxury you don't earn?'

'Yes, but I'm going to earn it. I don't live this way from choice, but because Julian says it is necessary and because I can't go on with my lessons if I don't go where he goes. But I'm going to pay it all back when I'm singing, and I'm going to do all I can for the people I've left behind there, my friends. I'm going to live my life for them.'

'Until you fall in love with someone and are idiot enough to marry him,' said Derek, eighteen.

She laughed rather sadly.

'I shall never do that,' she said, and thought of Bob, who seemed so remote a figure here in the heart-breaking loveliness of the jewelled Italian night.

They had strolled back and were turning into the gardens of the Villa Felicita almost they had realised it.

Claire still lay in her long chair, and Rothe sat beside her, the scent of her cigarette mingling with that of his cigar, their murmuring talk and a little ripple of her laughter drifting over the scented garden.

She looked up as they came to the terrace.

'Well, you two? What have you been doing? Dreaming Romeo and Juliet beside the lake, or lying on your backs in a vineyard moon worshipping?'

They laughed and looked at each other, aware suddenly that they had seen nothing of the magic of the night, and Jennifer, at least, had no idea where they had walked.

'We've been improving our minds and just saving our tempers, trying to save the constitution,' said Derek.

Claire made a gesture of mock dismay and incredulity.

'Just talking, arguing, on a night like this, and Jennifer's first night in Como? Oh, Derek, Derek! To think you're truly son of mine!'

Derek laughed and went to sit on the end of her chair. He thought how lovely she looked, how young and happy.

'It's hard to believe it, my sweet, tonight,' he said, and she caught the look of admiration in his eyes and laughed again, softly and more sweetly.

'You're terribly nice, Derek,' she said. 'Why is it my bad luck that you should be my *son*? What a waste of our two temperaments!'

'You forget that when I take a lady walking in Italy I talk to her of economics,' laughed Derek.

She shook her head.

'Not if I were the lady and other than your mother, you wouldn't,' said Claire. 'Jennifer, are you tired? You ought to be. I never sleep a wink on the way out here.'

'I'm not very tired,' said Jennifer, who had watched the little play between this modern mother and son with interest. She found it difficult to understand such a relationship, but then, she reflected with a touch of bitterness, the mothers she had known had not the time nor the money to look as young as Claire Ferring, and their sons, at Derek's age, were either down the pits or lounging about at street corners in hopeless, despairing, soul-destroying idleness.

Claire lifted her arms above her head, stretched a little and sighed.

'What a thing it must be to be twenty-two! I'm tired and I've done nothing all day. Let's go to bed,' and she rose and linked an arm in Jennifer's and one in Derek's whilst Rothe stayed to pick up her wrap and then followed them into the house.

'What a waste to bring you young things to Italy, the land of love and romance, of soft laughter in the darkness, of a song broken by a kiss. All that to choose from—and you quarrel about politics and economics! Heavens! A moment ago I envied you. Now I'm glad to be myself, Claire Ferring, forty odd and still able to feel romantic on a night like this.'

She paused at Derek's door to turn a queer, enigmatical smile on him, kissed him and took Jennifer along to her room overlooking the lake.

'You like your room, Jennifer?' she asked the girl, turning on the light and looking round to see that everything had been done for her guest's comfort.

'It's lovely,' said Jennifer, a little wistfully.

Claire hesitated a moment.

'I want you to be happy,' she said, almost passionately. 'Happiness is your right—the right of all young things. I wish I could take all the happiness of the world into my hands and break it into all the million parts which would give just one little bit, one perfect bit, to all the young things there are. Are you going to be happy, my dear? I wonder.'

After she had gone Jennifer opened her windows wider and watched the lights across the water as she undressed. They were like a string of diamonds round the lake, twinkling and glinting, sending a myriad reflections into the water to mingle with the mirrored points of lights that were the stars in heaven's blue night.

Somewhere, unseen, a boat drifted in the darkness and someone was singing. His voice floated through the velvet night, pure, effortless, heart-searching. Jennifer knew herself to be seeking something, to be restless and dissatisfied and incomplete without it. She longed passionately to be a part of all this beauty, and yet something held her back, kept her outside the charmed circle, left her wandering with hands outstretched to drag aside the curtain which would not let her pass. Claire was within it, and Rothe – and Derek, it seemed, had no desire to enter. Only she stood outside alone, clamouring for entry.

Would that curtain ever be drawn aside so that she, too, might step within?

Chapter Thirteen

Golden days and jewelled nights spun themselves miraculously into a week, and Jennifer felt almost as if she belonged to this lotus life at the edge of the lake.

They did nothing, for there was nothing to do, and Rothe declared himself too lazy for work, and yet the days sped by as they had never done before.

She and Derek lay one morning face upwards on the little raft which was moored just near enough to the shore for Jennifer to reach, with a frantic struggle, after a week's intensive swimming tuition from Derek, to whom water seemed his native element.

'I think you've learned to swim jolly quickly,' Derek told her with a condescension she did not at all resent. Physically he seemed like a young god to her, and as such he was within his rights in dictating to her and bullying her as far as physical prowess went, however much she might fight him and despise him on matters of thought and politics.

'I dare say I'm too tall and thin ever to make a really good swimmer,' she said regretfully, though she was secretly puffed up with pride in having been able to reach the raft and trying to forget that she still had to get back to the shore.

'Oh, I don't know. People taller than you can swim. Look at Brenner Mayne. He's tall and he won heaps of pots for swimming for Trinity. He can swim across to Ballagio from here and he's going to let me have a shot at it with him when he comes.'

'Is he coming, then?' asked Jennifer quickly.

'Yes. Didn't you know? We don't know exactly when, but it'll be one day this week. I'm jolly glad. I like him.'

She lay very still, her eyes closed against the fierce Italian sunshine, which it is so difficult for English people to treat as the enemy it often is. Claire warned her continually, made her wear a hat, cover her shoulders, and use various creams and lotions, and mercifully the girl's skin showed no sign of the hideous burns and blisters which might have disfigured it after so much unaccustomed roasting.

'What are you thinking about?' Derek asked her presently, idly.

'I don't know,' said Jennifer, but she lied. She knew that she was thinking of Brenner Mayne, remembering every least thing about him, picturing him here with them, living in the same house, sharing every meal – daytime and evening-time, sunshine and the magic of the blue Italian nights.

'Well, you ought to be. You ought to be thinking about getting back before you begin to burn. What about it?'

She turned over and rose to her feet on the swaying raft, a little sick at the thought of that struggle to a shore which seemed incredibly far away.

'Come on,' said Derek, standing for a moment on the edge, a muscular young giant, godlike, and then diving into the blue depths with scarcely a ripple on the water to show where he had cleaved it.

His head reappeared and he began to swim leisurely back towards her.

'Stand on the second step and push off gently,' he advised her. 'Don't make a splash or you'll get it in your mouth and it'll wind you. Come on. You can do it all right. I won't let you go under.'

Closing her eyes and feeling like death, she did as he told her, the water icy cold to a body half roasted by the sunshine, and from the grassy shore in front of the villa Rothe and Claire called encouragement. After what seemed an eternity of effort, she struggled to the steps of the stone embankment, climbed up and threw herself down, laughing and panting on the grass.

Claire had a telegram in her hand.

'The train to meet after lunch, Derek,' she said, fluttering it at him.

'Who?' he asked, with a frown.

'Brenner,' she said, and the frown cleared magically.

'Good egg! What's the time now?'

'Quarter of an hour to lunch. Can you do it, both of you?'

Jennifer scrambled to her feet, consciously glad of the need for effort and the excuse for taking herself out of range of Rothe's penetrating, inscrutable eyes. It was as if he could, if he chose, look into that secret place in her being into which she dare not even look herself.

'I can, after a style,' she laughed, and fled, with Derek at her heels.

Rothe looked after them complacently.

'She's beginning to look marvellously fit,' he commented. 'Derek's doing her good, too. Taking some of the premature staidness off her, making her young for probably the first time in her life, poor kid. She's beginning to look like twenty-two instead of forty-two. She's getting almost good-looking as well.'

Claire looked at him as she threw herself down in a long chair under one of the cypresses which are so essential a feature of Italy's lakesides, eternal exclamation marks to wonder at the unearthly beauty about them and to point for ever towards God in His heaven, their tops turning over into the question mark which is His sign manual.

'You're an inhuman devil, Julian,' said Claire. 'Give me a cigarette.'

He lit one for her and set it between her lips.

'No. Human,' he corrected.

'To make a bonfire of that girl's life for your own ambition?' she asked him.

'To make a bonfire of her self-satisfaction, the false mask she wears, believing it to be her face, the cotton wool and swaddling-clothes in which her soul is being suffocated almost before it is born—yes,' he said.

'I can't help having a sneaking pity for the husband,' said Claire reflectively.

She seemed quite impersonal about the affair, as she was just now about everything that did not touch her intimately. A lamp was alight within her, a lamp to beautify her, to illumine her and give her an unreal, magic allure, a lamp to cast about her a circle of light which shut into the darkness everything outside it – Jennifer, Mayne, her husband, Derek even. Inside the charmed circle she saw only herself and Julian Rothe.

'Why?' asked Rothe. 'I haven't any. He did a criminal act in marrying her. The only thing he can do to rectify it is to set her free at the first opportunity.'

'Free? To marry Brenner, you mean?'

He shrugged his shoulders.

'Why marriage at all? Free, I said.'

'He won't set her free, of course,' said Claire.

'No. He belongs to the class which says, "What I have, I hold, and what I haven't, I'm jolly well going to get." He's got Jennifer and he'll hold on to her, if she'll let him.'

'Which she will.'

'I don't know. She'll have Brenner Mayne to reckon with by then,' he said thoughtfully. 'Coming in to lunch?'

He drew her to her feet and held her at arm's length for a moment.

'Happy?' he asked her.

'Oh, Julian—happy!' she told him, with a little sigh, and with his arm about her they went into the dim, cool room, where Caterina waited to serve them.

Afterwards Jennifer and Derek set out to meet the train which would bring their guest, whilst Claire and Rothe went upstairs to sleep, in true Italian fashion, until the day cooled down.

Jennifer was never tired of watching Menaggio drowse under the afternoon sun, for she was quite unable to catch the trick herself, and Derek seemed never to need rest, never to feel the heat of the sun.

They climbed slowly up the steep, cobbled streets, where the brown canvas curtains were hung from the edges of the shop blinds down to the pavements, making dark avenues of shade beneath which the shopkeepers drowsed at their doors; even the children stopped their play to creep into doorways or into corners where boxes or piles of merchandise threw cool shadows.

They paused to look down at the lake's edge, at the covered curved tops of the boats beneath which protruded somnolent pairs of legs. Beneath a patched black awning, a stonemason lay on his side with his tools scattered about him, his head resting placidly on the tombstone he had been carving when sleep overtook him.

Outside the station horses slept between the shafts of the *carrozzas* which awaited possible passengers from the train, and inside the vehicles the drivers slumbered peacefully, sprawled across the seats. A porter had drawn his trolley into the shade of the open waiting-room and was curled up on it, fast asleep. Within the booking-office the station-master and general factotum lay back in his chair, his feet out at the open door.

It was a 'still' portrait of Menaggio in the sun, but the next moment it was as if some giant hand had switched on the power that turned the 'still' into a motion picture, for at the sound of the fussy little engine's shrill whistle the sleepers awoke and went about their business without even stretching themselves. The station-master came out on to his station with his flags, the porter pushed his trolley down the platform, the drivers climbed out of their *carrozzas* and on to the driving-seats, whilst from the various streets which converged on the station came the hotel porters, wiping their damp brows preparatory to putting on their gold-lettered caps.

Only the horses went on sleeping. They would be prodded into motion, anyhow, if they had to move, so with philosophic calm they waited for that moment to dawn. It might never come, for few people arrived in Menaggio by the noon train other than the peasants, who did not engage the *carrozzas*.

Jennifer's heart missed a beat and then went on racing again at sight of Mayne's tall, lean figure, at the eager, questioning glance around him which turned to gladness at sight of the two in their whites, with old Benedetto smiling behind them. He met every train of the day whilst Claire was in residence at the villa, though no one either asked him to do so or expected it. It was his job, and he did it mechanically – that and nothing else nowadays. It was pleasant dozing under the trees outside the station, he and his old horse, and if by chance anyone did come on the train, there would be a lira or two for him.

Brenner took their outstretched hands, Jennifer's and Derek's.

'Bless you, my children! Glad to see your old uncle again, returned from furrin' parts?' he asked them joyously. 'Derek, you look too healthy to be decent, and what have they done to you, Jennifer? You look—'

'Yes?' asked Jennifer laughingly, as he paused.

'I'll tell you about that another time,' he said. 'One suitcase, Benedetto. How's the *reumatico*? Though no one ought to have *reumatico* in this blessed land of the sun.'

He stood speaking to the old man for a moment, in his manner the same easy charm that made Claire blessed with good service. Jennifer resolved that if ever she were wealthy enough to have servants, she would cultivate just that same manner.

Benedetto found the suitcase and hoisted it into the old four-wheeler with which Claire would never dispense whilst he was alive, and the three started to walk down the hill, the world about them preparing to relapse into slumber again as soon as the train had been persuaded to go away and leave them to it.

'Are you liking it as much as you thought?' Mayne asked Jennifer as they went.

'I'm loving it. It's making me feel as if I had never lived before, certainly making me sure that I've never even dreamed of beauty before,' she told him.

He gave a sigh of satisfaction.

'That's how I wanted you to feel about it,' he said.

She looked at him quickly.

'You knew I was here?'

'Of course,' he said, very quietly, and Derek looked at the two of them and began to whistle a little tune and flick at the jessamine hedge as they passed beneath its fugitive shadow.

Jennifer did not speak again until they came to the pink villa, dreaming beside the lake.

'They'll be asleep,' she said. 'Claire asked me to apologise. She says when you see her at tea-time you'll see her radiant instead of limp.'

He smiled. 'Haven't you succumbed to the idea yet?' he asked her.

'I can't. I don't want to miss an hour of the sunshine. I've been starved of it all my life and feel I can't possibly have enough.'

They lay in long chairs on the terrace until tea-time, talking desultorily, dozing, now and then sipping gratefully at the iced lemon-juice which Caterina brought them, and which is so utterly different from what Jennifer had always known as 'lemonade', for Giulio had picked the lemons that morning from the grove behind the villa, and the sun-ripened juice had gushed into the glasses with none of the tardy reluctance of the sad little lemons of the English kitchens.

At half past four Claire came down to her cup of English tea which nothing could make actually like English tea, though she imported it herself and had to pay an enormous duty on it, and Luigio made it. It is the quality of the water itself, Claire averred, but she could not bring herself to substitute coffee or the iced drinks beloved of her guests.

Mayne thought again how lovely she was, how changeless and ageless was her charm that had so little to do with features or colouring or clothes, though all of them enhanced it. She would be charming at sixty, in rags in a slum, he thought, but was glad that her beauty should be so fittingly set, that she should have the riches which enabled her to exploit her fascinations for their delight.

'Brenner, how *satisfying* to have you here,' she said giving him her hands as he rose to meet her. 'You look in need of Italy, too.'

'Suggesting that I look old and haggard?' he asked. 'I felt both of them until I had left England behind me. They're having a spell of truly spring weather—rain and hail, with daily threats from the B.B.C. of new depressions from Iceland.'

'You're a fraud, Brenner. You know that in your heart you're fiercely British, and that one has only to utter a single disparaging word for you to go all England-my-England about it,' said Claire. 'We're out here, Julian, and the children have managed to tow Brenner in.'

The two men exchanged greetings, and it seemed to Jennifer as if there were something oddly wary in their attitude to each other, as if each waited for the other to make the move which neither of them did actually make.

'How's business?' asked Rothe. 'May I have orange juice, Caterina? With a lot of sugar?'

'Quiet for the moment,' said Mayne.

'No nice juicy murders? Bodies in trunks and what not?' asked Derek with relish.

'Not a thing, unfortunately,' replied Mayne, with a grin. 'I'm just waiting for something really sensational to happen, something with love and passion, and plenty of blood to entrance the female newspaper readers.'

'You ghouls,' said Claire.

'You're a fraud,' said her son calmly. 'You know you read them yourself.'

'I admit it,' she laughed. 'They're such a welcome change from the bloodless crimes against which there is no law because they are merely political murders and destroy in sufficient quantities to be called wars instead of mere murders. There's honesty in a man upping and killing a faithless friend, or a nagging wife. There's no honesty in men sitting in high places and sending men to kill other men against whom they have no grudge in order that personal and national greed may be satisfied.'

'That's an odd statement for the wife of a cabinet minister in the present government,' said Rothe, with a grin.

She laughed and spread out disclaiming hands.

'I'm not the wife of a cabinet minister out here,' she said. 'I'm just Claire Ferring on holiday, and the world may do what it likes so long as it leaves me Como for a while. Anybody bathing? I'd like to.'

They went to their rooms, to reappear in bathing-suits on the little patch of grass which the gardener watered continually to encourage it to keep green under the scorching sunshine, and for an hour or more business and affairs of state mattered not a jot to any of them. Derek and Jennifer and Mayne swam out to the raft, and then, encouraged by the two men, she swam between them further out, gaining confidence from their nearness and succeeding in reaching the jutting edge of rock which formed one of the arms between which the Villa Felicita was set. They helped her to climb it, and she perched there, laughing and triumphant, and feeling herself to be on top of the world.

Claire and Rothe, whom the others seemed instinctively to leave together, were in the battered old bathing boat drifting about on the almost motionless surface of the water, for Claire's desire for action had been fleeting and she loved this lotus life which made no demands on her of any sort. Rothe, pulling occasionally on an oar to keep them from drifting too far and scandalising the natives, looked supremely content.

A warning gong brought them reluctantly in, Mayne swimming very near to Jennifer in case she tired, and when they reached the shore they exchanged one of those long, slow glances which seem to mean so little but actually linger in the memory afterwards.

They had dinner on the terrace, a gay, friendly, intimate little meal so charmingly different from the 'affairs' in the great dining-room in Carlton House Terrace, and they were split up quite naturally into pairs by the arrival of Lotta, a little Italian girl, the daughter of a school friend of Claire's who had always had the run of the Villa Felicita during its few weeks of occupation.

She was a dark, vivacious little thing, gaily setting her cap at Derek, who admired her enormously, but was still of the age when he felt it necessary to hide his admiration zealously.

'Will you sing to us, Jennifer?' asked Claire, when they had finished and the table had been taken away, leaving them to their cigarettes and coffee and the soft Italian starlight. 'I feel in the mood for soft music.'

Jennifer glanced at Rothe inquiringly, and he nodded and went in with her. There was a piano in one of the rooms opening on the terrace so they could hear her without moving. She was glad. She liked the thought of singing to them whilst they sat there.

'Nervous?' asked Rothe, for she had not yet sung to them.

'No, I don't think so,' she replied serenely. 'What shall I sing?'

He made the choice for her, a little cynically. He found her serenity irritating and hard to understand. She had shown him she had emotional possibilities, and yet not even Italy and Como had brought her voice to life.

She sang beautifully the aria he chose first, followed it by a complicated setting of an old Italian song, and then he gave her one or two operatic airs which tried her powers considerably but which she sang artistically and in a manner which did him credit.

Outside, Derek listened with little appreciation, for he had no delight in music, and presently he and Lotta slipped down the steps into the garden and stole away guiltily.

Claire listened with understanding, critically, unhappily aware of what Rothe must be feeling, conscious of the lack in the beautiful voice, that lack which would for ever prevent the girl from becoming the great singer he desired her to be – unless something or someone supplied the thing lacking.

Mayne lay back in his chair and remembered the voice of the Singing Lady: the tenderness, the passion, the appeal with which she had sung the sweet, old songs which Rothe would have disdained, and which would have so little meaning in Claire's expensive entourage, for though life at the Villa Felicita was called by them 'the simple life', it was not the simplicity which included the deathless old ballads Jennifer had sung with her heart as well as her voice.

They congratulated her politely when she and Rothe rejoined them, but she felt that somehow she had struck a jarring note by her singing and, a little unhappy and forlorn, she made excuses as soon as she could and slipped away to her room.

By morning she was restored to normal, the slight shadow forgotten, and they spent the time until lunch wandering about the stalls grouped about the steps of the church and along the narrow streets, for it was market day and everyone was to be met there on such occasions.

The scene enchanted Jennifer with its gaiety, its colour and life and noise, its laughter and bargaining buyers and sellers appearing almost to be coming to blows at one moment, shouting and gesticulating, the next moment smiling and bowing and exchanging friendly greetings whether the bargain had been concluded or not.

Derek had chosen to spend the morning in the water, as usual, so Jennifer found herself with Mayne, whilst Claire and Rothe went on a search for a particular shade of silk to match a frock.

To her delight Jennifer found her own knowledge of Italian better than his, though both of them had recourse to the phrase book and dictionary, which she carried about with her unfailingly, and which they laid before them previous to completing a transaction and used with amusement to themselves and delight to the smiling Italian vendors. He bought one or two trinkets in the delicate filigree work which abounded, chose lengths of silk from the gaily streaming draperies which hung from the stalls, and, since it was unusual for anyone to want purchases wrapped up, carried them over his arm with an unconcern which delighted the others when they met again.

Claire felt frivolous. She insisted on buying hats for the two men, those round, shallow felts which look so essentially 'foreign', and in which they looked ridiculous but which they both wore with an air. For herself and Jennifer she bought huge cartwheel straws and laced sandals of red and green and blue stripes, which were delightful to wear in a climate where leather shoes quickly became an abomination to hot, swollen feet.

She wanted to call on Lotta's mother in Cernobbio, so they drove there for lunch, Jennifer and Mayne choosing to go to a small restaurant rather than to the luxurious and ornate Villa d'Este.

'Don't wait for us if you want to move on afterwards,' Claire told them. 'Derek and Lotta will probably swim, and Julian and I may stay in the cool with Alice till later.'

They found a little restaurant which had a balcony overhanging the lake and they sat under a striped orange awning, with jessamine sprays touching their heads when they moved.

'Let's have a real Italian lunch,' said Mayne. 'Nothing we have at home, if we can help it,' and they chose from the menu things which, at least, sounded unfamiliar, speculating with laughter and nonsense as to the constituents of the various dishes which were set before them.

They drank Orvieto, though he said they should have the thin, sour red wine of the district, and afterwards the fat, smiling landlord came out to them and offered them the luck of the house in a fruity, potent drink which went to Jennifer's head and made her laugh and talk, and even sing. What did that matter in Italy? Mine host produced a violin and played a sweet old Italian folk-song to them, and they caught the lilt of it, and sang it with him to no words that are in any known language, but which have been in the hearts of men and women since the world began.

Jennifer thought, 'Fancy doing this in England!' but it did not disturb her, and her lovely voice rang out clear and sweet and heart-stirring, and they all forgot everything in the world but themselves and one another.

The waiter came out in his greasy apron and joined in after a time, and Mayne sat Jennifer on the edge of the stone balcony and held her with his arm whilst Antonio swayed before them with his violin, and beneath the jessamine Giorgio, the waiter flung into the perfumed air glorious notes which would have ravished a Covent Garden audience, but which they would never hear.

Claire and Rothe heard the concert as they drove back and stopped in the road to wait for its conclusion.

'It's Jennifer,' she said softly.

'I know. Have you ever heard that note in her voice before?' he asked triumphantly, and when at last they went through the restaurant and out on to the balcony, it was to see a transformed Jennifer taking from Antonio a great spray of pink rambler roses, whilst Mayne, half laughing, half in earnest, crowned her dark head with jessamine, and Giorgio bowed to the floor in delighted approval of her.

Rothe told them that Jennifer was to be a great prima donna, and Antonio brought out his squat little bottle again and insisted that they must drink to her, and she sat on the balcony rail and held her first court, and her eyes went from one to another in gladness and laughter, and something akin to tears.

How kind they were! How good to her and how dear!

'Thank you—thank you—*grazie, grazie*!' she said, and gave them her hands and her heart.

Brenner Mayne was always to remember her like that.

Chapter Fourteen

Jennifer had been at the Villa Felicita for three weeks, twenty-one jewels, diamonds and sapphires and emeralds strung on a chain of gold and a chain of silver, and it seemed that she had never existed anywhere else but in this land of sunshine and laughter, nor lived anything but this lotus life of idleness.

Rothe insisted on certain hours of work, but for the most part she was free as he had intended she should be whilst Mayne was there. Derek and Lotta had discovered the gentle art of fishing, and most of their time was spent in an old boat catching the delicious lake fish which they ate at dinner. Claire, with Rothe never far from her, seemed entirely content to be lazy, and they spent their time for the most part between the garden and the lake, though once or twice she went to pay state visits, exquisitely dressed, at neighbouring villas whose ladies had called on the notable English visitor.

Jennifer and Mayne had no fault to find with the arrangements. They explored the lakeside together, often taking their bathing kit and their lunch and buying a bottle of wine, or of the delicious *aranciate*, to carry with them to quiet little spots they found by the water's edge, or up on the mountain slopes with trees interlacing over their heads and the ice-cold waterfalls babbling beside them.

Sometimes they hired a car, or old Benedetto drove them in his ancient vehicle to one of the little villages nestling beneath the rocky slopes or hanging precariously above the level of the lake. From there they would walk, losing themselves amongst the rough mountain paths but always knowing that they would come out again to some spot from which they could see the gleaming waters of Como and the white ribbon of the road which edges it.

On one such day they burrowed through a leafy tunnel high up on the side of the mountain and emerged to find themselves perched up above a little stone-built village, with half its houses in ruins, its church dominating them as it does in all Italian villages. However poor the people, however badly in need are their homes and their children and their poor flocks, the church was never in need of repair nor the priests hungry.

Jennifer was not thinking along those lines, though. She lay on a grassy ledge which they had found, Mayne's coat spread over their legs to keep off the mosquitoes and midges, a tree festooned with wild briony protecting their bare heads from the sun.

It was the magic after-lunch hour when the world about them slept. She had come to love that hour almost as much as the moonlit darkness of the night. At first she had been afraid of the loneliness they shared, afraid because it was so sweet to share it with him. Then came recklessness borne of the ecstasy she had never before known, and she let herself drift, refusing to look ahead, closing her eyes and her mind to everything save this gift of the gods – the magic of Como and of Brenner Mayne.

It seemed to matter no more to him than to her whither they were drifting. He woke each day of blue and gold to the glory of a world which held the woman of his dreams, and went to bed on each night of silver and diamonds with the memory of a day shared with her, finding new wonder in her, new peace and a new unrest.

It was difficult to remember that she was married. All that part of her life that did not hold him seemed unreal and unsubstantial. She never spoke of her husband, wore no ring, and seemed utterly content to be without him.

Where would it end? Where could it end? Mayne was not of the type to take marriage lightly, neither his nor any other man's, but it was impossible to think of Jennifer as a wife to another man. She was like a dreaming child, untouched, with none of the delicate bloom gone, and yet, with every look, every tone of her voice, a woman, standing on the brink of life's knowledge.

In their long talks they had plumbed many depths, had come to know intimately each other's minds, aspirations, ideals, and fears. For each of them was the dream of service to their fellows. She told him much of her early life and of the passionate desire to help which was the outcome of the suffering and privations which she had witnessed during all her most impressionable years. He came to know the essential honesty and sweetness of her mind, her total lack of artifice, her humility and lack of self-appreciation.

And Jennifer learned of the strength of this man, of a life which in its own way held as much struggle and privation as the lives of which she told him. His mother, deserted by her husband when her three children were still at school, Brenner himself only ten years old, had been and still was his guide, philosopher, and friend, a courageous, fearless woman whose boundless ambition for her children had thrust them up and out into a world which only sheer toil could master. All three of them had worked for their education by winning scholarships, the foremost ever stretching down a helping hand to the others, none of them ever neglecting anything which might benefit them or help to fulfil their mother's ambition for them.

And they had won out. Brenner, at thirty-two, had already made a name for himself and was spoken of as having a great future before him when he had added age and experience to his brilliance. Anthony, two years older, was a surgeon of some repute, and their one sister, Mira, had been head of a large training college for women, before she married, and married well.

All this he had told her during those long walks. Only one thing they had never said with their lips, nor had Jennifer ever dared to say it in her heart. She just knew that she was happy with sweet pain and that for a little while the world was standing still for them.

Below them, as they sat in their leafy shelter, the lake dreamed in loveliness. Nothing moved and, except for the chirrup of grasshoppers, there was no sound. There was not even a steamer on the lake, and a boat moored some distance from the shore lay motionless, a toy on a sheet of glass.

'It's like the old fairy tale of the Sleeping Beauty,' said Jennifer softly, whispering as if her voice might shatter the illusion. 'Everything has been sleeping for a hundred years.'

Mayne looked at her. During these weeks, her fine, mobile face had acquired some new, indefinable quality, something that was almost beauty. It was younger, gentler, more rounded, and in her eyes were dreams.

'And at the end of the hundred years, didn't the princess wake up?' he asked her.

'Did she? The prince had to come first, though, and cut his way through the thorns and brambles to reach her,' she said dreamily.

'Perhaps it wasn't in a house at all that she went to sleep! It may have been on the hillside, under a tree.'

'Oh no! That was the whole point of the story, you see. The hedge grew up and round the palace so that it should be hard for anyone but the prince to wake her,' said Jennifer.

'I wonder what would have happened to the rest of the story if when the prince had cut down the hedge and torn away the brambles and got into the palace, the princess had turned on him a look of blank dismay and told him he wasn't the right prince at all?' asked Mayne, watching the expressive face and the dark, changeful eyes of Jennifer.

A little flame of colour ran up into her cheeks and in her eyes was a hint of fear.

'That isn't the way it happens in fairy tales,' she said. 'It's always the right prince that gets through.'

'She'd know if the wrong one got through?' he asked. 'She wouldn't wake for any but the right one?'

She did not answer, but sat looking at him with face grown grave and eyes that pleaded with him.

When he spoke again, there was that in his voice which she had never heard before, which no woman had ever heard before from Brenner Mayne.

'Jennifer, my dear, my dear, why didn't you wait?' he asked her.

She could not take her eyes from him then, did not want to. She let him see that lovely thing that was there, that frightened thing, that wistful thing.

He groped for her hand in the grass and held it closely within his own.

'I shall love you till I die,' he told her. 'Oh, my love, my dear, give me a little of your love, a little of yourself.'

It seemed that neither of them moved, and yet she was in his arms, his mouth on hers and all the world about them forgotten in that moment that was heaven.

'I love you,' she said against his lips. 'More than life or death, my own darling,' and her lovely voice broke on the words and yet made of them the music of the spheres, for they were the first notes of a woman's soul.

Whilst time stood still for them, they kissed and clung, and when at last he released her and let her sink gently back on the grass beside him they knew that for neither of them would life ever be the same again.

She closed her eyes and he saw the slow tears well beneath her lids and bent to kiss them away, resentfully, pitifully.

'No tears for our love, my Jennifer,' he said.

She dashed them away and smiled through them.

'Oh, Brenner, it's too much to bear,' she said quiveringly. 'Too much happiness. It hurts me here,' with a hand at her breast.

It was so strange a revelation of their love, for there was no past for them, no future, nothing but the fleeting present.

Inevitably she spoke of her husband.

'Just now I can't feel anything but happiness, but when I am alone, tonight, I shall have to remember—Bob,' she said in a low voice which inevitably held shame, for she was no wanton, no light woman to whom a kiss meant nothing. She had given to this beloved man the heart from the body which belonged to another, and the knowledge was bitter.

'Jennifer, why did you do it?' he asked her desperately.

'You know. We talked about it that night before I went back. You remember?'

'Yes! I didn't know you then. Oh, God! I could have stopped you then and yet I let you go! Jennifer, you can't go back. You can't go on with that. You belong to me, for ever and ever.'

She shook her head and looked out across the still blue lake with eyes which saw a mining village.

'No! That's where I belong, Brenner—there and to Bob,' she said with such certainty of conviction that he felt already he had lost her. 'I must go back. I ought to have gone when—when you came here.'

'You cared for me then?'

'Yes, though I didn't know it. Ah, yes, I did, I did! I knew it so long ago that I've almost forgotten the time when I didn't know it.'

He gathered her into his arms again and held her there, kissing her unresponsive lips until he forced response from them and she gave him passionate kisses for his own and broken murmurs of love for the rapture he showered upon her.

'I have loved you since the beginning of time,' he whispered to her. 'I have waited for you, known that somewhere in the world God must have made you because he set your image in my heart to keep there until you came. Oh, Jennifer, my love, my dear.'

And so, above the dreaming beauty of Como, they told their love, in broken words and kisses, with always the tears behind them because of what might have been and could not be.

At last they rose to go, slowly, reluctantly, knowing that this hour could never come again for them, that life would never be able to give them just that ecstasy again, that first kiss and the touch of arms no longer withheld.

They spoke little as they went, Jennifer both exalted and abased, Mayne busy with more practical problems, not content as it seemed she was to let life beat them down and snatch from them this lovely thing for ever.

'You won't let the others know?' she asked in a low voice as they came down to the white road again and found old Benedetto still dozing peacefully beside the patient Edoardo.

'Of course not'; but he knew that Claire and Rothe, at least, had guessed how it was with them, even though Jennifer had been dreaming along in ignorance of her own emotions.

'I should hate anybody else to know. It would—would make it seem unclean, somehow, sordid,' she said. 'I couldn't bear that.'

'Nor I, my darling,' he said gravely.

'Oh, Brenner, I do love you so,' she told him with a little break in her voice.

He caught her hand and squeezed it hard for a moment. There was no time for anything else, for Benedetto had managed to wake Edoardo and was ready to move.

'Come, Edoardo,' he exhorted his steed. 'Think you that the signor and the signorina want to wait your pleasure all the day?'

'Why do you call him Edoardo, Benedetto?' asked Mayne as they ambled along in the dusty cloud made by the horse's hoofs.

'After your so great King Edoardo,' said the old man, who was proud of his ready English, acquired heaven knew how. 'Me, I *garzone* in hotel in Mentone when the lord Edward of England he stay there when he was lord of Walls before to be king. Very great man he was, very good, very large in the pocket,' and he slapped his empty pockets and sighed reminiscently, not offended at all by the laughter with which they greeted his story.

It was almost a relief to Jennifer and Mayne to find that Claire had visitors, for it kept them from thinking too much of themselves and each other, made demands on them which gave them leisure for nothing else.

When they had gone, Claire looked mischievously into Derek's dark, brooding face and moody eyes. He had contributed so little to the conversation that one might almost have accused him of boorishness, though Cora Hesselton's extreme brightness had served as a cover for it.

'Derek, my loved one, they've gone, so you can smile again,' she said with gentle malice.

He frowned.

'Why do you have people like that here?' he demanded. 'You know that you wouldn't dream of having them in Carlton House Terrace.'

'Agreed,' said Claire. 'Everything would shriek at me, "You can't do that there 'ere!" which is precisely the reason why I enjoy doing it now.'

'You seem to leave something behind you when you come out here,' said the boy in that slightly dictatorial manner which amused and seldom irritated her.

She had that rare quality in a mother of being able to look at her son from the point of view of an outsider, which was perhaps why they were such good friends.

She laughed.

'Oh, my dear, I do! I leave behind the overlay of years, the stiff conventions of England, the terribly confining bonds of being the wife of an Important Man. For just these blessed weeks I wake up and stretch, come out of my bonds and live. Darling, don't grudge me the tail-end of my fleeting youth whilst I can still hang on to it!'

He kissed her suddenly.

'Adorable, I grudge you nothing,' he said.

'Only Cora Hesselton,' put in Claire. 'Poor Cora! She bursts the bonds with a vengeance.'

'She must have known in the first place that Westman was the sort of brute to refuse to marry her after all that scandal,' said Derek.

'But they weren't in the least in love with each other,' said Claire. 'Why should they commit the ridiculous folly of tying themselves together for life when all the damage had been done?'

Derek looked at her in disbelief.

'You're saying things just to annoy me,' he said. 'They disgust you as much as they do me actually.'

'Oh no, my lamb. They amuse me and—make me a little sorry. The only disgust I feel is because they didn't know the rules of the game. Their lives are their own to do with as they like, of course, but for the sake of the game we all agree to play they must observe certain rules, and the first one is discretion.'

The boy looked at her uncertainly as she lay there, completely aware of her charm, of her power over all of them, so finished she was, so guarded and enclosed by that armour of her self-possession. She lived her secret life within it, but no one was given an opportunity of penetrating it – no one save probably Julian Rothe, and – Ferring?

The boy threw them all a casual good night and went indoors, his thoughts revolving round his lovely, elusive mother and that man for whose life he and she were a background, a man to be admired and feared but so little to be understood and loved.

The others had listened without interruption to the comedy of words and, in the darkness, Mayne laughed softly.

'Where did you get that boy of yours, Claire?' he asked. 'What's he really made of?'

'I wonder. Of dreams and hopes and fears, of endless possibilities and the almost certainty that he will eventually become the Fine Old English Gentleman, with capital letters,' said Claire.

For a few minutes the talk was desultory and general and then, as if by tacit consent, Jennifer and Mayne drifted away into the shadowy garden.

'You didn't like Mrs. Hesselton, did you?' he asked her.

'No! She's loud, isn't she? Was there a scandal about her?'

'Terrific. Westman, the financier, was co-respondent in her divorce case and, when it was over, he cleared out to America and left her, though I believe he provides pretty handsomely for her. It was a nasty, sordid business and I must admit I was surprised myself to see her here. I believe she lives in Cadenabbia, just along the lake.'

She was silent for such a long time that he looked at her questioningly.

'What's all that about, my sweet?' he asked.

'Don't you see? We—it might be you and I?' she said quiveringly.

'Jennifer, you don't mean you think that? That I could ever treat you like that?' he asked incredulously. 'Don't you know I'd give all I possess to be able to marry you?'

'Would you, Brenner?'

'But of course I would. Don't you know that?'

She shivered and pulled about her the light wrap she wore over her thin frock.

'Oh, it's so horrible, so sordid. It spoils everything. It doesn't fit in with all this loveliness.'

'There's a canker at the heart of most things,' said Mayne rather sombrely. 'No one knows that better than a lawyer. My dear, is it quite impossible for us to find happiness together?'

'Quite impossible,' said Jennifer in a low voice.

'Wouldn't your husband release you?'

'Well—yes, I suppose he would, though people of my class don't work things out like that or go in for divorce. It never occurs to us. We marry and keep married.'

'But if two people make a mistake and are horribly unhappy?'

'They just take it as part of life and make the best of it. Usually they can't afford to do anything else. The wife hasn't any money and there are generally children.'

'That isn't a parallel to your case, though, Jennifer. Even if I had to give up my profession, I've got a bit of money behind me now. We could start afresh somewhere else.'

'No! Happiness could never come for us out of the sacrifice of what means almost everything to you,' said Jennifer soberly. 'There's Bob, too. I couldn't do that to him. He's done his best for me and there's never been anyone else for him. It isn't his fault if he's crippled and poor.'

'But what an existence for you, Jennifer!' cried Mayne in impotent revolt against what he knew was fate.

'I shall have my profession,' she told him, and there came to stab her Rothe's words to her: 'You'll have to suffer first,' he had told her. 'Tortured, torn to pieces with unendurable agony. Then you might be a great singer.'

Was this what he had meant? Was this the beginning of the torture? Would she finally emerge from this rapture, this agony of pain and love, of grief and remorse and joy unutterable, as Rothe would have her be? Was this the price she had to pay for the fame that in this hour seemed so valueless and little worth the seeking? Already it was turning to dust in her mouth. All she wanted in life was this man who had opened the gates of heaven before her but who could not lead her within them.

'I shall have my profession,' she told Mayne, and he heard the unsatisfied note in her voice.

'An empty vessel, Jennifer.'

She turned to him at that, catching at him with her hands.

'Oh, my dear, do you have to tell me that? Do you think I don't realise how empty all the world is going to be without you?'

He caught her closely and they clung together for a moment.

'Risk it, Jennifer. Come to me. Let's give it all up, both of us, and make a new life together somewhere,' he said unsteadily.

She released herself and shook her head.

'No! There's always Bob. I couldn't leave him any more than I could leave a child,' she said.

A thought struck him suddenly. He knew so little actually about her life with this vague husband of hers.

'Jennifer, there isn't a child, is there?' he asked.

'No. There can't be,' she said in a low voice. 'He was—hurt, you see.'

Mayne was inexpressibly shocked. He knew so much more of life than she did. It was impossible for a man of the world to accept such a marriage in the calm way she seemed to accept it.

'Dearest, you mean—you're not actually, physically, husband and wife at all?' he asked.

The colour flamed into her face. It seemed dreadful to her to talk of such things to anyone, even to this man become so familiar to her.

'I'd rather not talk about it, Brenner,' she pleaded. 'I don't mind about it really. That sort of thing doesn't matter to me.'

'That's because you don't know anything about life,' he said gravely. 'It must matter in marriage. Without the physical, there can be no real marriage when people are young, like you and your husband. Can't you see that that is the real basis and meaning of marriage? That there's no other reason for marriage between young couples?'

'There's companionship, affection, friendship,' said Jennifer.

'That's all right for older people, for the later years of marriage, as the solid basis on which happiness in married life rests. It won't do for a start, though. How does your husband feel about this? Did he know before you married?'

'No. He—he minded quite a lot, but I think he's got over it now,' she said, hating the conversation.

'He hasn't, unless he's no man at all,' said Mayne shortly. 'Hasn't he suggested setting you free, Jennifer?'

'Yes. Naturally I refused,' she said.

'But, my dear, why? You don't love him?'

'But I do!' she cried.

'Not if you love me.'

'Not *as* I love you, Brenner. But—I can't explain how I feel about it,' she said in distress. 'We'd always been sweethearts, always been going to get married, and he's so dependent on me now. It would be wrong and cruel to desert him just because he's been injured, and injured in trying to save my own people. You've got to remember that, Brenner.'

He frowned. He knew in his heart that she was right, saw even more clearly than she the net which held her bound to Bob Haling, meshes not made by laws which could be twisted and broken, but by the finer cords of gratitude, decency, sentiment, the sense of obligation which must always bind her.

'Are you going to sacrifice your whole life's happiness for the paying of that debt, then?' he asked harshly.

'I married him because I thought I was in love with him, Brenner,' she told him quietly, though her heart felt as if it were breaking. Was this to be the end, so soon after the incredible sweetness of the beginning? 'I took my vows to him, for better, for worse, in sickness and in health.'

He was silent, feeling the impregnable barrier of that very simplicity of hers which he loved. She could not deviate from the path which stretched so straightly before her. For such as she there were no side-paths, no turnings, no by-pass road whereby she might avoid the direct route on which she had started.

Arm in arm they paced the mossy path beneath the lemon trees, the moonlight filtering between the dark leaves and the pale globes of the fruit which filled the night air with their subtle perfume, sweet and aromatic.

'Shall we go in?' he asked at last, unable to bear her nearness and to know her unattainable.

She clung to him for a moment, her face pale, her eyes dark with pain.

'Brenner, forgive me—forgive me!'

He held her closely, kissed her, felt her trembling beneath his touch, knew the wild temptation she was to him.

'For what, beloved? For being the woman of my dreams? For letting me know that such a woman actually exists outside them?' he asked.

'For giving you sorrow when I would give my life for your happiness,' she said in a low, quivering voice.

The perfumed night about them, the faint lapping of the water, the utter peace and silence, caught their senses in a rapture that was sweet anguish.

'Jennifer, I want to make love to you! I can't just let you go like this. Do you want me to make love to you?'

'More than I've ever wanted anything in my life,' she told him.

And suddenly he set her free, let his hands fall from her and stood leaning back against one of the pillars up which the stems of the lemon-trees twisted fantastically. She saw that his face was very pale and there were little beads of moisture on his forehead.

'You've got to go in, Jennifer,' he said. 'Do you understand? I'm only a man, and a man deeply in love with you—too much in love with you to take you and despoil you. Go in, my darling —and lock your door against me.'

She was afraid and yet exalted. She was seeing the man beneath the veneer of civilisation, beneath all the overlay of conventional laws, and that which was primitive and fundamental in all life leapt within her to meet him. Nothing seemed to matter to her in that moment save the satisfaction of that urge which brought her near to him again, to this man, her mate.

'I love you, Brenner. I want you to take me. I want to be yours, to know what love is, to fulfil myself, to find out the meaning of all this—unrest. Kiss me, my dearest heart—love me, Brenner!'

For a second he stood to watch her, fascinated, exultant, triumphant. Then he gathered her into his arms and she gave him her lips, her white throat, her breast, and a mad ecstasy held them both. Suddenly, with a queer, strangled sound, he let her go, pushed her away and went from her, leaving her standing there faint and sick from the suddenness of that parting.

She leaned against the scented pillar, trembling and white, her fingers mechanically arranging the satin of her frock where his lips had pushed it aside. Her feet were powerless to move and her mind was struggling to readjust itself to normal thought. Deep within her she knew that presently she would be glad that he had left her, glad that their love was still the sacred and beautiful thing it had been, that he had had greater strength than she. But just now, in that first moment of shock, she was angry with frustration, all her sense reeling at the sudden and brutal check to the uprising tide of her emotions, that tide on which she would have rushed to meet his love.

She did not know how long she stood there, but later, much later, he came to her again through the trees, wrapped her cloak about her with fingers which were warm and steady, and smiled into her eyes with that gentle, familiar look which told her he was master of himself again, though still he loved her.

'Come in, my dear one. You'll be cold. Southern nights are sometimes treacherous,' and slowly, quietly, they went in together, and he left her at the door of her room with no more than the touch of his hand on hers.

But Jennifer could not sleep. For almost the first time in her life she had a 'white night', and presently gave up the attempt, wrapped herself in a warm coat, and sat on her balcony to watch for the dawn.

She, like Brenner, had recovered her peace of body, but she knew that that night would stand forever as the gateway between her girlhood and her womanhood. Though she was still virgin of body, outwardly the same, she had passed through the gate into the realm of knowledge. So little had kept her virgin of body even, and she wondered, with a feeling that was both shame and exultation, at the unsuspected self that love had discovered within her hitherto complacent body and mind. Memory brought the hot blood in waves to her face and she covered it with her hands at such moments, for she had offered herself to her lover and it had been his strength that had defended her, not hers.

And the dawn came with its ineffable beauty to wake the world to everyday life again, to bring so much that was new, revive so much that had briefly been forgotten, for mankind.

To bring to Jennifer – what?

She could find no answer to that question and presently she went in, for she heard Maria's voice in the courtyard below and knew that the day had began.

Chapter Fifteen

Jennifer came down the next morning with white face and deeply shadowed eyes.

She had had breakfast brought up to her, though Derek had called up to her from the garden to come into the water, and she had not even gone to the window to call an answer so that he had decided she was still asleep and gone without her. From where she lay she could see his head far out, a speck on the sunlit water.

She had decided on her course of action. She would ask Julian to let her go back to England, back to Bob, and to stay until the lessons could be resumed in London. By that time she would have built a new barrier against this love which had come to her unsought.

She dallied over her dressing, however, pausing countless times to look at the lovely vista of the lake she might never see again, never with the man she so passionately loved, and when at last she went downstairs, it was to find everything in the wild confusion which can be produced in an Italian household over the merest trifle. One would have said that the whole house had met with disaster and that the dissolution of all its components and its inhabitants was imminent.

Men and maids ran about, calling excitedly to one another, pausing to have what sounded like a violent altercation and parting again with laughter to race upstairs or down with bags, time-tables, rugs.

In the midst of it stalked Rothe, the one calm thing in all the unrest, and he went immediately to Jennifer when he saw her coming down the stairs.

'My dear, I've got to leave you here for a bit. I've had an urgent summons which I can't refuse. It is to the bedside of my sister, my only relation, and I can't refuse though it may be too late by the time

I get there. I've just had a wire which had been sent to London in the first place, so valuable time has already been lost.'

Jennifer caught his arm.

'Don't leave me here, Julian. Let me go with you,' she said urgently.

He looked at her in surprise.

'My dear, that's not possible. It's not even as if I were going to England. She's in Norway with friends. I couldn't possibly take you.'

'Then let me go to England. I could manage quite well alone. Please, Julian.'

He was amazed at her vehemence of desire.

'But, my dear child, what's the idea? You'll be all right here, and if this affair keeps me there for longer than I hope, Mayne will take you home when he goes.'

'But, Julian, I don't want to stay on here without you,' she said in such obvious distress that he paused to look at her searchingly.

'Why not? Aren't you having a good time here? You haven't appeared to be languishing for *my beaux yeux*, anyway.'

The painful colour flooded her face for a moment and then receded, leaving her pale again.

'It isn't that, Julian. I want to go home, though.'

'You can't. The place is shut up and the servants are away,' he said shortly.

'I didn't mean that. I mean I want to go home to—to my husband.'

He made a gesture of impatience.

'What for? I may not be away more than a few days, and it is most undesirable and unnecessary for you to interrupt your work with any such nonsense as that. Have you forgotten your promise to me when you came back? Or are you just going to throw it aside when something upsets you for a moment?'

She swallowed. There was justice in his criticism. She had given him her promise that she would not go away from him again without his permission until her training was complete, 'All right,' she said with a queer note in her voice, a note which later he remembered. It held resignation, acceptance of something beyond and outside her control. 'I'll stay.'

Claire came from the telephone, where she had been conducting a sprightly conversation in her fluent Italian.

'An hour and a half to wait at Bale and then a through train,' she said. 'I've booked a seat on it for you so that you get the right section. You'll telephone me from Bale?'

'Of course. I hate to have to go like this, my darling.'

'I know you do. You'll come back if you possibly can?'

'Yes, surely.'

They had forgotten Jennifer and she had an odd sense of loneliness through their detachment from her. She wandered away, remembered some shopping she had to do, and decided she might as well do that as anything else. Certainly she was better out of the way of all this bustle and excitement and confusion, which she knew would die down as if it had never been once the train had fussed its way out of Menaggio with Rothe on board.

Mayne met her as she came out of the chemist's, in which she had been buying yet another preparation to defend her from gnat-bites.

'Rothe's had to go. Do you know?' he asked her, taking her parcels from her and slipping them into his pockets.

'Yes. I—I asked him to take me with him,' she said in a low voice.

It was strange to meet him here, in the sunny, busy little street, for the first time after those heart-searching moments of last night. It brought them back to normal with a jolt which was infinite relief to her.

'Why?' he asked calmly.

She turned to stare at him. He looked so calm and ordinary that she might almost have believed she had dreamed last night.

'You ask that? Don't you realise that—that it would be the best thing?' she managed to say.

His eyes searched hers and he shook his head and smiled a little.

'Why try to fight fate? To mould our own destinies? I am to some extent a fatalist, I suppose, and whilst I try to live my life to the best of my ability, something inside me always inclines me to believe that what is to be will be.'

She walked along beside him, past the shops where already the brown curtains were being put out, and into the quiet road between high walls, topped with roses and jessamine, which led down to the Villa Felicita.

'I shouldn't have imagined you, a lawyer, having a belief in anything as—as unsubstantial as destiny,' she said gravely.

'Greater men than I have believed in it,' he said with his whimsical smile. 'There is a destiny that shapes our ends, rough-hew them as we will.'

They came to the gate in the pink wall and stopped before it.

'I wonder if that's true?' she asked, and there was a sort of panic in her face and in her voice, and the words came a little breathlessly, as if the mind that conceived them had been running fast. 'I wonder if certain things come to us, *must* come to us, no matter what we do to—escape them?'

He held her eyes, and there was quiet laughter in his which reassured her, held her down to normality in spite of the wings which fear would have lent her imagination.

'Does it matter?' he asked, and she hesitated a moment, and then shook her head, laughed, and went through the gateway in the pink wall.

Within, all was peace and quiet. The servants moved about their work with their customary efficiency, Derek and Lotta lay on their backs on the raft, and Claire, her lovely face a little wistful and shadowed, lay in a long chair with a book which she was not reading.

'Come and swim, Jennifer,' said Mayne, and she ran to her room in thankful acceptance of the return to the familiar routine.

At the end of a week, during which Claire's two guests had pointedly attached themselves to a not too pleased Derek and Lotta, avoiding the necessity of being alone, especially in the evenings, Rothe followed his daily telegrams with a long letter, parts of which Claire read out to them.

It seemed that his sister, of whom he was deeply fond, had met with an accident whilst climbing, and injuries to her back had necessitated her removal to a big hospital in Oslo where an operation had saved her, they hoped, from the permanent invalidism which had at first been feared for her.

I know you have to shut the villa so as to be in Cannes by the end of the month [Rothe wrote]. I'm a little uncertain what to do about Jennifer, as I may be kept here for another week or two, so I suggest that you ask Mayne to see her safely back to England when he goes, which I believe was to be about the twentieth. If she wants to go back to her husband for a bit, she might as well. If however, she likes to stay in London, perhaps you would send a line to Mrs. Carter, the caretaker at 'Pesante', and get Mayne to deliver her there.

There was a lot in the letter which Claire did not read aloud to them, and Jennifer had a queer feeling of envy as she saw her refold the closely written sheets and put them back into the envelope with fingers which she knew handled the paper tenderly.

'Well, there's not much to add to that,' said Claire.

They were all sitting over their after-dinner coffee, Lotta curled up in a long chair with Derek at her feet, Jennifer and Mayne sitting on the balcony steps, and Claire poised as if for flight with her precious letter as soon as the necessary business had been discussed and settled.

'I shall have to go before the twentieth, I am afraid,' said Mayne. 'And though I don't want to cut Jennifer's holiday short, of course I should be only too glad of her company on the return journey and would deliver her safely the other end.'

'What are your own ideas, Jennifer?' asked Claire. 'Naturally I don't want you to go, my dear, but I've got to go to Cannes and you can't travel back to England alone. Derek's going to Milan for a few days when we leave here, or he could have taken you.'

'I'm quite able to travel alone,' said Jennifer, aware of her desperate desire to fall in with their suggestions and yet knowing how unwise such a journey might be.

They all disclaimed that with one voice, so she let the talk and the arrangement flow about her unresisting, and at last Claire was able to slip away, Lotta and Derek went off on some excursion of their own, and Jennifer and Mayne turned instinctively to each other.

'You don't mind, Jennifer?' he asked her.

She had consciously avoided being left alone with him, but now it seemed as if all her efforts were unavailing if they were to take that journey together, the day and the night and the day of strange intimacies which would inevitably link them still more closely.

'Will you?' she asked him.

'You know the answer to that one. Come out on the lake. I haven't had a moment alone with you for days and I'm getting restive about it.'

Feeling as if she no longer belonged to herself, no longer ordered her ways, she went with him to the boat and let him row her out on the spangled lake, out until the darkness hemmed them in.

He shipped the oars and let the boat drift, though there was so little to ruffle the water that they scarcely moved on its surface.

He leaned forward, and she saw his face, pale and grave, in the darkness.

'So we come to the end, my sweet?' he asked her very quietly.

She made a little, low, quivering sound of pain.

'You break my heart,' she said.

He left his place at the oars and came to sit beside her on the wide, cushioned seat and she shivered as his arm closed about her.

'How much do you care for me, Jennifer?'

'More than anything in the world,' she told him, her voice trembling on the words.

'And you're still sure there can be nothing in the future for us?'

'My dear, how can there be?' she asked him sadly.

'There can be—a memory, if you have the courage, Jennifer.'

She knew what he was asking of her, had known all through these days of armistice that this hour must come, that when it came she would rush to meet it with just this sweet pain which pierced her heart.

'Is that all it would mean, Brenner? Just—courage?'

The volcano had been smouldering all through these days of denial, and it needed only his lightest touch to make it burst out with renewed vitality for that compelled repression. Neither of them had the power, nor desired it, to keep back that ardent stream.

'We want each other so, my Jennifer,' he was whispering to her. 'It isn't possible to deny ourselves for ever, to part with no more than this for memory, with no more than this to take down the empty years. I thought I was strong enough to defend us both against it, but I'm not—and you're not strong, my sweet, my love. You're weak and helpless in my arms, putting up no defence against me. You let me take your lips and your breasts. I can take all of you, Jennifer. You won't resist me or deny me. You can't.'

His voice was heavy with passion and she closed her eyes against the flame in his which scorched her. She knew, with no sense of shame but rather with exultation, that what he said was true, that she had no strength nor desire to resist him, that now, at this moment, he could do what he would with her.

'I don't want to resist you,' she whispered to him. 'I love you. Nothing else in the whole world matters.'

'Listen. I'm not going to fight myself any more, nor fight you, Jennifer. The other night I couldn't have taken you, not like that, on a first mad impulse as animals take their mates. We should have spoiled something lovely and regretted it for ever. This is different. My body and my soul ache for you. I'm going to take you away with me, Jennifer, somewhere where I can make love to you without the need to be furtive, to make our love sordid by cheap little subterfuges. We'll go away tomorrow. I'll tell Claire. It will be easy and she'll really be glad when we go. She's miserable without Rothe.'

'Are they lovers, Brenner?'

'I don't know. Probably. I try never to speculate about it, as it's so entirely their own affair. She doesn't want to keep on here without him, though, and she won't try to stop us. We'll go together up into the mountains, Jennifer. I know just where I want to take you. It's high up, just a tiny village at the side of a mountain pool, no more than a drop of blue water in a shallow green cup. There's an inn there, a primitive little place, but very clean, and the people would make us welcome and trouble their minds about us not at all. It's a place very near heaven. It would be heaven itself for us. Will you come with me there, Jennifer?'

His voice had found its more normal tones again, and though he still held her with his arms, they were both more composed and self-controlled.

'There is—Bob, my husband,' she told him shrinkingly, though her mind refused to bring her any more than a vague memory of that other life in which this madness of desire held no place.

'I know. I know how you feel about that, which is the only reason why I don't try to batter down your defences and take you for good and all before the world. But we shouldn't be robbing him of anything that is his, should we? Your love is mine, not his, and—forgive me, beloved, if I hurt you, but your body can never be his as it could be mine, so I am not even robbing him of that.'

She was silent for so long that he leaned forward at last, took her chin in his fingers and turned her face so that she looked into his eyes.

'Well, my Jennifer?'

She drew a deep breath.

'I'll come with you, Brenner,' she said, and for a long time they spoke no other word and she lay back against his arm, her cheek touching his, the soft air every now and then brushing their still faces like the caress of a butterfly's wings.

When he turned at last to kiss her, there was more of tenderness than of passion in his kiss. It was a sacrament rather than an act of physical love. It offered her homage and loyalty and the gifts of the spirit. It brought her a strange sense of peace and rest after all the turmoil of the days which had culminated in that hour of revelation.

'I love you with my mind as well as my body, Jennifer,' he told her softly. 'That is what makes it so perfect. It is what I have always longed for and never found, had come to believe that it could not exist outside my imagination. No matter what life does to us, I shall love you till I die—and beyond the grave.'

'And I you,' she told him, her beautiful voice soft and warm and quiet. 'I have never dreamed of anyone like you because I didn't know what love was like.'

'You don't know even yet, my princess still asleep,' he said. 'Up there in the mountains I'm going to teach you all there is to know of love.'

She was a little wistful at that.

'You have loved other women before?' she asked him.

'Their bodies, yes. Most men have. Very few of us are lucky enough to have got through the callow years without meeting the predatory type of female who does her best to ruin us. I've done what most men do—experimented with sex and called it love. But I've never *loved* a woman before, Jennifer, never worshipped her, never wanted to live all the days and nights of my life with her by my side and to die with her hand in mine.'

Her face was beautiful in its tender pride in his love for her.

'That is the way you feel towards me, Brenner?' she asked softly.

'Yes. Do you see now why I left you as I did the other night? Before I had smirched the loveliness of the thing I could not believe I had found?'

'Brenner, will you—feel all those things for me, all those beautiful things—afterwards?' she asked him fearfully. 'Will you feel them just the same when I am your—mistress?'

The colour flooded her cheeks as she brought out the difficult word, so strange a word for her to be applying to herself.

His eyes were gentle and he set his hands about her face, framing it so that he held it there beneath his steadfast, tender gaze.

'You say that word as if it were a shameful one, my Jennifer. It shouldn't be. It isn't in origin shameful. Do you know what it really means? A woman courted and beloved, and you're that in truth. But we won't even think of the word if it hurts your mind. When I take you for my own, on an Italian night of stars like tonight, it will be as my wife, and what could a mere ceremony or the mumbled words of a man add to that? How could anyone make it more sacred and binding than my own love and loyalty will make it? You will be my wife, Jennifer. Whatever comes to us, whether I ever see you again in this life after we—part, there will never be any other woman in my life or in my arms or in my heart. Can you believe that?'

She was tongue-tied as ever, inarticulate for all the passionate love that surged through her, but he found nothing to cavil at, nothing missing so long as he could read her clear eyes, feel the trembling of her body.

'I love you so—so terribly, Brenner,' was all she could say, and soon, slowly, regretfully almost, they went back across the still magic of the lake to the house where Claire Ferring lay awake, alone with the ashes of her life, with bitterness and sweet memory, with pride, with humiliation, with eternal regrets.

She heard them come in. Were they lovers? Would they ever be, or would Jennifer, whom still she understood so little, blind herself with the belief that in her marriage she had found her unalterable fate? Passionately she found herself hoping that they would not miss the best things in life as she had done, would not grasp at the shadow and miss the substance, would take what lay on the lap of the gods for them before the hands, which would not offer for ever, pushed aside the gifts and sent them shattering into ten thousand fragments on the floor.

Jennifer and Mayne met next morning with a long, deep look into each other's eyes, a look which satisfied each of them that the night had brought firmer resolve rather than reluctance, and when Claire came down, he went to her with a letter in his hand.

'Claire, will you forgive me if I go earlier than we expected? It means taking Jennifer away too, of course, but we should have to break up the party very soon in any case.'

Claire gave a conventional smile of regret, but accepted it without demur. After all, with Julian gone, her zest for this lotus life had also vanished and she would be glad to get back to normal conditions again.

'I'm sorry, naturally,' she said. 'I was afraid that would happen once the first of my guests had gone, but it can't be helped. There are other years, we will hope. When will you have to go?'

So the conversation turned quite naturally on time-tables and packing, on necessary telegrams which Mayne undertook to send, all of them being in agreement that it was unnecessary to trouble Rothe with the details of what was only an advancing of the prearranged programme.

Jennifer lived through the remaining hours as in a dream, very quiet and gentle, saying nothing at all to Mayne and very little to anyone else. She had fought her battle, decided the issue, and let herself rest on it without futile repetition of argument. Later might come retribution and remorse, but her mind was tranquil now that it was made up.

Claire and Derek saw them off at the station. Their luggage had been registered through to London, to await their arrival, and they carried what they would need.

'I felt rather awful about that,' admitted Jennifer when the train had carried them out of sight of the Ferrings. 'I hate to deceive Claire.'

Privately Mayne wondered if they were deceiving her. There had been a look in her eyes, mischievous, understanding, the least bit unhappy, as she said good-bye to them. Claire was so essentially a woman of the world, and it must have been patent to her that the two were in love and that, for only one reason, temporary happiness seemed to be theirs. Jennifer could not have worn that look of calm content had she been about to part from the man she loved, nor would Mayne have been so happy at taking her back to another man.

But not for long would he allow the girl to think of anyone but themselves and soon he had her laughing and glowing, her body and mind steeped both in their love and in the beauty about them.

They left the train at one of the tiny mountain stations, a mere shed perched on the side of the slope with a white road leading down into the narrow valley between two peaks and losing itself in indescribable silence and solitude once the station lay far enough behind them to be forgotten.

They had brought food with them and they found a grassy hollow from which they could still look down on the lakes.

'Are you glad, my Jennifer?' he asked her.

'I didn't think life could hold anything like it,' she told him. 'I've never really had any idea of happiness before. It makes me feel—very humble and grateful. Just to be here would be heaven, but loving you is like living in another world.'

She spoke shyly still and with the reserve of a lifetime, for she had never tried to express her emotions before and only the knowledge that it would give him happiness made her struggle to find the difficult words.

He put his arm about her and they sat there in the perfect communion of silent voices and hearts that beat in tune. All about them nature was prodigal with her gifts, and splashed on her canvas every colour her palette could conceive, had fashioned the delicate petals of a thousand flowers and the great, rugged crags of rock and the little mountain streams that gurgled and laughed as they found their happy way down to the lakes below.

'Tell me what you're thinking, Brenner.'

'I'm etching it all on my mind so that it will stay there for ever,' he told her softly. 'So that I shall be able to come back here in my mind when I am quite old, and shall find you again as you are now, so sweet, my dear, so young and beautiful.'

She smiled and shook her head.

'Not even you can call me beautiful,' she said with a touch of regret. How glad she would have been to be able to give him such beauty as Claire Ferring's!

He set his hand beneath her chin and looked into her eyes.

'To me you are the most beautiful woman in the world,' he said. 'Other men just see your body. I see your soul that loves me, and there is no more beautiful thing on earth for a man's eyes than that.'

She drew a deep quivering breath.

'Oh, my dear,' she whispered, 'I am afraid to care so much.'

He rose and pulled her to her feet.

'I'm not having you afraid of anything whilst I am with you, my sweet. Shall we go on? We've several miles to go yet. You won't be tired? I wanted you to see this with me, but perhaps I ought to have taken you round the road by car.'

'I'm glad you brought me here instead. The roads belong to anybody. Things like this belong to just you and me.'

They had rested in their grassy hollow during the hottest hour, but it was still warm and breathless and they made their way slowly through the valley with many pauses, stopping to drink from their cupped hands at the clear, mountain streams, the water a little brackish but ice-cold and refreshing.

'Oriavi is just ahead of us now,' he told her at last. 'I wanted you to come on it just at this time of day, with the sunset behind it on the snow and reflecting in the water. Not tired, my darling?'

She shook her head and gave him her deep, slow smile.

'I feel I could never be tired again,' she told him, and they went on hand in hand, climbing up over a steep bluff and stopping instinctively at the sheer splendour of the scene before them.

They stood on the rim of a shallow cup of green, the green of grass and vineyards, of maize and corn, of the tall spears of the pines. Below them was the still water, that water which Mayne had told her was blue, but which was now as red as blood with the reflection of the sun setting in glory behind the distant snow-capped peaks.

Jennifer gave a little cry of awe and instinctively caught at Mayne's hand.

'Look! It's blood!' she whispered, and he felt her whole frame shudder, and looking at her quickly, saw that she was pale as a ghost.

'Why, Jennifer—darling! What's wrong?' he asked anxiously.

She clung to him, her eyes wide with a kind of fascinated horror, though the next moment she managed to laugh shakily.

'It was just—a stupid fancy. It looked like blood, an omen. Have we got to—go across it?' with another little shiver of fear which she knew was foolish and unreasonable, but which she could not help.

'Yes. There's a boat there as a rule. If there isn't one, you stand and shout for it. We could go round it, of course, but it's a long and very rough path,' looking at her doubtfully.

She began to draw him forward down the winding path they had followed for so long, a mere mountain track which in bad weather was impassable, leaving the tiny village completely cut off.

'No. I have a feeling we shall have to cross it,' she said in a queer, frightened whisper. 'There can't be any going round, not for us. Let's go on.'

As they dropped down to its level, the lake lost its uncanny appearance and became a sheet of greying water at the edge of which an old, flat-bottomed boat rocked gently, moored to a stake on the bank. Mayne helped her in, threw their cases in the end, and made all speed across to where the friendly lights of the few houses, little more than huts, welcomed them.

The largest of the houses was built in Swiss fashion, a chalet with long roof sloping almost to the ground on either side and wide eaves as a protection from heavy snows. The green shutters were flung wide to the evening breeze, and at sound of the oars a man and a woman came out on the broad wooden balcony and stood with hands shading their eyes for a moment before they hurried down to greet their unexpected and ever welcome guests.

Few but the seasoned travellers discovered their tiny village, for it was out of the path of the regular tourist and accommodation was limited and uncertain. Mayne had taken a chance on finding room at the chalet, and it was with relief that he saw they were being made welcome.

Oh yes, they remembered the English signor well and felt life had been worth nothing since he had gone until he should return to take all they had, everything they could give, all of their best – and so delightful that now he had brought his signora, and soon, oh, soon! there would be a room for them and food and wine of the best in all Italy!

Mayne called them Luisa and Tonio, took their eager, toil-worn hands, presented the shy Jennifer to them – 'My dear signora,' he called her and lingered lovingly on the words, and watched the simple graciousness which was so natural to her and which won the Italian hearts as simple as her own.

Tonio took them into the dark, earthy, smelling little bar and gave them cool wine to drink whilst the fat Luisa bustled up the stairs to prepare her best room for them, after she had filled the place with lamentations that she had not known that the signor and the signora were coming so that she might have everything ready.

Jennifer and her lover sat on a bench in the dark little place and sipped their wine and listened to Tonio with no need to reply to the jargon of Italian and primitive English with which he was delighted to entertain them.

'Do you understand what he says?' she whispered to Brenner once.

'Very little, but he's only offering us all Italy for our delight. All you have to do is to smile and look happy.'

'That isn't hard, my dearest,' she said, and they exchanged a long look which Tonio saw with ravished delight, for of all men on earth, your Italian loves a lover.

Soon Luisa, who had passed through once or twice with bundles of clean linen and paused only to give them a smile from black eyes and flashing white teeth, came to tell them that all was ready, and they went with her to her big front bedroom, plain and bare but spotlessly clean. On the floor were handmade peasant rugs and hanging on the whitewashed walls were crude pictures of the saints with the inevitable dark, scowling features of Il Duce dominating everything from its place of honour over the bed.

The furniture was the simplest imaginable, a chest of drawers, a table with a mirror standing on it, a huge wooden bed on top of whose spotless sheets and cover Luisa had triumphantly spread the pride of her heart, a fat, padded quilt covered in red satin and looking like an overgrown feather-bed perched on top of the coverings.

A three-legged iron stand held a basin and ewer, and Tonio came panting up the narrow wooden staircase with ice cold water fresh from the mountain stream, which they could hear gurgling and splashing a few feet from the house.

Luisa turned on her husband with a tongue like a flail.

Cold water, indeed! Did he not know that the English signor and signora would want hot water, and at once? Much, much hot water, and the bath from the outhouse which, through the mercy of God, she had scrubbed with her own hands only that week! Apologising, gesticulating, flinging back unintelligible retorts, pausing to give a sly wink to his guests, Tonio was bundled back down the steep stairs, to reappear in a few minutes with a shallow, round, tin bath, which he placed with pride on the scrubbed boards at his Luisa's feet to receive his reward in the renewed sunshine of her approval.

The hot water would be there soon – soon. Had she not, that very evening, as if she had known they were coming, filled again to the brim the iron pot over the fire? And was not the whole of the water in the pot very hot and at the entire disposal of these so welcome guests? Tonio should carry it up at once, but at once, whilst she, Luisa, attended to the supper, to the *minestrone*, than which was no finer in all Italy, and to the *risotto* with the little lake fish in it.

The lovers watched and listened and laughed. There was no need for them to say anything. Luisa and Tonio asked nothing better than to talk and to run about in their service. It was a new and fascinating experience to Jennifer to be in an Italian home like this, amongst the people themselves, to share as friends their essential kindliness, their happy acceptance of life as it came, their amicable wranglings which meant nothing at all, their boundless hospitality.

And at last they were alone again, the shallow bath filled with steaming, pine-scented water, big metal ewers of cold water standing beside it and a heap of soft towels, white as snow, on a chair. Jennifer had watched with interest when Luisa brought in a small wooden stool and covered it tenderly with a folded square of towelling, and now she went to it and regarded it more closely, finally touching it with her fingers and drawing them back to find them covered with rice powder.

She felt Brenner's eyes on her and looked up, and laughter robbed that intimate moment of the embarrassment that had threatened it.

'It's to sit on when you get out of the bath, my sweet,' he told her amidst their laughter. 'Save some for me. Don't sit too hard. I'm going to have a cigarette on the balcony, whilst you bath, but first of all there's something I must do,' and he reached up to the photograph of Il Duce and solemnly turned that pugilistic countenance to the wall. 'I couldn't possibly make love to you with him frowning down at us, and if anyone's to see you in your bath, it isn't going to be *that* dictator!' and he flung her a look of mingled mischief and laughter before he went out on to their balcony and pulled the door to behind him.

It had touched him inexpressibly to see the look there had been in her eyes when Luisa had left them alone in their room. It was a look which held both humility and pride, but there had been a hint of fear, of appeal, that had caught at his chivalrous soul. She had looked so young and defenceless, as if she knew herself to be at his mercy, her fate and her happiness in his hands.

He vowed himself to her service like some knight of old, swore that he would protect her and be as the solid rock beneath her feet whilst life lasted.

She called to him presently, and he went back to find her dressed again, her eyes soft and shy, and pleading for the gentleness he found it so easy to give her.

'I don't know how you're going to manage,' she told him. 'It looks as if I've used all the hot water, and in any case, I don't know how to empty the bath.'

He laughed and kissed her.

'You go down, my sweet, or wait on the balcony. There's a chair out there. I'm too old a campaigner to worry about details when there's hot water, soap and towels all to hand.'

'I'll wait outside,' she told him.

'Put a coat on then, dearest. It's chilly and you've just had a hot bath.'

'It's lovely to be looked after and treated as if I were precious and breakable,' she said, with a little shaky laugh.

'You're precious, but I'll never let you be broken if I can help it,' he told her.

Unwillingly she let her thoughts go back to the first night of her marriage to Bob, its bewilderment, its fear, the intensity of her relief when she found that nothing was going to happen, after all; of all the things she had dreaded with an agony of fear which should have been enough in itself to tell her that the feeling she had for her husband was not love. It was not until some nights had passed that she had begun to be aware of the true facts of the case, of Bob's desperate fear and self-contempt and humiliation and misery. He had talked to her wildly, harshly, in a way that had both shocked and pained her, for she had not been able to understand all it meant to a man.

Slowly she had struggled out of the morass of pain and shame that had been their honeymoon, had tried to understand him, had been aware all the time of her own relief, for Bob had never touched in her the springs of her own desire, and she was even more virgin than Mayne imagined.

Now, filled with her love for this beloved man, she could think with compassion, mingled with futile regret, of Bob whom she had never loved. Bob who had killed for ever any possibility of her loving him by the self-contempt which had made him harsh and unloving towards his bride. Mayne's tender consideration for her was to her one of the sweetest attributes of his love, and she repaid it by a passionate gratitude.

He came out to her in flannels and sweater when he had finished, and they stood together to watch the last reflections of the dying day, the tender light on the snow and the rose and lavender to which the blood-red hue of the water had softened.

'There's no blood now, Jennifer,' he told her. 'Look! There's only soft pink and mauve left—roses and lavender at the end of the day, our perfect day, my sweet.'

'I shall remember it all my life,' she told him, and they were silent for a while, that perfect silence which needs no words for understanding.

Each of them seemed to have lived a lifetime in that day, to have entered on a new world since the mountains had closed on them and shut from their sight Claire Ferring and Derek and all that their familiar forms represented. It seemed impossible to realise that beyond the green walls which shut them in, the world, with its problems and its obligations, still went on struggling, hating, suffering, grasping, cheating.

He was holding her left hand in his, and presently he took something from his pocket and slid it on her third finger and raised it to his lips.

'All my love and my worship and my faithfulness for ever, my one beloved,' he said to her, in a low voice.

She looked at her hand. It wore a circle of tiny diamonds, set in platinum.

'Oh, Brenner!' was all she could find to say.

'They call them Eternity Rings. That's why I chose that rather than an ordinary wedding ring. You like it?'

'For what it is, but so much more for what it means,' she said shakily. 'I wish I could wear it for ever!'

'Hush, my sweet. Don't let us make a future. Ours is today, our eternity.'

Their lips met and clung.

Down below them was a sudden clatter of voices, of chatter, of laughter, of Luisa scolding and praising, of knives and forks and the rattle of dishes.

'*Signora—signor—il pranzo!*'

Hand in hand they went down the stairs, no longer the narrow wooden steps of a village inn but the staircase of a royal palace down which they walked, the king and queen of an enchanted land, for they had come at last into their kingdom.

Chapter Sixteen

Jennifer stood, dry-eyed, to watch her lover go.

There were no tears for such grief as hers, no easing for such pain.

All yesterday they had travelled through Switzerland and France, gathering the last of their bitter-sweet memories, and this morning they had crossed to England and he had taken her out to Rothe's house, where he must leave her.

It had been impossible for her even to contemplate going back to her husband. Later, when the pain had eased a little, when the heart-ache was dulled and the poignant regret less piercing, she knew she must go. But not now – not yet – not so soon after the memory of all that bound her for ever to the man whose very name was the sound of love to her.

She had told him, on that last night they had had together in Oriavi, that she could not go back.

They had gone out on the lake in the moonlight for the last time, as they had done most nights before going to bed. There was never another boat on the water, for there were no other visitors in Oriavi and the natives would never dream of using the little lake for anything but a means of getting to the other side when need arose.

'Sing to me, Jennifer,' he said, as he had done more than once, and she had given him a long look and then had sung to him that most beautiful, heart-searching love song of Delilah's.

Rothe had taught her to sing it in French, for no translation can equal the lovely, melting softness of the original.

'Mon coeur s'ouvre à ta voix.'

The man who loved her lay back and listened to the glorious voice which he had touched with magic, giving it a depth and beauty, a tenderness which love alone could bring to its cadences. It had an unearthly loveliness as it floated over the still, starlit waters, and on the mountainside the Italians came out of their houses to stand enraptured.

When she had finished he had drawn her into his arms in a passion of worship.

'*Mon coeur s'ouvre à ta voix*,' he whispered to her. 'My heart opens at your voice—my dear—my love.'

Later he had reminded her of what he had once said.

'I was to hear you sing that at Covent Garden and to bring you camellias,' he told her. 'There are no camellias in Oriavi now. What am I to do?'

'You have already given me all the flowers in the world, my beloved,' she said softly, her eyes like stars, her voice quivering between tears and laughter in that adorable way it had when she was deeply moved.

And they had known, both of them, that she could not then go back to Werford, to Bob Haling, who in that last night had come out of the vague mists which had veiled him from them and stood menacingly in their path, barring the way to happiness for them.

So Brenner had taken her back to Highgate, where most of the staff had returned and were expecting their master.

Jennifer stood at her window and watched him until the shrubs at the gate hid him from view. Then she threw herself down on her bed and wept tears which seemed the very blood of her heart. Some day in the dim, distant future she might be able to think of Brenner with a mind that did not hurt. Just now her every thought of him was a stab of unendurable pain, nor would her brain evolve any thought that was not of him, that was not a memory of their days and nights in Oriavi, possessed and possessing.

Presently, realising the need for discretion before the servants, she rose and bathed and changed her dress, made up her face carefully, locked away Mayne's ring, and went down to her solitary dinner. She felt that she was the worst possible company for herself, and yet she could not endure the thought of talking to people like Jane Bettle or Merely God, or any other of the parasites who, at this time of the year, could so easily have been secured for company.

There were letters waiting for her, for she had telegraphed instructions from Menaggio that no more were to be forwarded to her, and these took her some time to read. There were one or two from Rothe, who gave good news of his sister and expected to be home in a few days. They were chatty, clever letters, bringing vividly before her the man's personality, the slightly mordant flavour of his wit, the impersonal attitude he adopted of being an onlooker at life. In her new knowledge and experience Jennifer could be understanding and gentle in her thoughts of Claire Ferring, and of Julian, who probably loved her as she and Brenner loved, though she could not understand how Guy Ferring held her in bonds which she could not break, bonds so different from those which held her. She felt that no mere worldly consideration could have kept her from Brenner. Only Bob, in his helpless dependence, could so hold her.

There was a short, bitter letter from Bob. It held nothing that was tender or thoughtful, and she was glad with a dreadful, shamed gladness that it was so. She sat down and forced herself to write to him, telling him that she had come back to London, but would be working too hard to manage the suggested visit to Werford, after all, until about October. She told him about Italy, about Menaggio and Como, about the Ferrings, and nothing at all of Oriavi and of Brenner Mayne.

There was a long letter from Lottie, a letter which made her frown and gave her food for long and painful and anxious thoughts, bringing to her mind some measure of relief from its thoughts of her lover.

Things were getting worse and worse in the coal-fields, Lottie told her. The men were constantly on short time now, and they were sick to death of the state of affairs, of the eternal questions which were being asked in the House and never answered, of the empty promises of politicians who had never intended to keep them but had merely used them for getting into Parliament. The men had too much time for standing about discussing their grievances, too little money to do anything with their time but talk. Everywhere rents were owing and landlords putting on the screw, women getting more and more deeply into debt for the sheer necessities of life, children getting less and less food of an ever-diminishing quality.

It would fair break your heart to see how thin the kiddies are getting, Jen. Mine are not too bad because of that work Ive been able to get, but my folk are going abroad for the winter and shutting up the house, so I shall get nothing then and I darent think of what Im going to do then. Bobs as good to me as he can, but he hasnt too much though he seems to have a bit more now. Perhaps youve been sending him extra money. I don't like him in with that Mallinger, but it isnt any good me saying anything because it gets him on his hind legs. Not that Mallingers any different to anyone else now. Theyve all got a grouse and all the talks of strikes and fights and revolution and heaven help us all is what I say if the talk comes to anything. Ive seen revolvers and loaded sticks and ugly things that make me afraid. Bobs got a revolver, but he wont say where he got it, and if the police find out hell be for it. Theres plenty of new police about here now, so they're expecting trouble and Im afraid. If youve any thought of getting Bob up there, nows the time before he gets in with this gang of tuffs any closer.

Jennifer was in a panic at the letter, at the mere thought of having to bring Bob to London, of making a home for him and with him, of living there where at any time she might see Brenner, where he might see her with her husband. Must it be? Was there no other way?

Whilst they were in Italy Rothe had begun to discuss her premiere, which was to be a concert, the few other artists to be very carefully selected to give her just the right background and create an atmosphere for her. That would lead, he hoped, to at least half a dozen concert engagements during the winter and the succeeding spring, and in the following autumn she was to make her debut in opera, either in London or Paris, in which latter city she was to spend the summer months perfecting the language.

Somewhere in that programme, stretching over eighteen months, Bob must come in. Bob must come up to London, as they had first planned, and though Rothe decreed that he must at all costs remain in the background, she was expected to make a home with him and be, at least in private, Mrs. Robert Haling again.

She knew now what she had refused to confess, even to herself, that she had come back from Italy intending to make the date of that permanent reunion with her husband as remote as possible, and here, at the very moment of her return, was Lottie's warning that she ought to get Bob up to London even sooner than they had arranged.

The very thought made her feel sick and ashamed. How could she meet him, look into his eyes, hide from him the thing which had come to possess her very soul? How could she accept again the travesty of married life with him when she knew what a real marriage of body and soul meant?

Lottie's letter had been lying there for some days awaiting her return, and the next day brought a second and more urgent one. Some of the most extreme of the younger men had now banded themselves together into a company which they called The Legion, and it looked as though their objective was nothing short of red revolution with all its attendant horrors, with its almost certainty of failure against the organised defences of army and police, especially since the latter had been reinforced from the public schools and the class most likely to defend the constitution at all costs.

> *Bobs hot and strong for them and they sneak about at night and hold meetings with locked doors and talk wild about altering all the laws and seizing the railways. Im worried about Bob and think it will be a good thing for him if you could come and see him if you cant have him there with you because hes acting so wild and talking wild.*

Jennifer read the letter several times. She could quite believe in Bob's wild talk and actions, for he was in a state to be easily inflamed, and he had always been inclined to the extreme party, always eager to strike, never listening to counsels of prudence.

It was inevitable that her feelings, if not her sympathies, should have changed a little from living amongst the rich instead of with the poor. Insensibly she had assimilated some of the beliefs of these people, adjusted her standards a little to theirs, learned to look at life from a different angle. She poured scorn on herself when she realised she was doing so, and struggled to get back to the standards to which she had been born and bred, to hatred of riches and a passionate eagerness for the formulation of some scheme whereby all should share equally.

She had talked long and earnestly with Mayne, especially during that magic fortnight which she felt must hold for her all the delights life had to offer. It had not been all love-making, for Mayne had delighted in her mind as he had in her body, finding it as fresh and virgin and tractable, as ready to respond to his least touch, eager and vital.

They had talked of many things, 'of shoes and ships and sealing-wax, of cabbages and kings', and Jennifer had learned such rudiments of economics as had never come into her vision before, had seen so many angles at which the country's problems might be viewed that her mind had reeled and she had begun to doubt the worth of anything she had ever before believed so earnestly.

Mayne was a man of wide understanding and sympathies, able both to feel for the under-dog and to appreciate how he came to be in such a position, and the practical difficulties in the way of releasing him, his probable reaction to such release. He had a respect for the constitution without a bigoted belief in its infallibility. He could see a clear way straight through a problem and yet appreciate the advisability of going round it sometimes.

And he had left Jennifer uncertain and bewildered, feeling strangely alien to the world to which Lottie and Bob belonged, grown apart from them and unable to conceive of her life running parallel with theirs again.

She longed to take the letters and discuss them with Mayne, but they had agreed that the only course possible to them was to part, to meet when chance brought them together and then only as friends.

There was to be no seeking one of the other, no surreptitious visits or stolen hours.

'I couldn't bear to have you like that, my sweet,' Mayne had said, when they discussed the future. 'It would spoil our love if we made a furtive, sordid thing of it, a thing of dark corners and secret coming and going. If we take the courageous course and let it end when we leave Oriavi, we shall have only splendid memories to take with us down the years.'

And she had agreed. How could she, knowing him, do otherwise?

So she could not go to him with these letters. She must herself decide what to do, and with everything within her shrinking from going back to her husband, from beginning the life of lies and deceit which henceforth must be theirs, she found it impossible to do as Lottie begged her and go to Werford.

It would have been easier had she been able to go on with her work, but in Rothe's absence everything was at a standstill, and no scheme of work arranged.

And in less than a week all England was shocked to interest in the collieries, and Jennifer sent headlong to Belsdale by the night train that carried officials hastily recalled from holiday, troops, police, newspaper men, politicians, and a host of those who had little or no business in that direction at all, but whose curiosity caught them by the scruff of the neck and hurled them wherever sensations might be found.

Not only had the men struck work, but they had done so in defiance of their sorely tried leaders, had taken possession of the collieries, commandeered the buses, taken forcible possession of the electricity works, raided the shops for food, clothes and weapons, and overcome the police and the officials of various undertakings who attempted to retain law and order.

The attempt was, of course, foredoomed to failure. It was on too small a scale, nor was it properly organised. Before the flame of Belsdale could ignite other and more inflammable towns of greater importance, additional armed police and troops hastily rushed to the scene, and by sheer force of numbers had ousted the rioters.

But Jennifer had fled there at the first rumours, for Lottie's frantic telegram had been worded in such a way that she knew something terrible was afoot, and she had found herself precipitated into Belsdale amidst a surging mass of soldiers, police, and shouting, excited civilians.

The station had been retaken by the officials and the police, for the affair had been too swift and badly planned to bring out the railway men, and when Jennifer gave up her ticket she was scrutinised by men in uniform who advised her against breaking her journey there.

'Better go further up the line, or else go back, miss,' she was warned, as were other women travelling unaccompanied.

'I live here,' she said. 'My husband is in Belsdale.'

'Would you like an escort, ma'am? There's a good deal of rioting going on still.'

She smiled, though with a conscious effort.

'No, thank you. I shall manage,' and she passed through the gateway and out into a street made unfamiliar by the boarded shop-windows, the fewness of private cars, and the presence of the military. Knots of men gathered to be instantly dispersed and told to move on, and in the tram she boarded soldiers sat at intervals.

Opposite her was a woman from Werford, who stared at her for a moment without recognition, and then smiled uncertainly.

'It's Mrs. Haling, isn't it?' she asked, and Jennifer was aware that the soldier sitting next to her pricked up his ears and watched her.

'Yes. I've just come from London,' she said composedly. 'Have you seen Bob? Is he in Belsdale, do you know?'

'I believe so,' said the woman, and closed up like an oyster with a frown of warning to Jennifer, which made her bewildered.

She got out at the stop near Bob's lodgings and realised that the man was following her, and it was with an unreasonable relief that she found from the landlady that Bob was not in the house.

'I'll wait for him, Mrs. Meek,' she told the woman whose belligerent attitude belied her name.

'If you want something to eat, it's in his cupboard,' said the woman ungraciously, and left her in Bob's bed-sitting-room, the cheap little room they had found for him when they broke up the home in Werford.

Jennifer found the remains of a far more plentiful meal than she would have expected, knowing Bob's circumstances and his refusal of late to accept any of the small sums of money she had been able to send him, sums saved from the allowance Rothe gave her. There were the remains of a good-sized joint and an apple tart, bread, biscuits, cheese and even bought cake, which had been an undreamed-of luxury in their former life. There were two bottles of beer, one of them unopened, and the remains of a packet of much more expensive tobacco than he had formerly smoked.

She got herself a meal, eating sparingly from force of habit now that the old life had claimed her again, and as she was clearing it away the door opened and Bob came limping in.

She saw that he was surprised to find her there, but his greeting amazed her after her first instinctive throb of relief that he did not offer to kiss her. She knew she had been dreading that moment, though she was ashamed of herself for the feeling.

'What have you come for?' he asked her abruptly.

'To be with you, Bob,' she said. 'Don't you want me? You don't look very pleased.'

'Why should I be? What do you want?'

She stared at him, the painful colour rising in her cheeks. It was so long since she had heard a woman spoken to in such a tone, and she was fresh from Mayne's innate courtesy to all women and his tender consideration for her in particular.

'I've come to be with you, Bob. I heard that you were—were not very well, and I felt that you would like to have me here,' she said courageously.

She saw the marks of dissipation in his face, in red-rimmed eyes and blotched skin and loose mouth, in restless movements of his hands and in twitching muscles.

'Why should I?' he asked again, in that surly, hectoring tone. 'I suppose what you mean is somebody's been telling you I've been drinking, eh?'

'Lottie told me you were not well, Bob, and naturally I came as quickly as I could.'

'What did Rothe have to say about that, eh?' he demanded. 'Eh?' as she drew back at his menacing attitude and did not answer.

'Mr. Rothe is not at home, but in any case it would not make any difference what he said if you were ill and needed me. I feel that my place is here with you.'

'Bit late to begin to think that, isn't it?' he asked her, with a sneer.

'I don't know what you mean,' said Jennifer steadily, though her mind was reeling from the shock of her reception.

'Don't you? I'll tell you then, if you're sure you want me to. You and Gentleman Rothe have been having a fine old time, haven't you? And before that, haven't you? Singing lessons and other kinds of lessons. I'm not talking without the book, either. Here—see this?' and he snatched a newspaper from an untidy pile in a corner and flung it on the table before her, pointing at a marked paragraph with a dirty forefinger.

Filled with distaste and a nameless horror, Jennifer looked at the cheap paper, which was headed flamboyantly, 'The Voice of the People', and consisted of a single sheet of badly printed type.

Gentleman Rothe with his Jennifer-Jenks-Haling-Rothe is to be seen daily, but not nightly, outside the villa of a certain famous lady in Italy. It's nice for people when their name is or becomes, Rothe, isn't it? We ourselves could do with a spot of Italy, but, then, our wives' names are not Rothe.

Her lip curled as she pushed the paper away from her.

'Filthy little rag,' she said. 'One could sue them for libel if it were worth it, I suppose.'

Unconsciously her voice and manner had taken on those of the people amongst whom she now lived, and the fact added fuel to the fire of his anger.

'You wouldn't dare—neither would he! You know it's true, but none of the so-called newspapers have the guts to show up people like you, so you're safe, or you think you are. My God, to think I was such a fool as to let you go! I actually believed you were going there to learn to be a singer!' and his laugh was horrible.

'I did go for that purpose, and you know it!' she retorted. 'I am learning to be a singer, and as for you letting me go, how could you have done otherwise? You couldn't provide for me here.'

His face was white with impotent fury.

'That's right! Throw that up at me! I thought you would. It hasn't taken you long. What have you come back for now? Has your fancy man got tired of you and chucked you back at me so that I can have what's left?'

She was sick with anger and fear and disgust.

'Julian Rothe's been nothing to me, and you know it,' she said.

He took a lurching step forward and caught her by the wrists and forced her so closely to him that she could see the bloodshot whites of his eyes and smell his hot, drink-laden breath.

'Oh, do I? Do I know it? Can you look me in the eyes and swear to me by God that you've come back as you went, untouched by any man but me? Can you? If so, swear it by Almighty God! Swear it, I say!'

White as death, with an icy numbness creeping over her limbs, Jennifer faced him, let his wild eyes search hers and look into her very soul, but not a word did she speak. The thing that lay between her lover and herself was too sacred to her to profane it by either denial or confession, and after a few moments, which seemed to her like hours, he pulled her nearer to him and spat in her face.

'You filthy harlot!' he screamed at her, flung her from him with such force that she reeled back against the wall, and with her last consciousness she was aware that he had stumbled from the room. A moment later the front door slammed.

She had no idea how long she had lain there when at length her senses returned to her, but it was growing dark, and she knew it must be well on into the evening. Her watch had stopped, and she saw that Bob had wrenched the winder off it when he had caught her wrists in that cruel grip. Already the tender flesh was showing black marks where his fingers had crushed it, and she gave a little shiver and drew the cuffs of her coat over them.

She had only one desire, which was to get back to London, away from all this horror and hatred and fear, and she put on her hat, found her bag and gloves, and went unsteadily down into the street. Her head ached both from the scene with her husband and from a bruise which she had made by striking her head against the wall, and she tried to find a taxi, but none of the drivers had ventured into the streets since the first day of the rising, when many had had their windows smashed by flying stones, their vehicles being regarded as perquisites of the rich.

Somehow she managed to reach the station, and the first person she saw was Rothe himself.

With a little gasping cry she threw herself into his arms, scarcely knowing what she was doing in the vastness of her relief at seeing him, so cool and self-possessed, so blessedly familiar after all the turmoil of the past hours.

'Oh, Julian, take me home!' she sobbed. 'Don't leave me!'

He pulled her into the buffet near which they were standing, ordered a whisky and made her drink it neat, standing over her and shielding her from the curious eyes of the other customers. She gasped and coughed, but got it down her and handed him back the glass, tears in her eyes.

'Thank you. It was horrible,' she said, with a brave attempt at a smile. 'Please take me home now.'

Neither of them imagined she might mean anything other than Highgate by 'home', and he left her whilst he went to inquire about trains, returning a few moments later with a frown on his face.

'God-forsaken line!' he said. 'I'm sorry, my dear, but there's no train till half past nine. You'd better come and get something to eat to fill in the time. We can't stay here.'

'I can't eat anything,' she said shakily.

'Well, I can. Where is the best restaurant here?'

'People usually go to Skedder's, in Small Street,' she said.

There were one or two taxis in the station-yard, and Rothe approached one of the drivers.

'All depends where you want to go, sir,' said the man.

'Skedder's in Small Street?' asked Rothe.

'I don't mind trying. Things seem a bit quieter now. Jump in, sir. Mrs. Haling going with you?'

Jennifer started when she heard her name and looked at the man. He was a native of Werford, and they had played together as children, and she gave him a small, half-shamed smile.

'How are you, Frank?' she asked.

'Fine, thank you, Jennifer. Been in foreign parts, haven't you?'

'In Italy, yes,' she said uncomfortably, and Rothe bundled her into the cab with a chuckle of appreciation.

'You're a local celebrity,' he said.

'We knew each other when we were small,' said Jennifer.

Rothe had no means of knowing that it was not discomfort because she felt superior to Frank Barter, but because she knew he was a friend of her husband's and would inevitably tell Bob of this meeting, and leave him to draw his own quite wrong conclusions. Then she lay back in the cab and tried to dismiss it from her mind. After all, what did it matter now what Bob thought? Things were finished between them, whatever else came about.

Skedder's was a pleasant modernised restaurant, the ground floor of which had long windows which could be slid back in the hot weather to make the whole place into an open-air restaurant. Some of the windows were still open, and Rothe made for a table near one of these.

'Too cold for you, Jennifer?'

'No, I like it. It's amusing to be right on the street like this, too. It's reminiscent of Menaggio,' she said, struggling to keep the conversation along ordinary lines and restore herself to normal for Rothe's sake.

'So long as they don't start rioting outside and break the place up,' he said.

The waiter who had come for their order smiled reassuringly.

'They don't do things like that in Small Street, sir,' he said. 'We're off the track for that here. Down the High Street, or in the market square, you *might* worry.'

'It isn't really serious rioting, is it? No shooting or real fighting?'

'Nothing bad, sir. One or two have been taken to hospital, they say, but you can't get the truth of it. The soldiers'll soon have them under, though.'

'I'm told quite a number of the rioters have revolvers,' said Rothe.

'I've seen one or two myself, but I don't think they'll use them. They'd be too scared here. It isn't like Chicago. Can I have your order, sir?'

Rothe ordered from his knowledge of her tastes, and she was thankful not to have to exert herself to make a choice.

'I didn't know you were even back in England, Julian,' she said when the man had gone.

'Lucky for you I am, isn't it?' he asked, with a smile. 'You'd only left the house about half an hour when I got back, and when they told me you'd come here by yourself I dashed off after you and got to the station in time to see the train go out. I had to wait nearly two hours for another, and it was pure luck meeting you at the station like that.'

'I thought you'd dropped straight from heaven,' she said, with a catch in her voice. 'I couldn't believe you were real when I saw you there. I don't think I've ever been so glad to see anybody in my life before.'

He laughed and stretched out a hand to touch hers across the table as she toyed nervously with the menu, revealing to his practised eye her strained nerves.

'Nor I to see you, for I hadn't any idea where to start looking for you. I wasn't looking only for my straying pupil, either, my dear. I was greatly concerned for your safety.'

The tears welled up into her eyes at the look on his face, at the kindliness in his voice, at the warming knowledge that this man understood her and cared for her, was her friend.

She let her hand cling to his and leant across the table to him.

'You're divinely good to me, Julian,' she said. 'I long for the day when I can begin to repay you.'

He opened his lips to reply to her, but before he could speak there was a shot, a cry, and he fell forward over the table with a little choking sound.

Jennifer screamed and rose to her feet, and instantly all was confusion, a crowd gathering in miraculous fashion inside and out, people pressing through the open window to stare at the man sprawled across the table and at the ugly red stream spreading already across the white cloth.

Two police pushed their way through the crowd, elbowing them out of the way, and Rothe was carried into an inner room, whilst someone telephoned for an ambulance, and Jennifer, appalled and frightened, tried to shut her eyes to the horror and her ears to the multitude of voices, and the insistent repetition of her name when someone recognised her.

'Can I go with him?' she asked, white-faced, when the ambulance arrived and Rothe, unconscious but alive, was lifted into it.

Permission was given, though the men stared curiously at her when she gave them her name as Jennifer Haling, and they were rushed to the hospital where, after an agonising wait in a draughty corridor, she was admitted to the ward and to the screened corner, where Rothe lay waiting for the second doctor who had been called.

'You can't stay, Mrs. Haling,' she was warned. 'The house surgeon is going to operate as soon as Dr. Blather arrives.'

There was no flicker of consciousness from the figure on the bed, and Jennifer turned to the nurse fearfully.

'Will he die?' she asked in a horrified whisper.

'We shall do all we can,' the girl assured her, with the false cheerfulness of her kind, and Jennifer was led away.

Never in her life had she felt so appallingly lost and alone. She had nowhere to go, no one to whom she could turn, and back there in the cheerless white building she had just left lay, possibly dying, the man on whom she had come to depend for almost everything in life. She longed inexpressibly for Mayne, but the memory of her husband's words was too vividly in her mind to allow her to send for him, though she knew he would come. It would be too horrible if Brenner and Bob were to meet, and she shuddered at the bare thought of it, for she felt certain that her husband would guess their secret and drag it and them in the mire.

She thought of Lottie, but how could she ask her to come, in the circumstances? She sheered away from that whisper she had heard, not once or twice but many times, whilst she had stood with the crowd and waited for the ambulance to take Rothe away. It was Bob Haling's name that had been whispered, and when she was out of the hospital grounds and in the street again, she found herself looking about fearfully, as if at every turn she should meet some corroboration of the horrible fear that possessed her mind.

They had told her at the hospital that there would be no news of their patient until half past nine at the earliest, and she might telephone then, or inquire at the door.

Half past nine! That was the time of the London train, the train on which they would have been going back to the safety and peace of that home she might never see again.

She wandered about the streets unhappily, and long before the appointed hour was at the hospital, standing on the steps trying to summon her courage to ring the bell. What if they were to tell her that Julian was dead? What if Bob ... She could not let that thought have place in her mind, and she rang the bell frantically.

'I want to know about, Mr. Rothe,' she said. 'I'm too early, but if I might wait?'

She was allowed to wait in the entrance hall, and at a quarter to ten a message reached her that the operation had been performed and the patient was comfortable. How many despairing, anxious people have had to content themselves with just that information and go away with the sense of futility, of utter helplessness against the giant, impersonal organisation which has swallowed up the dearest thing in life?

Lottie, good and faithful friend, telephoned to the hospital, hearing the bad news which flies fast, and before Jennifer left a message was handed to her that Mrs. Marsh would be waiting for her at the station when she left the hospital.

The two friends met and clung and wept in each other's arms for a few inevitable moments, and then Lottie's practical common sense reasserted itself.

'Well, it's no good doing this. I've arranged for us to go to Aunt Loo's for the night. You remember Auntie Loo? Mrs. Parr? I've been round there and got a key because I didn't know how late you'd be at the hospital. How is he, Jen?' fearfully.

'I don't know. They never tell you anything at the hospital, but I've been warned by the police that I mustn't leave Belsdale. Oh, Lottie, what if he dies?' and the two looked at each other with stark knowledge in their eyes.

'Don't meet that till you have to,' said her friend briskly. 'This is our bus. We get off at the market square.'

'You're so good to me, Lottie,' said Jennifer with a sob.

'Why not? Aren't we pals?' asked Lottie, and they sat in the bus with clasped hands and hearts too full for speech.

Chapter Seventeen

Night and day doctors and nurses fought for Julian Rothe's life, and never for an instant did the police leave his bedside in case in a moment of consciousness he should be able to reveal any definite facts about his assailant.

Jennifer haunted the hospital, a white ghost of a woman with fear in her eyes and a dull ache at her heart.

She never had an instant's doubt about Bob's guilt, and she tortured herself with imagining the result if Julian died. Her memory gave her back faithfully every word, every look of that interview she had had with her husband, and in the final insult he had hurled at her as he flung her from him she had seen the madness of hate for her and for the man who he believed had taken her from him.

She knew that the police were watching Bob and expected hourly to hear that he had been arrested lest he escaped them. Lottie had told her, fearfully and with averted eyes, that Frank Barter had been heard to say that Bob had known that his wife and Rothe were in the restaurant. Soon after she had left his lodgings, he had gone to the station with some vague idea of a reconciliation in spite of everything, and Barter, not guessing that anything was wrong, had told him that Jennifer was at Skedder's with a man whose description fitted Bob's conception of Julian Rothe, though he had never seen the man himself, and had formed his ideas from Jennifer's description and some snapshots which she had sent him from Italy.

Aghast at the position in which his free talk had placed his pal, Barter refused to be drawn by the police into admitting his own statements, but Jennifer knew that if legal action were taken against Bob, Frank would be forced to speak.

On the fourth day Rothe recovered consciousness, and Jennifer's hopes ran high, though the sister-in-charge warned her gently not to be too optimistic.

'He is very ill, Mrs. Haling,' she said. 'We are doing all we can, but you must be prepared for anything that might happen in spite of us.'

Jennifer swallowed hard and looked at her with her over-bright eyes.

'He can't die,' she whispered desperately. 'Oh, don't let him!'

The woman said nothing, but let Jennifer go alone to the bed, where at last the body was inhabited by its mind, and Julian lay with eyes open, ready for her.

She dropped on her knees by the bed, everything forgotten save that this was the man who had changed the whole face of life for her, had come to mean so much to her, and who now lay in peril.

'Oh, Julian—dear Julian!' she said brokenly.

'Don't worry, my dear,' he whispered, and his eyes went with a ghost of their old sardonic gleam to where the plainclothes man sat trying to look as though he were not listening.

'Are you in pain, Julian?'

'Not much. Jennifer—could you—I'd like to see *her*,' and his voice dropped to a mere thread of sound as his eyes closed again.

'You mean—Mrs. Ferring?' asked Jennifer gently.

His eyes opened and he smiled a little and made a gesture of assent. He could not say anything else.

'I'll write,' said Jennifer. 'Do you know where she is? Is she still abroad?'

'I—don't—think—' but the effort was too much for him and he lapsed into unconsciousness.

Jennifer called the nurse and went away. At least he had given her something to do, and she went at once to the small hotel near the hospital where she had taken a room.

'I want to put a call through to London at once,' she said and after a little delay she found herself speaking to the Ferrings' butler.

'Is Mrs. Ferring back yet?' she asked. 'It's—Miss Rothe speaking.'

The name sounded odd to her. These last few days had seemed a lifetime, and during them she had been Mrs. Haling and Jennifer

Rothe had become a stranger to her, part of some other life than her own.

'She came back about half an hour ago, Miss Rothe. Shall I ask her to speak to you?'

'Please do.'

Claire's voice came to her almost at once.

'Oh, Jennifer, I'm so glad you've rung up. Where are you? How is he? I came back at once, directly I heard.'

It seemed that all the barriers were down. There was no attempt to disguise Claire's passionate interest in Rothe, no suggestion that the girl did not know all that there was to know of these two. She was a woman in agony, and nothing else mattered, save that she should learn news of her beloved.

'He's very ill, but he's conscious, and has just asked for you,' said Jennifer, in a voice filled with tears. 'Can you possibly come?'

'Oh, but of course!' said Claire. 'At once. Tonight. Where can I find you? Or shall I go straight to the hospital?'

Jennifer gave her the name of her hotel and said she would meet the train.

'I shall go to Croydon and get an aeroplane,' said Claire.

'I'll stop in and wait for you, then, unless they send for me to go back to him.'

'Yes. He mustn't be left. Oh, Jennifer, is he going to die?' she asked, with a sob.

'I hope not. It's terrible for me. They think that—Bob did it.'

'Oh, my dear! But, of course, he didn't. I'm going to ring off now and go straight to Croydon. Pray for him to live, Jennifer,' and she was gone.

Jennifer went to her room and longed afresh, with a passionate intensity of longing, to see Brenner for a moment, just for a moment. She had never felt so terribly alone in her life. She knew that somewhere, never very far from her, was Bob, her husband, and that her lightest word or wish would bring him to her, but she shrank intolerably from the very thought of meeting him. She felt no resentment against him, nothing but a dull numbness which she knew would leap into something active and vital at the first moment of contact with him. Before she had loved Brenner Mayne his attitude towards Rothe would have been beyond her comprehension, but in the intensity of her own love, she could understand the feeling which must have actuated Bob when he saw her with the man for whom he believed she had betrayed him.

Suppose there had been truth there, that it had been Brenner with her in Skedder's, that Brenner lay there behind those walls that enclosed so much tragedy and suffering, fighting for his life!

She shuddered and remembered that Claire was suffering that very agony.

Claire had read of the occurrence casually in an English newspaper already two days old, and, cancelling without a thought every engagement, she had started for home within the hour, travelling in discomfort, feverishly watching the slow hours pass without rest or sleep, pacing the corridors of trains like some caged wild thing, chafing intolerably at the least delay, and arriving without warning at her London house.

Her husband was holding an important conference in the privacy of his study, and it ended a few minutes after the conversation with Jennifer.

A tap at her door heralded his entrance, and she turned to him with a look on her face which he had not seen there for years. She looked incredibly aged from that journey, and yet something about her made him remember what she had been like when he first married her. The careful mask of the society woman and the political hostess was gone, and she stood revealed as the woman herself, that woman whom he had not seen for nearly eighteen years.

'I have only just learned that you are back, my dear,' he said, with his usual punctilious courtesy, but his eyes asked a question, for she was obviously packing again, and the room was strewn with clothes.

'You know about Julian?' she asked, without preamble, pausing in her work.

She had not felt equal to the tears and protestations which always accompanied Luigia when she had to be forcibly torn from her own people again, and had preferred to travel alone and look after herself.

'I have heard, naturally. It has considerable political significance,' said Ferring, in measured tones.

'Oh, political! I'm not thinking of it in that way,' she said impatiently.

'Surely, my dear, you aren't thinking of it in any other way?' he asked steadily.

She faced him across the strewn bed, a desperate determination in her whole attitude which at least matched his own more steely intentness.

'You know I am, Guy. You know exactly how I am feeling about this and why I have come home.'

'Do I? And why have you come home?' he asked blandly, though his eyes were ice cold.

'I'm going to him, Guy,' she said.

'I beg your pardon, my dear, but you are going to do nothing of the sort,' he said, in that same inflexible tone. 'You will kindly remember that you are my wife and that nothing—*nothing* can justify your forgetfulness of that fact. You will remain here and do your duty as I do.'

'I can't do it, Guy. I'm going to Julian,' she said, but a faint terror had crept into her eyes as she realised what she was defying. 'He's—dying,' and her voice broke uncontrollably, though the next moment she had it under control again.

'What concern is that of ours, Claire?' asked the merciless voice.

'Oh, how hard you are! Have you never had an emotion in your life? Never one decent, human emotion?' she cried.

'Yes. One. You killed it so long ago, however, that I have managed to forget it, fortunately.'

'It was not such a brave thing, after all, was it?' she asked him bitterly. 'It wasn't big enough to forgive, was it?'

'Didn't I forgive? Aren't these years of comfort and pleasure and security proof enough?'

'That wasn't forgiveness. It wasn't love, not love of me. It was love of yourself, of your good name, of Challissey and all that it meant. And it was fear, fear of appearing ridiculous, of having men laugh at you and point at you for a fool. Do you think I didn't know why you were what you call forgiving, why all these years you have called me your wife and Derek your son? Why you have kept me chained to you for my boy's sake? Made me a travesty of myself, a mouthpiece for you, a catspaw to help you pull the chestnuts from the fire? Do you think I haven't known you for what you are all these years?'

Her voice was low and filled with concentrated bitterness, the bitterness of all her years of silence, of repression, of unending payment for one wrong done to this man of iron.

He was outwardly quite unmoved by her rapid, unconsidered speech, though inwardly he wondered if he had ever really known her.

'Even if I were all these things you say, by what right do you fling them at me as accusations? What other treatment did you expect? Have I ever ill-treated you? Denied you anything? Regarded you as other than a wife to be respected? Has the boy been denied anything? Has he or anyone else ever had cause to suspect that he is not my own son?'

She spread out impotent hands. He was always so terribly right!

'Oh no, there has been nothing—nothing!' she said wildly. 'I have always been the beautiful Mrs. Ferring, the popular society hostess, the perfect political wife! Derek has always been the son of Guy Ferring, the eventual heir to Challissey, the future Lord Bordray—and a prig and a snob into the bargain, thanks to you. Oh yes, we've had everything—everything except happiness, decent human emotions, love. There's not even been sorrow and sadness—except mine, which I could never show.'

'And these weeks every year in Italy with your lover?' he asked coldly, though the veneer was at last cracking and showing the anger and the bitterness and the hatred that Claire had always known must be there.

'You didn't give me those, Guy. I took them and you didn't dare to stop me because you knew that it would have strained these artificial bonds between us to breaking point and beyond it. You were afraid, not of losing me, but because you would lose Derek and, eventually, Challissey. Do you think I haven't understood all these years why you have let me remain outwardly your wife and acknowledged Julian's son as yours?'

Instinctively he looked behind him and moved a step further from the door and Claire laughed. It was not a pleasant sound.

'Oh, the door's shut. No one can hear,' she said scornfully, and she bent again over the case into which she had been cramming a few necessities.

'You're going then?' asked Ferring.

'Definitely. Nothing you can say or do can stop me,' and there was finality in her voice.

'Very well. I want you thoroughly to appreciate the position if you do,' he said in measured tones. 'I shall take immediate steps to divorce you, citing Rothe, and there is no possibility of my being considered as condoning the adultery because I shall quote the last few weeks at your Italian villa in evidence and shall not receive you back into my house after you leave it tonight. I shall also put in the facts of Derek's birth and disown him.'

Claire was very white, but her purpose was unshaken.

'You will ruin yourself as well, Guy,' she said.

'I know. I am prepared for that, regrettable though it will be.'

'And the future of Challissey?'

'I shall marry again. There is probably no reason at all why I should not beget a son. I have many times thought that all this possibly has been a delusion and that our three fruitless years of marriage may have indicated nothing. We probably jumped to conclusions.'

'And you think you would find revenge sweet even at the cost of your career and the furtive contempt of other men because you have pretended all these years that another man's son is your own and your wife blameless?'

'Yes.'

'What is it you're avenging, Guy? My going to the man I love when he is—dying, or that old, old wrong I did you? No, neither of those things. You're going to get satisfaction out of humiliating me through Derek because all these years you've hated me and regretted the bargain you struck with me. You've been jealous of me because of the influence I've had with men who have helped on your career and given you power. There is no hatred on earth greater than that which a man feels towards a woman whom he has ceased to love and yet on whom he is dependent. Everything she does and is, is gall to him and yet he goes on drinking the cup because of his lack of courage to live without what she can give him. Oh, I haven't lived with you all these years without understanding you, Guy. Well, our future is in your hands. You can do what you like with me and with Derek. I am going to Julian.'

'Have you considered what your position will be if he dies, as appears likely?' asked Ferring cruelly.

She winced, but her determination was unshaken.

'I have considered it,' she said. 'I shall be divorced by my husband for a man who cannot marry me. If it were otherwise, do you imagine I think you would still divorce me? You swore to me that you would never let me marry him, didn't you?'

He smiled, and she saw the devil beneath that cold, cruel movement of his muscles, for the smile did not reach his eyes.

'I did.'

'There is nothing more to be said between us then, Guy. Will you please leave me alone now to finish my packing? And if you prefer me not to use the car in the circumstances, would you be good enough to have a taxi ordered?'

'By all means use the car,' he said suavely, and turned and left her.

Like a woman in a dream, she closed and locked her case, saw that there was money in her bag, and went down the stairs and into the waiting car.

'Hurry, please,' she told the chauffeur. 'At all costs,' and she leaned back against the cushions and closed her eyes.

The scene through which she had passed seemed all part of the dream, easily pushed into the background, to be remembered later perhaps and wondered at, but not mattering at all whilst her mind held the thought of Julian dying, waiting for her, as surely he would wait, knowing that she would come.

'Oh, God let him live just till I've seen him again,' was her continual, wordless prayer. For his life she could not pray, dare not

251

ask. She remembered too well the tones of Jennifer's voice and knew that Julian would die.

The aeroplane which she had ordered by telephone was waiting for her at the air-port.

'Did you arrange for a car to meet me at the aerodrome the other end?' she asked the pilot.

'Everything is arranged, madam,' he assured her. 'Will you step in?'

She was usually air-sick, but today she was impervious to any mere physical sensation, and she sat so motionless as they flew at tremendous speed that the young pilot amused himself by seeing how much he could get out of his 'plane, getting her to the aerodrome in record time.

Claire thanked him absently and hurried to the car.

'Belsdale Hospital as quickly as you can,' she said, and she began to emerge from the dream and know actual physical sickness when at last she was walking behind the rustling nurse to where Julian waited for death.

'How is he?' she had managed to ask the nurse.

She looked grave and was still young enough to be pitiful.

'Well, of course, he's very ill indeed, but he is conscious and looking forward to seeing you, Mrs Ferring.'

She had had to give her name before they would admit her, and though at first it had expressed nothing to them, she could see that this girl knew who she was.

But she forgot everything when she saw Julian. Their utter absorption in each other cut them off from all else as completely as the red screens gave them privacy from the other occupants of the ward. The police had taken from him his assurance that he could give no light on the source or author of the attack on him, and they had left him at last.

'I knew you would come,' he told her in that difficult whisper of his. He had spoken little since Jennifer had told him she was coming, saving his voice and his strength for her.

'As soon as I heard, I started back,' she said. 'Oh, my darling,' and in spite of herself the tears rained down her face.

'Don't let me go away with the memory of your tears, Claire. I've loved your happiness so.'

'You've given me all I've ever had of happiness,' she told him brokenly.

'Does Ferring know you've come?'

'Yes.'

'How did he take it?'

'Rather badly, but he'll get over it.'

'I can't do you any more harm now, my dear,' he said with a little twisted smile that tore her heart.

'You've never done me harm, Julian,' she told him passionately.

'Yes, my dear, I have. If I'd let you go, eighteen years ago—can it be eighteen, Claire?—you'd have been happy with Guy.'

'I should never have been happy with him. He's too hard and cold to give any woman happiness. Don't let's have any regrets, Julian. I haven't any. I've loved every minute with you, every thought and memory of you.'

'And I of you, my dear heart.'

The effort had been almost too much for him, and he lay still for a long time, only his eyes and the thin, nervous hand she held telling her that he was still conscious.

When he spoke again, she realised that he was definitely weaker.

'Darling, I want you to look after Jennifer if you can. Get Lader to launch her, though she really wants another six months' training. I haven't provided for her. You see—this is purely for your ears, Claire—it was Haling who shot me. I saw him just as he fired, though I have told the police I didn't see anybody. She's dreadfully upset about it, poor girl, and it would be ghastly for her if they—got him for it. If I make provision for her, it might lend colour to what she says people think about us. You see?'

'Of course I'll do anything you like, dear,' she said, infinitely distressed by the need for such talk between them, but knowing that it would ease his mind.

'See Wontner—afterwards. I've left you and Derek provided for, in case—anything happens between you and Ferring. I've made it all right, though. There won't be any publicity the way I've done it.

Wontner will handle it all for you. He's a decent chap. You can trust him absolutely.'

'Don't talk about that now, Julian. The time's—so short,' with a sob.

'I want to be sure you'll be all right, though—you and the boy. I'd like to have seen him again, but it wouldn't have done,' he added wistfully. 'You've made a fine job of him, Claire.'

She shook her head and smiled through tears.

'He's much more what Guy's made of him,' she said. 'It's better that way. The respectable people like Guy are really the only people who can't come a cropper, the only safe people.'

'But they don't have any fun in life,' said Rothe, and in the long look which hung between them was memory which would surely go with him as with her. 'We've had fun, haven't we, Claire?'

'Marvellous fun, Julian.'

He had to be silent again, and as she watched him, she grew afraid and rose to call the nurse. He opened his eyes and shook his head feebly, groping for her hand again.

'No. Just—you—now—beloved.'

She knelt beside him, his hand growing flaccid between her own, and she leaned near him to catch the whispered words.

'If I should fall asleep—where no dreams are—I shall have known—the perfect hour.'

She knew the words. It was a poem they had loved, had whispered in the darkness together. She bowed her head on their clasped hands and his soul passed out as he would have had it pass, without pain and with only the beloved woman at its passing.

Claire knelt beside him until the sister came behind the screen, saw at once what had happened, and led her gently away. She went in silence, without a tear. This was too deep for tears. Her heart wept whilst her eyes were dry.

She went back to London without even seeing Jennifer. She had no desire to stay by the body of the man whose soul she had known and loved. Julian was gone. Why, then, should she stay for the pitiful rites with which we seek to dignify that which is left?

She sent a message to Jennifer and a telegram to Wontner, Julian's solicitor, and went quietly back to her husband's house. Her mind worked like an automaton. Part of it was dazed with suffering which presently would absorb the rest of it, but for the moment she acted with precision of thought which afterwards amazed her.

She had the business of packing her personal belongings as her first care, and she went about it methodically, sorting and listing and packing such small treasures as she would not trust to alien hands. It was long past midnight when Ferring came to find her so occupied, and she had had no food since luncheon on the train that morning, though the servants had tried to persuade her to eat the dinner hastily prepared for her.

She had wondered dully how much they knew, for they had been kind and a little curious, and ill news flies fast.

She looked up without interest as Ferring came into the room. She was in her own sitting-room packing into a case some small statuettes of marble and porphyry which she had bought on one occasion when she and Julian had been together in Italy. She was lost in her memories and seemed infinitely remote to Ferring. It was as if already she had gone from him.

'You've come back then?' he asked her without resentment. There was no expression at all in his voice.

'He's dead,' she said briefly and went on with her work.

'Is it any use my saying I'm—sorry, Claire?'

There was an unusual quality in his voice which pierced for a moment the fog which enwrapped her and she looked at him with startled eyes.

'Sorry?'

'It is—a grief to you, Claire. I know that.'

'Yes.'

She could not speak of it, least of all to this man who was both her husband and a stranger, who had never, save briefly in the first year or two of their marriage, dwelt within her secret life at all.

After a silence, he spoke again.

'Gage tells me you have had nothing to eat since you came home. Did you dine on the train?'

'No.'

He went out of the room and returned presently with a tray on which were sandwiches and wine. He filled a glass and brought it to her.

'Drink it, Claire—please,' he said, and again there was that arresting quality in his voice. She looked at him, took the glass and drank. 'And the sandwiches. I've cut them freshly.'

'You cut them, Guy?'

'The servants have gone to bed.'

She knew, with the part of her that was still alive, that at any other time she would have been profoundly touched by his unwonted consideration for her. He had always paid others to care for her. Now, for almost the first time in her memory of him, he was giving her personal service.

'Thank you,' she said simply. 'That was kind.'

'Must you do all this tonight, Claire?' he asked her next.

'But of course. It would be unnecessarily distressing for—for both of us if I had to come back another time to do it, and I should not like to leave these things in the hands of the warehousemen.'

'Will you at least go to bed now and leave it until tomorrow?'

She looked at him in surprise, with a little frown.

'I don't know what you mean. You aren't suggesting that I sleep here?'

'I was, yes,' said Ferring uncomfortably.

Something had happened to him during the short time of her absence from the house. She felt it without defining it, though it was of too little consequence to her to analyse it.

'Aren't you overlooking the fact that if I sleep under your roof tonight, with your consent, you may be—prejudicing your case?' she asked.

'But what will you do otherwise? Where will you go at this time of night? It's nearly two o'clock.'

'Is it? I had no idea. I ought to have gone before, but there was so much to do. I have taken a room at the "Overland" for a few days, and I told them I might be late. As for what I'm going to do after that, does it matter?'

'I think it does.'

'Oh—I don't know that I've made any plans. I shall see what Derek wants to do when he gets back. I shall have to send him a wire tomorrow. He'll be back then by the end of the week.'

She spoke with the utter indifference she felt, and he knew that it was no pose. That told him more plainly than any words how deeply she had cared for Julian Rothe and how bitter was her loss. Strange feelings stirred within him, feelings of pity, to which he had so long been a stranger that he felt awkward and diffident about them.

'Claire, as a personal favour to me, will you stay in this house tonight? If you prefer it, I will go to the club, but please stay here.'

'You're taking a risk, Guy.'

'I am prepared to take it.'

She passed a hand across her eyes.

'I think I must be very tired,' she said weakly.

'I am sure you are, my dear. If I leave you now, will you go to bed?'

'Yes. You must do as you think—wise about going to the club, Guy,' and her utter weariness was apparent in the way she spoke and moved.

He crossed the room and took her hand in his for a moment.

'Take some aspirin, dear, and try to sleep. We'll talk things over again in the morning. We were both of us—overwrought this afternoon. Good night, Claire.'

'Good night, Guy.'

As she lay staring into the darkness after she had gone to bed, she heard him moving in the next room and knew that he had not gone to the club. She knew what that meant. In all probability things were to go on just the same between them. There would be no scandal, no divorce, no wrecking of Derek's life, no need to humiliate herself before him, to make him turn on her in hatred.

It didn't matter.

Nothing mattered.

Nothing would ever matter again.

Julian was dead.

Chapter Eighteen

The next day's papers gave two items of news of not very great importance to the general public.

Julian Rothe was dead, and Robert Haling had been arrested and charged with his murder.

The papers were very guarded in their reference to Jennifer, little mention being made of her, and the general impression was that Rothe had been shot accidentally in the rioting and the charge of murder was intended as a deterrent, and as a check to the men who were stirring up the trouble in the coal-fields.

To Jennifer it was a blow, although in her heart she had expected it. What she did not expect was Bob's vehement denial of the charge, and her spirits rose as she tried to believe in him rather than in the openly expressed opinions which she heard on every side, though their own friends tried to hide them from her.

Lottie said very little, but her face was pale and troubled and she listened gravely to Jennifer's reiterated belief in his innocence.

'He ought to have a good lawyer, Jennifer,' was all she would say. 'One of the really big criminal lawyers, like Curtis Bennett or Brenner Mayne. Why, you know Brenner Mayne, don't you? Didn't you meet him in London once?'

'Yes. I don't think we could get him for Bob, though,' said Jennifer slowly, avoiding her eyes.

'Why not? You mean it would be too expensive?'

'Probably.' She caught at the excuse. 'I believe he gets enormous fees which we couldn't possibly afford.'

'Don't you think Mr. Rothe left you anything, Jen?'

'Lottie! Even if he did, could I possibly use it for this? And there is no earthly reason why he should have left me anything. I owe him hundreds of pounds as it is, and I can never repay him now.'

'Well, he won't want it, will he?' asked Lottie practically. 'And you'll be able to earn plenty, won't you?'

Jennifer swallowed a lump in her throat and tears stung her eyes.

'I don't know. I feel at present as though I should never be able to sing again, and in any case I may not be able to get engagements. I haven't finished my training.'

'But you did get them, didn't you? You must have had a good many before you went to Italy. You used to send us quite a lot.'

Listlessly Jennifer told her the facts about that escapade of hers. How long ago it seemed! How simple and primitive had been her enjoyment of it! How far she had gone from the girl who had sung in the streets in the grey velvet mask!

'Bob thought Mr. Rothe had given you that money, Jen,' Lottie told her gravely. 'That was one reason why I wanted you either to come back or to let him come up to London. I don't know how he knew, but he said he had found out that you hadn't had any singing engagements and—well, you know what men are. They are always ready to think the worst of a woman on her own, even the best of them.'

'Bob couldn't possibly have known I wasn't getting engagements,' said Jennifer. 'London's too big for that and there are too many concerts and dinners and things. He must just have been suspicious and jealous and—imagined things.'

'You never were—like that with Mr. Rothe, were you, Jen?'

Jennifer looked straight in front of her.

'No, never,' she said.

Unwillingly, Jennifer went to see Bob. It was a horrible experience for her, for they had not a moment's privacy and there were things that must be said between them after that last interview of theirs, things to which no third person should listen.

'Do you hate me, Jen?' asked Bob, a thin, white-faced, haggard Bob now that he was not wearing the false mask of the drunken man.

'Of course I don't, Bob. Why should I?' she asked pitifully.

'They say I shot Rothe. You don't believe it?'

'No.'

'Jen—what if they manage to—to make it look that I did?' She shut her eyes and her mind to the furtive look he gave her.

'How can they, if you didn't do it?' she asked with an assurance she did not feel. What would be the reaction of a court of law to that look in his face, that tone in his voice?

'Jen, you've got to get me a lawyer, a good one, one of the top-notchers. He'll get me off.'

'How can I, Bob? Where is the money coming from?' she asked.

'You can get it, can't you? Some of your rich friends will lend it to you, won't they?'

She shrank back in distaste. It seemed horrible to her that he should be able to make the suggestion, and she knew in that moment that in her heart she believed him to be not only guilty but a coward. He had shot the man whom he had believed to be her lover, and he would accept his freedom at the hands of her friends and those probably of the man himself.

'I couldn't do that, Bob,' she said in a low voice.

'Not to save my life, Jen? It may come to that. They're calling it wilful murder, and that means hanging if they bring me in guilty.'

She shivered, and the warder who mounted guard over them moved nearer to her. They always avoided scenes if they could, though she did not look the hysterical kind.

'Time's up now, ma'am,' he warned her.

'I'll see what I can do, Bob,' she told him shakily, and was glad of the excuse to hurry away.

She went to see Mr. Brigget, the old solicitor to whom she had gone at the beginning of all this business. He had known them both since they were children, and he was sorry for the mess in which they had landed themselves. He included Jennifer in the primary causes because, in his opinion, she should have stayed with her husband instead of going away to work out her own career, leaving him to get along without her and to fall into bad ways and make bad friends.

'Bob says he wants a first-class lawyer to defend him, Mr. Brigget,' she said nervously. 'They're charging him with—with murder, you know.'

'Yes. That was inevitable, I am afraid, after all the rather wild talk there's been, and of course your husband was not very discreet.'

'How does one get the very best lawyers, Mr. Brigget? How much do they cost?'

'Well, on a capital charge, the State will provide adequately for your husband's defence, of course. I don't suggest that they would brief men like—well, like Curtis Bennett or Brenner Mayne or men like that, but he would have a first-class counsel, with probably a very good junior as well.'

'How does one get men like—Curtis Bennett or Brenner Mayne?' asked Jennifer.

Mr. Brigget shrugged his shoulders expressively.

'Well, just as one can get most things, my dear young lady—by being able to afford them, or getting someone to afford them for you.'

'I see. You don't think—whom do you think Bob might be given to defend him?'

'Oh, men like Giles Mettling, or there is a very good criminal lawyer who has handled several cases successfully lately, a man called Bantery.'

'How much would it cost to have—Curtis Bennett, if he would take the case?' asked Jennifer.

'I could find out and let you know, of course, but it would naturally be a very expensive business, and Sir Henry might not be willing to take the case at all. If you care to wait a few minutes, my clerk could give me some rough idea of the probable fees. There would be the two cases, of course, the first in a magistrate's court and then probably in the High Court.'

When the approximate figure was given to Jennifer she looked stricken. Even if she could borrow such a sum from Claire Ferring, how could she ever hope to pay it back? Any question of earning large sums by her voice seemed endlessly remote of answer at present.

Mr. Brigget talked on, but she scarcely heard what he said and left his office without any clear idea of what had been arranged.

In thought she had flown to Mayne, was talking to him, watching him, listening to him. Dare she do that? Rather, dare she not do it? She felt a tremendous responsibility towards Bob for the crime which she believed in her heart he had committed. True, she had been blameless of the sin with Rothe for which he had taken his revenge on him, but actually she was guilty, for had she not covered Brenner by allowing Bob to believe his accusations against Rothe, Julian would be alive yet.

Lottie had gone with her to the solicitor's and was waiting for her. She gave her reluctantly the rough outline of what Mr. Brigget had said, and Lottie was vehement in her urging that Jennifer get a famous counsel, no matter at what cost.

'Oh, Jen, it may mean his life, and he's lost so much already. Everything's been against him, his health and his job, and—losing you.'

'He hasn't lost me, Lottie. I'm still his wife,' said Jennifer in a low voice.

'In name, yes, but not in anything else. You're lost to us, Jen. You'll never be able to live with us again, our sort of life. You've grown too far away from us. Do you think Bob doesn't realise that just as much as I do? Oh, Jen, if you can do anything that will get him free from this horrible thing, won't you do it? Whatever it means?'

She had no idea what she was asking of Jennifer, but her words rang through her sister-in-law's mind long after Lottie had left her and she had gone back to her hotel.

'Whatever it means' – and it meant asking her lover to defend the husband who had shot Julian Rothe for the sin which she and Brenner had committed.

The next morning, after a sleepless night, she took the train to London, leaving a message for Lottie that she had done so and sending instructions to Mr. Brigget to do nothing until he heard from her again.

From the London terminus she rang up Brenner's chambers to learn that he was in court.

'When will he be available?' she asked. 'It is a matter of urgent necessity, and I think he will make an appointment if you give him my name.'

The clerk was doubtful, but interested. It did not sound like a 'case', he decided.

'There will be an interval for lunch,' he said. 'I could slip across to the courts and give him a message.'

'Would you do that? Will you say that—that Miss Rothe is in town and would like to see him today if possible? I will call you again later if there is any message. Tell him I will keep any appointment he is able to make. Thank you,' and she rang off.

When she rang again, the clerk's tone was almost affectionate. He was sentimental and had long been looking forward to Mayne, who was his hero and idol, having an 'affair', and his sharp eyes had not failed to note the instant response in Mayne's when he received the message.

'Oh yes, Miss Rothe. Mr. Mayne says will you dine with him tonight at his house at half past seven? He says if he is detained, will you please ask for anything you want, and he will be with you as soon as possible.'

'Thank you,' said Jennifer sedately, but her heart was racing when she replaced the receiver and walked away.

She went, reluctantly but of necessity, to Rothe's house at Highgate to dress and to collect a few things which she could no longer do without. Everything was it as had always been save that the blinds were down and the servants subdued and sorrowful.

She had the blinds pulled up.

'He loved the light. He would hate to see it all darkened like this,' she told Simmons, and it was with relief that they did as she suggested.

'Will you be coming back to live here, Miss Rothe?' asked the butler hopefully.

'No, I don't think I shall be able to do that,' said Jennifer. 'You see, I was only a pupil and there is no reason why I should go on living here. I shall have to go back amongst my own people. I shall miss you all, Simmons.'

'And we shall miss you. Miss Rothe, if I may make so bold,' said the man, for she had been pleasant to serve, never exacting or fault-finding, never failing in gratitude for the smallest service.

She was glad that she had a very good black evening gown, one which Claire had helped her to choose, and though she was thin and worn and the events of the past fortnight had told on her severely, she knew she looked attractive and was glad of it.

In spite of everything, there was a flush in her cheeks and light in her eyes when Mayne came himself to open his door to her and take her into the remembered room, that masculine room of leather and pipes and books.

'My darling,' he said, and in the tones of his voice, the look in his face, was heaven for her.

She clung to him though she had vowed to herself that she would not even touch him.

'Oh, Brenner, just to be with you again!'

'Has it been so bad, my sweet?'

'Ghastly! You know all about it?'

'Of course. You understand why I did not write, or come? I longed to do both.'

'I know you did, Brenner. I longed for it, too. It was all I could do to keep myself from ringing you up and asking you to come.'

He took her cloak and she shivered as his fingers touched her neck for an instant. The contact made her almost faint with its ecstasy.

'Come and have dinner and we'll talk afterwards. It's been a rush job, but I've tried to get everything you like. *Hors d'oeuvres*, look, those queer little fish things you used to pick out. Remember?'

'Everything, Brenner,' she said tremulously.

'And I, my sweet.'

As they ate, he talked to her, deliberately entertaining her to keep her mind away from the tragedy which he knew had brought her to him, and after the table was cleared and they were left alone with their cigarettes and her special brand of liqueurs, he dropped the mask and turned to her gravely.

'Well, Jennifer dear?' he asked.

'Brenner, they're going to try Bob for murder,' she said with a pitiful break in her voice.

He nodded his head.

'Yes. That was a foregone conclusion if Rothe died. Why did he do it, I wonder?'

'Brenner, he didn't do it! He didn't! They can't prove he did when
he didn't, can they?' she cried.

'Well, no, not if he didn't do it. I don't think there's often a grave
miscarriage of justice in this country, not in capital cases, anyway,' he
said gravely. 'On what grounds will they charge him? It seems to be
an open secret down there that he was looking for Rothe, with the
avowed intention of killing him of course.'

'How did you know?'

'Directly I heard about it, I was afraid you might somehow be
involved and I sent a man down to see what he could find out about
the affair. It doesn't look too good for Haling, dear, but I still don't
know why he did it. What harm had Rothe ever done him?'

'Brenner, he—he believed that Julian and I were lovers,' said
Jennifer in a low voice.

He turned incredulous eyes on her.

'Jennifer! How could he?'

'I don't know. He had some horrible, privately printed rag of a
paper there that linked our names, Julian's and mine, and then there
was that money I sent him, the money I earned—you remember?' He
nodded. 'He must always have been jealous of Julian, though I didn't
realise it, and—he put two and two together and—'

'Made five of it? Oh, my dear, it's been ghastly for you, hasn't it?
Wouldn't he believe you when you denied it?'

She flushed miserably and looked away.

'I—didn't deny it, Brenner,' she said. 'At least, I denied it, but I let
him think I was—lying.'

'But—Jennifer?' he asked, startled beyond words.

'Oh, my dear, you know it wasn't true! You know there never has
been anyone, never could be anyone, but you, don't you?' she asked
him quickly as she saw the beginning of an unthinkable idea at the
back of his eyes.

He caught her to him and held her closely in atonement for that
thought that had never actually been as much as a thought.

'Of course I know, beloved,' he said.

'He knew I was different, Brenner. I didn't realise that I was, but I
must have been. I think Julian knew too. I felt—radiant, filled with

the love of you and the joy of it and—he guessed, Brenner, and I let him believe that it was Julian.'

He still held his arm about her.

'Why did you, dear?' he asked her gently.

'I was afraid for you, afraid he would find out somehow. I never dreamed that he would—would want to hurt Julian. He seemed to hate me so. I thought he'd just let me go. Instead of that, he seems to have followed me, to have seen me with Julian—and then all that happened.'

They were silent for a long time, each with a mind pregnant with thought. Then Mayne spoke: 'What is it you want me to do, Jennifer?' he asked quietly.

She turned to him with pleading eyes.

'I think you know already, Brenner. I want you to defend him.'

He shook his head.

'My dear, I can't. Don't you see that I believe he did kill Julian Rothe? That being the case, I could not possibly defend him. It would be against my honour to do so.'

She caught his hands in hers and faced him desperately.

'Brenner, don't you see that you must? If it had not been for us, for what we have done, Bob would never have run any risk of being charged with killing Julian because he would not have wanted to do so. That's all they actually have against him, that he was there, that he had a revolver, and that he had been foolish enough to make threats against Julian. Don't you see that actually Julian was in your place, Brenner? That he has died for what we did, you and I? It isn't easy for me to come and ask you to do this, but don't you see that we owe it to Bob? As reparation? As the only thing we can do? We can't let him lose his life as well—two lives because of our sin. Brenner, I do beg of you to do this! I beg it!'

He loosed her hands and began to pace the room. She sat there quite still, her eyes watching him every now and then, unable to gather any impression of his thoughts from the face which had baffled many better mind-readers than she was.

When she could bear it no longer, she spoke his name.

'Brenner!'

He came to her at once and stood looking down at her.

'You are asking me more than I thought any person had a right to ask another, Jennifer. You're asking me for what is more than life to me. Do you realise that?'

She did not and could not realise it. Like many people, she thought that a lawyer was to be bought with anybody's money, and she had no conception of what it would mean to a man like Mayne to defend a prisoner whom he believed at the outset to be guilty. The only saving grace was that he was not being bought, that he was not selling his honour for money.

'When you see Bob, you'll know he isn't guilty, Brenner,' she said brokenly, leaning her head against him as he stood beside her.

He put an arm about her protectingly. So bright she had been, so glad and joyous in her love, and now was bowed down and broken.

'Because you ask it of me, beloved,' he said heavily.

'I shall thank you all my life—and love you till the end of the world,' she told him, her voice thick with the tears she would not shed.

Presently he spoke again: 'I'm afraid you'll have to go now, dear,' he said very gently. 'It won't do to arouse the slightest suspicion of us now.'

For a moment they clung together. Then he wrapped her cloak about her with a tenderness that was lingering sadness. He wondered if she realised that this, at last, was their farewell. Whether he saved her husband for her or not, this must be the end for them. He knew that if Haling were acquitted she would cleave to him in self-immolation because she blamed herself for the whole position. And if he were not acquitted? He could not see Jennifer walking to happiness, even if happiness were possible, over the body of the man she had wronged. She would feel in that super-sensitiveness of the artistic mind, that his death lay at her door, just as she felt that Rothe's lay there.

'I shan't see you personally any more than I can help,' he told her in parting. 'Get your solicitor to put everything in motion for you. He'll know what to do. Just tell him you wish me to be briefed for the defence and that the fees have been arranged.'

Jennifer nodded. She was past speech. He waited at the door until her taxi had gone. Then he turned back into his study with an unpalatable mixture of bitterness and sweetness in his heart. Some words which had been ringing in his brain whilst he and Jennifer had talked came now to his lips, and he whispered them ironically:

'… drown'd my Honour in a shallow Cup,
And sold my reputation for a Song.'

Chapter Nineteen

Robert Haling was acquitted.

Those who knew the inside facts as well as those who merely read the accounts in the newspapers said that it was a miracle, for the case did not even go to the assizes and Bob was free after one day of agony which had followed the period of suspense whilst he awaited the first hearing.

'It was that lawyer chap you got who did the trick, Jen,' he told his wife jubilantly in the first hour of his freedom.

They had got away in a closed car and gone to Lottie's, and now he was alone with Jennifer, the remains of the meal cleared away and Lottie putting the children to bed.

'Of course there wasn't any evidence, and in this country they can't convict a man of a thing like murder without some sort of evidence, and the bullet that killed Rothe might have come out of anybody's gun. We all had the same sort, and there've been dozens of shots fired from them at odd times, as the police knew. This one didn't go wide like the others, and I was unlucky because for once they could fix it on someone who might have had cause. I bet the police are wild about it. Gosh! Mayne didn't half chew them up! I knew I should get off, of course, but when he started to speak in that quiet way of his, the other side knew it was all up too. Marvellous voice he's got, hasn't he? So quiet and easy and yet it bores right through you.'

Jennifer covered her ears with her hands.

'Oh, stop, stop! Don't you think I've had enough of it? All this time waiting, and now today—oh, horrible, horrible!' and she cowered shiveringly down into the chair.

Bob stared at her. He had never seen her go to pieces like this, and he was filled with amazement and wonder. Did she care as much as that, then? Did he really matter to her after all?

'Jen—I say, Jen,' and he limped over to her and placed a hand on her shoulder.

She drew away as if the touch had burnt her, and for an instant he saw her eyes. There was hatred in them, the hatred of a wild animal trapped and helpless.

'God! You hate me, don't you?' he asked stupidly, drawing away from her.

She rose from the chair and walked over to the window, looking out into the darkness with eyes that saw nothing whilst she struggled for composure, for new courage and strength to go through with this thing she had undertaken.

The past weeks with their culmination that day had set on her body and brain marks which they would carry to the grave. She had never visualised the unimaginable horror of sitting there in the tiny court-room, packed to overflowing with the ghouls whose minds feed on the sufferings of others, whilst her lover fought for the life of her husband.

To her, during that fight, the issue had changed. It became no longer a fight but a sacrifice. She knew that Bob was guilty; Brenner knew it; nearly everybody in that crowded room knew it; the solicitors, the barristers, knew that Brenner Mayne was selling his honour. Only Jennifer knew the price for which he sold it, not for money or for fame, but just so that the woman he loved might have peace of mind.

Bitterly she regretted that she had asked this thing of him, and as her eyes and her thoughts had gone from the frightened, defiant man in the dock to that other man whose strong, calm face made so great a contrast to Bob Haling's, she had realised what she had sacrificed on the altar of her own paltry self-esteem. Better, far better, that she had gone through all the rest of her life in self-abasement and remorse than that the man she worshipped should be giving more than his life to save her from it.

Dimly she knew that the case was being handled with diabolical cleverness, that Brenner was weaving a magic carpet with his adroit wit and the clever brain which knew just how to make use of every scrap and thread that came into his hand, how to work them into the pattern so cunningly that the other side could find no flaw.

And Bob Haling walked out of the court a free man, and the comment of friend and foe alike was, 'Lucky fellow!'

Brenner had not even looked at him as he left the court with a jauntiness which made Jennifer feel sick, and she turned to go where she could no longer see her lover, unfamiliar and remote in his wig and gown, but Mr. Brigget, fussy and elated at having been associated in a case with Brenner Mayne, had laid a hand on her arm.

'It is usual to speak to counsel,' he whispered to her, and she turned, white-lipped, to where he was speaking to his junior preparatory to leaving the court.

'Thank you, Mr. Mayne,' she said painfully, and held out her hand.

He took it, bowed gravely, and waited for her to turn away again.

Beyond and above every other memory of that day, the look in his eyes at that moment remained to stab her. She was remembering it now as she stood at the window and fought for the mastery of herself whilst everything within her cried for the relief of abandonment to her misery.

How hurt he had been, how stricken and abased by that day's work! Brenner, who had loved his work, his honour, his pride in the name he had made for himself, by his own efforts, by his utter honesty amidst a world of shame and intrigue and lying!

She had thought that when it was all over she could come with Bob and help to make a home, begin all over again, forgetting the past and making silent atonement to him for that which she could not forget.

Now she was wondering, with a sick misery, how she was to find the strength to accomplish it. Did she hate Bob? Did she not rather hate what he represented, the bondage to another man when her soul cried out for her lover, the ever-present reminder of all they had lost?

Mayne had told her that if he could not get Bob acquitted, he would almost certainly be able to get the charge reduced to one of manslaughter, but she knew that Bob was a murderer. She knew that he had gone there that day with the intention of killing Julian Rothe.

Round and round went her mind, unstable, inconsistent, unable through sheer weariness to think coherently, the same thoughts bringing the same bitter answers, and behind her Bob waited for an answer to his question.

She turned at last, a little less distraught, her eyes quiet.

'Don't let's go into that now, Bob. Don't let's talk about any of it for a bit. I'm—I suppose I'm deadly tired. My head's swimming and my throat hurts. My throat hurts!' she repeated wildly, becoming aware of it only as she spoke the words and putting her hand instinctively to where she had suddenly realised pain throbbed and burned.

Her eyes were frightened and her imagination immediately began to magnify the slight pain till she could think of nothing else.

'Bob! My throat!' she said again, as he did not reply.

'I guess we're both of us pretty well done,' he said gruffly, his mind still too much occupied with himself to take her seriously. 'What about turning in? It'll be a treat to be in a decent bed again. Are we stopping here the night?'

'Lottie said we could,' said Jennifer dully. Could she get to a doctor that evening? It was still early and she would not be able to sleep until she had done something about that pain.

Passionately she longed for Julian. He would know at once what to do. He would not have dismissed it casually as Bob had done. He would have understood how terribly important it was.

Bob went to the foot of the stairs and called his sister.

'Are we kipping here tonight, Lot?'

She came down with a pile of little garments over her arm and her eyes went at once from one to the other of these two. She longed ardently for their reconciliation. She felt that if anyone could keep Bob straight and give him any sort of happiness, that person was his wife. She did not entirely overlook Jennifer's side of the case, but she felt that where love had once been, love could come again, and with it contentment.

'If you'd like to, Bob. I told Jennifer I thought it might be best and then tomorrow you two can talk things over and make plans. I don't

suppose you'll want to stay in Werford, in any case, will you?' looking
at them both with a pleading look that stabbed Jennifer.

'I don't know what we shall do,' Bob told her roughly. 'Come on,
Jen. Put a jerk into it.'

He was not of the type to consider courtesy towards his own
womenfolk necessary, and Jennifer shrank alike from words and tone.

'I won't come up just yet, Bob. I'll stay and help Lottie,' she said,
and something in her look cut short the protest that was on Lottie's
tongue.

'Afraid to sleep with a murderer?' asked Bob nastily. 'Don't worry.
I shan't manhandle you,' and he gave a short, unpleasant laugh as he
turned on his heel and climbed the stairs in his difficult fashion.

Jennifer went into the kitchen and Lottie threw down the armful
of clothes and followed her, closing the door behind her.

'Jen dear,' she said pitifully. 'Be patient with him. He's suffered
cruelly. He isn't himself, not his real self. Everything's been against
him. It's made him hard and say things he doesn't really mean.'

'Do you mind if I go out for a little, Lottie? Can you manage?' asked
Jennifer, making no attempt to respond to her sister-in-law's lead. She
felt that she simply could not discuss it with anyone just then – and
there was this awful hardness at the back of her throat.

'Of course I can,' said Lottie, after a little pause in which Jennifer
felt she was offended by the rebuff. 'Will you be sleeping here?'

Jennifer turned to her desperately.

'I don't think I can, Lottie. Not tonight. Try—try to understand,
won't you? Bob isn't the only one that's suffered,' her voice shaking on
the words.

'Well, he's the one that's suffered most,' said Lottie with a touch of
acerbity. 'It isn't as if you were fond of Mr. Rothe or anything. You've
said all the time he was only your teacher, and all this time while Bob's
been out of work and in pain you've been enjoying yourself, haven't
you?'

Jennifer flinched. There was enough truth in it to make her feel
humble before Bob's sister, though she would not have been human
had she not also felt resentment.

'Don't let's quarrel, Lottie,' she pleaded. 'I know I've been to blame a lot, but—I've got things to bear as well as Bob.'

Lottie's face softened. It was not in her nature to resist a tax on her generosity, and Jennifer was her oldest and best friend.

'I don't want to quarrel either, Jen. I know Bob isn't easy to get on with these days, but he loves you dearly and always will. The way he goes on is only his manner and it doesn't mean anything. He's all right at heart. You're not going to leave him again, are you? Jen, he needs you so.'

'I've said I'll stay,' said Jennifer unemotionally. 'I think it's best if we don't see each other again tonight, though. We're not ourselves and we may—may say things we don't really want to say. I'll go back to the hotel for tonight and come here in the morning. Tell Bob, will you?' and she was gone.

Lottie watched her for a moment as she hurried down the street and then went back to her many duties which had had to be neglected lately. She had worked so hard to effect a reconciliation between Bob and his wife, believing in their eventual happiness. Now for the first time she began to doubt her own wisdom. Could they ever make a success of it now that they had drifted the poles apart? More than ever she was conscious that Jennifer had gone from them in spirit, however strongly they might bind the chains that held her body.

Bob came lumbering downstairs again.

'Where's Jennifer?' he asked.

'She's had to go back to the hotel, Bob, just for tonight. She told me to tell you she'd be back in the morning.'

'I didn't think she'd stay,' said Bob gruffly.

'She's coming back, Bob. She said so, and she'll keep her word. You know Jennifer for that.'

'Oh yes, she'll come back in the morning,' he agreed. 'The thing is, what's she going to say when she does, eh?'

'She wants to help you make a home, Bob. I know she does,' said his sister bravely.

'She doesn't *want* to. She wants to go back to her fine friends in London. But she'll stay because she thinks she ought to, because she's afraid I shall get into trouble again,' he said bitterly. 'Well, I don't want her. Do you hear? I don't want any of her blasted kindness and duty. Let her stay away and be damned to her,' and suddenly his nerve gave way and he dropped down in a chair by the table, laid his head on it and burst into the hard, dreadful tears of a man.

Lottie mothered him and soothed him, hoping and yet fearing that Jennifer would return, Jennifer with that strange look in her eyes, with her way of speaking which removed her so far from the girl they had played with as children, Jennifer who might look with scorn on a man in tears.

'I love her so, Lottie. I can't bear to let her go! And she hates me. I saw it in her eyes. I could hear it when she spoke to me after we came out of the court-room,' he said between those hard and terrible sobs.

She persuaded him to go to bed at last, stayed to tuck him up as she tucked up her own children and, with a rare understanding of the frightened child that he was, she came back with a night-light burning in a saucer and placed it where he could see the small, comforting light. Bob watched her. Why could not Jennifer have been like that? As simple and uncritical and forgiving?

He flung the thought from him. If she had been, he would not have loved her. He had always striven for the prizes, for the things difficult to win and hard to keep. He would rather have the crumbs that fell from Jennifer's table than sit at the feast with any other woman.

And Jennifer had gone to a doctor in Belsdale, a stranger. She did not feel able to face the kindly old man who had known her all her life and who would know at once what she feared and probably not tell her the truth.

This man was young and keen. She realised that he must know who she was and she told him at once that the past events had been a great strain on her.

'There's nothing actually wrong, Mrs. Haling,' he said at last. 'There are signs of general strain and fatigue, of course, but I think that with proper rest and care you will find everything normal again. I don't think I should try to sing for a little while, if I were you. Give the throat and vocal chords a complete rest for, say, three weeks or a month. I'll give you a tonic and a gargle, and you might get these tablets from the chemist. Don't worry,' and she went back to her hotel considerably relieved.

She told Bob and Lottie the next day, at an interview which proved the wisdom of her flight the night before, and though little was actually said about their future, it seemed to be tacitly agreed amongst them that they should remain together at Lottie's house for the time being.

'Matter of fact,' Bob said sheepishly, 'I've got the offer of a job in Norfolk, on a farm.'

The two women looked at him with interest.

'Where and how?' asked Jennifer.

'Well—er—through Brenner Mayne,' he said, and fortunately for Jennifer he felt so awkward about the matter that he did net look at her as he spoke. 'He left the message for me with his clerk, that he could get me an open-air job if I wanted one and thought I could manage it. He's got relations there who have a farm.'

How like him, thought Jennifer, though the very thought was a fresh stab at her heart. He never did anything by halves. He had not stopped at saving Bob's life for her; he must see that it was made worth having, must give him at least the chance of providing her with a home if her career had to be abandoned.

'Could you manage that, with your leg and all?' asked Lottie doubtfully.

'Well, Mayne knows all about that, and he isn't the sort of chap to send anyone on a wild-goose chase. The job he had in mind must be something a lame beggar can do or he wouldn't have suggested it. He's a jolly fine chap.'

Jennifer said nothing. It might mean salvation to Bob, and Brenner had piled that gift to her on top of all the others. She felt quiet and very humble.

They settled down to at least a semblance of peace. One more humiliation Jennifer had to suffer, which was Bob's jubilant acceptance of an offer from a Sunday newspaper to publish his 'story', which meant that they paid him a generous sum for the right to append his name and photograph to the page of copy which some young journalist had written up from such details as Bob gave him. The account contained references to Jennifer's career and gave florid descriptions of the training which had been interrupted by Rothe's death, explaining her abandonment of it by sentimental talk of 'devotion and the love that had hallowed the lives of these tragic young people'.

Jennifer had known nothing about it until she saw it in the paper, and her anger knew no bounds. Bob's ingenuous delight at the money he had received and his utter inability to understand her feelings did little to mitigate the humiliation she suffered, and when in the midst of it came Mayne's letter to Bob completing the arrangements for him to go to the Norfolk farm Jennifer snatched at an opportunity not to go with him at once.

'They're going to put me up at the farm till I see how I get on,' Bob told her rather sheepishly. 'They don't say they're expecting me to bring you with me, but I dare say it'll be all right.'

As a matter of fact, now that his first feeling of relief from the fear and helplessness at his trial had worn off, he was beginning to realise how far he and Jennifer had drifted apart. She took her expected place in Lottie's home, did more than her fair share of the work, seemed to prefer to labour endlessly indeed, and there was nothing in her attitude to give the impression that she resented her position or thought herself above it.

But the fact remained that she had grown away from them, that her mind held thoughts which her lips never uttered, that only her body lived with them, and Bob felt sulkily resentful of his own feeling of inferiority to her. He knew that it would be a relief to him to get away from her for a time, and she was conscious of a lightening of his face when she made her thoughtful answer to his half-suggestion.

'I think it might be better for you to go alone in the first place,' she said. 'As you say, they do not appear to be expecting me and it might be awkward for them if I turned up. I'll stay here with Lottie for a bit until you see what arrangements can be made for me to join you.'

So that was how it was settled, and when the train had gone both Bob seated in it and Jennifer leaving the station felt a guilty sense of freedom.

It proved well that they had chosen this course, for less than a fortnight later Bob walked into the cottage, threw down his bag, and lumped himself into the arm-chair with a defiant look at the two startled women, who had been washing up.

'Bob, what a surprise!' from Jennifer, and, 'What on earth have you come back for?' from his sister.

'I've quit,' he said. 'The job's no damned good to me. What do they take me for? A horse or a mule? Or a blinking machine? Up at five in the morning milking because of this blasted summer time, cleaning out pig-stys, swabbing up after the cows.'

'Well, other men do it,' said Lottie, whilst Jennifer sat in silence, horrified at her mental reactions to her husband's reappearance.

'Maybe they do. Maybe they like it. Well, I don't,' growled Bob, the more surly for their obvious disapproval, though he had known he would meet it and had a sneaking feeling that he deserved it. He had come away in a moment of anger, without giving notice to the farmer and with his usual disregard of the consequences of his impulsive actions.

'There's all sorts of jobs that people do for a living, whether they like it or not, Bob Haling,' said his sister sharply. 'Do you think Jennifer and I like scrubbing floors and washing the dishes and the clothes, and cleaning out the flues? We don't, but we do it because it's got to be done, same as thousands of women do it. Here, take your bag. You better go back, and go back quick before they give the job to somebody else—if they'll have you.'

He refused to touch the bag she tried to thrust into his hand.

'I don't want their lousy job,' he growled.

'Well, you're not coming to live on Jen and me, anyway,' she told him fiercely, and suddenly Jennifer rose to her feet and walked out of the house, not looking or caring where she went, concerned only with getting away before all the bitter thoughts in her mind could pour through her lips to brand their memories for ever.

It was not only that Bob had thrown up his job and come home. It was his ingratitude to the man who had stood his friend and helped him, had picked him up from the gutter into which he had fallen and stood him on his feet and given him a chance to be a man again.

Brenner had done this for her, had saved the life that stood between them, had tried to bolster up that life for her and make his gift worth while. And Bob had flung back the gift, had chosen the gutter, had shown not only to Jennifer, but also to Mayne, who must hear of it, how worthless was the thing which she had chosen, which she had kept as a barrier to their happiness, which, so far as she could see, must ever remain a barrier.

She returned at last to find Lottie alone, the children in bed.

'Where is he?' she asked fearfully.

'Gone to the pub, I suppose,' said Lottie bitterly. 'Oh, Jen, I feel so—rotten about all this. I've got you into it. If it hadn't been for me and those letters I sent you and the telegram, you wouldn't have come back and all this wouldn't have happened.'

Jennifer watched herself consoling the unhappy woman, It was odd how she seemed to be standing outside herself, a third person looking on whilst they talked.

'Don't worry about it, Lottie. Perhaps it was fate. Who knows? I haven't anyone but myself to blame. I made him marry me, after all. I thought myself so much better than I am, saw myself in heroics when actually I'm a very ordinary sort of person. Don't take it so hardly, Lottie.'

Her sister-in-law looked at her wonderingly. It was never easy for her to understand Jennifer nowadays, but this calmness was even more difficult.

'How can you take it like this, Jen? Don't you *mind* about Bob chucking his job when he'd got a decent chance and coming back on us like this?' she asked.

'I don't know. Do I mind? I thought I did. I could have screamed and behaved like a virago when he walked in, but perhaps I've got over it,' and she passed a hand across her eyes in a gesture of utter weariness.

She had been sleeping badly since Bob had been at the farm, for, in spite of herself and the iron will she had sought to acquire, the dread of taking up permanent life with him again had grown to terrible proportions. So, when he arrived like that she was ill-equipped to deal with any fresh problem, and Lottie realised how thin and tired she looked.

'Oh, Jen, what can we do? What can any of us do?' she asked anxiously. 'You can't go on like this, and what are you and Bob going to live on, anyway? I'll do my best, as you know, but it's job enough to make my bit of earnings keep me and the children, and—'

'We're not going to live on you, Lottie, that's certain,' said Jennifer firmly. 'It's been little enough I've been able to pay you these last few weeks, and now that Bob's chosen to throw up his job there won't be anything unless I earn it.'

'How will you do that, Jen?' she asked anxiously.

'I'm going to London to see a friend of Mr. Rothe's, Lader is his name. He's not such an important man, of course. There's nobody quite like Julian. But I think he'll do what he can to start me as a singer. I shall never be able to do the things we had planned to do, of course. I still had too much to learn when Julian—died, and nobody else will bother to teach me. Nobody agreed with his methods, and if I learned anybody else's methods it would mean unlearning everything I've been taught. I'll ask Mr. Lader to arrange a concert for me and perhaps I can get other engagements, broadcasting, making records and so on.'

She was quite calm and self-possessed, and it was obvious that she had been laying her plans carefully during the time she had walked alone in the lanes and fields, letting their utter peace lap her tired mind and their simplicity restore her tortuous thoughts to some semblance of order.

Lottie nodded and gave a little sigh.

'It's the only way, Jen, though it's terrible to think, after all this, you and Bob are going to part again. You didn't ought to have married him, Jen. I've seen that all the time. He isn't your sort and you aren't his. He isn't all bad. There's a lot that's good in Bob. It's just that—that you don't hit it off together. He ought to have found a wife more like me, just an ordinary, stupid sort of woman who wouldn't have expected too much of him but could have turned round and given him a mouthful of as good as he gave, or a sock on the jaw, and nobody any the worse for it.'

Jennifer smiled wearily.

'He would have been better off with someone like you, Lottie. You're so much—finer than I am, more honest with yourself. You don't set yourself up on a pedestal and paint yourself in fine colours and think how splendid you are. You just get on with your job and take all the worries and the hardships and the sorrows in your stride, and never think of trying to dodge them or feeling hard done by,' and before the open-mouthed and wide-eyed Lottie could think out a reply to that amazing speech Jennifer had gone to the room she had perforce to share with Bob and locked the door behind her.

It did not concern her at all what he would do for the night. She felt completely detached from him by his entire lack of thought for her and care as to how she should live. This was the end. She made no plans for any future which held him; she made none for a future with any other man; her plans concerned herself alone.

When she had packed all her belongings save those which might be of use to Lottie personally, she undressed and went to bed. Very much later she heard Bob come in, his uneven tread heavy and unsteady. He swayed against her door, its light frame creaking at the onslaught, but when he turned the handle and found that the door would not open, he stood breathing heavily outside for a minute and then went down the stairs again, and she heard the springs of the old couch in the living-room squeak as he flung himself down on it.

In the morning she went down ready for her journey. Bob, still unwashed, dishevelled, heavy-eyed, stumbled to his feet and looked at her morosely. Jennifer hated the look of him, drew herself away from any possibility of his touch had he shown any signs of offering it.

'I'm leaving you, Bob,' she said quietly. 'Whether it is for good or not depends on you. I am going to London to try to get concert engagements. It is obvious that I shall always have to earn my own living, but I will not earn yours now that I realise how little care you take to earn it yourself. Whilst you were really unable to get a job I was willing to do anything for you, but now that you have deliberately thrown up the chance that was given you, for no reason except that it was hard work, I refuse to do anything for you. I shall let you know where I am, and, as I say, any future we may have together depends entirely on you.'

Her very self-possession invited his unsteady nerves to put him into a fresh rage, but he tried honestly to keep a check on himself, setting his teeth and clenching his hands whilst she spoke.

'You don't mean to live with me again, whatever I do, do you?' he demanded, face and voice ugly with pain and temper.

'I have already answered that question,' said Jennifer steadily. 'It is up to you. I don't ask you to keep me. I only ask you to keep yourself, and when you are doing that I am prepared to discuss our marriage again.'

He moved a step nearer to her and she shrank instinctively from the menace of his clenched fist and bloodshot eyes. For one sick moment she thought he meant to strike her, but he kept his hands at his side with an effort of will for which she did not give him credit.

'I know what you mean by that, for all your fine words. You'll dig yourself in with your fine friends again, come out as a singer—Jennifer Rothe! Ashamed to use either your father's name or your husband's! You'll dig yourself in there and then want to get rid of me so that you can marry one of these lah-di-dahs, perhaps one with a handle to his name that you won't be ashamed to use! Well, Jennifer Rothe, let me tell you that I shan't do it. You can't divorce me because I can't commit adultery, and I won't divorce you and give you the pleasure of being Lady Tom-Noddy when you're tired of being Jennifer Rothe. Jennifer Haling you are, and Jennifer Haling you'll remain. See?'

She was very pale and the shadows seemed to deepen beneath her eyes, whilst at the back of her throat there crept insidiously that terrifying constriction that was not actual pain but was far more frightening to her than pain. She put her hand to her throat instinctively and Bob laughed. It was a horrible sound, jarring her nerves and filling her with nausea.

'Oh, you needn't be afraid I'll choke the life out of you,' he jeered, misinterpreting her action. 'I don't mind telling you there's nothing I'd like better than to get hold of your white throat with my two hands and squeeze it till you're dead and can't look at me like that any longer. But I'm not going to do it. I've had one taste of trial for murder and I don't want another. I might not get off so easily when I'd done you in. Everybody said I was lucky, didn't they? I know I was; I killed Rothe—I meant to. Murder that was. Did you know that? Did you?' as she refused, white-lipped, to answer.

'Why talk like this, Bob?' she said at last, her voice shaking and queerly hoarse. 'It doesn't do either of us any good. Let the past be the past. I—I think I'll go now,' and though she had intended to wait for breakfast and to see Lottie, who was helping the children to get ready for school, she felt she could not stay another minute in the house which held her husband. She took her suitcase in her hand and turned to the door.

'Tell Lottie I'll send from the station for my trunk,' she said, and he stood to watch her go, a stricken and dreadful look on his face.

He had loved Jennifer passionately, loved her with all the best in him which had become the worst by physical frustration. His mind had not been able to rise superior to the deprivations of the body, and in that rare moment of self-revelation he saw it and knew how Jennifer must also see him.

Lottie came down to find him hunched in his chair again, that stark, dreadful misery in his face. She hustled the children off to school with a final warning about the main road they had to cross, tucked baby Jennifer into her cot with a crust to suck, and came to put an arm about her brother's bowed shoulders.

'She's gone, Lot,' he told her heavily.

Lottie nodded.

'Yes. I saw her going down the street. Well, maybe it's all for the best. It's been a dreadful time for both of you. You can stop with me, Bob. You know that, old pal. Where I've got a home, there's always one for you, but'll mean getting a job. I've wondered a lot whether it's any good going to those people who help you to get to the colonies, whether they'd help us.'

He lifted his head and she saw in his sombre eyes the slightest flash of hope, though instantly it was lost again.

'It's no good, Lot. I'm not the sort they help. They only send men who can work hard and keep fit, not a crock like me. Besides—there's Jennifer,' he added slowly.

Lottie gathered his head closely to her, mothering him as she mothered her fatherless children, for was he not a lost and frightened child?

'Bob, it's hard to say it, but you'll have to let Jen go,' she said gently. 'She doesn't belong to us and our sort any more. You know that as well as me. Why not make up your mind to it and start over again, and let her start over again?'

He shook his head and freed himself from her gentle hold.

'Nix to that. She's mine, and mine she stays,' he said, and lurched out of the house. If he were quick he might be in time to catch a glimpse of her before she left. He did not know what train she was catching. If she caught the 9.10 he might just do it.

Chapter Twenty

Jennifer sat a little apart in the artists' room behind the stage of the great concert hall.

The others, the fat little tenor with the sentimental eyes, the enormous, deep-chested baritone, the somewhat over-blown soprano, who were making a background for her, all knew one another and chatted amicably together, glancing now and then with speculative interest at this new star in their firmament. They wanted to be friendly, but Jennifer was too shy and nervous to respond to their overtures.

Claire had chosen her frock and insisted on paying for it, though already Jennifer felt unhappily in her debt, for her debut had been delayed for anxious months following a complete breakdown in her health.

She had gone, immediately on reaching London, to the great throat specialist, and Sir Samuel had been kind and sympathetic, but grave. Jennifer had told him her position, and he had remembered her from association with Rothe, but he could do no more for her than advise complete rest of her vocal chords together with a treatment which she felt wretchedly was impossible.

Claire had come to her rescue.

'My dear, let me do this for you,' she said. 'I shall feel I am doing something for Julian. He had set his heart on your career.'

'You loved him, didn't you?' asked Jennifer wistfully.

Every barrier seemed to be broken down now between her and this famous woman who had once appeared as a star in the firmament rather than as a human being like herself. Grief had aged Claire perceptibly, had robbed her of that garment of radiant youth which it seemed had belonged to Julian Rothe and which he had taken with him, leaving her still beautiful, still with the charm she would take with her to the grave, but a woman who had passed the milestones of youth and who never even wanted to look back.

And so, quite simply, Jennifer was able to ask that question, and as simply Claire Ferring answered it.

'More than my life,' she said. 'You knew that when you sent for me, didn't you? I shall always bless you for that, Jennifer.'

'I think I knew in Italy.'

'It has been a long story, a sad one, and yet sometimes a marvellously happy one,' said Claire. 'Oh, my dear, don't throw away the substance for the shadow, as I did.'

For a while they sat in silence, and then Claire spoke again.

'You're going to let me help you, Jennifer? Actually Julian left money for that purpose, but he wouldn't make a new will because he was afraid it might hurt you in some way—your reputation.'

Jennifer nodded.

'Yes. That would be like him,' she said sadly.

'I think, of all people in the world, you were the only one to know him as he really was—the only one beside myself,' said Claire. 'I treated him badly, but he repaid me with a lifetime of love and service. Jennifer—have you ever realised that Derek is Julian's son?'

The girl came out of her reverie to stare at Claire, to link up half-forgotten memories and impressions and fleeting thoughts with this amazing revelation which, possibly, was not a revelation at all.

'No one knows, no one but—my husband,' said Claire slowly. 'It all happened so long ago, but Guy has never forgotten or forgiven. Julian and I became lovers after the bloom had worn off my marriage, but I hadn't the courage to do what he pleaded with me to do. I was afraid of poverty, for he was quite poor and unknown then and we had met when he was having a week's holiday in Italy, a holiday he had scraped and saved for for years. That was why, afterwards, he always went to Como. He was away when I knew Derek was coming. I was so frightened and ill. I didn't know where to find Julian, and before I could get in touch with him Guy guessed how things were with me and assumed that the baby was his.

'I was weak and a coward, and by the time I plucked up courage to confess the truth, he had blazed his triumph to the world and made an utter fool of himself because of my condition.

'I can't bear even now, after all these years, to remember that scene, but in the end I struck a contemptible bargain with him. I agreed to stay with him if the child were a boy so that he could be brought up as the Bordray heir. If it were a girl, I could do as I liked, but in any case Guy said he would never divorce me. Julian came back with his future looking rosy, and—Derek was born, though I had prayed for a girl, thinking that Guy might relent, after all, and set me free for Julian if that were so.

'And that's how things were. Julian never married. I stayed with Guy year after year for Derek's sake, to give him not only a name but a peerage and Challissey. Once a year, most years, Julian has been able to come to me at Menaggio and Guy has known it, but has never questioned it, or refused to let me go.

'And now—Julian is dead, and there is only Derek. He loves Challissey, loves the thought of being Lord Bordray some day, and will never know the price I have paid to give him those things.'

Her quiet voice ceased, and presently Jennifer spoke gently.

'Derek loves you, Claire.'

The sad face brightened.

'Yes. I have that—that and the loveliest memories any woman ever had. And now, my dear, you'll let me do for you what Julian would have done?'

Jennifer had not been able to refuse, even had she wanted to do so, and Claire had sent her back to Sir Samuel with a *carte blanche* order, which had resulted in three months in his private nursing-home, and then Lader had taken her and put her through a short course of training and promised to launch her.

So here she was, waiting for her first big concert, her name unknown to the general public, though the critics were watching her with keen interest, impressed by her work in the two small, semi-private affairs which had been arranged for their benefit during the weeks preceding the present occasion.

She had sent a half-hearted invitation to Lottie and Bob to come up for the concert, but they had refused, and she was thankful. Somewhere in that vast throng there would be, she knew, the one man to whom she would be singing.

She and Mayne had not met since the day of Bob's trial, and though heart and body ached with the need for him, Jennifer tried to be glad and to think it best. But she knew that tonight he would be here, though he had sent her no word.

With a sad and bitter-sweet pride she had searched the newspapers day by day for any mention of him, thankful to realise that what she had feared had not come about, that he had not lost prestige for that betrayal of his honour when he had defended a man he knew to be guilty. Steadily, with an occasional leap when he figured in some notorious case, he was pushing his way up the ladder of success, and Jennifer watched with a jealous eye for every reference to him personally when he handled such cases successfully.

This man, this famous, respected man whose name was steadily growing one to be revered – this man was hers. She had lain in his arms, had listened to his inmost thoughts, knew him as no other human being would ever know him, and the thought was sweet anguish to her.

Someone opened the door and came into the artists' room and spoke her name.

'Chennifer!'

It was Valnor, the violinist, a great friend of Rothe's, who had interrupted a successful season in Paris to come to her premiere and play in her concert.

She turned to him with a nervous smile.

'I'm here, Val.'

He came to her and took her hand, warming it in both of his.

'So? A leetle troubled? Pain under ze pinny?' with one of his odd colloquialisms.

'Yes, a big one,' she said.

Lader came in behind him, pompous, fussy, anxious, and Valnor waved him away as if he were a troublesome little fly.

'Go your ways, Lader. Me, I talk to Chennifer. You make her more troubled, more have the nerves. Look now, Chennifer. You go to the platform—so. You walk three steps—so. You turn to look at the other side of the platform—so. You look. You see befront you nothing—nothing at all! And you say to yourself "Cabbages, cabbages, cabbages", and why for do you want to be troubled to sing to rows of cabbages? *Hein?* And so you sing—you sing like the birds. They like cabbages, hein? And so—we go. I take you the one hand and Lader, he take you the one hand,' and between them they led her out to the platform, to where the lights blazed and the orchestra played softly and the great crowd of strangers out there waited for her – and somewhere one man sat with his soul in his eyes and to this man she would sing.

Julian's own accompanist, Roy Lindsay, was at the piano, and she caught his heartening smile and had a strange feeling of Julian's presence.

For one moment she hung back, feeling as if her feet touched the edge of a vast sea that threatened to engulf her utterly. Then she began to sing, and forgot everything in the world in the joy of singing.

After the first song there was no possible doubt of the result. Round after round of applause invited her back to the stage, and, laughing, a little breathless, her cheeks flushed and her eyes bright, she let Lader bring her back time after time, until at length she stood alone and gave them the encore for which they clamoured.

It was a slumber song, tender, brooding, heart-stealing, and Mayne, listening to that lovely voice, poured out his soul in silent homage and love to the woman who sang to him and to those unborn children of his who might never lie at her breast.

In the artists' room they gave her respectful homage which held a little envy, for they knew how seldom was such a voice born, how few could ever reach the high places where such as she would so easily climb.

Valnor kissed her, his scrubby moustache and little beard all part of the unreality of it all.

'I salute you—queen of song, my divinity! The all of the world is at your little feet,' he told her, in ecstatic admiration.

She laughed tremulously.

'I take six in shoes,' she said.

Lader came fussing to her with an egg beaten in brandy and milk. She hated it, and Julian had had no belief in it, but she drank it out of sincere gratitude to Lader, who, after all, had taken a risk for her.

'The next part will try your strength more than the first,' he warned her. 'Now that we have interested them, made them keen, you must show them that you've got fireworks as well.'

'You think I'll be all right?'

Her nervousness was returning and she could almost imagine that there was that old feeling of tightness about her throat. Valnor pushed the impresario aside without ceremony.

'You leaf her to me, Lader. She is like the angels. They will adore her whatever she does out there.'

Jennifer looked up at him between tears and laughter.

'Not if I crack on the top notes, Val,' she said, and though he laughed at her, he knew she was really afraid.

He stood where he could watch her when she went on again to sing a modern and very difficult setting of a Shakespeare sonnet, and he frowned his disapproval of Lader, who had chosen it for her. She ought to have sung only simple things on that first night, things like the 'Berceuse' she had chosen earlier – and suddenly he bent forward to listen intently to frown, to catch at his little bristly beard with a nervous hand, for on a high note Jennifer's voice cracked a little, hesitated, and then took up the note again with superb ease.

Scarcely anyone noticed it, possibly a few of the critics, but Valnor, with his ear attuned to the faintest shade of variation in sound, had heard it, and he knew, from the sudden clenching of Jennifer's hands on the velvet of her frock, that she herself had been aware of it.

When she came towards him her face was white and she seemed not to hear the tumult of applause which followed her.

'Did you hear?' she asked him, in a terrified whisper, and he took her hands in his and held them reassuringly. They were as cold as ice, and she was trembling.

'This place, eet ees as the grave vaults,' he said fiercely. 'Cold. Ice cold. Someone should think shame to ask a great prima donna to sing in so terrible cold.'

But he did not deceive Jennifer, and she let his voice ripple over her without being able to derive comfort from it, and still the people clamoured for more.

Lader came to her. He had noticed nothing, and he was rubbing his hands and chuckling with delight.

'Better go back, Jennifer. Give them something simple and easy, a little bit of sugar to be going on with, eh?'

Her eyes implored him.

'Please, Mr. Lader, let me just bow my thanks this time. I—I can't sing again just yet.'

'Nonsense. Mustn't be too niggardly. Later on, perhaps, when you're established, but for tonight we must be generous. It gives a better impression,' and he took her hand from Valnor's and began to lead her back through the door to the platform. She hung back a moment to cast an odd, fateful look at the violinist, and then walked on to the platform by Lader's side as one in a dream.

'I'll sing "Softly Awakes My Heart",' she said to him, between pale lips.

'Oh, nothing operatic at this juncture, surely,' he objected, but she insisted, and they could not stand before people arguing.

Lader went forward to speak to the conductor, and Jennifer stood quite still, waiting for the opening music, waiting with that queer look of fate in her face and with ice gathering round her heart.

Her voice came out clear and pure and ineffably sweet, in that most beautiful of love songs devised, originally, for such an unworthy purpose. She sang it in French as she had done in that other lifetime, when she had drifted in a boat on a tiny lake in the Italian mountains and had sung to her beloved.

'Mon coeur s'ouvre à ta voix.'

Valnor, watching her, saw that presently her hand gripped a fold of her gown again, and he could see the little pulse at her neck beating and the way in which her mouth seemed to drag, and suddenly he came on to the platform, his violin beneath his chin, to take up the air just in time to save Jennifer, for, without warning, her voice went, and though her mouth remained open, no sound came.

Gradually the audience began to realise what was happening, that she was no longer singing, but stood there with a look of frozen horror on her face whilst Valnor drew sweet magic from his violin, and the orchestra, startled into awareness, followed his lead rather than that of the singer.

Uncertain applause followed the last notes, and Valnor took Jennifer's hand, bowed low over it and raised it to his lips in the deepest homage before he presented her to a bewildered audience. For an instant she stood there with him. Then she broke from him and ran from the platform, the tears blinding her, her throat a tearing searing instrument of torture.

Lader came to her, frightened and concerned, but Valnor followed and brushed him aside.

'She is ill,' he said briefly. 'Come, Chennifer. Come with Val,' and he found her cloak, wrapped her tenderly in it, and took her to the dressing-room, which, as the most famous artist of the evening, had been placed at his disposal.

Sir Samuel, who had been in the audience, came to her there, kind and sympathetic as ever, but unable, she could see, to reassure her.

'You don't have to tell me,' she said to him in the queer, harsh voice which seemed all that was left to her. 'I'm done for, isn't that it? I'll never be able to sing again. It's—over.'

'My dear young lady, it is impossible to say a thing like that. How can one tell? There was some of the weakness left, that is clear. Perhaps we ought to have waited a little longer.'

She shook her head, her face white and tragic, her eyes strangely bright, her hands trembling as they held the cloak about her chilled body.

'No. You mean to be kind, Sir Samuel, but I know. I think I've known really all the time, but—I hadn't the courage to admit it. Oh, Mr. Lader, forgive me—forgive me!' as the fussy little man, quiet and awed by the sight of her, came to stand beside her.

'Never mind, Jennifer. They loved you. You'll be all right again later.'

Somehow between them they got her away, and Lader left her with a kindly chambermaid at the hotel where she had for some time been staying on his advice.

The maid waited on her, but there was little she could do save help her undress, brush her hair for her and warm her cold hands and feet. She left her for a little while, to return with a large cardboard box and a telephone message.

'Mrs. Ferring wants to know if you would like her to come to you, Miss Rothe.'

Jennifer shook her head. She felt she could not bear even Claire's tenderness just then.

'No. Just say—thank you. I'd rather be quite alone for a little while,' she said.

'Yes, Miss Rothe. And the box?'

'Leave it,' said Jennifer indifferently, but after the girl had gone she went to it without interest and read the florist's label. The lid was not tied, and she lifted it, moved the layer of tissue paper and stood staring down at the flowers that lay in their green nest beneath.

They were pink camellias.

With a little cry, as if her heart were breaking, she took them from the box and pressed the fragile, waxen blooms against her breast, their crushed sweetness drifting to her nostrils to bring her a thousand memories.

'Brenner—Brenner—my darling, my love,' said her pale lips, and she bowed her head on his flowers and wept.

October ... October in Italy, without the dreariness and the chill of an English October.

Jennifer lay in a long chair on the terrace of Claire's pink villa. Before her stretched the cloudless blue of the lake, above her the cloudless blue of the sky, whilst from the road behind the villa, screened by the arches of the lemon grove, came the sound of unhurrying feet and the rhythmic, drowsy song of the harvesters, that song which in the last weeks had become indissolubly woven into the fabric of her memories of Italy.

Harvest – fulfilment – the fruit of all the months of care and work and hope and fear.

She closed her eyes against the beauty of the scene before her so that she might the better listen to that happy, contented song which was both triumph and humble gratitude.

There was a step on the wooden floor beside her. Caterina with letters perhaps.

'Put them on the table, Caterina,' she said sleepily, without opening her eyes, and presently, when she roused herself to sit up, she found only one letter on the table, a letter which bore an English stamp.

She took it up slowly. It was from her husband. Odd that there was no surcharge stamp on it, for he had put only a three-halfpenny stamp on it. She looked at it again and saw, with a little puzzled frown, that it was addressed to her at Claire's London house, where she had been staying before she came out to Como, and that it had not been re-directed to her here. How, then, had it got here?

She slid her linger beneath the flap of the cheap envelope and drew out the closely written sheets. She knew what a work it must have been to Bob to write all that, for a letter to him was a matter not of minutes, but of hours.

Dear Jennifer,

You will be surprised to get this but not so surprised as me writing it. Well, Jennifer, there is another surprise you will get for me and Lottie and the kids are off to Australia. I dont quite know what day but Mrs. Ferring is going to fix it all up.

Well, Jennifer, this is to say things that have got to be said between us and perhaps ought to have been said long enough ago. I was sore about you when I ought to have been sore about myself more and I did a silly thing trying to keep hold of you when I knew for sure I couldn't.

Well, Jennifer, this is to say good-bye and good luck and to let bygones be hasbeens as they say. Mrs. Ferring has been real kind to us and it looks we shall have a new chance out there. She is going to pay our passage and when we get there we are going to work together Lottie and me for some friends of hers there, Lottie

*in the house and me in the garden and a little house of our own
with the kids that will be all right for us.*

*Well, Jennifer, this is about all. All you got to do now is to see
about getting yourself free from me and good riddance I am afraid
you will say. I dont know much about the law so I wrote a letter
to that Mr. Mayne that helped me in my trial and put it all to him
and asked him to see you and explain what you have to do. I dont
think much of old Brigget here but he says you wont have any
trouble because the marriage hasnt been consecrated or something
like that. Anyway Mr. Mayne will know.*

*Well, Jennifer, I guess thats all to say except that I hope youll
be happy. Mrs. Ferring seems to think you will be able to fall on
your feet all right once you are quite well again and she says
Mr. Rothe left you some money which I try not to think about.*

*Well, Jennifer, this is all, hoping it finds you as it leaves me at
present,*

Your loving husband, Bob

Jennifer sat with the slow, difficult tears running down her cheeks.
She scarcely knew why she cried, save that there seemed to her
something infinitely pathetic in this surrender to fate at last of this
man who had fought so hard to keep her, who had once shared her
dreams and her hopes, with whom she had set out valiantly along the
road that had proved so hard and tortuous, so difficult to tread.

It was a long time now since she had seen him – months before
that night which was both her triumph and her downfall. He had not
been to see her when she lay ill, sick in mind and body, in Claire's
London home, and Jennifer had appreciated the unexpected delicacy
which had made him refuse the invitation which Mrs. Ferring had felt
obliged to send him. Lottie had come instead, a shy, large-eyed Lottie,
who had felt unspeakably uncomfortable, had spent a difficult week-
end there, and had gone back thankfully on Monday morning, refusing
even Claire's offer to send her to the station in one of the cars.

That had been September, and Jennifer had come out here soon
after. Claire had spent the first week with her but had been glad to

return to London for the villa would forever be haunted by memories too sad to be borne.

And now it was October, and she was well again, and Bob had sent her this strange, unexpected letter, a letter which showed her how deeply Claire's friendship had hedged her round and upheld her.

She became aware that she was no longer alone, that with the shadows of the cypresses mingled another, a tall, thin shadow that drew nearer to her until she turned to look into the face of the man who had come so quietly, unheralded.

'Mrs. Robert Haling?' he asked her gravely, and in his grey eyes lay laughter and gladness. 'I see that you have read the letter which I brought out to you from my client, Mr. Robert Haling.'

She rose from her chair and came to him, and when he saw that there were tears in her eyes, the laughter in his own gave place to a deep tenderness.

'Oh, Jennifer—my love—my dear!'

And from the white road beyond, the road that wound upwards into the mountains, came the song of the harvesters, the song of fulfilment and contentment, of triumph and of humble gratitude.

Menaggio, Italy.
Warlingham, Surrey.

Give Back Yesterday

Helena Clurey has it all – a devoted husband, money and family. She is happy and secure, but her apparent contentment is about to be shattered by a voice from the past. Mistress she may have been, but that is not the way it is put to her: 'you were not my mistress - you were, and are, my wife.'

The Weir House

Philip wants to marry Eve. It is her way out - he is rich, not too old, and has been in love for years – but not a man she can accept. He has even secretly funded her lifestyle, such that it is. Eve feels trapped. Unlike her friend Marcia, who cheerfully accepts an 'ordinary' life without complaint, Eve has known better and wants better. A chance encounter then changesthings – Lewis Belamie pays her to act as his fiancée for a week. Adventure, ambition, and disappointment all follow after she journeys to Cornwall with him, where she eventually nearly dies after what appears to be a suicide attempt because of a marriage that has seemingly failed. However, the mysterious and mocking Felix really does love her. Just who is he; how does Eve end up with him; and what part does 'The Weir House' play in her life? Has Eve's restlessness and relentless search for stability ended?

Through Many Waters

Jeff has got himself into a mess. It is, on the face of it, a classic scenario. He has a settled relationship with one woman, but loves another. What is he to do? It is now necessary to face reality, rather than continually making excuses to himself, but can he face the unpalatable truth? Then something beyond his influence intervenes and once again decisions have to be made. But in the end it is not Jeff that decides.

Misadventure

Olive Heriot and Hugh Manning had been in love for years, but marriage had been out of the question because of the intervention of Olive's mother. Now, at last, she was of age and due to gain her inheritance and be free to choose. A dinner party had been arranged at the Heriot's home, 'The Hermitage' and Hugh expects to be able to announce their engagement. Things start to change after a gruesomely realistic game entitled 'murder', which relies on someone drawing the Knave of Spades after cards are dealt. Tragedy strikes and other relationships are tested and consummated – but is this all real, or imagined?

Printed in Great
Britain
by Amazon

31954382R00174